# STILLWATER

Books by Nicole Helget

The Summer of Ordinary Ways
The Turtle Catcher
Stillwater

FOR YOUNGER READERS
Horse Camp

# STILLWATER

Nicole Helget

Houghton Mifflin Harcourt
BOSTON   NEW YORK
2014

www.hmhco.com

*Library of Congress Cataloging-in-Publication Data*
Helget, Nicole Lea, date.
Stillwater / Nicole Helget.
pages cm
ISBN 978-0-547-89820-9
1. Twins—Fiction. 2. Brothers and sisters—Fiction. 3. Children of mentally ill mothers—Fiction. 4. Life change events—Fiction. 5. Underground Railroad—Minnesota—Fiction. 6. Minnesota—Fiction. 7. Domestic fiction. I. Title.
PS3608.E39S75 2014
813'.6—dc23
013001719

Printed in the United States of America
DOC 10 9 8 7 6 5 4 3 2 1

Nicole Helget is a fiscal year 2011 recipient of an Artist Initiative grant from the Minnesota State Arts Board. This activity is made possible in part by a grant from the Minnesota State Arts Board, through an appropriation by the Minnesota State Legislature and by a grant from the National Endowment for the Arts.

MINNESOTA
STATE ARTS BOARD

*For Aaron. Still waters roil beneath.*

*To the great state of Minnesota, to every last noble tree, fresh waterway, glittering fish, singing fowl, woodland creature, field rock, swaying prairie, March skunk, October monarch, star-splattered November night sky, head-clearing January wind, and rich black clump of soil. To all the citizen stewards, sinners, orphans, mothers, and myths.*

Part I

# SINNERS

# I

## The River

STILLWATER, MINNESOTA

MAY 1863

THOUSANDS OF WHITE PINE and tamarack logs were hung up, crisscrossed, and tangled to form a dam as tight as a sinner's fingers on the St. Croix River. North of the logjam, the surface of the great river shimmered and reflected the sun, haloing the town of Stillwater so that its citizens shielded their eyes as they watched rivulets creep toward their homes and stores. A dry spring had depleted the water level, and an easterly crook in the riverbed caught the trunks, one after another, until they stretched shore to shore. The usual roar of the St. Croix was eerily quiet, and stagnant pools sat rank among the logs. The backed-up water breached Main Street, flooding the lower roads, the railroad tracks, and the basement of the state prison.

The women of Stillwater walked from one side of town to the other on boards men had thrown over the miry roads. Mud dangled like lace along skirt hems. A young woman, laden with rattraps, tripped and fell and was nearly hit by the wheels of a passing wagon, but Mr. Barton Hatterby, a local politician, grabbed her wrist and pulled her into his own arms just in time. Her heart beat hard. Mr. Hatterby was handsome and had more than

once charmed a young lass out of her knickers. Everyone in Stillwater said his wife, Millicent Hatterby, was "touched" and, worse,
had been a poor mother to their daughter, Angel. When Millicent Hatterby heard about her husband's good deed, she flew
into another jealous fit and threatened to throw herself down
the stairs. Mr. Hatterby tied her to the bedpost and sent for the
priest.

Father Paul, from St. Mary's Basilica, who'd been overseeing
the building of a clay berm to hold water back from his church,
rushed away to pray over the affected woman. While he was gone
administering extreme unction, the laborers he'd hired skulked
into the warm church and stared up at a ceiling fresco of the Virgin Mary's Immaculate Heart until they fell asleep upon the dry
padded pews. While they slept, the river water poured over the
berm and rippled down the marble stairs into the church basement, destroying relics such as a wood sliver from Christ's cross, a
bone chip from the apostle James, and a thread from Judas's hanging rope.

Stillwater horses found themselves stuck in the sludge up to
their bellies. One fought so fiercely against the sticky matter that
he worked himself into a heart attack and died where he stood.
The rest of the horses looked as though they wore thigh-high
stockings of grime. On the outskirts of town, Beaver Jean's hogs,
drowned when the waters overcame their pen, floated, their legs
up and bellies bloated. Beaver Jean's two wives lassoed the carcasses together, pulled them to dry land, and disemboweled the
animals. The women hadn't seen Beaver Jean in days. But they
were content in each other's company, with or without him.

On the north end of Stillwater town, the whores of the Red
Swan Saloon waved colorful handkerchiefs and whistled to pro-
spective clients from the safety of the dry balcony. They ordered
the hot-footed men to leave their dirty boots on the stairs. And

rather than visit each woman individually, Father Paul stood on the bottom steps and threw general absolutions up to all the doves at once. He came to hear their confessions weekly, yelling, "For your fornications say a decade of the rosary and sin no more!" The women crossed themselves. They giggled and shouted down, "We won't!"

Mr. Hatterby, who liked to wear his boots in every situation, bought an extra pair, which he kept on the third stair and would exchange for his sodden ones before he ascended to the room of Miss Daisy, the best whore at the Red Swan as far as he was concerned. Mr. Hatterby showed no shame as he passed Father Paul on the stairs. The politician had promised in his will to bequeath a great gift upon St. Mary's Basilica, and so Father Paul prayed forgiveness for the politician's lust and adultery too, even though the man's shadow had never graced a confessional.

Mother St. John, headmistress of Stillwater Home for Orphans and Infirmed, sent her children out with pails. Frogs teemed from every corner of the earth, as if sent forth in a biblical plague. The children captured them, knocked them out against rocks, and brought them to Mother St. John, who butchered them, then floured and fried the legs in hot grease. After the frog-leg feasts, prayers, and bedtime, Mother St. John's helper, Big Waters, lifted her feet for Mother St. John to tend. The withered old things were drenched, wrinkled, pale, bleeding, and dropping skin in leaves. Big Waters was called "The Beggar" in town for her frequent trips to the backdoors of the wealthy, appealing for pennies for the orphans. Big Waters had the tale of the north in her. She knew the story of the place all the way back to creation if anyone cared to ask, which no one ever did.

Stillwater children squealed with delight and were head-to-toe wet from frolicking in the water during the day. But many of them took sick with fever and chills at night. Thomas and Angel Lawrence's youngest daughter, Goldenrod, caught a chill and would suffer a cough for the rest of her short life. Thomas Lawrence was heir to and operator of the largest timber outfit in the entire north. He spent little time at home, though his wife, Angel, was considered by many to be the most beautiful woman in Stillwater. Some said, though, that if you looked near enough, you could see that her eyes were too close together and pitch-black and that her nose and chin were too pinched to be considered beautiful. Everyone agreed that she had strange ways, like her mother, Millicent Hatterby, and kept suspect company. There was something about a hidden affair with an army deserter, some gossip about a Negro lover, and more speculation about an illegitimate child kept hidden in the basement of the Lawrences' mansion. And some said she wasn't even a natural child, that she'd been abandoned by one of those prairie mothers who every year popped out a baby she couldn't feed and was then adopted by the Hatterbys when she was but a few days old. Some said her rich husband, whose Lawrence lineage went all the way back to French aristocrats, would never have married Angel Hatterby if he'd known the truth. Some said that if he found out now, he'd divorce her and disown the children and marry someone more suitable, and there were plenty of willing prospects in Stillwater. Some of the women from other prominent families of Stillwater had a good mind to send Thomas Lawrence an anonymous note. Angel Hatterby Lawrence never saw a friendly female face in Stillwater.

After three weeks of the logjam, the whole town stunk of wet wood, rotting foliage, overflowing outhouses, drowned animals, and moldy potatoes and onions. Insects of every miserable biting and stinging kind proliferated by the millions and hung over the town in a buzzing fog. Workers from Lawrence's company and all available men from the woods, the riverboats, the farmlands, the businesses, and the mills ran to the river with picks and shovels. They jabbed at logs. Everyone had a stake in it. The freedom of the river affected the livelihood of all. The mayor demanded that the logjam be freed. "Blow it up," he said. "Get that river going again." He picked at his ear, where a malarial mosquito had bitten, as he watched a thin man hack at a log near the front of the jam.

# 2

# The Key Log

A TRUMPETER SWAN, A large white fowl with black eye-bands, had taken advantage of the quiet waters dammed between the logs to build its nest and lay two eggs. For days, the mother nudged her beak against the shells now and again to encourage the babies out. She cruised the waters, ignoring the chaos around her. Only when a logger came too near did she flap her long wings and jerk her neck and honk warning.

Loggers chipped with axes at logs here and there. But the hodge-podge was enormous and dense. The odds of freeing the jam by finding the key log and chopping it were slim. Sawmill foremen, whose empty warehouses and idle employees made them frantic, raced up and down the jam. They swore at one another and at the loggers, whose pace ebbed and flowed with the approach and departure of the foremen.

The foremen kept a close eye on the logging barons, the men dressed in suits and top hats who stood on the shores and stared up and down the long knot. The barons smoked pipes and cigars, which might have suggested calm, but the foremen knew that their smoking nonchalance masked an icy fear and anger. The barons worried their logs might be lost, their profits gone. They were concerned that the logging companies of Michigan and Wisconsin would jump on the contracts for the railroad ties, the fences, the wagons, the sidewalks, the barns, and the houses of the growing country. American people of every breed and station seemed to be headed west, building cities on lakes, rivers, and railroad outposts. They put barns on the prairies, general stores in the river valleys, and depots in the crags. Those brave adventurers and entrepreneurs needed lumber. Wood was king in 1863. The barons worried they'd be left behind if they couldn't deliver it. The reputation of their infant industry would be ruined. They smoothed their mustaches and watched the water level and eyed rogue gullies streaming toward Stillwater, toward their own mansions. They'd all seen logjams before, a common enough phenomenon. But the depth and scope and compression of this one were unparalleled in anyone's memory.

When the key log was found and freed, the mess would unravel and all the logs would float on down the St. Croix toward the boomsite, where they'd be sorted by catchmarkers according to each baron's mark, where they'd be loaded and shipped and cut and sold and fashioned into barns and houses, schools and courthouses, beds and rocking chairs, pitchforks and hammers, kitchen tables and fireplace mantels, armoires and desks, floorboards and shingles, picture frames and window frames, ox yokes and fence posts, shoe soles and shirt buttons, serving bowls and knife handles, traveler trunks and train cars, smoking pipes and field plows, apple barrels and flour boxes, and sturdy baby cradles and strong unyielding coffins for the living, moving, settling, and dying pioneers of expanding America.

Someone would have to soon find the key log, bust it up, and unlock the jam. Either that, or the mayor would bring in the dynamite, devastating the inventory.

Clement Piety was one of the men searching for that particular log. Many of the other loggers weren't convinced of the key log's

existence. But as he climbed and crawled over the logjam, Clement
Piety remembered that even as a single stray thread could unravel
a cloth, so too could a single log untangle a logjam.

Clement had been born in this river valley, which once had
been surrounded by the trees now felled and knotted together in
this river. Sometimes while he was working, he swore he could
identify a single log, recognize a knot or a gnarl in it, and remember the place where it once stood as a tree. He swore he could
recall the animals that had made a home in it and the shape of
its green foliage against the blue sky. Water from this very river,
when it had been cold, clean, and free, had quenched his thirst
and washed his face since the day he was born in the tiny orphanage, a building that was then hidden and protected by dense wood
cover. Though those canopies were now nearly gone, victim to this
ruthless industry and Lawrence's greed, Clement still knew the
ways and whims of the rivers, lakes, animals, plants, and weather.
Clement Piety was a man of the trees. They grew together, thrived
together, suffered together. These other men were from countries
and lives far away. They complained of the branch-cracking cold
in winter, the tongue-thickening heat in summer, and the blood-
thirsty mosquitoes in between. They didn't understand this place.
Clement Piety didn't like them. And they didn't like him.

At twenty-three, he was still slight among his peers. Thin and
short. Gaunt and jumpy. His long sideburns aged him somewhat,
as did the two furrows in his forehead, one for each year he'd spent
at war. In May of 1863, Clement Piety had been a half-year home,
a veteran of Bull Run and Edward's Ferry, where he watched his
best friend die. He was a deserter of the Union army, a fact he
didn't advertise, though neither did he hide it. Deserters were
everywhere. No one took their capture terribly seriously this far
north. Though he'd been gone only two years, he hardly recognized Stillwater when he returned.

Lately, he'd had the feeling that someone was watching him,

following him. At first he had convinced himself that the strange feeling came from the fallen trees. He supposed that he felt exposed and vulnerable, now that the long branches, solid trunks, and hovering leaves were gone. But then, at the Red Swan Saloon, where he now rented a room, he'd heard footsteps in the hall outside his door late at night. He'd awakened to a floor creak. His heart beat so loudly that he had to wait for it to calm before he could listen for any other noise. Just as he was about to nod off again, secure that no one had been at his door, another floorboard groaned. Clement sat up, put his feet on the floor, and waited. He wondered if it was a customer of one of the ladies of the house, lost in the hallway on his way out, but somehow knew it was not. The slight scent of fur and leather and drying meat made his nose bristle. And he could sense the weight and shape of a body on the other side of the door. Clement stared at the crack between the door and the floorboards. Though it was dark, he could clearly see the silhouette of two boots. He wondered if it was a bounty hunter looking for deserters. He put his hands up in the dark as if to ward off whatever might come through the door. He was about to call out when the phantom boots twisted on the floorboards, heavily and firmly in the way of a man, and then walked away. Clement threw himself back onto his bed and stared up at the ceiling until morning. He turned his mind toward the logjam. In the dark, he found great satisfaction in visualizing it and dissecting the problem.

Now, as he climbed over two slippery logs near the nest of the swan, he thought about his sister, Angel. He wondered if she thought of him as often as he thought of her. Unlike the logjam, his problems with Angel were not easy to dissect with his imagination. There seemed to be no key log. He recalled how, as children, he and Angel would stand along the shores to watch the swans fly in and land. They'd laughed at the doddering birds arriving on the waters, lilting to one side and then the other before crashing with a splash. He remembered how he used to count the swans with Angel, hundreds of them, so prolific that every other pond and lake around here had once been named Swan Pond or Swan Lake by the Indians. But where were the flocks now? Why didn't they swarm to Stillwater any longer? Clement looked around. He wondered if perhaps they no longer recognized the place from above, now that the trees were gone and smoke from the sawmills filled the air and only stumps and brown earth and wood shavings and pine needles remained.

Clement pulled a tin of sardines from his pocket and dangled a small fish toward the swan. The bird considered him. Clement knelt slowly until they were eye to eye.

"Here," he said. "Here you go. Come and get the fish."

The swan turned and swam away from him, toward its nest, but in a sideways, coy way. Clement Piety lowered his arm. He tossed the sardine into the water, watched that silver, flickering fish float toward the swan. The bird dipped its black beak into the water and snapped up the sardine.

"Pretty good, yes?" said Clement. The swan paddled in circles. He dumped out the rest of the tin before he stood and returned to the search for the key log.

Clement Piety had been working for St. Croix Valley Lumbering for five months. He was employed as a river pig. After the winter cuttings when most loggers headed home to farms or to the towns to spend their money, Clement and the rest of the river pigs herded the logs on the river, guiding them with pike pole and peavey to the boomsites. He spent all the working day soaked to his skeleton.

Angel's husband had given him this job, and Angel had warned him not to make a mess of it. Clement despised Angel's husband, Thomas Lawrence, for his warlike assault on the trees Clement loved so much. The man didn't deserve the money he made or the wife he had. He didn't appreciate the beauty he destroyed in the landscape or in her.

But for now, Clement kept his mouth shut and did his work. If he ever found himself in the position to care for Angel, he'd need money. He was a good worker, better than most, with his wiry build and quick thinking and knowledge of the river currents. These qualities, thought Clement, should have earned him a foreman's position, whereby he could exert some control over the sweeping clearings and lead the men toward saving a stand here and there to grow and seed. But no promotion came, nor would come. So the forests came down wherever Thomas Lawrence turned his eye.

As Clement walked away from the bird, he nearly tripped over the top of a log wedged straight up and down in the tangle. Though it appeared to be stuck tight, when Clement touched the top of it and put his ear to it, he could feel and hear tension. Though it looked taut, it was humming against the strain, vibrating like a railroad track as a distant train approached. And just like that, Clement knew he'd found it. This was the one. This was the key log.

His heart pounded. Clement stepped back and looked. In his mind he speculated how, once it was broken, the adjacent log would untangle, and then the next one would curl around it, and then the one to the side would bob but then straighten out and flow downstream. It was the one that, once busted, would free up this whole mess. Clement jumped and climbed over the other logs between him and the bank. He grabbed his ax and went back to the log. He put his hand on the end of it. Then he backed up. He swung the ax up and then back down, landing a perfect blow. Another and another. The swan glided over to see what he was doing.

"Better go away," he said to it. "Shoo."

It did.

Clement swung and pecked and chipped for half an hour. Finally the log was halved.

Nothing happened. He bent to look closer. The swan came back too and gave him what he took to be a smug look.

Had he been wrong? Was there a deeper log keeping it stuck? Clement lay on his stomach and peered down through the entanglement.

Then the log split an inch more. Water trickled through the opening. Clement heard a creak. Then he saw a thicker band of the river current coax its way between the pine log's two halves, which pushed the top half up, making a space just big enough for a larger rush of water. What was, at first, a moaning of log pushing against log and a slow trickle of water between became an explosion of white pine, tamarack, water, and foam. Clement scrambled to his knees, but he had no time to get off the jam.

When the gridlock ceased to be, Clement Piety was lofted into the sky, battered in the chest by a tamarack, grazed in the face by a birch branch, and flushed in the mouth and nose with river water. His arms cycled in the air, like the wings of a teetering swan coming in to roost, and as he approached the bank, he put his hands out in front of him to soften the fall.

He landed on the bank of the river, face-down in the mud. The air left his body. He groaned. And then he heard ringing in his ears and tasted iron in his mouth. Blood trickled down his throat and, for a moment, he thought he was back in Union blues at Edward's Ferry. Clement opened his eyes to see the river racing past and roaring happily. He tried to sit up, and pain came in his chest, and he relaxed. With the relaxation came more pain and the awareness of where he was and where he was not.

"Dummy," he whispered. He moaned and turned onto the side that didn't hurt. "Ohh," he whined. He gazed up at the blue sky and oriented himself in time: 1863, not 1861. In space: Stillwater, not Edward's Ferry. In event: a logjam, not a war, not a cannonball explosion.

"OK," he whispered to himself. "Time to sit up." Clement sat, coughed, and spat out blood and the fragments of a tooth. His chest hurt. He couldn't breathe deeply. He ran his tongue over a jagged incisor. "Shit," he said. He thought intently about his sister.

*Help me, Angel,* he thought. *Please come help me.* Angel sometimes had shown a comforting knack for materializing at the moment he needed her. *Please come now too,* he thought. He hoped. Was it silly to believe in such supernatural communication, to think that one twin could call for the other through a mere thought and expect the other to hear? But didn't the religious call to their guardian angels? Didn't the braves call to their ancestors? *I need help,* he thought again. *I'm hurt.*

Clement sat for a while and waited. Though he was all wet, he felt parched. After a few more minutes, he crawled to the river's edge and lay on the ground. He lifted his head and watched the logs untangling and floating down, just as he had imagined it before he chopped the key log. The river moved freely. He had done it. He reached in with his hands to cup water and splashed his face. Clement pushed himself up and sat back.

Where was Angel? Was she so mad at him that she wouldn't help him now? She was very stubborn. And also wrathful. If she were in a fresco in St. Mary's Basilica, she'd be an angel with a halo, cradling a dove in one hand and wielding a sword in the other.

Clement decided to rest awhile before trekking back toward the other loggers. He had the feeling, again, of being watched. He looked around, but he saw no one there. His head hurt. One arm hung corrupted. It might be broken, but Clement felt no pain from it yet. But his chest hurt him strongly. *I'm in a bad way,* thought Clement. *But at least I am alive.*

Once the ringing in his ears dulled, Clement heard the faint sound of a bird. He turned his ear toward it and filtered out the rumble of the water, the alarm of other birds, and the knocking of log against log. He listened again. A peep. Again. Clement's eyes followed the sound to the river's bank. Wedged among the reeds of the shore, the swan's nest rested in a precarious position, close to the current. One side of the nest had broken apart and succumbed to the flow already, but the two eggs remained in the center, though one was crushed entirely. He could see the broken baby, dead. From a hole in the other egg poked the gray head of a cygnet, with beady black eyes that watched him. He looked around but saw no sign of the white mother swan. Clement watched as the river took another few strands of the nest, and he was reminded of what happens when one thread is pulled from the cloth.

"All right," Clement whispered. He swallowed. He pushed himself up and stood. "Where's your mama, huh?" Clement waded into water up to his knees. He steadied himself against the current. He parted the reeds and grabbed the egg with the cygnet head sticking out of it.

"Hi there," he said to the baby. "You're not even fully hatched yet." He patted it on the head with his finger. As he peeled away the eggshell, he forgot about how his body hurt. He felt like sharing what he had found. He looked up and around. He was sure he could feel Angel nearby, but there was something else too.

# 3

## The Death Blow

BEAVER JEAN WAS AN OLD man, minutes from death, though he didn't know it. He'd been watching Clement Piety from the scrub brush along the shore and had seen him fly through the air. Now he walked to where he thought the boy might have landed.

Beaver Jean's killer lurked near the shore as well. She was tiny and pushed aside bushes as she dragged an ax through the mud. Angel watched him with her soil-colored eyes, considered his shambling gait and crooked back. He would be easily smote, she thought, and not make trouble for her, her brother, her husband, her children.

All his life, Beaver Jean had been a tracker and trapper of animals and humans. From the time he was small until this moment, Beaver Jean had hunted. He had caught all kinds of creatures, beaked and sharp-toothed, four-legged and upright, winged and weighted, slow and dumb or smart and fleeting. Beaver Jean had rarely lost a mark. He guessed the creatures' diversions and could predict their aggressions and smell their hiding places. He anticipated leaps and thwarted dives into underground holes and defended attacks. But being hunted was something new, and for it Beaver Jean was unprepared.

His eyes were bad. His hearing, not too good. He was oblivious to the murderous fate that now crept toward him. The lifelong predator had turned sad old prey.

In Beaver Jean's hand was the Union army's lengthy list of deserters, with rewards next to their names, posted in all the post offices and sheriff's departments and army forts. Most of them went yellow and curled with disregard. The whole country was tired of the war.

Clement Piety's name was hidden in the middle, with a brief but efficient description: *Smallish man. No remarkable features. One eye blue and one eye brown.*

When Beaver Jean had first taken the list of deserters, he'd resolved to bring in a couple of wayward soldiers for the bounty and buy his wives a new copper pot and a hairbrush, as the pair fought over those things, to his never-ending discontentment. He'd skimmed through many of the entries but stopped cold when he read about the mismatched eyes. The description sent a twisting ice auger up his back. That particular anatomical anomaly was one Beaver Jean remembered well but hadn't seen since he was a young child.

Beaver Jean had been following Clement Piety for a week, trying to get a good look at him. On this day, Beaver Jean thought to finally confront him and introduce himself. In his mind, the young man would be initially startled, but he would soon be happy to finally meet Beaver Jean and they would shake hands and perhaps embrace each other in a hug. The young man would tell Beaver Jean that he'd been waiting for him all these years. Beaver Jean imagined all the good advice he'd give the boy: early to bed, early to rise, makes a man healthy, wealthy, and wise; a man is the king of his castle; you can lead a horse to water, but you can't make it drink; children should be seen, not heard; a penny saved is a penny earned. He had just broken into a smile when he heard the explosion of water and logs. He hurried in his old man way, all knock-kneed and belly-led, toward the noise.

Then he saw Clement Piety, knee-deep in the river. Already Beaver Jean could sense that this meeting was not going to go as he imagined. Clement Piety was cradling a bird. The river frothed and rumbled all around him. Beaver Jean thought hard about what to say at this, their first meeting.

"Watchee got there?" Beaver Jean yelled.

Clement startled. He jerked his head toward the shore and the giant with a scraggly beard, and he shielded his eyes from the sun's glare. "Who are you?" Clement asked.

Beaver Jean wondered how he should answer. Should he shout "A bounty hunter"? No. That would scare the young man, and he just might try to swim for it. How about "Your long-lost father"? No. That too might be too surprising. He searched his mind and saw Clement's eyebrows lower and shoulders cower in suspicion as he waited for an answer.

"Just a body who heard the rumble," shouted Beaver Jean. "Are ye all right?"

Clement put his hand down and touched his sore ribs. "I saw you yesterday," he responded. "You been following me?"

Beaver Jean stepped carefully toward Clement. "Come on out of there," said Beaver Jean. He pointed his cane at Clement. "I wanna talk to ye." He waved the paper clenched in his fist.

"You a bounty hunter?" asked Clement. "I served enough time. I only signed up for three months, but the army tricked me into serving three years." Clement cupped the cygnet to his chest and searched up and down the shore for a place to advance out of the reach of the man.

"Yep," said Beaver Jean. "Boy ye. That blast was something."

Clement said nothing.

"Think I saw a log a rod and a furlong up in the air," said Beaver Jean. "I heard about that scam they ran on ye First Minnesota recruits. Pretty dirty." He picked a few more careful steps closer.

"Yes, it was," said Clement. "You let me be then, if we under-

stand each other. I got dysentery in Maryland and lice in Virginia."
Clement looked up and down the shore. *Where is Angel?* he wondered. "Got used as target practice at Malvern Hill and Antietam,"
he went on. "Never got the glory they promised us." His voice
quieted, but he kept talking to the old man.

"Lost my best friend at Edward's Ferry too," said Clement. He
was again sure he felt Angel's presence nearby, but then wondered
if he was only confusing a sad memory with a present sensation.
His eyes blurred.

"Them's your natural eyes?" Beaver Jean yelled. "Come out of
there before yer get swept away or hit by a log." The river ran fast,
sweeping random logs down-current.

"No one's enforcing those desertion laws," said Clement. His
voice got stronger. "You're not taking me in. All right?" Clement
picked a careful route through the water toward the bank. His
chest pained him fiercely. It hurt to talk, but he couldn't stop.

"Let me help ye there," Beaver Jean offered.

"Are my eyes how you knew me? They got a description on
paper about my eyes?"

"They do got paper on ye," said Beaver Jean. "But I'm not taking ye in." He reached out his cane toward Clement and tried to
get a look, but the sun and the water and the tears played with the
young man's eyes, so Beaver Jean couldn't see clearly.

Clement put the cygnet in the hand on the sore side of his body.
He reached for the cane with the other. "I served brave enough in
that danged war," said Clement. "Ate hardly nothing."

"Now, grab on so I can help ye up," Beaver Jean said. "I'm an old
man and can't be standin' crouched over like this for so long."

"Got paid hardly nothing. Slept on the ground. Got shot at.
Shot down some gents I didn't even know and who never did
nothing to me. I preserved the Union, all right."

"I'm sure ye did," said Beaver Jean. "Put down that bird and pull
yourself up."

"I want it," said Clement. "I'm keeping it. My sister will like it." Holding the cane end, Clement pulled himself up toward the shallows.

"Sister?" asked Beaver Jean. He pulled hard on the cane. "Yer mama get a husband?"

Clement stopped pulling himself up and dropped his end of the cane. "What do you know about my mother?"

Beaver Jean blinked. He tried to remember that long-ago wife, round and burdened with his child, tried to recall exactly what she looked like. He was surprised to realize that all he remembered of her was red hair. "Don't know nothin'," said Beaver Jean. He shook the cane at him.

Clement stood below him on the bank, in Beaver Jean's own shadow. In that way, Beaver Jean saw clearly the eyes, the blue one and the brown. "I'll be damned," Beaver Jean said.

Clement raised his eyebrows. "You gonna pull me up or not?"

"I only knowed one other person with eyes like that. Up ye go." He heaved Clement out of the water, and they both fell onto the shore.

"Goddammit," moaned Clement. "My chest hurts." Clement coughed and cleared his throat of water and blood. "I've got a twin sister, but her eyes are brown. Both of them."

"Ye ought not to talk that way," said Beaver Jean. "Probably got some broke ribs. Feel like ye can't get a full, whole breath?"

"Yeah," said Clement. "Like I can't." The cygnet peeped. Clement smiled at it.

"Ye gonna fry him up or something?" asked Beaver Jean. He leaned over to look at what kind of bird it was. "I ate swan meat a couple times but never them young ones. So ye got a twin, huh?"

"Yes, a twin. But no, I'm not going to eat it," said Clement. "So you think my ribs are broken?"

"Without a doubt, but ribs heal up quick," said Beaver Jean. "She with yer mama?"

"No," Clement said. "I'm going to save this swan. It'll die otherwise, with no mother." He picked the piece of shell from the bird.

Beaver Jean and Clement sat for a bit. They watched the river go by, the logs floating on down the way they ought to. They heard men hooting and hollering. On the opposite bank, downriver a ways, some men were waving their hats. Beaver Jean wondered if, when those men looked at Clement Piety and himself, they thought they looked like father and son. He hoped so. Then the men wandered away.

Clement had a strange desire to sit close to the man. The same leathery smell he'd noted in his room came to him now. He wasn't repulsed by it. Rather, he felt intrigued.

Clement looked at Beaver Jean. *Who was he?* he wondered. But as soon as that thought passed, he felt he already knew. Clement swallowed. All these years he'd been thinking about his mother and had rarely, if ever, wondered about his father. He had always thought about how he'd embrace his mother and forgive her for abandoning him and Angel. He'd never imagined the man. Still, he couldn't bring himself to ask and be sure, though he felt certain. He turned and regarded the old man.

Beaver Jean stared back. Mist from the roaring river condensed on his black-and-gray beard and on the whiskers of the young man. They shared a high brow and the familiar furrows. They were both sure now. Neither said a word and neither made a move until a shadow fell over them both. Clement looked up and Beaver Jean turned his head toward the figure standing behind him.

Beaver Jean saw a flash of silver descend as if out of heaven and felt a heavy strike on the top of his head. Then he saw white. He heard the young man say, "Angel!" He felt something warm pouring down his face. He said, "Humph," and toppled over on the grassy bank.

· · ·

Upon the delivery of the deathblow, Beaver Jean was surprised to find a convergence of all the religious beliefs about the afterlife he'd ever heard of. To this point, he'd been an unbeliever. As his brain swelled inside the cranium and slowly cut his blood supply, he wondered if it was too late to change his mind about God and to offer a proclamation of belief. He wondered if God required a public statement or if thinking his allegiance to Him might be enough. Beaver Jean had the sense that he could come back to the regular world if he wanted to and take care of the declaration properly, so that there'd be no mistake about it when his time came. He had the feeling he could stop the death process, turn from the path he was on, and come back to the right world. He had the dim feeling of being tethered to the two people who now stood over him. He felt a desire to roll his eyes back properly into their sockets, sit up, and ask the pair if they were from the womb of Lydian, the little girl wife he'd lost all those years ago.

But in the center of his being, Beaver Jean was and had always been a voyager, and he could not turn from this most important journey, a unique crossing. The desire to go forward was stronger than the desire to go back. The desire to chart a new way, forge a new path was more urgent than the desire to return to the known.

At the onset of this journey, Beaver Jean saw the light that his minister pappy had always described. True to the man's sermons, Beaver Jean understood he should go toward it. The long path some of the Indians promised lay before him. While minutes passed on the shore of the St. Croix River, running wild and fast now, while his son and daughter stared gape-eyed at each other, Beaver Jean sank into a weightless and painless place where he saw his own mother waiting in the light at the end of a long wooded lane. On either side of him, brown tree trunks rose to green foliage, and above that, stars. He had the sense of falling backward and going forward at the same time, like leaning back in a canoe as it glided ahead. He saw all the waterways he'd traveled, the rapid ones with boulders and falls and the smooth ones, quiet and mirroring. He saw all the wildernesses he'd hunted, the animals he'd trapped. He saw again the bear he killed, the one that had swiped his thigh before landing in his lap, dead. He smelled again the animal's sour fur, like the odor from the underside of tree bark. He saw the women he'd loved. There'd been so many. But he lingered on his three wives; first, the two moon-faced squaws. He heard again how they bickered when he first brought the Lakota one to meet the Ojibwe one. He saw again the spritely girl Lydian, with the distended belly full of his seed, her red hair dancing away from his grip. And though he hadn't been there, he was able to see the babies knotted together in a cradle as though he had been. *Oh, dying is a marvelous adventure,* he thought.

Beaver Jean floated on ripples of earth toward his cooing mother, beautiful with her dark hair and lines around her eyes, with all their love and wisdom. Beaver Jean had always loved the wrinkles around his mother's eyes and was pleased to see them again. As he got closer he realized that the light was coming from them, that the wrinkles were like rays of the sun. The trees stretched their branches like arms and passed him along gently down the lane. Toward her. Finally toward her. "Mother?" he said. If this was heaven, it was good enough. She reached out her arms, and he could see her eyes, one blue, one brown, and was then sure. "Mother," he said. Then everywhere, fireflies.

# 4

## Clement's Fall

ANGEL UNCURLED ONE FINGER at a time, slowly releasing the handle of the ax that was planted in the man's head. Her hands hung as if ready to grab it again, should he leap up and need another whack. When she was sure the ax and the man would remain still, she stood up straight. *My God,* she thought, *I put an ax in a man's skull. I am a murderer. I have now become more like my mother than I ever wanted to be.* She felt a headache coming on, and her eyes blurred. *But where Mother is selfish and cruel,* thought Angel, *I am only protecting my family. That must make a difference.* She cleared her throat and swallowed a sour taste.

Clement's mouth opened and closed like a baby bird's.

"I didn't know those axes were so heavy," said Angel. She put a hand to her mouth. "It took every ounce of strength I've got." Her voice was shaky from nerves and hissy from trying to speak without opening her mouth very much. "I've got to get home to the girls." Saying that felt natural and true. She conjured an image of her plump, healthy little girls, which calmed her. She tried to dust droplets of blood off her skirt, but they smeared. "Oh darn," she said. She tried to think of normal things. "Would you look at this mess?" The skirt, pure lavender silk, had cost her husband ten dollars, a mighty sum.

Clement, still seated, leaned away from the old man. Finally, he stood. He stepped back from the victim. He searched Angel's face. He had tried to hear exactly what she said, but she spoke with her hand over her mouth and often mumbled, making it difficult to understand her. Had she said something about her messy skirt? He observed her as she licked a finger and scratched at a drop of blood. Then he watched her catch a glimpse of his own face, which was contorted in horror, no doubt. Then he saw her expression change from wide-eyed shock to the lowered eyelids and clenched jaw of serious displeasure. This was always how she looked after she had done something wrong and was about to shiver off the blame, like a fowl shaking the water off. "What did you do?" he asked her. "Why did you do this?" His voice was high and hoarse, which he knew would bother Angel. He had wanted those words to come out firm and deep. He knew she hated it when he sounded weak or behaved as if he was.

"That noise," she said. She put her hands to her ears as though recalling the sound of the logjam explosion. "It was something, wasn't it? Did you get hurt? Hit by a log? What do you mean, why did I do this?" she said. She laughed, a forced sound that came from the back of her throat. Her voice was steady now, and she was pleased by that. She hated it when Clement displayed the slightest vulnerability, and she thought to teach him how to be strong. "Oh, him?" she said. "I did this for *you*, dear brother." She smiled at him, but her face was tight. "That's what you want, after all. For me to do something for you. To prove my sisterly devotion." She had learned that the best way to avoid getting into trouble was to make an accusation. "Isn't that right?" Her lips whitened. "I did this," she said. She waved at the man on the ground. "So you wouldn't have to go to some military prison like that awful Camp Sumter, or worse, face the firing squad. You know they shoot deserters, don't you?" There was some truth to that, she was sure.

Clement sneezed. His eyes and throat burned from the water he'd inhaled and swallowed. Water from the river ran out of his nose. "Angel, they wouldn't send me to a Confederate military prison, and no one's enforcing—" He stopped. Trying to explain anything to her was futile once she'd decided that she was in the right.

She continued to brush at the blood on her skirt. She looked down as she spoke. "Well, how should I know that?" she asked. Then she looked at him again, at his eyes, and suddenly disliked them. "What? Now I've come to save you, and you're not grateful?" She placed her hands on her dainty hips. She inflated her chest and raised her chin. She wondered what would happen to her if anyone found out she had been here, if her husband heard she'd been talking to a laborer, if he asked her about it.

She wondered if Clement would finally reveal her as the pauperous mutt that she was. She couldn't let that happen. She smiled at him in her charming way. She put her hand on his shoulder and pulled him toward her. "Oh Clement," she whispered. "I just wanted to keep you safe. I didn't want that big brute to arrest you and have you in the big stony prison."

Those were the kinds of words Clement always hoped to hear from his sister. He wished she'd offer to take him home and fix up his wounds, but she didn't and wouldn't. He wasn't allowed near the Lawrence mansion, come what may. "He was about to tell me something about our mother," Clement said. He pulled away from Angel and spit out a mouthful of saliva and blood. His sheared tooth was beginning to sting.

Angel fought the desire to run away and go back home and lock her doors. She wondered what the man had told Clement, how much he already knew, whether he'd meander the saloons telling this new bit of his story, their story, to anyone who'd listen. Clement was a terrible nuisance. She hoped she'd quieted the trapper in time, so that no one would know that Clement was his child, that she was his child, that she wasn't a natural child of the Hatterbys, that she didn't have the pedigree to be married to a man like Thomas Lawrence, that her children's blood was soiled with the filth of a fur trapper and his witless child bride. Angel touched his head. "Are you going to be sick?" she asked him. "Take a deep breath." She took out her hankie and wiped the corner of his mouth. She smiled again. She hated it when he, when any man, was sick or hurt. She despised it when men trumped up the slightest of aches or illnesses.

Clement wanted desperately to lay his head in her lap. He wanted Angel to dab his forehead and cheeks with her hankie for hours. He craved her tenderness. But he shook his head. "I'm all right," he said. He thought of what else a strong man might say. "It hardly hurts at all." Then he knelt and touched the chest of the old man. "He knew our mother," he said to Angel. And then, trying hard to warp his voice so that it was at once low and quiet and serious, he added, "I think this is our father."

Angel scoffed at him. "My father is the attorney general of Minnesota," she said. Then she laughed again. Here they were, standing over a murdered man, possibly minutes from discovery and arrest, and all Clement could think of was his sad old story, his wretched pitiful abandonment. He'd said, "I think," which meant he didn't know for sure. "And you don't have a father. Now stop with that nonsense, would you?" she said. "That's ridiculous. Look at him." She did and was repulsed.

Clement was getting teary again.

"For God's sake," she said, "you're twenty-three years old." How could he be so sentimental? Where were his will and his courage and his stoicism? The urge to lift the ax one more time flared across her brain.

"But, our mother, she could still be alive or—"

"Our mother was probably a whore," Angel snapped. Anger rose in her throat. "In any case," she spit, "she didn't want us, and it's best to forget about her." This man was her brother, her twin, but he seemed so foreign now, so unlike her. How could they have had the same mother? Though once she loved him more than any other, now she recoiled at the sight of him. A man should not be so weak.

Clement's lips turned down. "You don't know that," he said.

Angel turned away from him. She thought of her own daughters. She had to get back to them. Whenever she was apart from them, she felt unsettled, dark, and worried. She resented Clement for pulling her from her children, for not understanding that she was a mother now. She resented him for threatening her marriage, which in turn threatened the safety of her girls, his own nieces. She resented his attachment to the past, his desire to fix it or return to it or hold on to it. Even his devotion to her, rooted in fantasies and glorified memories of their childhood, seemed pathetic and silly.

Clement watched Angel turn fidgety, noted the way she wouldn't look him in the eye and the way she drummed her fingers on her hips as if impatient, all signs that she was about to leave. He couldn't let her. Clement shook the old man a bit. He was stiffening. "Well, what are we going to do about him?" he asked her.

Angel gestured toward the river. "Push him in. If he turns up, people will think he got hurt in the log explosion." She turned to go.

Clement couldn't believe it. She was going to leave Clement like this, hurt, next to the man she killed. "But there's an ax in his head," he called after her. His voice was high and squeaky again.

Angel was already stepping away. "Pull it out," she said.

Clement looked at the dead man, at the whites of his eyes and the ax in his head. The cygnet peeped. "Could you at least take care of this little guy?" he said.

This was always his way: to nag her into turning around after she'd already determined to go, to beg her to stay another minute or two, to commence vacuous talk that lengthened her time with him. She wanted to sprint away. But Angel turned and walked back to her brother. She tried to keep calm. "Here," she said. "Let me have him." She reached out her hand.

Clement handed the cygnet to Angel. She took it. Clement was about to say, "Careful," but he could see the writhing annoyance beneath her controlled countenance, so he didn't. "Thanks," he said to her.

"Get him in the water before someone comes," she said.

"I can't push him in the river," he said. "It's not right."

The noise of approaching loggers fell upon the pair. "You'd rather I go to jail?" She raised her eyebrows and then tried to make her eyes water and voice quaver. "Is that what you want? To see me in prison?"

"Of course not," Clement whispered to her, and waited until she seemed calm. "But I can't treat him that way. You could go talk to your father."

"Don't even think about my doing that," she said. She looked around. "People are coming, Clement," she hissed. "Push him in the goddamn water." And then she added, "You spineless weakling."

Clement's shoulders hunched. He hung his head. He'd asked too much of her and now she was angry with him again. He wanted to slap her and embrace her at the same time. He inhaled. "You go," he said. "I'll figure this out." How was he going to bury the body and prove to Angel that he was brave? Why couldn't she see it? Hadn't he been a soldier? Hadn't he risked his life for the lives of countless others? Why was she so cold to him? So icy? He was the only real family she had. What was it going to take to make her see? Resolve took him over. "I would do *anything* for you, Angel. You remember that."

"I know," she said. She spun around and hurried away without looking back. Her skirt flapped behind her like a magician's cape. Clement searched the riverbank for a place to hide the body until nightfall, when he could return and bury it proper. But in another

minute he looked up and saw the boys whose hooting and hollering he and Angel had heard. They were standing on the opposite
shore, pointing at him.

At the trial a couple of months later, Clement's appointed lawyer,
an ambitious man from the East who'd come to Minnesota hoping
to represent escaped slaves, drummed up a couple of river workers
as witnesses. They claimed to have seen a woman near the scene.
Some said she was young and well dressed. Others said she was
old and small, with slumped shoulders. Clement claimed ignorance of these apparitions and seemed resigned to go to prison. He
gave his lawyer little to work with. He confessed. "The man had
been following me," Clement said. "The man threatened to arrest
me for desertion," he said. "I had my ax. I swung it in his head."

To the judge, the list found on Beaver Jean's person seemed to
confirm this. The judge had no legal education, nor did he enjoy
legal wrangling. He lit a cigar and waved away Clement's lawyer even as the lawyer wondered how, with several broken ribs, a
cracked arm, and severe bruising, Clement Piety could have done
the murderous deed.

"This act," the lawyer argued, "would have required a person's
full strength. An upright stance. A full swing. This man, Clement
Piety, could not have done it. I plead to the court."

"He confessed!" shouted the judge. He threw his arms this way
and that. The smoke from his cigar wafted up and curled in the
humid air. "It wouldn't matter if he was paralyzed from the neck
down. He confessed and that's good enough for me! Now close
your argument, sir!"

"But what if he's taking the onus for someone else?" the lawyer
asked. "What if this confession is nothing more than theatrics?"

The judge relaxed in his chair and reached one hand up his
sleeve to scratch his armpit. "You better watch your mouth, son."
Under his sleeve, he herked and jerked his hand, removed it from

his sleeve, and studied an extracted coarse black hair before he dropped it on the table. "In any case, that's not the concern of this court. Now close your argument! I'm not going to tell you again without consequence." He yawned.

"Then God save the corrupt courts of Minnesota, which do not remember the toils of the men now embroiled in the noble cause of righteousness and freedom and who fight and die daily, nor give representation to the vulnerable and weak—"

"You can quit your preaching. Everyone's sick to death of that war and war talk. I'm cousin-in-law to Mary Todd Lincoln. My employment here is secure, young gun. And your words don't play on me." He slammed his gavel and turned to the sheriff, who sat picking a wart on his finger with the blade of a small knife. "Sheriff, take the man, this murderer, this cowardly deserter, to the warden and task him to find a nice warm cell and some good labor to busy this prisoner's idle hands and redeem his wayward acts. Tell this prisoner about what's happened to the rest of his good, brave company at Gettysburg and tell him to enjoy his rest on his cot and be thankful to God he isn't right now splaying his innards to the crows of Pennsylvania." Then the judge turned to Clement. "Eighty percent casualties among the First Minnesota regiment, boy. You keep that in mind when you're sleeping on a clean cot tonight."

And then the judge turned to the lawyer. "And you, representing deserters and Negroes and wild Indians." The judge shook his head in deep disappointment. "And didn't I see you in here trying to work up some nonsense about women's property rights? I don't know where you think you are or who you think you're talking to, but this here is Minnesota, an infant state but fulla experienced men who know more than a little bit about governing. You better watch yourself and put down those rebellious notions." Then he pounded his gavel and farted.

# 5

## Angel and Big Waters

O N  T H E  D A Y  T H E  L O G J A M  unraveled, downriver a short
way Angel Hatterby Lawrence and Big Waters passed each
other on a path. Angel wore a dress of lavender silk, splattered
with blood drops, and white side-laced boots, caked in mud. As
she raced away from the death scene, she worried over having to
ask Thomas for the money for a new gown and another pair of
boots. He would ask many questions. She carried a quiet cygnet in
her dainty palm.

Big Waters hobbled along, slowed by old age, and blood spots
bloomed through her animal-skin slippers. In her arms she held
the dead mother swan, its neck broken in the blast. She had
picked it up downstream from under a branch. The beautiful bird
reminded her of the many stories she knew that no one was interested in hearing anymore.

When they met, the two women understood each other and
swapped the animals, so that Angel took the dead fowl for its beautiful feathers and Big Waters took the living cygnet, for it needed
a willing mother. Each woman fiercely disliked the other, but they
accepted that their lives, through Clement, were entwined.

"The trapper is dead," said Angel.

"It is for the best," said Big Waters. She looked hard at the young woman, remembered those same fierce eyes in the face of a robust infant, long ago.

"Keep Clement away from me now," said Angel.

"You are all he wants, but I will try," said Big Waters. "Your debt to him is now paid."

"I never owed him anything," said Angel, knowing the words to be false.

# Part II

# MOTHERS

# 6

## The Reluctant Mother

LYDIAN, RUNAWAY WIFE of Beaver Jean the trapper, lay in the thin, stiff bed of Stillwater Home for Orphans and Infirmed, repeating, "Whoo-whee, whoo-whee," and sighing loudly. Her newborn twins lay right next to her, nestled stomach to back, the girl screaming, the boy sleeping through the racket his sister raised a mere breath from his ear.

"I can't believe I lived through that," Lydian said. "If that's how birthing feels, I can't believe any woman alive would suffer it knowingly." Lydian patted the head of the crying infant a bit too hard, and she squalled louder.

"You don't know what I've just done for you," she said to the babe. She rubbed the child's chest. "If you knew, you wouldn't cry at me like that."

Lydian thought of the four births she'd witnessed in her seventeen years: a standing cow who plopped her offspring onto a shit patty and commenced grazing lackadaisically while her calf struggled to stand on its trembling legs, a dog that licked the slick membrane off her pups and then snoozed lazily while they yanked at her teats, a garter snake that squeezed out a hundred or more baby snakes and then turned up on her back and died while they dispersed into the grass, and her own stepmother, who popped out Lydian's little sister.

"I can't believe it," she said. "I can't believe there's a body on this world at all if that's how it feels for all ladies squishing out babies. No right-thinking woman would ever let that baby get in her to begin with."

"It wasn't so bad as that," said the woman who'd delivered the twins. "If you're a married Catholic woman, bearing babies to be baptized into the Holy Catholic Church is your duty." The woman tried to put a rolled-up cloth soaked in water into the crying baby's mouth, but she wouldn't take to it.

"You're too old now," Lydian asked the woman, "but did you have some children like I just did? Did you push out some babies back in the old days who are grown now?" Lydian tried to imagine this woman lifting up her skirts and birthing a baby the way she had just done. She wondered if the woman would have had the same tight-lipped look to her then.

"I'm not yet thirty years in this world, girl," said the woman. "But I've not had any children. I made a vow to the Lord. I'm a bride of Christ." The woman made clucking noises at the baby.

"You took up the nun life?"

"I did. The sister's life, more accurately. Nuns are cloistered. Sisters do good works in the world. You can call me Mother St. John."

Lydian wondered why all the nuns she'd ever encountered always talked about women's duties. She wondered if it was because they couldn't have any woman's duties of their own and coveted woman's natural ways. But from where Lydian was positioned, the life with no rutting husband nor crying babies looked easier. So then she wondered if the nuns always talked about women's duties in order to keep girls like her from flooding the convents and becoming brides of Christ. Maybe there wouldn't be enough room for all the girls who'd want a nun life if they knew how nice it was with no big belly and baby sickness and then the deathly birthing and then the loud crying with no relief in sight. And that's not even mentioning the leg-spreading to endure. The nun life sounded like the life to live.

"Do all babes yelp so noisy?"

"No," said Mother St. John. "This one seems a bit fussier than most."

Lydian very much longed for the moment she could creep from this bed and out the door away from here, far from these babies and anyone who'd ever known her. Above all else in the world, she wanted to find a nice, warm place where the folks ate sweet food. But she'd have to bide her time.

The girl child was as heavy as a sack of coffee and had a head full of black hair, while the boy was much lighter and bald as a new possum. When the babies opened their eyes, slate gray irises big as coins peeked out. And though Lydian would not be there to see the change, in the coming months, the eyes of the girl would darken to mink brown. The boy's left eye would match his sister's color, but the right eye would live a blue life all its own, like a little pool of water.

Lydian was worn through from the journey, labor, and delivery, but the woman who had delivered the twins said that she would be up and moving about in a few days. She told Lydian to think of all the women who brought children into the world in dark, cold, and lonely places with a lot less fuss than Lydian had made.

"You scared away the turkey I was going to butcher for supper," she had told her. "When your husband arrives, he'll have to pay for it."

"Maybe you should have tied that tom up if he was the kind to run off." She pulled a greasy strand of hair over her mouth and sucked on it. "Maybe I'll just clean up and be ready for when he gets here, my husband."

"Soon enough," the woman said. She patted Lydian's leg. "The babies are not ready to travel quite yet. I'd like to see them each latch on proper before you're off."

"Just a little while perhaps," said Lydian. "Do you have any sugar here?" She looked out the window at the snow coming down and was happy to think of her tracks being covered. She sucked harder.

"Spit that out," said the woman. "It's a dirty thing to do."

"Hmm?" said Lydian. "Sure is snowing."

"Yes," said the woman. "We should say a prayer that your husband will find us quickly and safely."

Lydian thought of Beaver Jean, hairy as a goat and lumpy as a turtle shell. She supposed he'd be eager to bring a wagon to gather his wife and babies, if he knew where to find them. But when the laboring pains began several days ago, Lydian had sneaked away to the one place she knew he'd not look for her first. He'd come here second or third perhaps, but not first. He'd first go to her stepmother's and look for her there. But that gave her only a two-day start on him. He'd eventually think to come to the infirmary, though Beaver Jean tried to avoid the religious sort. He said their eyes gave him nervous fits and put his stomach in a weasely way.

Lydian had lived with Beaver Jean and his two squaws, who hated her, for nearly two years, since the day Lydian's stepmother had sold her to the trapper for a couple of pelts. Before Beaver Jean had even gotten Lydian back to his cabin, he'd bent her over and staked her like a landmark, grunting throughout the ordeal. After that, he pushed his groin against her in daylight and dark and created a mighty racket as he thrust about until he collapsed in a smelly heap and fell asleep. He was never-endingly kissing and touching her hair. And when she'd crawl out from beneath his massive body or entirely escape his affections, the other women he lived with as wives beat her with their bare fists and pulled her yellow-red hair. The squaws tried to do away with the life that had grown in her belly by starving her when Beaver Jean was away from the cabin.

When the laboring pains had started days before, in short tight coils every few hours or so, Lydian waited until nightfall and then crept out into the night, fleet-footed, considering her condition. When it was all over, she wanted to head toward Mexico, where she heard ladies could wear lace in all colors, even red, and where it never snowed. She'd marry a Mexican cowboy and raise colorful roosters on a farm and drink coffee like a lady. But first, Lydian turned north and went to the place where she knew she could deliver and leave her baby. She'd heard some farmers had gone there to adopt a boy for their own family. Lydian supposed someone would adopt hers too.

Lydian was thinking of Mexico, its red sun and red soil, when the girl baby started screeching again as if an owl had torn her skin with its talons. Lydian panted, shallow breaths. She felt faint. She looked again to the babies on the bed beside her and stroked their heads. She once had a bitch that had birthed two pups and protected them like they were bricks of gold. Lydian wished she had a brick of gold.

She picked up the girl child, the one who cried. The baby's lips opened and her head shook back and forth, seeking the breast. Lydian indulged the girl, who latched on ferociously.

"Ouch, you greedy little thing," Lydian said. The baby tugged and swallowed.

Lydian's belly cramped and relaxed, already working to put her middle back to trim, and with that pain all she wanted to do was to place these babies on someone else's lap, curl into a ball, and sleep. Her thighs pounded with aches, and they sometimes shook with powerful chills. Bouts of nausea came and went with each cramp. The very thought of all the blood she passed from her body onto the rags under her bottom nearly sent her into a faint. All her seventeen years she'd trapped and hunted, skinned and gutted, filleted and butchered carcasses of every sort. The ground behind her father's shack was stained red with the blood of the animals she'd prepared. And never had the sight, smell, or thought of that blood made her ill. She put her finger in the corner of the baby girl's mouth and released the suction. Then she placed her next to her brother. Lydian put the girl's own fist to her lips to suck, which the baby did.

"I'm feeling quite sickly," she told the stern woman. "Maybe you could put these babes on another cot for a bit so I could rest a spell."

"Look around here, missy," said the stern woman. "I got orphans and sick ones and old ones in every nook and cranny. I don't have a bed to spare."

Lydian fought to keep her thighs steady and her teeth from chattering and breaking off into little bits. She'd often had troubles with her teeth and couldn't afford to lose even one more. Willing herself to control her body, Lydian focused on how nice it would be to not be pregnant anymore but couldn't remember a time when she'd felt so cold and so pained. She recalled how her stepmother had given birth at the cabin and how she'd been up and frying griddlecakes for supper a few hours later. Lydian remembered the strange smell of the woman, blood and milk and earth and animal.

A jumble of thoughts and feelings kept her from a peaceful snooze. The babies would stay here. She knew that. She would be crawling out from under the warm blanket and off the worn straw mattress at the first opportunity. She'd pull her boots from beneath the bed and carry them out the door. She'd put them on outside and walk away.

But as she looked at the babies, she couldn't deny the feelings of . . . what? Care? Tenderness? Affection? Or love? She'd hardly ever heard that word used, except when her stepmother would say, "I love syrup!" as she tapped the maples and licked her fingers clean like a raccoon, or when Beaver Jean would say, "I love an Indian on firewater!" and then hurry away from the tribe, tripping under the weight of the pelts he'd swindled from the drunk ones and not paying any mind to the plight of the Indian woman looking for a scrap of food or a covering for the little ones. Lydian didn't know, for certain, what the word *love* meant. The sight of these babies' little lips made her throat feel like her tongue was swelling up and choking her.

Lydian wondered if at some time someone felt for her what she now felt for these babes, which was an odd urge to ladle them up and lick them. Doubtful that such a thought had ever crossed the mind of the ma who birthed her, her pa, or the stepmother who raised her and then sold her to Beaver Jean, Lydian did scoop up first the boy and then the girl and licked them both on the cheek. Neither seemed to mind. She lay them back on the bed.

Lydian realized that the stern nun must've given up her own bed for Lydian and the babes. Above the bed hung a picture of the Virgin Mary wearing a blue gown, with her heart exposed and circled in roses. A strand of praying beads lay on the bed table, and a crucifix lorded over the fireplace at the foot of the bed.

She heard, coming from another room, Mother St. John telling a story about a little man named David having a quarrel with a Philistine giant who wanted to kill him and enslave his people. She heard one child ask, "Was it a sin for David to kill Goliath?" She heard Mother St. John answer, "Yes. I suppose it was. But we have to think about how many good Catholics Goliath would have enslaved and murdered, had David not killed him. And I'm sure David offered his confession shortly afterward."

Lydian puzzled on that.

"What do you do with all those children?" she asked Mother St. John when she came to change Lydian's rags.

"Baptize them," said Mother St. John. "Keep some. School

some. Sometimes farm families come looking for children too. So sometimes we find them families, which is what we prefer, of course."

"Do some of them go to rich folks sometimes?" Lydian asked. "Or folks who have a mother who can make sweets?"

"Sometimes," said Mother St. John. She looked at Lydian oddly, then left to tend to the children's bedtime rituals.

This was where Lydian would leave the twins. So these moments offered Lydian her last chance at holding them both, cradled in complete innocence. But for now, Lydian was overcome with the pain in her own body and with the strange things happening to her womb and her breasts and her heart, which was full of an ache she could not explain. She had to get away. She had to get out of the infirmary before Beaver Jean found her and dragged her back to his affections and the squaws' wrath. Perhaps, Lydian told herself, the children would be adopted by a nice family. More and more, men were dragging women to this remote part of the country and sticking up wood houses or stacking together soddy huts in the middle of the forests. Towns grew up here, with proper churches and schools for children to be raised in a civilized way. Lydian knew of orphan wagons that brought little children from far away to the farmers here, who would adopt them. People here wanted children.

# 7

## Beaver Jean the Trapper

I F THERE WAS ONE THING Beaver Jean had learned from his pappy, it was that there was a wrong way to do something and a right way to do something. "It's the wrong way, the way yer doing that" was what his pappy would say to Jean if he was baiting a fishhook or tying a knot or eating an egg. "That way too is not right," his pappy would say when Jean would attempt a correction. "Watch me, and learn ye the right way," his pappy would go on.

No matter what it was, his pappy would do the task as quickly as possible, his back to his boy, and in a way that was hovered over, almost as if he didn't want Jean to see and learn at all. So, if the task was pulling a rotten tooth out of a calf's head, he'd place Jean behind him and tell him to "watch and learn if ye can." His pappy's arms, from behind, would look like lightning bolts flashing here and there. Then his pappy would turn around with the rotten tooth in hand and say, "Easy as pie," which was strange because making pies didn't come easily to Jean's mother apparently, as Jean had seen his pappy take bites of a hundred pies baked by his mother, spit each one out, and say, "Something has gone terribly wrong here." If, after watching his pappy's demonstration, Jean still didn't get the task right, his pappy would say, "Go on up to the house with yer mother before ye cause all sorts of ruination on a biblical scale."

His mother spoke only French, which was a language Jean's father thought to be flashy and fussy and the wrong way to talk. Though Beaver Jean rarely spoke with his mother, he preferred her over his pappy. She was a gentle woman and often petted his hair and stroked his earlobes. Jean loved his mother very much, and she doted on him until the one day when, even though his pappy had told her a hundred times that lighting the stove while wearing hoops beneath her skirt was the wrong way to do it, she did it the wrong way, and her skirt hem caught fire. Before Jean's eyes, she blossomed into a pillar of flames. She hustled outdoors, which his pappy later said was the right thing to do and a miraculous display of wit from a woman who would pick up the wrong end of a snake. Her right-minded thinking saved the house from burning down. She ran to the horse trough and dived in, putting out the fire but suffering a terrible sight of black, peeling, pus-oozing wounds all over her legs and belly.

She lived a few days, but not many. She died on a Sunday, on a day when the magnolia leaves were falling from the trees. Though losing her felt very wrong to Jean, having the flowers falling down at the time of her death felt right.

Pappy said that the right thing to do was to bury her and move on ahead. He moved the young slave woman, Jessie, into the house the next day to do the cooking, cleaning, and such, and she took up the place where his mother had slept. That did not seem to be right to Jean's thinking, but he was only just becoming a man at thirteen, and he wasn't sure whether it was he or his pappy who was right. So Jean asked his pappy. His pappy said, "Questioning the dos and do nots of my actions is the wrong thing to do." Not more than a year later, Jean bent that slave girl, Jessie, over a chair for himself one afternoon, and she told his pappy on him, which Jean did not think was right since she had seemed eager to go along with the transaction in the first place and shouted, "Yeah boy! Giddap, boy. Uh, uh," all throughout. His pappy told him that taking the slave girl, Jessie, for himself, even one time, was the wrong thing to do and sent him packing, saying, "Come back here ever again, and ye will see nothing but your life flash before yer eyes and ruination on a biblical scale." So Jean had called his dogs, neither of whom came to him as they were as disloyal creatures as any that had ever been born on this earth, and walked off the property, never to see Jessie or his pappy again. But to this very day, when he thought of bending Jessie over that chair, his loins flooded with blood.

Though his loins had not flooded with blood upon the sight of his first wife, In the Trees, nor his second, The Girl with Friend Eyes, the women proved vital to his survival in the great unknown north, where he found himself in the months after his banishment from his father's house. Beaver Jean had never seen so many different kinds of faces or languages as he discovered near the headwaters of the Mississippi River, which is where the whole world seemed to converge. To his luck, everyone was looking for someone or something, and Beaver Jean was a skilled finder. If a timber man needed a harmonica, Beaver Jean could locate it. If a river pig wanted tobacco wrappers, Beaver Jean could produce them. If an Ojibwe needed a hairbrush, Beaver Jean would remember the one sitting on the mantel of the pioneer family's fireplace a few hours away. He would recall that the pioneer family had needed meat, and he would thus negotiate a buffalo tongue in exchange for the hair groomer. He'd picked up his wives in such ways, and they were useful women, translators in this Babelic place, with maps of it imprinted on their brains.

He had found Lydian, his third wife, back in 1837 by way of smoke from a chimney. Above the winter trees, Beaver Jean had seen the black plume rising like hell and considered it a good omen. After four days of traipsing through the drifts and sleeping under buffalo-skin tents, he had been aching for four walls and a bed. He adjusted his heavy pack and stepped forward.

The Galtier cabin rested deep in the woods along the Snake
River. All winter, the women of the house fended for themselves
while their man worked north in the lumbering camps. Beaver
Jean couldn't quit thinking on the little white girl Lydian. Each
year he'd make an offer on her—a barrel of wild rice, a shotgun,
a couple of heavy beaver pelts, whatever he had, and the mother
would always laugh and turn him down as if he was teasing.

"Little Lydian?" she'd say. "Too young to be a wife. Too stupid."

It was true that her girl Lydian looked spacious behind the eyes.
But he had a witless wife already and found her to be the least
trouble. No. It wasn't Lydian's manner or smarts he wanted. He
only wanted a fresh body, a little one. One who smelled different
from his own women. One whose hair wasn't so thick, whose body
wasn't so dense or dark. He wanted one to climb all over him like
a squirrel on a tree, rather than rub like a heavy bear against his
trunk, as his wives were apt to do. One who offered tender white
meat like that of a prairie chicken or grouse, rather than the tough
red meat of a buffalo or bear. He wanted a little delicacy.

When the woman of the house finally agreed to give up Lydian
for some coffee and a few shoddy pelts, Beaver Jean nearly leapt
out of his boots. Negotiating with women was never predictable.
They were particular and flighty and enjoyed bantering in a way
that men did not. Whereas a man would grow tired of talks after
an hour or two, a woman would prefer that the back-and-forth go
on for days, weeks, and, in this case, five years before settling the
matter. In any event, Beaver Jean was happy to finally have her and
determined not to lose her once she was his.

Beaver Jean was a man of the wilderness, a hunter, trapper, liquor
runner, and tracker. As a child in the South, he'd been given his
first pair of bloodhounds at age eleven, a gift from his pappy to get
him started in the lucrative fugitive-slave-tracking business. This
work suited Jean well, but the hot weather did not. His skin was
highly sensitive, and hours in the sun made it red, sore, bumpy, and

itchy. As soon as he was able, Jean worked his way north, where most months were cool or cold, where there was more opportunity and less competition for the skills that Jean possessed.

So when he'd come home and discovered that his only white wife, the only one to ever get big with his child, had up and run away, Beaver Jean didn't panic. The Indian wives sometimes left too, when they got to missing their mothers or brothers and sisters. He would find Lydian and bring her home.

A little jolt of excitement struck him, in the way that some men get excited over pulling the fish out of the water or the wolf carcass out of the trap. It made him feel useful and alive. He told this plan to his wives, who had gleefully danced around him upon his return and played wholly ignorant about Lydian's disappearance. If Beaver Jean hadn't seen his older horse was gone, he would have suspected the pair of a murderous act on Lydian to be sure. He'd have to let his horse and dog rest awhile, but at first light, he'd be off again. There wasn't a man or boy, criminal or fugitive, who had ever evaded Beaver Jean when he was on the bounty trail. But women, mothers or mothers-to-be, could prove a bit more trouble. Women were craftier than men and boys. Their desperation made them willing to try anything. Once he'd heard of a slave woman who took up shelter in a bear's den rather than face the catcher. Though the bear did maul her to death, it didn't touch her little pickaninny, so the catcher shot the bear, skinned it, and got paid for the child and the fur.

Beaver Jean pulled out the document he'd ripped off the Fur Trade Post that afternoon.

*$100 Reward. Eliza and child. Ran away from kind and generous Mistress Winston who wants the pair returned safely to her and unharmed if possible. ELIZA, average height. Slim face and body. Comely face with black gums, snaggly teeth, and plaited hair. A very elegant girl who was given too much education and trust and*

*took advantage of the kindness of her owners who only worked
her around the kitchen and house and never had her lift a finger
to hard labour. About 20 years old. DAVIS, child of close to three
years. Very white eyes and small teeth. Has a downcast disposition
when spoken to and blinky eyed. The pair ran away from Stillwater last Friday after they were reported at the general stores
collecting supplies for the Winstons' return to Mississippi, a trip
which has now been postponed herewith and until further notice.
REMINDER slaves of the south are considered property of their
masters even if the masters take them to non-slave states or territories. Please contact Wm. Winston, the Westerly Hotel, Stillwater.*

A hundred dollars. Jean refolded the paper and put it back into
his pocket. He pulled the rocker close to the fire, sat down, and put
his bare feet toward the flames to relieve his aching toes, which
had been frostbitten when he'd passed out in the snow a couple
of weeks before. The things had turned first green, then blue, and
were now black and creating a terrible pain up his ankle and calf.

Those toes looked like hell. And it seemed to him that the
green color was creeping up his foot. This was a damned problem,
he knew. Something that'd have to be taken care of sooner than
later. The toes would probably have to go. Who could do it? Could
he cut them off himself? He wasn't sure. He knew he could get
drunk enough to dull the pain, but he didn't know if he could get
drunk enough to dull the pain and chop straight.

He thought of his pappy. He wondered what he would've done
with toes like these. Would he chop them off himself? Or would
he get someone else to do it? Would he use a saw? A hatchet? It
was hard to know the right way about everything. Beaver Jean
thought that when his son came, he'd be careful to teach him the
right way and the wrong way to do things too, just as his pappy
had taught him. Only he would do it better. And he would take
care not to scare him with talk of ruination on a biblical scale.

# 8

## *Mother St. John the Sister and Nurse*

MOTHER ST. JOHN gathered up the rags and blanket on which the girl had given birth. She'd have to boil and soap them thoroughly. Father Paul had recently told her a story of bears near here waking sporadically from their winter's sleep to seek food. She looked at the dreaming infants and shivered as she imagined one of those heads in the jaws of a black bear or their bodies being torn by a bear's long claws. Why did her mind work in such ways? She had no trouble envisioning the most dreadful things: snakes wrapped around a child's neck, spiders laying eggs in children's ears, tapeworms sliding out of a child's bottom. Sometimes she worried that the terrible images were sinful, or a sign that the devil had hold of her mind. But when she confessed the sights to Father Paul, he asked her if those imaginings didn't heighten her vigilance over all the Lord's children in her care, and of course, she said they did. And after that, she had felt better about receiving them and began to regard them as a gift from the Holy Spirit and another sign that she was indeed doing what the Lord had called her to do.

Mother St. John glanced at Lydian, who was studying the ends of her hair as Big Waters rubbed her legs, a thing the Indian women always did for each other after birthing. Surely no dreadful dream or complex thought had ever come to that girl. But something about her was quite familiar. Mother St. John sensed that the girl had been to the infirmary before. Mother St. John thought back to her first days in this place and soon her mind became confused over all the years and all the faces she had seen.

"Say," said Mother St. John. She brought a lantern close to Lydian's face and sat on the side of the bed. She too stroked Lydian's thigh. "You look quite familiar to me, now that I see you without so big a belly. Have we met before?"

"No," said Lydian. "I don't know a body in the whole world."

"I suppose I've been mistaken," replied Mother St. John. "There's just something about you that's got my memory working." Big Waters opened the door then and walked to her bed, where she flopped down as though exhausted.

"I can't keep them," Lydian said. She spoke to, but didn't look at, the nun. "You'll have to keep them."

Big Waters clucked her tongue.

Mother St. John raised her eyebrows and closed her eyes. She lowered her head a moment, and then raised it to look at Lydian. "Mothers shouldn't do such a thing," she said. "You can't just have children and then abandon them."

Lydian sealed her lips together.

"It can't be as bad as you think," said Mother St. John. "You'll feel better in a day or two."

Mother St. John considered the girl who'd just birthed these children. She could see through the eyes and into the pain. What had brought this girl here? Who was she? Where was her husband? Her family? Mother St. John imagined all the possibilities: the young mother couldn't afford the twins, couldn't feed them; the father was dead or had run off. Or perhaps these children were illegitimate and the girl had been run out of her house by her angry father. Perhaps even worse. Maybe the children were the product of incest. Perhaps that was why the boy looked so pale and sickly.

"You think on it some more," said Mother St. John. "If you don't change your mind, we'll think of something."

"Please take them," said Lydian. "Maybe they could get a good mother who lives on a farm with some animals or in one of those mansions that's been put up by the river. Or you could keep them here with that Big Waters. She favors this boy babe. I know it."

Big Waters perked up.

"You can't be telling him premonitions, though," said Lydian to the Indian woman. "I don't like that."

Big Waters came over and picked up the boy child. She took him back to her own bed and held him as he slept.

"I'll have to write some papers if you're sure," said Mother St. John. "To make it legal, you understand. You'll have to sign them."

Lydian nodded. "But I can't write anything but an L. I can make a nice L, though."

# 9

## Stillwater Home for Orphans and Infirmed

LYDIAN AWOKE TO HER babies being placed beside her. Through the night, Big Waters had tended the boy babe and Mother St. John the girl babe. Lydian had slept. Now, as she stirred, the two women crept quietly out of the room to leave the mother with the children. Lydian watched their skirts sweep behind the door before it closed. A waft of air ruffled the pages on the table next to her bed. There too sat a quill and ink. Though Lydian couldn't read, she knew what these things were. And she tried to remember, exactly, which way an L faced. She had learned once and recalled scratching the letter in the dirt.

In the outer room, Mother St. John and Big Waters looked at each other. Then they began preparing breakfast for the rest of the children. Big Waters peeled potatoes, and Mother St. John added bacon fat to a skillet.

"I suppose we'll find room for the babes," Mother St. John said. "I know a couple who lost a baby recently, and maybe they'd be interested in the pair."

Big Waters circled a paring knife around a potato eye and popped it out.

"I was thinking that whenever a baby is born or people move to this territory, papers ought to be drawn up, so that it's possible to track population growth and such. Someday people will be interested in such things. I have a notion to begin such recording myself."

The papers she'd left on the table next to Lydian had been created and written based on language she'd read in the Indian treaties, documents that she'd helped translate for the Indian chiefs, and in the papers she'd drawn up to get the Indian mothers to allow their children to come to the white school. Mother St. John had spent so many years learning to read and write that she liked opportunities to use her scripting skills.

"Maybe the girl won't sign them. Maybe she'll change her mind and keep the children herself."

Lydian put the babies in the center of the bed. They tangled together. The boy's fist clenched a handful of the girl's hair. The baby girl's mouth pursed into another wail, so Lydian gently pried his hand open. Lydian looked at the paper. She dipped the quill into the inkwell. She scraped the tip along the rim. She brought the quill to her nose and smelled. Then she closed her eyes and saw the shape of a ropy tornado. She thought that shape to be similar and put the quill to the paper and scratched the ink into her recollection of the tornado. She wondered about this mark. What did it mean exactly? When her stepmother traded with the trapper or traveled to the general store, the mark she made meant that she owed something, that she'd eventually have to give up something to pay for the supplies she'd taken. Is that what this mark meant? Was she now beholden to the nun and the squaw? Would she someday have to repay this favor? How could she ever settle such a debt? The horse, she thought. Though the horse was an old wreck and disagreeable, she'd leave it to the women.

Lydian stood. She was careful with herself. Her body was a mess of pains and seepages. She squeezed her thighs together to keep the blood from dripping. She paused over the bed and considered these children. She told them, "I wish there was a way I could keep you." It was a simple sentiment, but the words were, for Lydian, hard to come by and harder to say. She leaned over and put the tip of her tongue on each child's forehead. She had seen how a horse nuzzles its colt, and she did this too. She put her face close to the girl baby and rubbed her cheek against hers, then did the same for the boy. She walked out the front door of the infirmary. The minute she closed the door behind her, she heaved up a dry sob.

A feeling of such dread came over her that she stumbled in the snow. She turned back, put her hand on the door, and listened for the babies. She told herself that if they cried out, she would return and keep them herself, raise them as best she could. She would find a way. She would even go back to Beaver Jean if she had to, or maybe to her stepmother. Or maybe even go to the woods and look for her father. She waited. The babies did not cry, so she bargained with herself again. *I will wait two minutes, and if the babies cry, I will return to them,* she promised herself. Lydian waited for five minutes. They did not cry. Lydian turned around, tightened her coat and scarf, and walked into the wild, with no specific route in mind, intending only to go south and stay off the fur-trapping routes so as not to run into Beaver Jean.

In the outer room, Mother St. John heard the front door open and close. She knew it was the young mother leaving. Mother St. John didn't move to stop her. She thought it probably best, perhaps God's will. She had a vision of the girl freezing to death in the snow, with her eyes and mouth wide open, but Mother St. John shook it out of her head. Since the girl had made it to the infirmary in winter weather, Mother St. John supposed she'd get to wherever she was going. She pulled her rosary from her belt and crossed herself with it and kissed the crucifix. She offered up a prayer for the girl's safe journey. Sometimes she wondered why she spent so much time praying if God's will was already known to Him. Did all that praying point to some lack of trust? Was she praying for Him to change His mind? Did God change His mind? If He did, wouldn't that mean that things were not preordained and known to Him?

The spiritual aspects of being a sister seemed very complicated to Mother St. John, but the daily work was not. She liked the nursing and the caring and the teaching parts of being a sister. But the Church's tenets, the words, the prayers, the required beliefs were sometimes difficult to accept. There were many things Mother St. John did not understand. So, always, when she felt doubt or questioning come into her heart or her mind, she got to work. Mother St. John returned to the girl's cot and found the babies asleep and the papers resting there too. She read them over. She admired her own words, the care with which she formed the letters. Then she scolded herself for vanity.

She pulled the quill from the ink. Where Lydian had left blanks for the children's names, Mother St. John wrote Scholastica and Clement. She couldn't remember for sure, but she thought them to be the names of pious twin saints who'd prayed together in inclement weather. Mother St. John took great care to select proper names for all her children. The only person at the infirmary who would not accept a Christian name was Big Waters, though years ago Mother St. John had tried to christen her Sarah. Mother St. John kept careful record of each Indian child's tribe and tribal name but baptized all of them with the names of saints. These children needed the protection of all the patrons and matrons she could muster. For a surname, Mother St. John chose Piety, a gift of the Holy Spirit. Scholastica Piety and Clement Piety. Goodly names, she thought.

The babies slept for many hours, until hunger woke them. Mother St. John fixed a cloth soaked in sugar water for the girl, and Big Waters did the same for the boy. The two women marveled over the children's features. They let the babies clutch their fingers as if they were aunts or grandmothers, even. The two women smiled and smiled down upon the faces. An onlooker would never guess that these infants were in any sense abandoned, orphaned, or alone.

The babies, more aware now and opening their swollen eyes to their surroundings, searched the wrinkles of Big Waters and the broad nose of Mother St. John, but their little brains made no connection to these elders. They fidgeted. They listened but couldn't hear the beating-heart lullaby they'd grown dependent upon. They sniffed but could smell nothing familiar, and so they began to cry.

Mother St. John gently bounced the girl up and down. She swayed her to and fro. She laid the baby across her lap and patted her back. Still the girl cried. "Hungry, maybe," suggested Mother St. John. The noise of his sister inspired the boy to louden his whimper to a wail. Together they sounded like clamorous cats. Other little children left their mats and peeked in through the crack between the door and its frame.

"Go back to bed," Mother St. John urged them. One little boy pushed a stuffed sock through the door. It was filled with cloth scraps, and he'd stitched eyes and a nose onto it. "Elmer, the babies don't want your bear. Get that dirty thing out of here."

Elmer scrambled in, picked it up off the floor, and then rushed out. He was new here. His parents had died the past winter, frozen solid in a soddy to the south. They gave every last bit of food they had to Elmer and starved themselves. Elmer was found by a Sioux youth who'd come by to check on the German family. The youth had bundled up Elmer and brought him to Mother St. John. For days, the boy had slept with her in her bed, whimpering and sucking his thumb. Now she felt sorry for yelling at him.

"Elmer?" she called. "Elmer, come back. I think I was wrong. I think these babies would like your doll, thank you."

Elmer crept back in and handed her the doll.

"Bless you, Elmer," said Mother St. John. "Now, I left a little

sweet roll in the kitchen. You go get one and share it." Elmer
walked out with his head down, again not watching where he was
going, but she didn't scold him for that.

Even as a girl, Mother St. John had wanted to be a mother. She
had wanted a dozen children to hug and kiss and guide. Now she
had so many, she hardly could keep them straight. But she asked
for God's strength and patience and kindness, and she worked very,
very hard to be a good mother to all the children. She believed,
more than anything else, that they needed to be filled up with love.

In her earlier years, she had been assigned to other orphan-
ages and had witnessed how badly the sisters treated the children.
How they beat them with spoons or paddles. How they withheld
food. How they kept them in dark rooms for wetting themselves.
How they called them names. She remembered those sad faces
and determined to never, ever treat a child in such a way. And now
that she had her own place for the sick and unwanted, she could
organize it like a regular family, with God as the head and her as
the wife and mother. She was glad that Big Waters, a grandmother
of sorts, was there to help.

The babies whimpered persistently. Mother St. John speculated
first that they were too cold, then too hot, hungry, too full, gassy,
constipated, tired, bored, lonely for their mother, stirred up too
much, sick, premature, colicky, swaddled too tight or not tight
enough. Then, when she was at her wit's end, she put the children
side by side and watched. The boy curled around his sister like a
shell around a nut and became quiet. "Well," said Mother St. John.
"Why didn't I think of that earlier?" The girl fussed until Mother
St. John dabbed the corner of a cloth in sweet water, twisted it, and
put it in her mouth.

The girl babe sucked happily and quickly fell asleep. The boy
could smell an elemental scent, hear a common heartbeat, feel a
familiar breath and an ancient link. Here was his sister. His twin.

His blood and bone. And he would never let go of her. Clement Piety's little fist again took hold of a handful of his sister's hair. But she did not cry this time.

As quickly as the children quieted, Mother St. John's frustration and panic disappeared. She looked at them and wondered if there was anything in the world sweeter than a sleeping infant.

"Big Waters," said Mother St. John. "If I wasn't a believer in Mary and Jesus and their love and forgiveness, my heart would break over all the abandoned and orphaned children in these parts. Do you think it's so bad everywhere?"

Big Waters nodded.

"Certainly," said Mother St. John. "How does the world take it? How can any woman know of an abandoned one and not want to take the poor thing to her heart?"

Big Waters crawled into bed and pulled up the blanket.

"If I ever had a baby," said Mother St. John, "I'd move heaven and earth before I'd choose to desert it upon the world for some other to care for. But I took the vow of celibacy, so I suppose my love is for children like these." She draped another blanket over the babies. "When you hold the orphaned ones," she asked, "does it take you over like it does me?"

Big Waters rubbed her feet together beneath the blanket. She sniffed, and Mother St. John wondered if she was crying.

"Like a flock of night birds," Big Waters whispered, "landing on your chest."

"What?" said Mother St. John, even though she'd heard the old woman. "Goodness. Yes. That's what it's like. Heavy and grave."

Mother St. John turned down the lantern.

"I suppose we will be awakened a few times tonight to feed these." Mother St. John went on about keeping the fires burning all night and how little babies make a place feel special. She talked of a young mother who died in childbirth maybe a year back. She told of the woman's husband, who'd been away in the timber camp. She recalled how she'd kept that baby for a week or so until two of the woman's sisters came to claim him. She told Big Waters how each thought she was better qualified to raise up the baby right. One was married with a family already. The other was a single schoolteacher somewhere east of here. Mother St. John said she didn't know which woman took him, in the end. Either way, she said, he was lucky to be so much wanted, even if those women were some kind of Lutherans. She told Big Waters how Father Paul had baptized that boy before the women had ever arrived, so he'd go in the correct direction when he died.

Big Waters snored boisterously. She wasn't sleeping but clearly wanted to be. Mother St. John pulled the door shut and went about other business, mumbling the Joyful Mysteries of the rosary as she did so.

# 10

## Eliza and Child

JUST AS MOTHER ST. JOHN was hanging the last of the laundry to dry, a shadow crept past the window.

"Now who could that be?" she said, talking to herself, a thing she did often and didn't mind. "At this time of night." It occurred to her that perhaps the mother of the babies was returning. She rushed to open the door for her and called, "Up, Big Waters. Put hot water on for tea."

She'd invite the mother in, warm her up, tell her these fears were natural. But when she opened the door, she found not the mother of the twins, but a young Negro woman holding a small child by the hand.

"Oh," said Mother St. John, looking behind the woman, and then to the left and right. She was looking for white people, for minders, for masters, for caretakers. But no others were there. Only the night and the wind and endless drifts of snow. Mother St. John had never seen a black person unattended. "Oh," she said again. "Hello?"

She stared into the Negro woman's face. She'd heard that the Virgin Mary and her people were not white, but closer to a brown color. Mother St. John didn't know whether she believed this or not. But the woman in her doorway, now that she looked, was closer to brown than black. And she had a blue shawl draped over her head, so that the idea of a brown Holy Mother seemed more feasible.

"Help us, please," the woman said. She stepped into the doorway. She couldn't have been more than twenty. Mother St. John had read that the Virgin Mary was just an adolescent when she birthed the Lord, and she imagined that the Mother of God must have looked as pitiful as this woman when she and Joseph arrived in Bethlehem and were turned away time and again.

Then the woman pushed the small child into the room. "This boy's my son," said the cloaked woman, "and they mean to take him for a slave." She leaned over and coughed. Even through her dress and cloak, Mother St. John could see how bony her spine was.

Mother St. John stepped aside to allow the child and then his mother to pass. "Come." She closed the door while Big Waters went to the kitchen to light the stove. Mother St. John patted the boy on the head. It was too big for his body, in the natural way of a child of four or five years. He clung to his mother. His eyes were wide, but they had the stare of curiosity rather than panic or fear. "Hi there," she said to the child. She noticed now that his skin was lighter than his mother's. "Are you alone?" she asked the mother.

"Long as we can help it, we are," the cloaked woman said. She put her hand upon the boy's shoulder. "They'll come if they can find us."

"Sit down for a moment," said Mother St. John. "Calm down now. You're scaring the boy." Mother St. John moved to pull out the chair, but tipped it over instead. "Oh my," she said. She set it upright.

"My boy's real bright," said the cloaked woman. Her voice was raspy and soft. "Smart as any white boy." She put her hand to her chest. "I can't let them take him south and slave him."

Mother St. John prickled at the word *slave*. She simply didn't like it and wished that the woman wouldn't use it. In polite company, Mother St. John had heard the term *servants* used to describe the Negro race of the South. She preferred that. "We'll have a cup of hot tea," she said. "Who is it that will come and make a servant of your son?"

The young woman's gaze flitted around the room and behind her as though she was worried that at any minute something might manifest out of a corner and snatch her up.

"I don't want any trouble here," Mother St. John said. "I have small children to think about."

The woman sat down and pulled the child onto her lap. He fell against her breast and closed his eyes. "I heard you help us. Have you?" She searched the space again. "Have you helped others? A man. Lighter than most? I heard you had ways of getting us into Canada or Chicago or New York?"

Mother St. John searched her brain for who might have said such a thing. Without thinking, she was shaking her head no. She stopped.

"Have you seen a big, skinny, kinda yella man come through here?" asked the woman. "Goes by name Jim?"

Mother St. John's head began shaking again. "Who told you that?"

"You mean he was here?" said the woman.

"No," said Mother St. John. "I mean, who told you we do such things?"

The woman face changed, suddenly, as if her jaw and cheeks had been pulled down. She pushed back the chair and stood. The weight of the boy nearly bent her over in half. "Maybe I come to the wrong place." She looked around nervously. "Not supposed to ask who sent me. That's one of the rules. Know that for sure." She rushed toward the door.

Mother St. John went to the door too and put her hand on it. "Wait, wait," she said. She wasn't sure why she was about to convince the woman to stay, but the words were out before she could stop them. "You must calm down. I'm going to help you, of course. I'm only confused." Mother St. John laughed lightly at herself. "I've had a long day already. I'm just not clear on what it is you want." She sat down and crossed her arms over her middle. Her cramps were bothering her terrible.

"Some people told me you took care of all kinds of troubles and problems."

Mother St. John felt a chill blast from under the door and into the little room. She wondered about the young mother who'd left not too long ago. She wondered about this young mother now. She wondered if God was testing her in some way. A test of righteousness? A test of will? A test of intelligence? A test of intuition? She considered her little Home for Orphans and Infirmed, which was already packed with needy souls.

Mother St. John decided. "You're safe here," she said. "I can be trusted. No harm will come to you here. I would never put a child in harm's way. Never."

The woman examined Mother St. John and at last her gaze rested on the nun's eyes. "Thank you," she said. She swayed on her feet.

Mother St. John put her arms under the child. "Let me carry him." She took the boy from his mother's arms. The woman leaned against the door and coughed again.

Mother St. John stepped away from the woman. "He looks like a bright boy. Let's put him in a bed for the night."

The young mother nodded, crossed her arms over her chest, and slipped to the floor.

Big Waters came in, saw the woman, and waddled to her aid. She put the young mother's limp arm over her own aged shoulders and helped her stand. Together they shuffled toward the bed where Lydian had so recently birthed the twins. Mother St. John followed with the sleeping child. Big Waters helped the young woman into the bed, then she stepped back.

"He stays with me no matter what," whispered the young woman.

Mother St. John placed the child in the bed too. "It's clean," she said.

"Name's Eliza," said the mother. "Prolly seen the posters about me and my boy?"

Mother St. John searched her memory for such a thing. Certainly she knew what kind of poster Eliza referred to. There were only two reasons for a person of black heritage to be featured on a poster, for sale or for reward. "No. I've not."

"We're with the Winstons, of the Missouri Winstons, if you're wondering, which I'm sure you are, being you're a woman and a religious one besides."

Mother St. John spread a blanket over the boy.

"He's Davis, my boy." She kissed the top of his head and closed her eyes. "He's such a smart boy," she whispered. "Just like his daddy."

Mother St. John closed the curtain over the window. "I don't know the Winstons, but I know of them. Visitors to the fort, right? Trying to help the territory get organized and put down the Indian revolts?"

"Uh-huh," said Eliza, her eyes still closed. She went on then, her words fading in and out. "I been . . . that fort fixin' teas . . . suppers for . . . and that one. Been shinin' . . . tall boots . . . and all the while planning . . . from those people."

"Sleep now, if you wish," said Mother St. John. "You're safe here."

Big Waters tucked the blanket all around the pair.

Eliza whispered on. Nonsense mostly, about some man named Jim and freedom for her son.

Mother St. John was familiar with the phenomenon of runaway slaves, of Negro servants escaping their masters, but had never really developed an opinion about it and wasn't sure if the Church had decreed an official position on the matter. She had read something about the Missouri Compromise but honestly couldn't remember what it had determined. So much was going on in the country, Mother St. John had a difficult time staying abreast of the new territories being purchased, new states being formed, new railroad tracks being laid, Indian attacks, and wars. So little of it seemed to affect her daily life with the children. Way up here, in the north, slavery hadn't ever touched her.

Eliza then seemed to be asleep. Mother St. John crept close to her and noted the dry, scaly texture of her skin. Big Waters went to her own bed and fell into it. Mother St. John pulled a chair from the corner and sat in it, determined to sleep upright. She had closed her eyes for all of thirty minutes when Eliza's coughing shook the bed. Mother St. John opened her eyes to see the young woman, head pressed into the pillow, trying to stifle the cough. Mother St. John reached over and stroked the top of her head.

"Do you need water?" she whispered, so as not to wake the boy, Big Waters, or the babies.

Eliza nodded.

Mother St. John stood and walked across the room, careful not to step on the creaky boards, to the table where she kept a small pitcher of water. She poured some into a tin cup and brought it to Eliza.

"Lift your head now," she coaxed. She helped Eliza sip a bit. Eliza drank and then lay her head back down with a sigh. She began to whisper again.

"My mama ... four little boys sold ... shoulder high to her ... Joseph and Solomon and Willie and one we called Pumpkin Bottom ... can't even remember ... name. Can't let him be sold." Eliza's eyes opened, enormously wide.

Mother St. John looked into them and was pulled into memories of another person's owning. "Shhh," she said, to soothe Eliza. "You're safe here, both of you. Sleep now." Her mind took hold of Eliza's words and manifested the most awful scene: four small boys clinging to their mother's skirts and being ripped away from her by an awful brute of a man who, holding a tree limb and a horsewhip, was hitting the legs of the little boys. Was that what it was like? How horrible. Mother St. John had no idea what she'd do with these two. If she helped them, could she get into trouble? She needed Father Paul. He'd know what to do. He'd know about the Church's position.

Eliza mumbled for a while longer, about her boy, about a piano. Mother St. John caressed Eliza's head and worried over the consequences for harboring fugitives. She didn't want to threaten the safety of her own children for helping just one child. But the laws here were loose yet. Jurisdiction was a fuzzy matter. The territory hadn't yet defined what it wanted to be, how it wanted to govern.

"Gotta have papers . . . free document," Eliza murmured. "Keep moving."

Mother St. John thought about the paper she'd created for the twins. She could easily create a free paper for Eliza. But would it be a sin? She needed Father Paul. Should she wait until she spoke with him or create them in the meanwhile, so that they'd be ready when he arrived? Writing was so formal, so clear, so civilized. Mother St. John's heart pattered at the thought of the looping letters and lovely words she'd get to inscribe in the morning. She liked the smell of the ink, the sound of the quill dipping into the inkwell, the sight of the ink dripping from the quill tip, and especially the scratch of the inked quill on the paper.

Eliza coughed again. Mother St. John recognized that deep-chested but dry hacking. She had heard that type of cough before. Eliza was very sick. "We'll talk in the morning," said Mother St.

John. She imagined poor Eliza, sick with consumption, scrubbing floors and pounding bread dough and shining boots. She pictured Mistress Winston sitting up in bed and ordering Eliza about, even as she doubled over with coughing and chills. Mother St. John asked, "Were they terribly cruel?" but Eliza was asleep again. In her slumber, she looked no more than a girl herself, sixteen, eighteen at the most.

Here, in this exact moment, Mother St. John made a decision that would forever change the course of her life, of her calling, her work on the earth: *There's no harm in giving refuge to a mother and child. There's no harm in writing a paper. This isn't much different than the Virgin arriving in Bethlehem.*

Mother St. John pulled the blanket up again, and then checked on the twin babies. She covered them both too, and unclenched the boy's fist from his sister's hair. She covered Big Waters' feet, which were sticking out at the bottom of the bed like two gnarled tree roots. She wiped up the floor in her room, where Eliza, Davis, Big Waters, and the babies slept, and in the infirmary entry. She stood and straightened her back. Then she opened the door and stepped out into the black night. What a strange few days. She wondered if she should go after the young woman whose babies lay sleeping in their baskets. She wondered whom that girl was running from. She wondered who might come for the other mother and her child. Mother St. John wished for a bit of tobacco, but stepped back inside and closed the door. She drew the heavy board down across the door but then lifted it again. What if the mother of the twins changed her mind? How would she get in? But what if whoever was chasing the two runaways was approaching? So she drew the board down again. She pulled a blanket from a shelf and lay it on the floor in front of the door. If anyone came, she'd hear. If the mother knocked, Mother St. John would know, and welcome her with an open mind and an open heart. She stood up again and took an ax down from the mantel. If there was a knock and it was a chaser looking to collect Eliza and Davis, well, she'd have to chop him, wouldn't she? She'd have to be David protecting the people from the wild, hairy, dastardly Goliaths of the world.

# 11

# Beaver Jean's Troublesome Wives and Toes

BEAVER JEAN UNTIED THE NAG from the cart shaft and rubbed her nose some. Snow blew around his little cabin and settled into big drifts in front of the window. But even through the blowing snow and over the drifts, he could see his Indian wives inside, waiting for him. He put his mind to dealing with their antics tonight. He determined to come in firm and loud and not allow for any foolishness. He considered the cold and thought it would be wrong to keep the nag outdoors.

"You'll have to come inside with us tonight," he told the animal. He led her to the door, rested his shoulder against it, and pushed it open.

"I'm hungry," he yelled into the dim room. "Yer man is back, women. Help me with Alice here. She's cold."

Beaver Jean's breath could rip bark off a tree. His fat wives, who typically bounced at his feet and yapped in his face like wolf pups the moment he came back from his excursions, stepped away from him, covered their faces with their hands, then pinched their noses and pointed at his mouth.

"Shigog," they giggled. They looked at each other. "Shigog." The one with the droopy eyelid, The Girl with Friend Eyes, hid behind In the Trees, the one whose arms dangled long in front of her. The one with long arms reached behind and slapped at her sister-wife.

"Skunk, skunk," The Girl with Friend Eyes shrieked, brave under the protection of the other wife. They were both smiling like mules, their teeth white and horizon-straight.

Beaver Jean raised his hand and shook it as though empowered with prodigious might. "Ye'll bring down the lightning!" he warned them. "Now get this animal some water if ye haven't used it all for yerselves!" The wives sprung, quick and nimble, toward the coat he'd hung on a nail beside the door. They dug into the pockets and turned them inside-out, searching for treats or bits of leftover meat. Eventually, the one whose arms dangled long, chewing on a sliver of jerky, slapped the backside of the nag and moved her toward a corner.

"Come, come Alice," she crooned. The horse moved compliantly. The woman had a way with animals, Beaver Jean had always thought.

"My toes is like to fall off, if it matters to ye squaws," he said. He limped farther inside and took off his satchel, which the wives bore down upon. The Girl with Friend Eyes had her hands on the bag of coffee beans and In the Trees had her dangling arms wrapped around a jar of molasses.

"Get ye outta there!" Beaver Jean yelled. He swatted his arms at them. "Dammee, ye two." The molasses was intended as a gift for Lydian, who liked sweet things more than most.

He looked around for a container of some sort in which he could soak his foot. "My toes is aching me like a sonofabitch, I said. Dammee."

His wives had their fingers deep in molasses and cheeks stuffed with beans. In a time and a place when he needed comfort and care, they mocked him and made him uneasy, thought only of their own selfish wants.

"Get outta those beans," he commanded. "There won't be a one left for grinding. That's Lydian's sweet, ye wenches."

They were getting too bold for their own good, those two squaws. They'd gotten their nerve back and dander raised since Lydian left, as if they wanted to punish him for ever bringing her to his family in the first place. He wasn't a man to take such silliness from women, but his foot was paining him, he was tired, and he was cold. He didn't have the gumption to put them back in their right place and right mind, but he'd have to do it soon. Beaver Jean trusted in a firm hand. It was the right way for a man to handle his women.

He roared a few more times: "Get that fire going! Fix me something to eat, dammee! Cease that cackling, ye wenches! I'll put ye through the window! I will! Give me some peace, ye shrieking hawks!"

He spoke Ojibwe fairly but always yelled in English. He could understand some of the other Indian languages and a little French too. Since most of the French trappers were gone now, he hardly heard French at all anymore, except among some of the lesser tribes who always had a woman who could speak it a little. Those French-speaking women always made him lonely for his mother, who had been a real lady, the likes of which he had never come across yet in these parts. All these native women were ruffians, and the white ones were uppity yet on the verge of fainting at every inconvenient moment.

"Bring me that chair!" he yelled. His wives sucked in their faces and puckered their lips.

"Salmon face," the long-armed one said. But she lugged the chair closer to the fire and patted him on the head. Then she shook her hand and stuck out her tongue as though she'd caught something deadly from his hair. Beaver Jean didn't have the vigor to strike her, and anyway these days he was just as likely to get struck in return as not.

Beaver Jean had been having a tough time eking out a decent living over the past few years. After a long, steady business of selling beaver skins to be made into fancy hats for the Easterners and Europeans, Beaver Jean felt betrayed by the sudden lack of interest. Now they wanted silk and were buying hats from the Orient. Well, how could he compete with that? Where could he get silk? For a while, Beaver Jean thought he might be able to make thread out of the webs of tree caterpillars, but the material was too flimsy, and it easily disintegrated.

For now, he'd have to pick up more bounty hunting and such. Life was about adapting to the changing times, and if he didn't change with them, he'd get left behind and be a pauper too. Trading with poor tribes wasn't making him much money these days. Those Indians had gotten themselves into quite some trouble after they agreed to sell their lands without getting their payments up front. That was a mistake Beaver Jean would never make. He always got payment upon delivery. Since then, the tribes had little money to pay with and few things to trade, so Beaver Jean had to find other ways to make a living.

But he couldn't do a single useful thing until the blessed hellion toes quit afflicting him. As the cold wore off and feeling came back into his foot, the damned things throbbed as if weasel teeth were embedded beneath the nails. He lugged his foot onto his lap and peeled off his sock, then unwound the soggy wrapping from his toes. The middle three were swollen and discolored, and when he touched them, yellow pus bubbled from the sides of the nails. Only the big guy and the little guy had a regular pink color to them. He exhaled and squeezed the bad toes a little. The skin and muscle gave in easily, as only dead things can. The small black hairs, proud as cockleburs, that once erupted from those toes now rubbed off. This foot was going gangrenous, surely. So the poison wouldn't climb up his leg, he'd have to get the foot fixed up, toes chopped off, while hunting down Lydian and while keeping an eye out for that Negress and child.

He didn't consider himself sentimental, but he thought about some of the good times he'd had with those toes: as a small boy, he'd dangled his legs in a muddy pond and the minnows would nibble at them. Yes, he'd miss those old toes, but he had to get on with the good work of finding the women and putting them back where they needed to be. Lydian with him and the squaws. The Negro woman and boy with their rightful owners in Stillwater. And he'd put the fear of God into the squaws. With the money from the bounty, he intended to buy a pillow from a catalogue for Lydian and a paddle to swat those other two.

He spent the whole night worrying about this and that: his toes, money and supplies, how Lydian had gone missing and was no doubt ready to give birth at any moment, how these wives wouldn't give him one second of pity. Where had he gone wrong? Giving them too much learning and too much traveling? Paying them too much attention? And since there was no peace to be found at home, at first light, Beaver Jean packed up his belongings again. He grabbed his liquor bottles and sucked a nice gulp out of one before he packed some food. He coaxed the nag back outdoors and let her sniff the wind.

"Which way do ye think, Alice?" Beaver Jean said. He trusted the animal's instinct in these matters. The horse turned with the wind, toward the home of Lydian's stepmother, a wildcat of the prairie. Though he dreaded it, he would go to look for his pregnant wife there. Then he would go to the infirmary to have his toes seen to. He hoped his leg wouldn't be rotten by the time he got there. He hoped too to see some sign of the runaway pair before someone else caught them and collected the fee. Beaver Jean sighed with the weariness of a man with a lot on his mind.

# 12

## *Albertina*

On the prairie lands a few days south of Stillwater, Lydian's stepmother, Albertina, heard the creaking and the whinnying of Beaver Jean's cart and horse before she saw him. She ran to the window and spied him rising up like a god from between the snowdrifts. She hoped he wasn't bringing Lydian back to live with her. She looked hard and saw only Jean. Albertina ran around the house, tidied the supper pots, swept ashes off the fireplace, and started a pot of coffee. She pulled the pins out of her bun and shook down her hair, which was full, wavy, and golden, with graying strands at the temples. She pinched her cheeks and wiped her armpits with a rag. Albertina hadn't seen her own husband in years. After coming home and learning that Lydian had been married and moved on, he'd decided to stay in the timber camps all year. He sent packages with money, which Albertina spent on food and cloth for herself and her other little girl, and on improvements to their house.

For two years, she'd hired handymen to add rooms and amenities to the little cabin, so that it was now a comfortable house with a porch and a proper kitchen, an extra bedroom, and a sunroom where Albertina kept her plants, which grew green and lush all year round. In the corner was the table upon which Albertina had carnally known a Norwegian farmer named Ole, who had made that very table and who had a wife expecting their eighth child. On the north end was the additional bedroom in which Albertina had known the traveling preacher, Pastor David, who said, "Oh Lord, forgive me," over and over. Over the new stairway banister is where Albertina had bent for a German handyman named Gunther, who had eyes that crossed. Beneath the new stone fireplace, Albertina had ridden the son of her nearest neighbor, Hans, a man Albertina had also known when he and his son came to carve and install the mantel. Hans had sent his son to Albertina alone once, to finish the mantel and, he hoped, to turn the boy away from lusts that seemed unnatural. Albertina rode the boy gently then forcefully, but she had not been able to satisfy him and had insulted him so badly that he never came back to complete the job, and she'd had to hire a Winnebago man to do so. The Winnebago man was insatiable and grew to love Albertina. He had scratched an eye into the fireplace mortar, which meant he was always watching her.

Albertina was forty years old, still attractive to her own eyes whenever she gazed in the mirror. "Upstairs!" she yelled to her little girl, the only child to whom she'd given birth. "Go on. Now!" She shooed her up the steps and ran to window. Her breath fogged the glass, and she drew a circle in the mist and then added a dot in the middle. A nipple. Albertina was burning up with lust.

"Now you will finally come to a good woman," she said to the approaching figure. "I will be so naughty!" She undid her apron and tossed it onto a chair. She bent, and peeled her stockings off her legs. "Oooooh. You will like my legs around you, Mr. Jean. Big Mr. Jean-Jean. Albertina will rub you so naughty. Eeee!"

"Mama?" called the little girl. "What are you doing, Mama?"

"Go to your bed and play with your dolly!" snapped Albertina. "Right now!"

"Is Lydian coming home?" called the girl.

"I told you no!" Albertina yelled. "Now go on and do not bother

Mama anymore." Albertina ran to the kitchen, slathered jelly onto half a loaf of bread, ran to the stairs, and tossed it up. "There you go, sweetie pie! Take the treat to your room and be good."

The girl crept from her room and snatched up the bread. "Thank you, Mama!"

"Do not come out of your room until I tell you to, sweetie pie," Albertina sang. "Promise Mama you will not. Not even if you hear funny noises!"

The girl went to her room and closed the door, used to such orders.

Albertina returned to the window. Jean was approaching very, very slowly. "Come, come, Mr. Jean. I am waiting for you!" she said. "Albertina is so impatient!" She unbuttoned her blouse and let her breasts hang free. She put her arms up and grabbed the top of the window. "Come, come, Mr. Jean." She twisted back and forth, rubbing her nipples against the glass. "You like, Mr. Jean?"

Beaver Jean saw the sun reflecting off the Galtier cabin windows. The closer he got, the more certain he was that Lydian would not be found there. He hadn't noticed a sign of a person coming or going along the path. And he became sure that Lydian would have selected a more hospitable place to birth his child. In his few encounters with the woman of this cabin, he had concluded that she was as mad as a wolverine. But because the cold snow was numbing his toes, they ached badly, and he wondered if he should stop at the cabin for a simple rest before heading to the infirmary to have the nurse fix his toes. The closer he got, the stronger the scent of coffee, which made him quicken his step until he glimpsed the woman standing in the window, naked and writhing.

Beaver Jean stopped and stood in the snow. "Dammee all," Beaver Jean said. "What are ye doing with yerself?"

His horse whinnied. "Easy now, Alice," he said. "We'll be turning around from here. I'm sorry to trouble yer old legs with more wandering, but we can't rest here. The woman of this house is mad, and it pains my heart to think of my Lydian withstanding the wretched mothering of this one."

Then, just as Beaver Jean was about to turn his cart around, a man appeared from behind a snowdrift, and he sprinted toward the house. He was dressed in European clothing, but Beaver Jean recognized him as the blundering son of a powerful Winnebago chief to the west. The man was shouting at the woman in the window. When she saw him, she pulled back. In a few moments, the door to the house flew open and she emerged, completely nude but holding a rug over her shoulders as though it was a shawl. She ran to the Winnebago man, and he ran to her. And when they collided, he pulled out his penis and threw her down in the snow.

"Animals," shouted Beaver Jean. But the pair paid no mind to him. "Filthy behavior." He tugged at Alice and turned her around. They began their slow walk to the infirmary. Beaver Jean thought all the while about how lucky it was for Lydian that he had rescued her from such a stepmother, how lucky it would be for his son to keep her away from that sort of grandmother.

# 13

## The Arrival of a Blizzard

MOTHER ST. JOHN TENDED to Eliza and the child for several days while Big Waters went to summon Father Paul. Big Waters relayed his message: he promised to come as soon as he could. Eliza's cough, which had seemed bad enough that first night, was worse than Mother St. John first thought. Eliza's shoulders would quake a bit as she fought to suppress a cough, but soon she'd be bent over, hacking and spitting blood into a hankie.

Mother St. John led her into bed. Though it was only late afternoon, the sun had gone down, which made Mother St. John eager to get everyone fed and settled. She boiled chicken bones and innards with strong onion and pepper and proffered the broth to Eliza.

Eliza sipped. She nodded toward Davis, who sat in the corner with Big Waters and the babies. "Davis is tired," Eliza said.

Davis's arms were draped over the baskets in which the babies lay. The little girl curled her hand around Davis's finger as Big Waters tended to the nappy of the baby boy.

"Don't worry about Davis," said Mother St. John. "I'll put him to bed." She lifted the bowl to Eliza's lips again.

"This baby likes me," said Davis. He shook his hand and the girl child's fingers remained clenched around his pinkie.

Mother St. John wiped Eliza's mouth, then set the bowl on a

table. She stood and went to him. She'd come to like Davis very much. He was bright and spoke clearly, with an intelligence far beyond his four years. "Well, why wouldn't she?" said Mother St. John. She took his hand and led him to a cot she'd prepared on the floor beside Eliza's bed. "Say your prayers to Saint Mary and go to sleep." She gave him a kiss on the head. She couldn't help it. In him, she smelled all the things that would never be hers.

"I'm not tired," said Davis, though he yawned and stretched his arms.

Mother St. John turned down the lamp and left the room, carrying the bowl. She cleaned the kitchen and spooned flour into a large bowl for dough. Then she went to the children's ward and shooed a couple of rapscallions back into bed and stoked the fire to keep the place warm. She went to the kitchen, picked up a pitcher, and was about to head to the barn to milk the cow when she thought she heard the squeaking of wagon wheels. Just then, the front door of the infirmary flew wide open and a gust of wind blew through the entry and into the kitchen, whipping flour out of the bowl.

"What in the—" Mother St. John started. She hurried to the entry.

Wind and snow rushed in, and a huge man filled the doorway.

"What in the—" she said again. "Close the door!"

From head to toe, the man was dressed in furs and skins. Though the light was dim in the infirmary, Mother St. John could see a mustache and beard, a mangled forest of coarse and matted hairs. She approached. "Close the door!" she said again.

He did. "Pardon me," he said. The breath that came with the words emitted a foul odor, a scent somewhere between sour meat and silage.

The giant stomped in, shaking snow off. "It's a blizzard," he said.

Mother St. John glanced to the left, toward the room where

Eliza and her child rested, and then quickly caught herself and looked at the man in the doorway again.

"Mighty fierce weather," he said. "Been riding in it all day." He clapped his hands and arms together. Snow fell onto the floor.

"What in the—" she said. *He must be here for them.* Her heart leapt, and she prayed that little Davis would know enough to keep quiet. Then she heard the door to her room open and saw Big Waters pop her head out and then back in.

Mother St. John lifted the lantern to her face. "We're full," she said.

"I need tending," Beaver Jean boomed. He stomped his boots on the floor to loosen the snowy clumps. "Yi! That smarts." He unwound strands of rabbit skin from his hands. "My foot's rotten."

"What?" asked Mother St. John. Her intuition, or rather a feeling she attributed to the guidance of the Holy Spirit, told her that this man was up to no good. But she'd taken vows. She couldn't turn away a child of God in need of help, not even a child of God as hideous and smelly as this one. Didn't Jesus touch the leprous and the dead, pull them forth from their stinking decay in a place where the dead weren't buried but were left to petrify in humid, hot caves?

Beaver Jean breathed into Mother St. John's face. "My toes is like to kill me if I don't have 'em off," he said. "They look and feel mighty, mighty wrong."

Still, though, she wasn't Jesus and could do only so much for so many. Mothers and children first. Hairy Philistines later. "I don't have a single spare bed. Not one. Perhaps you could come back in a few days?"

Beaver Jean untied a wolf pelt from around his neck. He tossed it to the floor. "Find me a chair," he told Mother St. John. "I've got to sit and rest these bones." He sniffed at her as an animal might. "You got a name?"

Mother St. John went to the back of the room and drew a heavy curtain across a rope, a barrier that separated the quarters of the children and the sick from the chill of the front room on cold nights. Then she pulled a chair from the table for the man.

"You may call me Mother St. John," she said. "We must be quieter. Everyone is sleeping."

"Mother? What's that supposed to mean?"

"My name. I'm a sister."

Beaver sat down with a humph and tugged off his boot. He moaned as he stretched out his leg and wiggled his toes.

"We nurse the sick and care for orphans," she went on, taking a seat across from him.

Beaver Jean pulled his foot up onto his lap. "There's a contingent of souls who need a mighty dose of religious guidance a couple days south of here. Ye wouldn't believe what some of them prairie folks is up to." He rubbed life into the sole of his foot.

"I'm afraid I have my hands full here," said Mother St. John.

"I'm sure ye do," Beaver Jean said. "But my dearly departed pap used to say that having hands full was better than having them empty. Oh my toes!"

Mother St. John sat forward on her chair and smiled. Maybe he was just another soul in need of tending.

He jabbed his foot toward her. Even during the day, the light in the infirmary was bad in winter, shadowy and dull. She knelt and pulled the lantern close to the toes.

"Let's have a look then," she said.

He tried wiggling all of them, but only the outer two moved. The others were black and swollen, like a trio of bats. The nails were long claws.

"That smarts mighty good." He leaned toward Mother St. John and nodded at his toes. "These look to be spoilt."

"My," she said. "Yes, they're infected certainly."

From behind the curtain, from behind the door to the room where Eliza, Davis, and the twins slept, rose a mighty wail.

Mother St. John's breath stopped in her throat. She leaned back and smiled at the man, hoping to appear relaxed and sure of herself.

Then Big Waters, never a woman to miss anything, slipped among them, walked past the man and into the kitchen, made a milking motion with her hands to indicate she'd take care of the cow, and retrieved milk for the baby. When she passed the man again, she handed him a cloth and pointed to the mess he'd made on the floor. Then she faced Mother St. John and pinched her nose. Mother St. John nodded to her and then looked her in the eye. Big Waters slipped behind the curtain. Soon the baby was quiet.

Beaver Jean took the cloth and set it down on the table. "That baby sounded mighty fresh to the world," said Beaver Jean. "Sure does. Sounds like it just been borned." He rolled up his buckskin pant leg and rubbed his calf.

"Oh, don't do that," said Mother St. John. "You'll encourage the infection to spread up the leg." She sighed a bit, comfortable in knowing that Big Waters seemed to understand so completely without any words spoken and had the situation in hand. She gave a short prayer of thanks to the Lord. "Frostbite?" she asked.

"Got drunk with some Indians," he said. "Lost my boots in a card game and mighta stepped on something. Woke up in some bad weather, with my bare foot in the snow." He folded his arms over his enormous belly and shook in laughter at the memory. Then he sighed and looked back over his shoulder. "It be a boy or girl?"

"Hm?" said Mother St. John. She feigned serious inspection of the toes.

"That baby that was crying." He pointed a thumb over his shoulder. "It be a boy or a girl?"

"Oh. Uh. She's a girl child."

"Huh," said Beaver Jean. "I got a boy child coming pretty soon. Wife's about to birth." He put his foot back down. "That Indian woman looks familiar to me. Could be I know her from somewhere."

"Big Waters?" said Mother St. John. "I don't think so."

"I've got to get these toes off and get sober and then go and fetch my wife back."

"Back from where?" She picked up the lantern and lifted it toward his face. "Are you drunk right now?"

"Don't know for surely," he said. "She likes sweets. Maybe she come through here? I been drinkin' all through this voyage to keep my bones warm through the blizzard."

Mother St. John thought to avoid the question by asking a different one. "She didn't tell you where she was going?"

"Nah," said Beaver Jean. "She tries to run off sometimes, and I always got to go fetch her back. She been here?"

Mother St. John took a measure of the man, the way he looked, the way he talked, his arrival on her doorstep at such a time. The way that even the weather seemed to herald his arrival with a wicked blowing and snowing.

"No," she said. She was surprised by how easily a lie slid off her tongue. "That baby you heard is an Indian child. Its mother died of pox."

He was the type of man a woman would run from, the type of man who could drive a woman to abandon children and chance bad weather and death.

"Also, that baby is a girl," she said. "Sickly. I don't expect her to live."

Beaver Jean sighed. "That's too bad," he said. "Thank ye for all that information, lady."

Mother St. John felt sick. Maybe she'd given herself and the children away by too eagerly offering up untruths.

"Happens, though," said Beaver Jean. "Don't it? Hard and cold place for anyone. Little ones specially."

"Yes," she said quietly.

"Now let's get to this foot," he said.

"I'd better get some clean cloth for bandages." She stood. "I'll be back momentarily." Mother St. John disappeared into the kitchen and gripped the edge of a table to steady her breath. She poured hot water from the kettle into a large bowl. Then she selected a brown bottle of ale from the shelf and stuffed it into her apron. She returned to the patient. She set the bottle on the table and placed the bowl on the floor and lifted his foot into it. Her hands were shaky.

"Hot." He hissed through his teeth.

"We just need to get them clean first. You'd best keep drinking this if we're going to take those toes off," she said. "I'll get you a proper drinking vessel."

"No need," he said. "I been drinking plenty out of a bottle like this." He quaffed a bit from it. Then he reached inside his coat and pulled out a paper. He unfolded it and set it on the table. "The other ones I'm lookin' for are these two." He tapped his finger on the paper. "Ye seen a Negress toting a pickaninny?"

Mother St. John emitted an audible exhalation. She cleared her throat. This time when she lied, she'd be more restrained and believable.

"What?" she said. "Why, no. Drink up. I've got a lot of work to do before I can rest my head on my pillow, so let's get these taken care of quick."

Beaver Jean gulped down another swig. He pointed to the paper.

"Can ye read?" he asked her. "Never mind. Ye work on that foot, and I'll read this to ye." He cleared his throat.

"Hundred-dollar reward," he began. "Eliza and child. Ran away from kind and generous Mistress Winston who wants the pair returned safely to her and unharmed if possible. Eliza, average height. Slim face and body. Comely face with black gums, snaggly teeth, and plaited hair . . . Davis, child of close to three years. Very white eyes and small teeth. Has a downcast disposition when spoken to and blinky eyed."

Mother St. John gently rubbed the area around the toes. "Sounds like a pair I heard about who ran off to the Dakotas."

"Dakotas, huh?" Beaver Jean refolded the paper and tucked it back into his pocket. "Gonna find these two here for a nice reward. Gonna buy my boy some dogs to be a tracker like me."

Mother St. John knelt before the man and peered into the bowl. "Seems cruel to talk of tracking human beings like animals."

"Tribes here been engaging in slavery forever," said Beaver Jean. "It's natural. Anyway, it's not my concern. The rights and right-nots of it aren't for ye or me to decide."

"There are no laws here, really," she said. She shrugged.

"Lady, all this thinking is mighty interesting, but could ye just tend to my toes?" He pushed closer to her. "The pain's like to kill me any moment." He drank some more.

She handed the lantern to the man and showed him where to hold it. She lifted the foot from the water and turned it one way, then another. Beneath the toes, big yellow blisters grew. "I may have to take the whole foot," she said. "Looks to be spreading."

"No," he said. "Just the toes. I need the foot." He tipped back the drink again and took a nice long pull.

"Well," said Mother St. John, "we can pray that the poison will come out once we take the toes, I suppose."

"Ye pray then. I'm sure a prayer from ye will be abided, lady."

"Perhaps we should say a prayer together." She crossed herself and bowed her head. Perhaps if she got him good and drunk, he'd pass out and she could get Eliza and Davis to Father Paul before this man even woke. She could wound him enough so that he'd have to be put up here for another day or two. Though that'd be a mighty sin.

"Never had use for it, but ye go on," Beaver Jean said. "Dakotas, ye say?"

Mother St. John closed her eyes, but then opened them and looked up at the man. "You don't pray?"

"Get on with it now before I lose my nerve."

"Our Father," she began.

"The cutting, I meant," said Beaver Jean. "Get on with it."

"Oh," she said. "Well, then. I'll just get the knife."

"Be better ye bring a hammer and chisel for the bone," he said. "Quicker too."

"Yes." She stood. "I'll have to get them from the barn."

"Why don't ye wear those black trappings most other nuns do?" He waved his hand around his face. "With the veily watchathingy where only the face peeks out?"

Mother St. John raised her eyebrows. His eyes looked loose in his head, and his cheeks had turned red. "A habit, you mean? Impractical for life here," she said. She reached up and smoothed her hair back into its bun. She replaced a pin that was coming loose.

"I'll be back shortly. Stay here." She bent and picked up the bowl. "Keep drinking."

He relaxed in the chair and folded his hands over his gut. "Nowhere to go," he said. "Not right this moment."

Mother St. John opened the door and threw the water out. She could see the path of footsteps from the window of her room to the barn. *God bless Big Waters,* she thought. But she'd have to do something about the tracks or pray for a more powerful storm before she could let the man go. Then she scooped up a bowlful of snow and went back inside and set it before the man. "Put your foot in there for a bit."

"Yep," he said. "That'll numb my old paw real good. Ye heard that pair run off to the Dakotas? How would they'a got a ride there? No one's heading that way now. Not that I heard of, anyhoot."

"Keep drinking," she said. "It'll help too."

"Don't need much encouragement there," he said. He guzzled a healthy dose. "Nah. I'd a-heard something of a caravan going to the Dakotas. Less'n some missionaries goin' that way 'scaped my attention. Maybe then."

"I've got to use the outhouse, mister."

"Freezin' out there. Be quick or ye'll freeze yer womanly parts shut."

"I don't like that talk, mister."

"Sorry, lady. The drink's gettin' to me now." He shook with laughter.

# 14

## *In the Barn*

MOTHER ST. JOHN WRAPPED herself in a shawl and opened the door again to the weather. "Keep that foot in the snow," she said to the man. She took another look at him before she closed the door behind her. She heard him singing a drinking song as she walked to the barn, a sturdy thing built back in the woods a bit, out of the wind. Inside, the air was moist and warm. Big Waters had the stove going and was forking manure into a wheelbarrow. Eliza held one of the newborn twins and, hunched over, was slowly pacing and peeking out the little window, stealing glances at the infirmary. Davis was at her hem. He had his hand around the baby girl's foot. The other baby lay curled up on a blanket, sleeping soundly in the hay, like the infant Jesus.

No, thought Mother St. John, the Nativity family didn't have one tribulation more than this hodgepodge of misfits. An old red woman, who was a discarded wife. A runaway woman slave. Her child. Twins so young and helpless, they couldn't save themselves from hunger, thirst, predator, or cold. No, she thought, she'd never seen or heard of such a sorry collection of human beings as were in this barn, where every sad tale seemed to converge and look to her for comfort. Even Jesus had his mother and the protection of a stepfather, and at least the weather was warm where he was born. These children wouldn't survive five minutes in this winter. And

these women and children didn't have one man under the heavens
they could look to now. Except Father Paul, maybe. Mother St.
John was eager for him to come. She needed help and guidance.
*When will he get here?* she wondered.

"Forgive my blasphemy, Lord," she whispered. Eliza's eyes were
upon her like the glare of an owl. Mother St. John raised her finger
to her lips. "Quiet," she said.

Eliza nodded.

"He's got a paper on you and your son," Mother St. John said,
"but he's hurt and drunk. Stay quiet and calm. I'm going to get you
to safety."

Davis sat down in the hay and reached out to Eliza. She walked
slowly over and let him hold the baby. Mother St. John smiled
at him, then said, "When that man's asleep, we'll move you and
Davis."

"I'm staying here with her," said Davis. He put his finger in the
baby's palm, and she wrapped her fingers around it again.

Eliza pressed her fingers to her temples. "He say anything about
a man goes by name of Jim?"

Mother St. John shook her head.

"Got to have some paper and ink," said Eliza. "Got to have
them free papers quick so my boy don't wind up a slave too." She
closed her mouth to trap a cough. "Be terrible if you let that happen."

"I'll get them," said Mother St. John. "I'll make them. You'll
have them."

The baby girl began to fuss. Davis plugged his thumb into her
mouth.

Eliza mumbled about driving an awl into the man's heart,
something about poisoning him. Mother St. John went to the tool
table and took the mallet and chisel. "God will bless our intentions
if we heed His commandments," she said, as much to herself as to
Eliza.

"God doesn't seem to mind it too much from what I seen, ma'am," Eliza said, softly but clearly.

Mother St. John pretended to be searching hard for the tools by shifting them noisily back and forth. Though she would never admit it to anyone and didn't like to indulge the idea for very long, Mother St. John did sometimes question the very existence of God. She was confident that Jesus had lived and died. The Bible said so. But the Bible also said a lot of other things that didn't make much sense. So on the long winter nights, after reading a story to the children and trying to answer their questions (Why did Jesus raise Lazarus from the dead, but not my ma? Why did God let Herod kill all the babies who were innocent?), she knelt at her bed, reciting her rosary, all the while wondering whether that time on her knees was wasted. She tried to work out the contradictions inherent in her belief and was hard-pressed to do it.

"We can't know God's plan," Mother St. John said, again to herself as much as to Eliza. "We just have to have faith," which is what she'd heard people say all her life, though she knew it sounded as hollow as an autumn pumpkin.

Big Waters began sweeping again, sensitive to the need for a diversion.

# 15

# The Amputation

T HE MAN WAS TALKING nonsense when Mother St. John returned to the infirmary. Something about tobacco pipes and salt pork and a tree he once saw at Christmastime, with candles all over it. She laid out her tools on the table and set the man's foot up on a stool normally used for milking. She took the lantern from him and set it on the floor.

"This should do," she said. "You want something to bite down on?"

"I brought a piece of leather that'll do." Beaver Jean unrolled the top of a little pouch that held his tobacco and jerky. He pinched a dangly piece of jerky between his fingers and then rolled it in his palms until it was as round as an eyeball. He opened his reeking maw and tucked the leather far back in his cheek, between teeth that looked few and far between.

When he did, the bad smell rolled around Mother St. John and her supper came up into her throat. She swallowed and coughed. "We're ready, then." Mother St. John placed the chisel where one of the bad toes met the foot.

Beaver Jean leaned over and shook his head. "Bigger chap first."

She moved the chisel over to the longer toe and picked up the mallet.

"Whomp it straight and certain, lady."

"Holy Mary, guide my hand and make my aim true," she said. When she smacked the head of the chisel with the mallet, the black toe popped off and flew a few feet away. She was surprised it had gone so easily. "Oh my."

"Didn't even feel it," said the man. He sunk back into the chair. "Oh wait. Now I feel it. Quick, do the next one." He swigged a drink of ale. "The pain's coming fierce. Oh, hell yes." Beaver Jean turned his head to the side and spit on the floor. He swayed to and fro. He cupped his crotch. "Feels like I might lose myself."

"Be still." Mother St. John moved the chisel and smacked it with the mallet. The next toe popped off too, and flew farther than the first. Yellow puss and thick blood spat out from the man's foot. Then she moved the chisel once more and smacked the third toe.

Beaver Jean wet his trousers. "Donkey-fucker!" he said. "Ye didn't warn me ye was doing that last one. Dammee."

"What?" said Mother St. John, but the man only rocked and moaned. "Anyway," she said, "there you be." She wrapped the foot tightly in a cloth and lifted it back into the snow. "Keep it here for another little while, mister."

"That smarts fierce. Jesus Almighty. I wet myself."

"I hope that ends your troubles, mister."

"I'm sure it will," he said. "I might need to rest here for a bit." He toppled off the chair, spilled the melted snow, and collapsed on the floor.

"Oh," said Mother St. John. "Are you all right?"

"Put my nag in the barn, would ye?" he whispered. "Alice gets cold." Then he moaned a little, hummed a tune, and passed out.

# 16

## The Priest

JUST AS THE SUN set the next evening, blowing orange over the snow, an ox and cart, driven by Father Paul, croaked to a stop in back of the infirmary. He'd been summoned by Big Waters, and when he considered her advanced age and arthritic posture, he wondered again how she could be so sneaky and quick, especially in the wicked weather of late. Some talked of the powers of the Indian people to transform themselves into animals. Because of his belief in miracles, he did not dismiss the possibility that such wonders could occur. He only wished she'd be baptized and convert, so that he would be assured that any such transformation was the work of God and not the devil.

The priest groaned as he leapt from his perch. His back and bottom ached from the long ride. Though he knew he had an important job to do here, he hoped to sit inside to rest for a while. Though he loved his basilica, he loved the Home for Orphans and Infirmed more. Whenever he walked inside, round, happy faces greeted him. Little hands pulled on his. Little voices called for him. Big Waters cleaned the place immaculately. Mother St. John made the infirmary a home, and the Virgin Mary's presence cloaked it in motherly warmth and matronly blessings. Every room glowed, with fires in the stoves and fireplace. Simple curtains, embroidered with scenes of chickens, cows, horses, deer, and buffalo, dangled from the windows. The frost on the windows was scratched with the names of children who'd dared challenge Big Waters' order to never touch her clean glass. Every nook held a place to sit down: on a rug, a blanket, a stool, a pillow. Small children and dogs and cats curled up on the laps of older children. Games and dolls and socks draped from the tables and beds. And there was always room for one more at Mother St. John's infirmary.

But he knew that the enormous responsibilities wore her out, that she was stretched thin, worried about the health of the sick ones, the comfort of the little ones, the education of the big ones. She had said so in her last confession, rendered right here in a closet transformed into a small shrine to the Virgin Mary, where the children were sent to say their prayers or sit alone after being naughty. Together, he and Mother St. John had mashed in there and stood face to face. He had taken her hands in his, and she had said, "Forgive me, Father, for I have sinned." Outside the confessional, the cacophony of fighting and crying and whining created a distraction. The children were as wild as boars. There was a crash, and she had said, "Oh. I'm so sorry. I have to go and see." But he had stopped her and said, "Big Waters can handle it. Relax." Then her eyes squinted and filled. Her lip tightened a bit, and he saw that she was holding back a sob. She tried to take her hands back and raise them to her face, to cover her crying. But he held them fast in his own. He noticed then how young she was. She couldn't have been out of her twenties, though he had never asked her age. To him she seemed very mature, experienced. "There, there," he said. "You're a marvelous sister." He pulled her to him and let her cry on his lapel. "You do the work of a dozen women," he continued. Sometimes he imagined that he was the husband and she the wife, and all the children were theirs, together. He imagined lying next to her at night and whispering in the dark about the antics of the babes. He imagined all the things that husbands and wives do, but then would feel guilty and go back to his small room and thrash himself with a horsewhip for his lust.

Now Father Paul put his hands on his lower back and arched backward and said a prayer of thanks for arriving safely. He didn't bother tying up the animal, as it was the sort that would never flap an ear or even sneeze if its survival didn't depend upon it.

"It's a good thing it was an ass and not an ox who burdened the weight of the Virgin to Bethlehem," he told the animal, "or the Lord would've had to wait until December thirtieth to be born in the nice warm stable." The ox flicked its tail at him.

Despite the ox's flaws, Father Paul felt affection for it. He gave the animal a slap on the back. The ox had come to him a few months back, in exchange for the cloth, sugar, turnips, and potatoes he'd brought to a starving settlement of about ten Norwegian families near the Dakotas. Life on the prairie was hard, more so than life in the woods, where animals and timber were abundant, or in the towns, where supplies were at the ready. These Norwegians were like other prairie settlers he'd seen: ambitious, hopeful, adventurous, but completely unprepared for this type of hard winter, the impossibility of travel, the frozen wells, rivers, and ponds, the lack of firewood and food to hunt or fish for, the madness that sets in with the imprisoning cold and snow and tedium for five months of the year. At the beginning of December, the families had been holed up for weeks already, and they were almost out of flour and down to their last buffalo chips for fuel. They already wore a doomed look: a certain round-eyed gaze, the cords of their necks jutted, the shoulders curled forward. These were not the kind who'd come through winter in great numbers.

Sometimes, come March, whole families would be discovered dead. Last spring, some fur traders told him of a Dutchman who had slit the throats of his four children and his wife, rather than let them starve to death. It had been their first winter. There was food left in the house, a bag of beans and even a ham, which made Father Paul wonder whether it hadn't been the devil getting into the mind of the man, rather than the threat of starvation.

Father Paul hadn't wanted to take the Norwegians' ox, but those tall men were prideful and insisted, tying it alongside his borrowed horse, which took one look at the broad-shouldered animal, flapped its lips, and kicked at it. The ox sniffed at the horse's oat pack. Father Paul shook his head and waved his hands to reject the beast, but the Norwegians wouldn't be deterred.

"Take," they had said. "Works good." They flexed their muscles.

"Ya," they had said. "Go." They pointed eastward, eager for him to leave, it seemed. Father Paul thought they were ashamed to be seen in such dire conditions, and so he acquiesced. He pulled a few Bibles and writing tablets and pencils from his wagon and gave them to the settlers. These were all he had left to offer, and the quiet women came forward and reached for them with their long, skeletal fingers, some of which were red or charred at the tips from continually stoking the fires, to get the last bit of heat from every ember. When it came time, he knew those women might soften the pages of the Bibles and tablets in milk, if they had it, or water, if they didn't, and feed them to their children. He'd heard of such things and worse — people eating their mud walls, chewing on their boots, consuming the flesh of the dead. He felt ashamed he hadn't brought more for the Norwegians. He knew the ox was an extravagant gift in exchange for a few supplies, which wouldn't last them through January, but Father Paul decided not to insult them. He told the men he'd pray for them.

"We be good here," they had assured him. "Yes. Good." They tucked their hands under their armpits and nodded. Father Paul hadn't yet met a nationality or tribe whose men weren't like this: proud, to a deadly degree. It was the blight of his sex, and in his worst moments of silent prayer, Father Paul wondered if this bane was a remnant of God, the creator and the master male, the most prideful of all, perhaps. He punished himself for thinking such things by hitting his thighs with a hammer or refraining from a drink of water. Father Paul left the Norwegians, headed back east, and, as he had promised, prayed for their mortal and divine salvation.

Within a few hours, he learned that the ox grunted for food and water incessantly, moved reluctantly, and emitted gas at every other step. Before they could return to Stillwater, the horse, whether by coincidence or a yen for suicide Father Paul didn't know, ate an entire bag of flower seed—foxglove and lily of the valley—that he'd collected from the tribes, and lay down and died. The ox seemed pleased at this. Father Paul gave the horse carcass to the Indians to feed to their dogs, which apparently weren't affected by the poisonous seeds, except for expelling some fragrant diarrhea. Those dogs, he knew, would be in the stew by winter's end. "God works in mysterious ways," Father Paul always said. Since that moment, he and the ox had been inseparable.

After he slapped its back, the ox lifted its back leg to kick at him. But it was getting old and Father Paul easily avoided this limp attempt. "You're not so ornery," he said to it. Father Paul liked his role in this feral place. He knew he was witness to a great change in the wilds. Once, only the smoke from Indian fires rose in the sky. Now it was blurred with the dust kicked up by pioneers' wagons and plows. Once, only Indian would meet Indian in confrontation or negotiation. Now white women traded wares with squaws in sod houses. Indian healers brought herbs to soothe the aches and pains of old white men hobbled by rheumatism. And where disagreements erupted, Father Paul rushed in. He saw himself as a negotiator, an agent smoothing the transition from savage wilderness to Christian civilization.

As he expected, once he opened the door, a waft of warm cinnamon air met him. Mother St. John must have been baking. He hoped she'd have a bit of hot water or coffee for him too. "I got here at least," he called. Three girls in brightly dyed flour-sack dresses and lacy bloomers bounded down the hall.

"Mary, Lucy, Lizzie!" he cried. "Come give Father Paul a hug."

"Father Paul," said one. "There's a big smelly man here who never wakes up. Can we go pet Queen Victoria?"

"Well," he said. "Queen Victoria is fussy today, so don't bother her." He pulled a couple of slivers of jerky from his pocket and gave them each one. "Now go find Big Waters and ask her to tend the ox."

Big Waters appeared from behind a door. Father Paul had gotten used to the way she appeared like a sudden rain cloud in a clear sky. He didn't ask how she had beaten him back to the infirmary.

Father Paul nodded at her.

She ignored his greeting but walked past him out the door and took up the reins of Queen Victoria. She was no good with animals, but the ox was used to her, sniffed her pocket for sugar, and went along when Big Waters coaxed her toward the stable.

"Bless your kindness," Father Paul called after her. Big Waters didn't turn around but groaned in acknowledgment. Try as he did, he could not get that woman to like him, and he had serious doubts that he'd ever be able to baptize her and save her immortal soul before she died. It was a failure that afflicted him. He'd recently thought he might baptize her in her sleep if he had the chance.

Father Paul walked down the hall toward the kitchen and opened the door. On a pallet in the middle of the floor lay a big, snoring, slobbering man. Mother St. John stood at a table, throwing onions and pepper into a big pot, her remedy for the children's sniffles and sneezes.

"Oh goodness," said Father Paul. "What did you do to him, Mother?"

"Only what he asked," she responded. "And maybe a bit more."

She gestured for Father Paul to have a seat. "I amputated his frost-bitten toes and dosed him with morphine."

Beaver Jean slept fitfully, full of drink and morphine, on a pallet strewn on the floor near the fire. His big shoulders rose and fell as he snored like an old bull. The floorboards outside the kitchen creaked. Elmer and some other little boys tiptoed into the room and cheerfully waved their fat hands at Father Paul. He pointed to the sleeping man and put his finger to his lips to shush them. But they proceeded to approach the lug on the floor. They looked him over and poked him with the tips of their boots until Mother St. John turned and saw what they were up to. She took her spoon and spanked them each on the behind. "Out!" she whisper-shouted. "All of you. Out!" She followed them out of the kitchen, and Father Paul heard her scolding them in the hall.

When she came back in, she said, "You shouldn't encourage them to misbehave." Mother St. John lifted her hem a bit and stepped over the man.

"Oh, Mother. They're fine boys you have there. I hope you didn't punish them badly."

"I sent them off to search for that turkey, the one that trotted away. Should be easy enough in the snow, I hope." She knelt next to the man's head and pulled an envelope from her apron. She pulled back his lip. "He stinks terrible," she said. She tapped a good dose of the envelope's contents into his mouth.

"Don't kill him," advised Father Paul.

"He's big," she said. "He can take this whole bit." And she tapped out the last of the dust onto his tongue. "That should hold you for a while longer, mister," she said. The man tried to open his eyes, but he was too groggy. The lids fluttered and closed again. He smacked his lips and turned over to sleep once more.

"He should sleep like Lazarus now," said Mother St. John. Then she produced the document she'd made for Eliza and showed it to the priest. He took it, brought it close to his eyes, and read:

*The said executor, Thomas Freelord, does hereby remove Wilhelmina Christmas, complexion black, height 5 feet, weight quite slight humble servant since birth to wife, Christine, to her own recognizance on said day, April 26, 1835, this day emancipated along with whatever future children she may bear. Signed, Thomas Freelord, April 26, 1835, Biloxi, Mississippi. Signed, Wilhelmina Christmas, April 26, 1835, Biloxi, Mississippi.*

He raised his eyes and looked at her.

"You know what this makes you?" he questioned her.

"Yes," she said. "I do." Her lips whitened. "Will it do?"

"Freelord?" said the priest.

She shrugged. Mother St. John seemed particularly proud of that surname. She'd chosen it as an adaptation of her favorite gift of the Holy Spirit, Fear of the Lord, and after knowing Eliza only a little while, could ascertain that it was the gift the woman most needed, what with her brazen character and bold person.

"Christmas?"

"Eliza wanted it."

She gestured to the document. "What do you think?" she asked.

"Certainly," said Father Paul. "I'm sure it's fine. In truth I haven't seen many of these so I'm not sure what to look for, but it certainly has an officiated air." He handed it back to her. "You did a fine job, Mother, as always."

Mother St. John exhaled and wiped her hands down her apron. "They're out in the barn with Big Waters and your ox."

Eliza hacked up something that resembled a small frog and spat it onto the barn floor.

Father Paul covered his mouth. "She's not well?" he said to Mother St. John.

"No," said Mother St. John, "but she can't stay here."

Eliza slit-eyed the priest and her brows gathered like two angry

grackles squaring off. Father Paul sat down and kicked the snow
off his boots. He smiled broadly at Eliza.

"What's he want?" Eliza asked Mother St. John.

"He's your ride," she said. "He's here to help."

Davis looked up at his mother's face. "Where's his ears?" he
asked.

Eliza went to Davis and stood in front of him. Davis peeked
around her skirt. Father Paul removed his black hat and said,
"Good day, ladies. Good day, little one." He knelt to greet the
boy. "I can still hear, despite my ears," he said. "See here?" he said,
pointing to them. "The Indians got me."

Eliza crossed her arms.

"My apologies," said Father Paul. He touched the wrinkled buds
that used to be his ears and then scratched his head. "I believed
little boys to be interested in Indians."

Mother St. John shoved the paper at the priest.

"All right then," said Father Paul. He stood and took the paper.
"Yes." He folded it and tucked it inside his coat. "In case we're
stopped, though I doubt that'll happen. Those men don't usually
interfere with the comings and goings of the religious."

Eliza reached out her hand. "I'll keep hold of that," she said.
Father Paul handed the paper to her. She took it, smoothed it.
And for the first time since Mother St. John had met her, Eliza
allowed her lips to rise into a smile. "Looks mighty good," she said.
"President himself could have written it." She folded it carefully.
Then she pointed out the window and turned her attention to the
priest. "The ox cart, then?" she said.

"It's a comfortable ride, if slow," he said.

# 17

## Eliza's Hurt

A FEW HOURS LATER, Davis lay asleep in Eliza's lap as she tried to sit still in the cart, which bumped and staggered over the road. Her legs tingled, but she dared not move lest she wake her child, who she knew deserved a good strong doze. She rested her head uncomfortably against the wall of the cart. The priest told her they were headed to a brothel, where her journey would begin. Eliza found herself in a strange mind.

She felt like laughing. Or giggling at least. These people, the nun, the priest, even the squaw, were silly in their righteousness. Eliza's humor lurched up and came out a cough. All those white folks were always thinking they were doing the Negroes so much good. Making themselves feel good was more like it.

Eliza looked over the edge of the cart. Since the day he'd left, Eliza had the feeling that at some moment, Jim Christmas would round a corner, emerge from behind a tree, or step down off some porch and that she'd see him and love him again. She had never quit expecting him. And he seemed somehow closer than ever. The pull of him seemed strung right through the snow and ice crystals in the air. Every sharp, tiny contact with the snowflakes falling from the trees seemed a kiss from Jim Christmas.

Until her move north, she hadn't considered seeking him.

She had been content to wait for his return to her. But the move changed everything. Before, she'd have never considered running away from the Winstons. But here, so many talked of escape, abolition, and freedom. Here, Eliza was suddenly barraged by white folks and free blacks intent on freeing her from her terrible bondage. That's what they always said, "terrible bondage." She endured their righteous talk about freedom, but she couldn't conceive that such a thing would honestly be possible or even desirable. Who would take care of her? Where would she live? How would she get food? As it was with the Winstons, every night she knew that she had a clean bed to sleep in. Every day she knew she'd have three meals. For practicality's sake, Eliza was comfortable in her position with them. Especially with a child to care for, Eliza relied upon the Winstons to help her. She didn't worry about them selling him off. Really, they weren't that kind. They had only a handful of slaves. Eliza knew that the buying and selling of children happened. She'd seen it. Her mother had endured it. But that was mostly on the big plantations. No, her state wasn't that bad. Eliza knew plenty of poor white folks and free black folks who had lives much more difficult than her own.

But once she got here, she suddenly became aware that this was her chance to go looking for Jim. And especially when the cough set in, she knew she'd have to find him. She gave up comfort and protection for uncertainty, for the hope that she could find Jim Christmas and see him and know what happened to him before she was gone from this earth. It roiled like hot broth in her gut. She wanted so badly to look upon him one last time. No, it wasn't freedom she was chasing. It was love. Eliza wanted Jim Christmas more than anything. She wanted to know if he had abandoned her or if he'd been sent away. In her heart of hearts, she couldn't believe that he had left her. Not after the things he had said to her! Not after the way he'd touched her! Even if he had, thought Eliza, if she could just find him and show him the fine son that they'd made together, that he'd be proud, that he'd love her again, and keep all the promises he had made.

Things hadn't gone exactly as planned, of course. Weeks ago, when she'd gone into town to get Davis's hair cut at the black barber, a free man who vacillated between offers to buy her from the Winstons if she would agree to marry him and attempts to grope her hips and buttocks, he'd tried to impress her by telling her that he'd arranged for several slaves to escape by going to the woman of the ugly habits. She'd been too busy fending off his advances to ask for clarification, so she gleaned that he had meant the nun, but now realized that rather than referring to the nun, he must have been talking about the women at the brothel. Now Eliza smiled at her own mistake. It was a story that would make Jim Christmas curl over with laughter, she knew. He would laugh in the way that made him wheeze and sneeze and need a slap on the back. That image made her smile and cry at the same time. She felt very close to an end and a beginning.

She breathed in deeply, and with the smell of hay and animal manure and wood came a swell of sorrow and relief from her belly, and she leaned into her son and cried full on now. She coughed and tasted the ever more familiar taste of blood on her tongue. She was running short on time, she knew. If Jim Christmas could just see the boy. If she could just see Jim Christmas one last time.

The cart had four wooden wheels and no springs nor anything else to dampen the bumps. Besides Eliza and her son, the cart held split wood, some paint, tools, and bundles of twine. Oak trees could grow from acorn to the moon in the time it took the ox to walk half a mile. The ox took many rests, stalling in the middle of the path, then lying down under the weight of his yoke. The beast would not move until plied by Father Paul with a treat of some sort—a scratch behind the ear, a bit of sugar, some kind words.

"Comfortable back there?" asked the priest.

Eliza didn't respond. She put all her energy into holding her boy and realized that a thing that had once been so easy, supporting her son's weight, now demanded every bit of her strength and endurance. She adjusted her legs to help prop up her elbow on which the boy's head rested. He moaned and adjusted his position.

The cough had started months ago as an itch in her neck. Now her lungs felt full, furry, and warm, and they would allow only shallow breaths. She was waning. Though she didn't really believe it helped, she prayed to God to watch over her until she was able to find Jim, to get Davis settled somehow, somewhere. The wagon lurched on over the frozen road and rolled through the woods.

Eliza opened her mouth and inhaled as wholly as she could. She could feel herself separated into two incongruous but nevertheless simultaneous experiences, life and death. Her body was dying, her chest and heart quickening, panicking, attempting to live. But her mind, slowed in pristine clarity, was calm. An airy sense of existing in two worlds fell over her. She peered over the cart and focused on the place where the wheel encountered the snowy road, at the exact moment of impact, when it hit the snow and either dashed it into the air or drove it into the ground. She listened to it. The sound was like hot milk hitting the pail or an ax hitting a rotten tree or a butchering knife hitting the breastbone of a quail. It was the sound Davis made in the seconds after he'd come rushing out of her, when she'd twisted her finger into his mouth and cleared his throat and he gasped to life. She delivered him into this being, this living, this earth. Now he breathed in sleep on her lap. She had made him. She had made it possible for him take in that air. If she had not cleared the mucus and blood from his newborn neck, he'd not be here, on this untethered and nonsensical and impossible journey. How had she known how to do that? Who had told her to clear his throat, to get him inhaling? No one. But she had done it. And then he knew what to do. And he was of her. Though he was heavy and burdensome, she worried little about him. He, without her, would be fine. He was of her. His mettle was hers. Another dying mother might have left him safe in the care of the Winstons. Another might have searched high and low for a suitable woman to replace her. Another might have settled him in with the nun and squaw. Not her. Together they were taking their last chance at finding Jim. What would come, would come.

Then she concentrated on the trees, which should have been dormant in winter, but as she watched they folded their limbs across their trunks, the thin branches and pine needles dangling like the sleeves of robes. Then they offered up a song in chorus. They hummed for her in a way that made her throat vibrate, a thing she had not experienced since Jim Christmas put his lips to her neck and moaned sweet, slow-burning, pretty words.

The road to the brothel was crude but well used. At first, when she'd heard someone approach on the road, she'd quickly covered Davis and herself with an Indian blanket. Now, at the end of her journey, she was too weary to do so. And no one looked twice at the priest's cargo anyway. Eliza had been in this area long enough to know that it wasn't entirely rare to see Negroes here. Some fur traders used black accomplices to make deals with the Indians, who trusted black skins more than white skins. Railroad companies hired black surveyors because they were cheaper and worked harder than white surveyors. At Fort Snelling, Southern generals, who'd been commissioned to prepare the green troops, brought their slaves to keep up their houses and take care of their horses. Steamboats with Southerners and their servants, escaping the malaria of the Southern summer, came frequently.

Always, Eliza searched the faces of these men, looking for Jim Christmas. She wondered what happened to him. She wondered if he wound up as a king in Haiti, as he claimed he would. Or whether he'd gone to Chicago. Or New York. Or Canada. Until the end, she'd look everywhere.

Now, in the back of a frozen ox cart in the cold North, she compared this day to those in the warm Mississippi air. When they were at the Winstons together, Jim Christmas would laze his big body alongside the corn furrows she dug in the garden and then follow her into the cooking shed, where she baked the cakes and tarts. He'd filch dill from the garden to gnaw and pinch berries from the tops of the tarts to suck, all the while bragging from day-smile to day-sigh, and from one end of her chores to the other, about his connections in Haiti and the high life he planned on making for himself once he bought his freedom, only half a year away. While she beat the rugs, he'd comment about the dry, hot weather there and how it was perfect air for ladies with lovely hair like hers, which was so sensitive to humidity. Had it been ridiculous to believe that he really cared about whether her hair poofed up like a wasps' nest? Now she reached up under her headscarf to touch that same hair that Jim Christmas had found so beautiful and found it greasy and matted.

In those Mississippi days, while she darned the socks, he'd remark about the colorful and cheery dresses the women wore in Haiti and how especially lovely they looked on ladies with ankles as dainty as hers. While she squeezed lemons along the window-sills to murder the army of ants incessantly attacking her pies and tarts, he'd talk of the charming pink flamingoes sleeping on one leg and the creeping green iguanas changing colors throughout the day. When she tried to sneak looks at books, he'd talk of the schools in dire need of good teachers in Haiti. He'd say that in Haiti, all the children were taught to read. At the end of the day, when she got ready to rest her head, he'd talk of the little hummingbirds that lived in flowers bigger than any magnolia she'd ever seen. When he started talking about blacks who ruled their own destinies and about how she could live like a queen there, she finally gave herself over to him.

Those were the glorious moments, ones that would not be gone from her head, ones in which she forgave him all his faults. She

remembered how he'd sneak her to the small rapids and lay her
down on a soft blanket and how his long, skin-and-bones frame,
his elbows like sharp gravel-road turns, his knees like pulley wheels,
his foot bones like strings would urge against her, and even now
her body quaked, and she wondered, she hoped that it might mean
she'd live. Does a dying body want for carnal pleasures? He had
been just a bit bigger around the middle than she was, and she was
hardly nothing herself, a fence post. When he lay on her, his hips
and ribs ground into hers. They had too little flesh to soften the
crash of their bodies. In a collision of joints and bone, they joined
their desperation and love. It was a hard and necessary union.

Within four months Eliza was pregnant. On a morning when
a fierce kick from inside her womb woke her, she'd risen to light
the kitchen fire. There Mrs. Winston had been waiting for her,
told her that Jim Christmas had paid the Winstons what he owed
them and gone off without her.

Eliza remembered the sudden sensation of her heart dropping
to her toes and her eyes not seeing quite right. She remembered
panting and feeling sick. Mrs. Winston noted wryly that Eliza
looked upset. Eliza responded with the obligatory "No, ma'am,"
and absentmindedly ran her hand over her belly. Mrs. Winston
said she'd known it, said she'd suspected all along that Eliza was a
filthy, dirty girl.

The following spring, on the day when the petite roses blossomed, Eliza crept into her room and squatted over a basin in
the corner and delivered the baby out of her body. She called him
Davis, after King David in the Bible, who loved Bathsheba, the
beautiful wife of Uriah.

Eliza supposed then it had been ridiculous to ever believe a
word Jim Christmas had said. But believing Mrs. Winston was no
easier. She preached Christian living and the Bible constantly, but
took praise for pies made by Eliza when her husband gushed over
the flavor, charged Eliza for a plate that she herself had chipped.

Eliza grew to wonder if the Winstons had gotten rid of Jim Christmas and then lied to her about it. She sometimes thought that maybe he was out there somewhere, trying to get back to her, return to his boy; perhaps he had a pouch full of money to sail them all to Haiti.

Whenever she thought about Haiti, she imagined a colorful world with pink birds and orange fruits and warm winds and crystal waters where little children swim, and she felt something close to happy.

She reoriented herself, got her mind right. Breathed the cold air. Snow air. Her lungs then felt as open and free as they had in some time. Her chest opened like bird wings and she respired full. The winter winds rushed in and swirled inside her chest, around the heart that had always loved Jim Christmas. "Someday we'll swim in warm waters and all be together," she said to her child, his deep-sleep breath floating off his lips. Lies, she knew. But what did it matter to lie now? She pulled her arms around her son again and then loosened them and produced a little coo. One more breath. Clean and sprightly. Then Eliza Christmas exhaled her last ghost of air and discovered herself ankle-deep in seawater surrounded by flamingoes. A long-legged man fished its waters. Her loins stirred and prepared once more for the violence of it.

# 18

## The Red Swan

B EYOND A STAND OF pines, their branches heavy with the
weight of snow, appeared the Red Swan Saloon, a tall, thin,
ordinary building but for the red swan on the sign above the door.
The ox, sensing a warm bed of straw and a handful of oats, quickened its pace. Father Paul turned to look at his cargo. They were
clasped together in sleep.

The Red Swan Saloon on the outskirts of Stillwater was built
through the patronage of the logging men who worked along the
St. Croix River and in the far northern timber camps, which began
appearing in the late 1830s as the fur trade declined and men had
to imagine a new industry. The first gaggle of ladies of pleasure
arrived by steamboat in 1835.

When the women stepped off the boat, they looked to be of
the Southern aristocracy, wearing white gloves and hooped skirts.
Behind the upstairs bedroom doors of the Red Swan Saloon, these
women swore most unladylike, squatted over men of every shape,
color, and size, and dabbed their foreheads with powder puffs
afterward, sighing, "My, I broke into a little sweat," as if amazed,
as if they hadn't said it fourteen times already that week.

But the real work of the brothel was its quiet embrace and then
covert moving of those whom the world of men had mistreated.
Several of the disgraced Southern belles came to the North with

memories of mistreatment and sympathized with their darker-race neighbors. From their lacy beds the Southern whores rebelled against the practice by coercing money, wiling secrecy, and ascertaining connections from their wealthy, powerful patrons to aid their Negro charges. A web of brothels across the country quivered with the movement of men and women escaping the confines of slavery. Very soon after its construction, the Red Swan Saloon joined the crisscross of assistance to the slaves.

Father Paul, in one of his first trips to the brothel to bring the good news and Holy Reconciliation for the whores' sinful deeds, instead found himself accomplice to the whores' good if illegal exploits. Now he intended to leave Eliza and Davis here for the ladies and their private benefactors to deliver on to freedom. These benefactors were something of a mystery. Father Paul knew much money was needed for the tasks, but he wasn't sure exactly from whom it came, as none of the women would utter the name. Though he wanted to know, the secrecy comforted him too, as he suspected his own participation in the work was kept anonymous as well.

"Here we are," he said. He pulled back on the reins and the ox stopped compliantly. Father Paul turned again to look at the mother and child. Neither moved. He hopped from the seat and moved to the side of the cart. He reached over and touched the young mother on the shoulder. He shook her, and her whole body moved. There was no reaction.

The jerk woke the boy clutched in her grip. He pressed his head to her chest. "Mama?" he said.

Father Paul outstretched his arms. "Here we go," he said. "Come."

The boy lifted his fingers to his mother's lips. "Mama?" he said again.

"Come, come," said Father Paul. He opened and closed his hands. "Come here now."

The boy pushed against his mother's arms. They gripped him stiffly.

"Oh," said Father Paul. He reached into the cart and broke the child from his mother's rigid hold. The boy grimaced, understanding. He crawled off her lap and slid away. He stood, and she fell back against the wall of the cart so that her head faced the white sky and her eyes stared up at its gray clouds. Her mouth was slightly parted, as if in rapture.

The boy sighed. "Will you close her eyes?" he said to Father Paul.

Father Paul cleared his throat. "Yes," he said. "I will." He reached into the cart, grabbed the boy beneath his armpits, and lifted him down. "Don't worry," he said. "I'll take care of her."

Father Paul entered the Red Swan, had a quick exchange with Miss Daisy, and put the child in a velvet chair. He coaxed the bartender into helping him bring Eliza's body inside. The women gathered around her in a strange, somber pall; white women in every color and texture of dress surrounded the frail, listless body of a Negro woman dressed in the muted hues of a household slave. The whores pulled lace handkerchiefs from their bodices and pressed them to their eyes and noses. One fixed a stray curl on Eliza's forehead, and another straightened her dress. Father Paul said the obligatory words, and afterward the whores cursed all the men who had probably done the dead woman wrong, confusing their own tales of misery with what they assumed were Eliza's. The boy watched and listened quietly.

Father Paul helped the bartender dispose of Eliza's body until the ground thawed for burial and took care to acclimate Davis to life without his mother by telling him about the Kingdom of Glory. He pondered what to do with the boy. Take him back to the Home for Orphans and Infirmed? Could Mother St. John manage another child? Would the Winstons recover him there and drag him to the South and into a life of bondage without anyone, not even a mother, to protect him? Should Father Paul send him on toward safety and freedom? When he expressed this conundrum to Miss Daisy, she scoffed at him and behaved as though she'd been insulted.

"I'll love him like a natural mother, of course," she said. "I've always wanted one. He almost looks white anyway. Like he could be mine anyhow."

It was absurd, Father Paul knew, but who would object?

As he got ready to leave, the ladies crowded around him. They teased Father Paul's hair, rubbed his chest, pinched his buttocks, blew on his neck, and patted him from top to bottom. Miss Sunny asked him to say her name, as it tickled her to hear him say it. Miss Cornflower raised her leg onto the piano bench and lifted her skirt to reveal her pink stockings. Miss Bluebell bobbed her bosoms so that they looked like a pair of gophers poking their heads out of a hole.

Though they were goodhearted women, they were devilish at times and could not, with their daily experience of the basest desires of men, believe that the priest did not want to expel his buildup. Instead he asked if they wanted to render their confessions. The ladies fought over who got to go first, feigning all seriousness and then spouting the filthiest deeds imaginable: I sucked a trapper's pole. I got poked by an Indian for four continuous hours. I ejaculated a logger between my bosoms. I took it like an animal on all fours from a boy of not yet fifteen, with a rod thin and hooked like a peavey. Miss Marigold and I bopped a dwarf railroad man between us. I cried out to the Lord in most unholy ways. I took His name in vain.

Father Paul listened to each lady and then gave each the same penance: an Act of Contrition and some serious imploring for the Virgin Mary's intercession, all to be done while kneeling so that each woman knew the Heavenly Father's true motivation for fashioning human legs to bend midway. Then he lined them up and offered them the Holy Eucharist, which he placed on each tongue without judgment, without wondering where that tongue had been last or what sacrilege had crossed it. He understood that the women confessed crude sins to shock and arouse him, but he was wise, empathetic enough to know that in this place was much pain, despite the carousing atmosphere and jolly décor. In the few years he'd known them, he'd tended to these ladies after beatings, broken noses, and twisted arms, after abortions, and after letters from loved ones who told them they were considered dead among their relatives. In the way that Jesus gently urged the prostitute to sin no more, so would he free these from wrongdoing. Most were still nearly children, lambs wandering in a land of wolves. When he considered the way men used them and turned them into animals, Father Paul came as close to hate as he could allow himself to.

When he was finished, he bid the women to join him in special prayer for Eliza and thanked them for their promise to care for Davis. He assured them that they'd all have a special place in heaven, for their good works far outweighed their sins. He made the sign of the cross over each of the ladies of the Red Swan and commissioned the bartender to teach Davis some tunes on the piano. Then he opened the front door and walked outside. As he coaxed his ox to stand, the ladies stood in the doorway, as colorful as a collection of priestly stoles in an armoire at the Vatican. They set to corrupting their lips with observations about the blessed endowment of the priest: "Looks like he put a ferret in them pantaloons." Davis, hearing language he knew he ought not hear, put his hands over his ears, then looked at the priest. And, as if not to hurt his feelings, he removed his little palms from them and waved to the priest. The women, upon seeing this act of empathy, erupted in laughter and hugged the child. Davis smiled, proud to cause such happiness and entertainment.

# 19

# The Schmidt Brothers

BEAVER JEAN CAME TO ON the floor of the Home for Orphans and Infirmed. His eyelids weighed more than they used to. His forehead felt as though it had been stomped upon. His tongue had grown dry and fat. He groaned, turned over on his side, and slowly sat up. He tried to orient himself and figure out how long he'd been here. A blanket lay beside him. There'd been a pillow under his head. He'd been cared for. He remembered the nun. He remembered her saying that the place was full, and he felt no anger that he'd been confined to the hard floor for his recovery. He wiggled his toes. He could feel blood rush from where the sick ones had once been. He sat still and waited for the seeping to stop. He thought about where he'd go and what he'd do next.

Beaver Jean didn't like the Schmidt brothers, who lived in the woods two days east of Stillwater, but he knew of no one else, aside from the religious types he tried not to get involved with, who knew as much about the comings and goings and whereabouts of folks as they did. They were the nosiest pair of badgers this side of the river. One of the brothers was fat. The other was skinny. Like him, they were trappers, and Beaver Jean often found himself in competition with them over productive river locations or animal paths. They were forever accusing Beaver Jean of thieving from them, but this was only rarely true. Now, though, he needed them, so he stuffed his sore, bandaged foot into his boot, yelled for someone to bring him Alice, and prepared to take leave of the infirmary and the nun who ran it. She came running. He told her about his powerful headache and that he felt as though he had slept for three years.

"Only two," she said. "And it was a fitful, restless, and gaseous slumber."

"Well, I'm off and grateful to ye for yer help," he said to her.

She followed him out into knee-deep snow where his horse was saddled and waiting, thanks to Big Waters.

He braced his hand on her shoulder and hoisted himself into his saddle. The leather whined as his weight settled into place.

"Bless you, mister," she replied. She waved.

"Thank ye," he said. "I'm sure it means a lot. Take good care of that newly borned one. The one ye said which was a girl." He nodded toward the infirmary.

"I will," she said. She waved again and turned away.

"Ye'll need to send me word if ye see any of my lost wanderers," he said to her back.

"Yes, I will," said Mother St. John over her shoulder. But she didn't look him in the eye.

Beaver Jean urged Alice down the path and into the dense woods. He rode for hours into the winter wind. His foot hurt in the stirrup. He sometimes pulled it out and lifted it onto the horse's neck, so that the blood didn't run so hard and hot. That type of riding provided some temporary relief. He thought about In the Trees and The Girl with Friend Eyes and wondered what they were up to. He considered what they might be eating. He remembered the little games they played, such as hit-the-other-on-the-top-of-the-hand-before-she-pulls-it-away, and how they would braid each other's hair. They were good women to have, he decided. Even if they were troublesome quite a lot. He rode all day, camped, then rode all day the next. When he spotted the Schmidt brothers' cabin, he cleared his throat and prepared to shout, but the brothers' dogs, a trio of hounds with long ears and tongues, bounded off the porch and dashed through the drifts toward Alice, who reared up and kicked at the ruffians.

"Ye Schmidty boys!" Beaver Jean yelled. "Ye call yer hounds down now, dammee. I'm an injured soul and can't fight these bastards from hell. They smell the blood on me, I think."

The front door opened, and the fat brother emerged. The thin brother poked his head out but then went back inside and closed the door. The fat brother pointed a rifle at Beaver Jean.

"What do ye think yer pointing at?" Beaver Jean called out. Several of his encounters with the brothers had come close to fisticuffs, but never had either of them aimed a rifle at him. He tried to remember an offense he had recently committed that might inspire such a reaction of implied violence. He undercut the Schmidts in a deal with the Ojibwe, but they had done it to him first. He took a wolf off their territory, but he had used his own trap. Beaver Jean thought maybe they were angry over his marriage to In the Trees. Years ago, the fat Schmidt had negotiated a deal with the chief for In the Trees. But the chief had changed his mind and reneged, coming to an agreement with Beaver Jean instead.

"Put that rifle down, ye old coon," yelled Beaver Jean. "I come with a deal for ye to consider."

The fat brother widened his stance. "I'm not maken any deals with you, Beaver Jean. Getten the hell out of here or I'm gonna blasten a hole in you."

"Ye do that, and ye might break this bottle of fire I brought for ye." Beaver Jean kicked with his good foot at the dogs, who were leaping up at him without much effect. With his boot, he popped one in the jaw. "Ye shut up, ye son of a bitch," he said to it.

The fat Schmidt shouted, "You betteren not maltreat them dogs! What you wanten for that liquor? And don't tryen to cheat me, neither!" Then he brought the gun down and put two fingers in his mouth, high-pitch whistling for the dogs. The dogs jumped over one another through the snow and hopped back onto the porch and sat down, huffing and puffing happily, as though they'd saved the world from evil.

"Ye heard any news about any Negro ones heading west?" Beaver Jean yelled. He adjusted his position in the saddle. His rump was quite sore, and his foot was throbbing terribly.

The fat Schmidt rubbed his chin for a while, then shouted, "Mighten heard something about some caravans headen off to Dakota but I canten be certain." He looked back toward the house and then turned to Beaver Jean again.

Beaver Jean saw the thin brother pull aside a curtain inside and slowly put it back. "Ye better tell me straight, ye scoundrel," said Beaver Jean. He thought these two were behaving mighty shiftily, as though they were hiding something.

The fat Schmidt raised his gun, and the dogs started barking. "Donten you scoundrel me, you Beaver Jean! You owen me a spring's worth of muskrat pelts after whaten you pulled last year."

"I don't owe ye nothing!" Beaver Jean was getting mad now, and the blood seemed to be pooling in his boot.

"That trap you setten upriver of mine was a sneaky a thing as I've everen seen in these parts," said the fat Schmidt. "You donten have rights to that part of the St. Croix and you knowen it without me haven to tellen you it! So donten you tellen me to tellen you straight. Why, I oughten to come over there and pullen you down offen that old nag."

Beaver Jean leaned back and screamed to heaven, "By the time ye got over here, I'd be in Canada, ye old possum!" He calmed down a little and added, "Now have ye seen my little wife with the red hair?"

The fat fellow shifted his weight from one foot to the other. He rubbed his jaw and looked again toward the house and back at Beaver Jean. "Jest what are you accusen me of, you Beaver Jean?" He moved his mouth some more but no words came out.

"I'm simply asken if ye've seen my little wife," said Beaver Jean. He sure hated dealing with the Schmidt brothers. They were about as contrary a pair of humans as he'd ever encountered in these parts. "I lost her and she's about to birth."

"You comen all the way outen here to accusen me of taken your wifey?" said the fat Schmidt. "Well, I ain't seenen no women about to birth and wouldn't tellen you if I did, ye crippled beaver."

Beaver Jean thought that the man was a tad more ornery than usual. "Well, have ye seen that pair here what are Negro and run away from their master?" He held up the notice on Eliza and Davis.

The fat Schmidt scratched his armpit. "No, I haven't seenen your woman or the slave pair neither. But for a bit of that potato liquor I mighten be able to tell you what I knowen about a caravan mighten be headen somewhere. For a side of that bacon them dogs can smellen on you, too."

Beaver Jean leaned forward. "I don't have no bacon, ye scoundrel!" he shouted over Alice's ears. "That's the smell of my bleeding foot that's got yer dogs all scallywagged." He raised his foot in proof. "Now I might be willing to swap you some potato liquor for some whereabouts of those people I'm searching for, but only if ye swap me some of that rhubarb jelly I know ye made last spring and kept down in that cellar of yers."

The fat Schmidt stepped back and peered through the window and into the confines of his own house. He turned back to Beaver Jean. "Don't you talken about my cellar! You don't knowen if I got a cellar over there or whatnot, and I tellen you what. I catchen you sniffin' near my cellar and I will thrown you down in it and locken you up good 'til youen nothin' but bones for the worms."

"Ye can't throw me anywhere, ye old whelp! Not ye or ye and yer brother both. Ye old turtles!" Beaver Jean wondered why the fat Schmidt kept such close watch over the contents of his house. He speculated that the Schmidts must have some mighty good food-stuffs in there. The Schmidt brothers weren't friendly, but they were good cooks. Beaver Jean salivated. "What do I care whether ye got a cellar or not? Ye sure is acting fidgety." He pounded his chest. All this yelling was giving his chest pains. "Now I would consider given ye my liquor and a warm fox rug I got rolled up here for that information ye were yapping about and a bit of that jelly with a bit of bread, if ye got it."

"Bread!" roared Schmidt. "Of course I gotten bread! We eaten like royalty here! You thrown me that rug, and I will tellen you the first bit."

Beaver Jean untied the rug from his saddle and heaved it to the Schmidt cabin. It landed just short of the porch. One of the dogs scrambled down and retrieved it, and dropped it at the fat Schmidt's feet. He kicked the dog away from it then, and the dog yelped.

"Seems to be true," said the fat Schmidt, "that the Frenchy priest who baptizen those Sioux bein' massacred by the Chippeways at Black Dog Village on the St. Peter River hasen organized . . ."

Beaver Jean put up his hand and said, "Whoa now." He took a deep, sanctimonious breath. "That river is called the Minnesota River, ye turkey. And them Chippeways are supposed to be called the Ojibwes." Alice whinnied as if in agreement. Beaver Jean pat-ted her neck.

"You donten tellen me! That river is calleden the St. Peter after the saint. And Chippeways and Ojibwes is the same. Now you bettern be quiet or this deal is overen!" He swiped his hand in the air.

"Go on, ye sensitive old coon. But it is too called the Minnesota River, now."

"Monsignor RaVoux hasen it in his head to taken those Sioux which canten get along with the Chippeways and moven them westward toward what they're callen Dakota." The fat Schmidt pointed his shaky arm toward the west.

"That right?" Beaver Jean remembered his own grandpappy, who'd come down with fierce shaking toward the end of his life, how the man could hardly manage a sip of water without upsetting the whole of it onto his chest.

"Well, I'm tellen it to you, arenten I?" said Schmidt. "Course it's right."

"What's them Sioux running away to Dakota from the Ojibwes got to do with the three I'm looking for?" Beneath him, Alice relaxed her hind legs, as though she was going to sit down in the snow. Beaver Jean heeled her in the belly.

The fat Schmidt pretended not to notice. "If you'd shutten up, I'd tellen it to you. For one, it ainten got nothin' to do with your wife. I hearden something bout a girl runnen to Texen or Mexico, though." He leaned back on his heels and cracked his back.

Beaver Jean wondered if Lydian had really run off to the south. She was always babbling about that place. He supposed if that was where she really wanted to be, he may as well give her a chance to see it. He thought she must have the traveling spirit, as he did, and that made him happy. He'd have to go get her, though, in time. She belonged with him. And certainly, his boy belonged with him. No one else could teach his son all the important lessons he knew. He wondered if his son living in Mexico would make him dark-colored or if he'd stay light, like him and Lydian.

"For B," Schmidt continued, "I hearden some Negro servants

stayen at Fort Snelling defected their duties to them's masters and found asylum in the bosom of the monsignor."

Beaver Jean puffed up with an important thought. "That is not right thinking on the part of that monsignor. Why, that makes him guilty of harboring fugitives, and I mean to bring him in too for a fine reward!" said Beaver Jean.

"No, it donten! He's a man of God and those rules donten apply to him." He pulled up the waistband of his pants again. "He sayen himself that he is subjecten to no laws except the ones which God hasen given onto man and I for one agreein' with him."

"Well, if yer so smart, which way they taken out to them Dakotas?" Alice felt weak in the rump again. Beaver Jean kicked her up.

"You mean you donten know how to get to the Dakotas? What kind of trapper are you if you canten even find the Dakotas?"

From inside the house came the high vibration of a harmonica being played. The fat Schmidt went to the window and rapped on it. The music stopped.

"I know where them Dakotas be!" shouted Beaver Jean. "I been in that territory lots of times and took bears and lions out of that craggy wilderness. I asked if ye know which route that holy caravan is taking so I don't have to wear Alice out looking down the wrong path when I could simply take the right one that's been paved by the monsignor and his caravan of wrongdoers!"

Alice sniffed.

"If I dinten have that blind brother of mine to take caren of, I mighten ride along out there and seen what kinds of critters they gotten out there in that territory to catchen and sellen," said Schmidt.

"I'd never travel with yer crotchety self," said Beaver Jean. "But that's pretty good information, I must say. Now I'm gonna give ye the liquor, and maybe ye can let me sit by yer fire for a bit to warm up. My foot is hurt from an amputation I had to endure."

"You're not comen in here. I'll shooten you in the eye dead on if you thinken you're comen in here. Now getten out of here and don't you comen back!" He stepped off his porch carefully, so as not to lose his pants.

Beaver Jean pulled a bag out from between his legs. "I was keeping it warm in there," he said. He untied the bag and pulled out the bottle. "Here ye be." He tossed it to Schmidt. "Share a bit of that with the skinny fella in there."

Schmidt caught the bottle, then yelled back, "Donten you be tellen me what to do with my own bottle." Then he turned his back on Beaver Jean, slapped his fat thigh for the hounds to follow, and headed into the house.

# 20

## The Disquieting Mother

BARTON AND MILLICENT HATTERBY blew into the Stillwater Home for Orphans and Infirmed on a mid-April morning, hollered for Mother St. John, and demanded to see what white babies were for sale or adoption.

"I've just got to have one," said Millicent. Her brown eyes were warm as coffee.

Mother St. John welcomed them down the hall, past all the rooms of children, toward the kitchen, where she'd put Lydian's twins in a crib while she cooked. Big Waters pounded bread dough in the corner. She groaned disapprovingly when the couple entered.

"I've got tea," she said. "Would you like some to warm up?"

"No, we're looking for a son," said Mr. Hatterby. He tucked a hand between the buttons of his coat.

Millicent tightened her lips into a smile. Her husband was always wandering off to Fort Snelling to negotiate with the regiment men, to Grand Portage to bargain with the fur trappers, to the timber camps to collaborate with the foremen, to the sawmill to parley with the barons, to the river to consult with the steamboat captains, to the church to make deals with the priest, or to the Indian camps to sway the chiefs. He had big ideas about this town and territory and imagined himself at the center of organizing it. She wished he would stay home with her. She hoped that maybe a new baby would tether him to her.

The babies lay tangled together on a blanket of red-and-black plaid. Millicent noted the aged Indian woman standing nearby.

"Hello," Millicent said.

The woman nodded. She was chewing tobacco and moaning a little chant, conjuring up some wicked Indian spells, no doubt, thought Millicent. The nun laid one hand on the crib and stretched her other over the babies, as if to introduce them.

"These are our newest additions," said Mother St. John. "The bald one's Clement. The other is Scholastica."

At the sight of the infant with swirling black hair, the muscles in Mrs. Hatterby's neck swelled, and her throat felt as if she'd swallowed a thistle. That old itch, the kind she'd first felt months before when she'd birthed her own, returned to her fingertips. This urge, for her, was a thing hard to explain, both loving and hurting, teetering between care and pain, between the desire to stroke the heel of a tiny foot and drive her fingernail into the head's soft spot. It was a baby's vulnerability, its resilience, the thinnest ledge between life and death that made Millicent barmy with glee. She pulled a porcelain baby brush from her pocket and ran her thumbs over the bristles.

"The boy's the little one?" asked Mr. Hatterby. "The one that looks pale?"

"I brought this," Millicent said. She raised the brush a little to show Mother St. John. "I had hoped."

"Well, yes," said the nun. "As you can see, the girl has a headful of hair—"

"She's got a darling widow's peak," said Millicent.

"The boy is small, but he is doing well," said Mother St. John.

Mr. Hatterby pushed down Millicent's arm. "Let's not get ahead of ourselves," he said.

"Yes," Millicent said. "The hair, though." She smiled. "I'm sure about it." Millicent had to get her hands on that child. She had to brush that hair. She didn't want to appear too desperate because Barton didn't like it when she behaved hysterically or fitfully, and he often said, "Easy now, Millicent." She hated to disappoint him. Early when Barton was courting her, they'd waded in freezing water and waited to see who could outlast the other. It was the first day the robins had returned. At first, the water stung her legs. But eventually, Millicent's thigh above water cooled and numbed and her calf below the water felt amputated, as though it were not there. Millicent knew about this strange, little-known aspect of pain. Pain doesn't hurt for long. As soon as you think you can't stand it one more second, you do. And as soon as you think the pain's unbearable again, the pain's gone. She could've stood all day in that water. But she'd let Barton win at the little game and took care to display her ankles as she dashed out of the water. The good pain of that cold water reminded Millicent of this yearning to touch that baby. She could've just stuffed those hands and feet into her mouth and eaten the child up. She wanted her so desperately. Millicent had spent her entire thirty-five years waiting and wanting for people.

The baby girl screeched like a stringed instrument.

"Noisy one," said Barton. His mustache twitched.

"She's upset from all this excitement," offered Millicent.

"Yes, I'm sure that's right," said Barton. "The boy. He doesn't have much vigor, does he?"

"He's sleepy is all," said Mother St. John.

Barton Hatterby leaned over the crib and pulled the bald one away from his twin sister by the foot. "There we go," he said. "That's better. Now get a good look at them and decide," he told his wife.

Mother St. John cried out a little. She said, "We've learned that they're really only satisfied if they're together. They're hardly any trouble at all when they're together."

Millicent caught the wide-awake eyes of the boy. Such a strange look he gave her. He had uneasy control over his eyes, looping around in the sockets, but she knew that to be common in babies. He had the look of a cat she once saw and didn't like. She felt known and invaded, challenged suddenly by the infant, as if he meant to unnerve her. His skin had the dull white pasty look of a newly born but already dead animal.

"We're not taking the boy," she said.

"Maybe we should wait awhile," said Mr. Hatterby. "Perhaps another baby will arrive soon."

"No," said Mrs. Hatterby. "We'd wait forever before there'd be another white baby. I know you wanted a son, but—" She studied the boy again. He was bluish and small. He looked like the zombies she had heard tales of.

When Millicent was a small girl, her mother threw herself into the ocean and died after relentless attempts to get the attention of her husband, a captain in the French army in Haiti. After Millicent's mother was gone, a Haitian nanny had cared for her and filled her head with talk of zombies and spells. A tapestry of a blue Jesus dying on the cross hung above the table where Nanny had prepared Milly's food. Nanny had fashioned a small altar of colored bottles and a red-and-black rooster made of cloth, to which she presented three kernels of corn on the window ledge next to the tapestry. Milly had asked her nanny if she prayed to Jesus, to which her nanny had said of course. One must respect and fear all people who can come back from the dead, so that they don't get mad and bite the necks of the living.

Millicent considered the bald boy again. "No," she said, "we won't be needing him. Only the girl."

"But they're really so much more content when together," said Mother St. John. "As soon as I try to separate them—"

"No, no," said Mr. Hatterby. "We'll only be leaving with the girl. Maybe we'll have our own boy someday soon." He gave his wife an obliging, sideways squeeze.

"She's really lovely," said Millicent. "I'm her mother, certainly. I already feel like her mother, as though she belongs to me."

"I've got lots of other little girls in need of good homes," Mother St. John went on. "Many past this delicate, crying stage—"

Mr. Hatterby asked, "The baby girl, is she healthy enough? The boy's not going to work out, and I won't take a sickly one. Does she have worms or the croup? Are you sure these others didn't contaminate her?"

"They're both healthy." Mother St. John leaned over and moved the boy back near his sister and covered them both.

Mr. Hatterby lowered his voice and leaned toward Mother St. John. "We lost one, you know," he said. Two months before, Mr. Hatterby came upon a scene he'd never forget. His wife sitting, in the nursery rocking chair, was humming a lullaby, cupping the dead baby's mouth around her nipple. Pale blue milk spilled down the porcelain cheek, running, running onto the wood floor. Mr. Hatterby discharged all the servants and help. He didn't want the story getting out.

He had nailed together a little box, dug a small hole in the frozen ground with considerable effort, and called for the priest. Together, as light snow fell, they buried the girl, just six weeks old, while Millicent watched from the window. For days, Millicent asked after the baby. Who was minding her? Other times, he'd found her sobbing, the front of her blouse soaked with milk. Millicent's mind was as fragile as a prairie hen's egg. Mr. Hatterby couldn't determine whether she understood that the baby was dead and buried. Because he was a busy man and didn't like getting involved in women's troubles, he consulted with the priest, and they together decided it was best to quickly get her another baby and proceed as though the entire event had never occurred.

Millicent felt a tingling rush of milk come to her breasts. "I think she's hungry," she said.

"Yes," said Mother St. John. "I heard about your loss from the priest. I'm terribly sorry." She pursed a smile. "It's hard getting such little ones through the winters here. I've had some troubles myself over the years. We had some Indian children with smallpox a couple years back. Terrible illness."

The Hatterbys didn't respond.

Mother St. John cleared her throat and fell quiet.

Millicent thought the nun's silence was a good thing. She hoped Mother St. John wouldn't say anything that would make Barton change his mind about the baby, make her leave this place without that child in her arms.

"We'll take her," said Mr. Hatterby. He took up the little girl and handed the babe to his wife. "There you are now. Your daughter."

"She looks of me, a little," said Mrs. Hatterby. The girl child squirmed. Mrs. Hatterby brought the baby to her own face to kiss the little pink lips.

Mr. Hatterby reached inside his coat and pulled from it a bag of coins. He pressed it into Mother St. John's hand. She opened her lips but said nothing. Big Waters rumbled in the corner, but no one paid any attention to her.

The baby boy squirmed restlessly.

When they got into the wagon, Mrs. Hatterby lifted her shawl, unbuttoned her blouse, and plugged the infant's nose until she opened her mouth and latched on.

"She's hungry, I bet," he said to his wife. He clicked at the horses to move and put a hand on his wife's thigh to steady her and the baby. "Everything will be all right now, won't it, Millicent?"

"Oh yes," she said.

"Mmm-hmm," he said. "I knew it."

"This angel will get nice and fat," said Mrs. Hatterby. And Angel is what they called her.

# 21

## The Unwanted Ones

NOW THAT THE BOY CHILD had been stripped of his mother, as well as his sister, Big Waters thought to convince him that she would not leave him. She rubbed the baby boy's legs with lard until they glistened and were warm and limber. She wrapped him up tightly and brought him to her own chest. She chanted a little song, telling him he would be a strong warrior, a brave hunter, the rock for his family. The baby whimpered softly but soon fell asleep against Big Waters' breast.

Arthritic aches racked her body. Each movement sent switches of lightning up her back. Her own mother had been humped over by such pains as these. By the time Big Waters was a woman with children, her mother could stand no taller than a deer, no matter how many layers of bear fat Big Waters rubbed and pounded into the woman's crooked spine. One day, the old woman disappeared into the prairie. Big Waters watched her hobble away, her head no taller than the tips of the Indian grass until she was a specter, and then gone. Big Waters wanted to call to her to come back, but she hadn't. Perhaps if her mother had known what a help she had been to Big Waters. How her children had loved their granny's stories of the old days and of Jesus. The old woman told many stories of Jesus and his spirit of fire. Fire, that constant source of entertainment, captivated the children. Big Waters had once caught her oldest trying to set fire to Granny's hem as she slept. Though her hem was singed, Granny was patient with the boy and laughed at his antic. Those were days when Big Waters was young, with a strong husband and many healthy children. Now she moaned when she moved. She prayed to the warm west winds. When they came, her aches subsided. Soon they would bring longer days, more sunlight, better health for her. Then she would be more of a help to Mother St. John. To the little ones.

Big Waters patted the baby boy on the back tenderly. She disapproved of the way the Hatterbys had stomped through the infirmary, their heavy boots waking any sleeping child within earshot, and taken Clement's sister with them. They passed all the other children without reaching out to touch or smile or bother about them at all.

Big Waters massaged the back of the baby's head and neck. It felt good to have one so vulnerable depend upon her again. Clement. He weighed less than a rabbit. He was pale and cold. He nuzzled in close to her breast. Already her pains eased. She brought him to her mouth and dripped a little tobacco juice into his. He livened at that. His arms pushed against his blanket, and his eyes watered.

They were a good pairing: he young, she old. He an orphan, she a discarded wife. He tended toward the chills, she toward hot flashes. He bony, she full of fat. His skin dry and peeling, hers shiny with oil. His eyes wild and mismatched, hers black like tree knots and steady. He ugly, she ugly too. Both unwanted but for each other.

Big Waters took the child to her own bed that night, and she tucked herself and the child into the blankets. When the baby cried, she leaned toward the table and dipped a corner of cloth into milk, then placed the cloth in the child's mouth. When he sucked it dry, she repeated the process until he was sated. They slept like mother and child, warm and cozy as bears in the sun.

At first morning light, Big Waters strapped Clement to her back and carried him to the kitchen, where Mother St. John stood drinking coffee and chewing on a piece of pemmican while she scraped the frost off the window with her fingernails. Loaves of grainy bread sat cooling on the counter for breakfast, raising a yeasty steam. "He will be as my own," said Big Waters.

"Very well, old woman," said the nun. "Though he is small and sickly, surely he'll thrive under your care."

Big Waters understood. She brought Clement to the barn with her and placed him in the straw on his blanket while she fed the mules and milked the cow.

Big Waters was born in the time when the voyageurs sought the water passage from the East to the West. Each new season, new men came. Yellow haired, red haired, brown haired. Many with blue eyes, some with green. Dressed in strange clothes—hooded capes the color of the sky, red caps, cloth pants. All of them stroking canoes up the river, waving the flags of their people. As a girl, she had learned English and French and even a little Spanish. In that time, Big Waters spent her days traveling with her father, and then later her husband, to make negotiations or trades or help the voyageurs navigate the maze of waterways or the land routes to the best trapping places. In her opinion, and among the talk of many other women, Big Waters had saved the people from certain starvation many winters. How quickly the men could be tricked into bad deals after a few drinks of whiskey. They never seemed to learn. Each time they'd come away from such an affair, their heads would hurt, they would vomit on the trail, they would be ashamed by how lightly the horses and women could walk under their empty packs. They would begin the cursing of the white man. They were cheaters. They were devils. This was an endless conversation. It had already lasted many generations.

Each season, the people would bring their pelts to the trading station or fort where the French or the British, for a while even the Spanish, and finally the Americans staked claim by raising big cloths that waved on tall poles. For many seasons, the men had given away more of the people's hunting grounds, their fishing places, their settlement lands, while singing and drinking with the white ones, while making fools of themselves, dancing with broomsticks and with tin buckets on their heads. At each session, Big Waters and the other women were expected to stand off along the wall, to wait to carry the goods, and to be quiet. They had been silent so often that many children had died from hunger. The next season, Big Waters simply stepped forward among the men at the long table at the fort and said, "I would like to read that paper before these fools put their marks on it."

That was the end of her time among her people. Though she'd saved the people from giving away another parcel of place, from agreeing to remain confined in a bare space with no animals or water, she'd insulted the men, her husband in particular, and he had declared her banished.

The next day, he had a new wife. In the same way her mother had disappeared all those years before, Big Waters then walked into the tall grasses. Her children were directed to turn their backs to her as she left.

Her own children did this. The one Big Waters had nursed until he could ride a horse. The one she had tended to night and day for many months while he lay crying and recovering from burns suffered in foolish play, in dares of manhood made by one child to another. Had he forgotten how she had held him in the cold river water day and night? Or how she held her hand over his mouth so the other boys would not hear his crying and think him a coward? Even her only girl, the one who was betrothed to a Spanish brute with a withered arm until Big Waters begged on her behalf to her father, saving her from the bad marriage, even she turned her back to Big Waters. She from whom Big Waters later pulled the upside-down baby after three days of pain and delirium, saving both their lives, also turned her back. She who had been stolen by the enemies for a slave and whose return Big Waters had negotiated by trading her own fine beadwork and tunics, she turned her back. Even the two she had taken into her own heart as her own after their mother succumbed to disease. They all turned their backs to her. Never to call her mother again. These were the events Big Waters could not speak of to anyone except the small baby in her arms, the one whose little ear was so near her lips. She would be a good mother to Clement, and he would be an obedient son.

Big Waters introduced Clement to the finicky horse, left by the girl who had birthed the twins. The beast snorted at the baby's scent. The baby sneezed at the horse's. Big Waters let the animal sniff the child again, then laid Clement in the straw while she worked; but she didn't take her eyes off that horse. He showed her his teeth but didn't try to bite her this time. The warm, stewy air of the barn entered Clement's lungs. He breathed deeply in a way that swelled his chest, like a river about to overflow. He slept soundly and snored. When he woke, Big Waters mixed milk with molasses and sugar and let him suck. She tried to make peace with the horse and offered it a bit of sugar too, but it snapped at her finger, and she kicked its leg. This horse had a bad spirit. Big Waters called him Hole-in-the-Day, after her husband. But Hole-in-the-Day's spirit wasn't as bad as her husband's. Whereas his breath had smelled of throat fire and bile, the horse's smelled mealy and grassy, and only occasionally of stomach odor. Even then, its breath worked magic on Clement. While the boy slept beneath the horse's nose, he grew and strengthened. The vapor healed whatever ailed the baby.

Within a few weeks, Clement was smiling at the animal, which showed an odd tolerance for him. Clement's cheeks grew fat. His legs plumped from arrows to clubs. Within a few months he reached for the horse's ears to pull and gnaw at them. The beast was patient. Soon Clement used its nose to pull himself to standing position, which the horse resigned itself to without complaint, even when the child's sharp fingernails scratched into its delicate pink skin. Because of this, Big Waters forgave the horse its bad disposition. Still, she looked forward to the day when the child, instead of her, could be charged with its care. For Big Waters knew the horse would have a long life, as did all males who were particularly bothersome to her.

# 22

# Beaver Jean Ponders Changes

I F BEAVER JEAN WAS GOING to set out for the nation of the beef, he'd have to get supplies and bundle up his wives and pack them along. Beaver Jean coaxed Alice away from the Schmidt brothers' place and back toward his own cabin near Stillwater and then on to Fort Pierre, about a month's journey west. Alice was getting old and tried to sit down every few minutes. The rides with her were getting longer and longer, slower and slower. Beaver Jean had a lot of time to think.

That Schmidt brother had made him mighty mad, suggesting he didn't know the way to the Dakota lands. Of course he did! He'd practically written the maps! He'd been out on a voyage that way with a couple of French railroad cartographers who'd worked for Jedediah Smith himself, before Smith got mauled by that bear. Beaver Jean had snatched up poisonous rattlesnakes, eaten the meat, and sold those skins for a good price. Beaver Jean would have bet the toes he had left that neither of those Schmidt brothers had ever handled a rattlesnake. Whoa boy! He chuckled to himself now, imagining the shaky one handling a rattlesnake. Ho! He imagined the snake rearing around and biting Schmidt on the nose. Beaver Jean laughed so hard, he nearly fell off Alice. He righted himself.

"Move along, Alice," he said. "We've got a long way to go yet before ye can sit down and rest awhile." Alice clopped along the icy path. Beaver Jean reached down and patted her neck. She was a good horse, but she probably wouldn't last much longer.

Beaver Jean now worried. The last trek he'd taken to the big portage had not been fruitful. The men, different from the old traders and trappers, had told him that nobody wanted beaver pelts anymore, that the English now preferred silk hats.

Beaver Jean had hoped for many years to discover some kind of new material that could make him rich, but he'd had no luck yet. Some said there was copper to be found in these parts, but Beaver Jean was sure that was nonsense. He knew there was gold in the Dakotas, but the Indians from those parts would never allow a white man to stick a pick or shovel into their sacred land. Others said that trees were the way to wealth, and Beaver Jean saw truth in an economy based on timber, but cutting and shipping trees didn't seem very exciting or noble. The trees were in plain sight and didn't fight back when you chopped them down. Where was the thrill of the hunt? The contest between man and beast? Others were talking of moving the Indian nations farther west to open up land for planting crops, as they'd done in the East and in the South. Beaver Jean hoped agriculturing wouldn't happen to these wooded parts, but he supposed eventually farming would come here, the way it, along with Bible preachers, smallpox, and bad smells, accompanied the New Englanders wherever they went. These parts had recently been overrun with New Englanders, the kind who talk a lot about politics, money, exploration, farming, fine clothes, good tobacco, abolition, and even privileges for women.

Though men like Beaver Jean and the Schmidt brothers had lived here for decades and should rightfully have been in charge, the newcomers were claiming this spot and that one, putting docks and nets and boats in the river, building bridges, developing stores along the main roads, naming places and pounding stakes into the ground, and building up houses with deep basements, churches made of limestone, a courthouse with jail cells. Everything they made now was built to stay. They were staying, and the world was changing from wild to civilized. Beaver Jean's pappy would have said these changes were right. Beaver Jean felt they were wrong and that the natural order should prevail. Beaver Jean intended to teach his own son the right ways, the traditional methods of hunting and trapping, once he was old enough. Beaver Jean was eager to teach all he knew to his own seed.

Beaver Jean turned Alice toward an abandoned dugout left by a trapper who died in it one winter and wasn't discovered until the next spring.

"We'll warm up here for the night," he told Alice. Into the darkness, Beaver Jean shouted, "Jean-Pierre LaFoilette, if yer half-bred ghost be in here, it's yer old friend Beaver Jean askin' permission to spend the night out of the wind with his poor ol' nag, Alice. We both got achy feet, one of which had some toes removed from it not so long ago. We remember how ye in life were as pleasant a person and skillful beaver trapper to ever have walked these woods." Beaver Jean listened for a disagreeable spirit but heard no objection, so he brought Alice inside with him.

It was cozy in there, and he and she would keep each other warm. He built a fire, took off his boot, and unraveled his bandage. The place where the toes used to attach to the foot was swollen and very white and puffed up like the underbelly of a fish. "That looks better than I thought it might," he told Alice. "We'll both of us rest our feet tonight and then pick up them squaws tomorrow. Then we'll head out to get that runaway woman and child and hopefully find Lydian, the one who used to braid your mane, somewhere along the way. A girl like that won't likely last long without the care of her man."

Beaver Jean rested alongside Alice's belly. He spread a buffalo blanket over himself and over her hind legs. He dreamt that night of a man who was his son, but grown up and sitting across a log floating on a river.

His wives packed up for the journey agreeably. For thirty-three days, Beaver Jean and In the Trees and The Girl with Friend Eyes enticed Alice across the long prairie, through cold rivers, and into the land where the Dakota fought with the Arikara, a farming group with feisty work dogs running around. When last Beaver Jean had been out this way, the Arikara had been a robust and populous group, spreading from horizon to horizon across the world, it seemed. But now their numbers were sorely diminished, and their earthen homes sat abandoned on the plains. According to one old one, who'd been left behind because of her sore eyes and old age, a terrible disease had taken many, and big fighting with the Tetons chased away the others. Beaver Jean moved his horse and wives along. They passed among grave mounds and over burned fields now sprinkled with snow. The wind talked to him and told him this place was haunted.

The Girl with Friend Eyes shamed In the Trees by saying her Dakota people ought to stop pestering the Arikara and quit burning up their corn and scaring the little Arikara children and dogs. In the Trees slapped The Girl with Friend Eyes and said the Ojibwe started it by pestering the Dakota out of their lands and pushing them to this barren territory in the first place.

Beaver Jean used the reins to slap both of them in the legs. "Ye both make right points, but now is the time to be peaceful squaws and quit bickering amongst yerselves." Beaver Jean sighed. Then he raised his arm and pointed from one side of the earth to the other. "Look, ye women. The world is empty, with enough places for everyone to lay down their head or plant their corn or fish the rivers or hunt the buffalo." He pointed at first to one wife, then the other. "No need for fighting. There is, always has been, and always will be enough room for all of you if you don't get too greedy, which ye women tend to get."

He thought to himself that he had managed the women's troubles with great skill. Finally, after more days of walking, the trio spotted a stone fort to the west, surrounded by encampments.

"We made it," said Beaver Jean. "That Negress and boy should be here and will hopefully agree to come dutifully."

Among the tipis and mud houses, In the Trees found some people who knew her sister.

"Stay and enjoy yerself for a while if ye want, but take yer other one too, and I'll take Alice with me to ask about our bounty." In the Trees and The Girl with Friend Eyes sauntered off.

Beaver Jean entered the fort and swelled up with air. Trappers draped in capes and skins walked here and there. Soldiers sat on stumps, spitting on their boots and wiping them shiny. Some Arikara men led a pack of dogs pulling a cart of tubers and onions toward a shack that looked to be a store. After so many adventuring weeks, it was nice again to see people alive and well on the earth. Even Alice lifted her nose and seemed to be smelling the interesting scents. Beaver Jean showed every other person Eliza's wanted paper.

"Ye seen this one?" "Ye know her?" "Ye heard about a runaway woman and child?" But no one knew anything. Then a Negro blacksmith motioned for him to come near. Beaver Jean showed him the paper.

The blacksmith scoffed at him. "Yull come all dah way from Stullwater? Yull don't even know how dumb yull are. Whatchu chasin' hepless woman and chile for?" he asked, holding a horseshoe in blazing red tongs. "Big man like yursuf. Whyn't you chasin' sumfin else, that's hurtin' somun."

"This woman ran away from her rightful owners," said Beaver Jean. "If she were a free woman, I'd not hound her in the least bit.

But this be a fair pursuit of a criminal according to the law." He stepped back as the blacksmith sunk the horseshoe into water. It sizzled and fizzed and splattered.

"Yull talk like dat round me more and yull fine this tongs up your asshul," the blacksmith said. He smacked his tongs against the side of a hot cauldron.

"There's no call for yer foul talk."

The blacksmith launched into a rambling then. "I'll talk what I wunt to talk. Um free with papers whut saw so. Yull better nut threatun me. Ill thretun yull better thun whut yull can say to me. Ill threatun a brand yull on the face and burn that beard uff yull stupid jaw."

"I don't have to stand here and take this abuse from ye!" said Beaver Jean. "I don't tell ye how to do yer employment, do I?" Beaver Jean crossed his arms and leaned back, satisfied that he had made a convincing argument.

The blacksmith went on. "Yull too dumb to find anybody. I knowd lotsa bondaged ones prolly going right under yull nose in dat Stullwater place. Yull sure is dumb. They be long gone by now. Yull prolly passed 'em on the road. But they bes flying away from yull and all yull dummies chasin' 'em. Yull sure is dumb." The blacksmith threw back his head and laughed.

Beaver Jean was confused by the blacksmith's talk. "Come on, Alice." Beaver Jean pulled the horse away from the blacksmith. "And ye just lost a customer with yer bad mouth. This horse needs new shoes real sorry, but ye won't be getting money from me even though I'm limping under the weight of how much coins I have! Ye'll be sorry now as I walk away to do my blacksmithing business with a less abusive smithy!"

The blacksmith's eyes widened. "Imma send erry Negroed figure I know to dat Stillwater place to get dem sum freedom. If all dem slave catchers dumb as yull, they be safe un soun in broad daylight even if day'd be carryin' signs whut say 'I's escaped my massas. Catch me quick.'"

Beaver Jean didn't turn around and moved farther into the fort. He sat down at a table where a man served bread and beer. He asked a young soldier if he knew of a monsignor leading the committed souls away from their rightful masters, and a young soldier said, "The father to the Indians and Negroes? Yeah, he's here. Been back in the quarantine for a neary a month."

"The quarantine?"

"The pox afflicted a lot of the people. We put 'em on the south end and put up some fleety walls. The father's been hauling water for 'em from the Bad River. You can catch him coming back anytime."

"I believe I will do that just after I finish my sup," said Beaver Jean. "Thank ye for yer kind help," he said.

"Surely," said the soldier. "But I'd turn wide of that pox infestation if I were you."

"Thank ye for the warning, but I never been sick a day in my life unless it was induced with hard liquor. And once I had some toes removed for infections, but that too was a self-inflicted affliction."

The soldier held up his two-fingered hand. "I lost these digits in the raising of that wall yonder." He pointed toward where Beaver Jean had entered the fort. "Now alls I got left is this gristly pair. When you find the father, will you ask him if my digits will be returned to me in my heavenly way?"

"For yer kind help, I will," said Beaver Jean. "Yer a good boy. As fine a one as I hope my own to grow up to be."

"Thank you, sir," said the soldier. Then he farted loudly. "Excuse my disturbance. I feart I have worms of some kind in my inter workings."

"Drink some clear water mixed with a little turpentine. It'll clear ye right up," said Beaver Jean. "Same concoction works for lice in yer beard and armpits." Beaver Jean told himself to remember those two bits of wisdom to teach his son.

Beaver Jean got up and wandered around for a while. He talked with some trappers about beaver prospects. He talked with some traders from the American Fur Company who told him money was now in buffalo. Finally, the people who had been crossing this way and that way, brushing shoulders and talking mouth to ear, moved away from the main thoroughfare, opening up a wide space down which a skinny old man tugged a cart full of water buckets. The people on either side raised handkerchiefs to their noses and mouths, and many turned away from the man. Beaver Jean approached him.

"Well, ye must be the monsignor every soul's avoiding," Beaver Jean said as he passed. "God bless ye and all that."

The old man wore dull black pants, a black wool shirt so dusty it could have been gray, and a handkerchief around his neck. "Terrible, terrible disease," the monsignor said.

Beaver Jean joined him in step. He helped the old man with the handle of the cart.

"If your soul's not pure as snow, you better back away from me. The Lord's my only protection from the affliction, and you're like to get it, should you follow me to where I'm going."

"I'm healthy as a horse," said Beaver Jean. "Heard ye rode with some runaways out here."

The old man walked quickly and breathed heavy. He seemed quite tired but moved despite it, pressing forward. Then he dropped the handle and said, "Yes, man. Here, take this if you won't be deterred like a body with an ounce of God-given sense in his head." He plucked a clean handkerchief from inside his shirt and wiped his brow. He straightened his back and walked quickly now. "Come along," he told Beaver Jean. "Hurry up."

"This cart weighs considerably and is left-leaning to boot," said Beaver Jean. "I shall take my time, sir. God bless ye and all that." But he did pull a bit harder and pick up the pace a little. He remembered how infuriating it was when Alice would walk so slow as to let the snowdrifts pile around her hooves, even as the angry, cheated Indians were gaining on them. "About them that runned away?"

"What do you want to know about it?" he asked. "I don't lie. But I'm not inclined to offer information to those that needn't have it." He pointed out a gopher hole to Beaver Jean so he wouldn't trip in it.

"I heard maybe ye took up some scallywags what did run away from their master back in a town called Stillwater on the St. Croix River," Beaver Jean said.

"What happened to your leg?" asked the priest. "Or your foot? I see you have a gimp."

"Had to be relieved of some infected toes," said Beaver Jean. "Ye bring some runaways out here?"

"Well I might have done something like that," said the old priest. He looked ahead, seemed to be gauging how much farther he had to pull the cart. The water sloshed over the bucket rims as the cart jerked over a rut. "You're welcome to look if you want, but you won't find any help here in getting anyone you find back to where you want them to be. In fact, I say the word, and you might catch hell for it."

"This place be runnin' over with soldiers," said Beaver Jean. "Ye think they don't have the correct sense of right and wrong? Where's the general or the man in charge of this outfit?"

"So long as I been here, these men have all figured right and wrong from the good book and no other place. We serve, all of us, only one master here. And when these men are confused, they come to me for answers."

"Well, I figure to just look around and see what I can see." Behind them and the cart, the thoroughfare closed again with people.

"Suit yourself," said the priest. "But I warned you about the pox and such."

# Part III

# ORPHANS

# 23

## Angel's Doll

ANGEL HATTERBY WOULD SPEND most of her infancy banging her pink fists on what turned out to be, for her, death's sturdy locked door. Millicent laced Angel's food with whatever household poisons the child would drink without objection. Sweet liquids, such as borax mixed with sugar, worked well. Jimsonweed caused fever and shaking, enough to alarm Barton and bring him running from wherever he might be. Millicent only wanted him to be with her. She wanted him to see what a careful and dutiful mother she was. She wanted him to compliment her, smile at her, stay with her. But again and again, he'd wait until the child pinkened, sat up, and felt better, and he'd be off again. Millicent became more creative, more clever. Ashes from the fire caused an eerily similar ashy color in the baby. She'd send for Barton and cling to his arm as he pulled back the blanket to see if he too could see the odd color. She sometimes dabbed chloroform tenderly onto a handkerchief and wafted it soothingly under the child's nose. Millicent simply had to take care not to let the little girl inhale too much and to hold her tongue forward so she didn't swallow it and suffocate. Millicent had learned her lesson about that. She'd been careless with the first, but not with this one.

Millicent did these things to Angel not because she didn't love the baby. She did. And she tried to be very careful, so as spare

Angel from what happened to that first child. She hadn't meant for that to occur. No one could say she wasn't a good mother. Everyone could see how difficult that loss had been on her. She had been, of course, completely devoted to the baby, like any good wife should be to the child of her husband. But to have Barton turn away from her after the child's death, not touch her or kiss her or share a bed with her unless he was roaring drunk and confused, was too much. She needed Angel to bring him back home from his many, many trips, his many, many distractions. So she was restrained with Angel, and Millicent's self-control had succeeded. Angel was alive, after all, and growing like other normal five-year-olds, unlike the first child, the poor dear.

Angel's curiosity about where her mother went at dusk compelled her to be naughty, but to be naughty while also being good. She saw her mother creep past the bedroom door and heard her mother's hand sliding down the banister. Angel climbed out of bed without thumping. In her bare feet, she padded down the stairs, but she did it without putting her filthy handprints on the wallpaper or smudging the butternut handrail Father had specially made for Mother when she cried and cried about him leaving on business again. Angel crept through the lavishly wallpapered blue dining room, but she didn't touch Mother's silverware, nor the candlesticks, nor the stuffed peacock Father bought for Mother when she threatened to jump into the river and never be seen again. Angel didn't smear the stained glass windows on the dining room doors or put her fingers through the lacy ruffle of the sofa pillow. Angel sneaked through the winter kitchen, but she didn't filch bread or get too close to the new stove, which had come on the train all the way from Boston, the stove that Father ordered for Mother when she said she'd throw a rope from the rafters of the livery and hang herself if he ever left again. Angel did go outdoors without Mother's or Nanny's supervision, but she stayed inside the fenced yard and didn't pull petals off the flowers, which Father had arranged to be planted by the former gardener to Andrew Jackson's wife when Mother threatened to lie down in front of the stagecoach and get trampled to death if he took another business trip south without her.

Angel scrambled out the door and behind a cottonwood tree. Angel counted to ten and peeked around to look for Mother. Angel loved the trees. She loved how they towered over the Hatterby house like protective grandmothers. She loved their green glow and the homes they made for all the little animals. She didn't get scared when thunderstorms came and scratched the branches against her bedroom window or when in autumn the trees dropped all their leaves and looked like her nanny's crooked fingers.

Angel had never known her mother liked the trees too. Her mother seemed to favor only her cats and her dresses and her parasols and her father, of course. But here she was! Under the trees too! Angel tried to be very quiet. She held her breath. She stood like a statue. Her mother knelt in the grass. Her skirt would get dirty! Angel was so surprised, she gasped. Her mother spun around.

"Angel?"

Angel froze, quiet as could be. She closed her eyes.

"I see you, Angel," said her mother. "Come here."

Angel swallowed. She stepped alongside the tree.

"Come," said her mother. "It's all right." Her mother waved her over.

Angel ran to her and crashed down beside her. She put her head in her mother's lap and looked up at her mother's face. Mother had been crying. Her eyes were all wet and red. Angel didn't worry because her mother cried a lot.

"You're supposed to be in bed," said her mother. She petted Angel's hair and placed a strand behind her ear. All month, Angel had been laid up with various stomach illnesses. Angel's stomach often pained her, and she only had one memory of a time when it hadn't grumbled and pinched and barked at her like a dog. It was when her father had invited her mother along on a steamboat ride down the Mississippi River, and they had been gone for a month and left Angel in the care of a nanny, whom Father insisted upon hiring the last time he'd had to leave.

Among the trees, curled on her mother's lap, Angel clenched her stomach muscles when she felt the gurgling noise coming. She tried to quiet it. She asked, loudly, "When is Father coming back?"

"Angel," said her mother. "You needn't shout. I'm right here."

"I'm sorry, Mother," said Angel.

"In a week or two, I suppose," said her mother.

"What's he doing?" asked Angel.

"Business, dear," said her mother. "He's trying to make a state here, or a territory first, I think. I'm not sure which. Don't worry your silly brain with it, dear. It's a man's concern and women only look foolish when they try to discuss such things."

"What are you doing out here, Mother?" asked Angel. She played with the hem of her mother's skirt. "Your skirt is getting dirty."

Her mother paused and breathed and said, "Hmmm." She pulled Angel onto her lap and pointed to a flat granite rock in the grass, about the size of the big Bible in the house. "There's an angel down there," she told Angel.

"Like me?"

"Yes," she replied. "But no, that's not what I mean."

Her mother stood up and took Angel's hand. "Come along, now," she said. "Come away from here." Her mother seemed sad.

Angel's curiosity about the site overcame her. That same summer, she waited for a day when her mother was confined to her bed, sick, and Angel sneaked to the gardener's shed and took a hoe. She scampered to that same place and dug and dug around in the peat, looking for angels. She dug and dug and got dirty until her shovel hit the top of a box. Angel wiped off the top and saw the letters O-P-A-L followed by HATTERBY, Angel's own last name. She recognized that. Angel saw that name on the stone outside the gate of her own house.

Angel tugged the box out of the earth and pried it open with a stick. A cool breath and milky scent escaped the box. Inside was something wrapped in some white cloth. She picked up the gauzy bundle and unwrapped it. And between her hands unfolded a cherub doll, perfect with a creamy complexion. A doll! One unlike any she'd ever seen. Angel clutched it close to her chest and decided it was hers to keep. She filled in the hole and hid with the doll behind a stump in the woods. She pretended to serve it supper and coffee.

After only a few days, though, Angel's cherub melted and distorted into something ugly and began to smell of wet bread. Bugs crawled from the eyelids and a sticky mess pooled where clean, cool limbs had been. Angel found a branch with a forked tip and pushed the bundle through the woods and down to the St. Croix River. She watched it bob on the current before finally getting lost in the froth. She collected a few clamshells and skipped back to the house.

When she was older, Angel would wonder whether she had actually done this, whether she had actually seen what she saw. The smell permeated. And Angel remembered this too: one evening as she lay in bed, trying to sleep but biting her nails, her mother darkened the doorway. She dropped the box onto Angel's floor and walked away. Angel didn't dare get out of the bed, but the smell from the box was familiar. She turned over and gnawed at her nails until they bled. When she woke, the box was gone, and she wondered if it had ever really been there. She wondered if she had dreamt her mother's dark shape against the faint light in the doorway. But the smell hung over her, cold and moist and dead.

Later in the morning, her mother came up with soup in a white bowl, black swans gliding along the rim. Angel loved the bowl. Steam clouded above it. Her mother's eyes had tightened and grown small. Her lips formed a thin smile.

"Here we are," her mother said. "Drink it all gone."

Angel sat up, and her mother arranged the tray over her. She dipped the spoon into the broth, blew on it, and sipped it obligingly.

"Hot," said Angel.

"All of it," said her mother.

Angel swirled the spoon, which twisted the floating cream into the shape of a winding river.

"Don't play. Eat."

Angel filled the spoon and brought it to her lips again. She swallowed. Overwhelming the cream and stronger than the onion, pepper, and salt, a bitter and sour flavor bloomed on Angel's tongue and in the back of her throat. She felt her stomach clench.

"That's a good girl," said her mother.

Angel swallowed it all.

For Angel, the next few weeks passed in a haze of steam, darkness, sweats, and otherworldly visions. She felt they were real, but, as in a vivid dream, she couldn't be sure. She heard a voice, over and over again, as she drifted in and out of sleep. A child's voice, talking and playing, at once familiar and foreign to her, tinkered in her brain as though speaking in a room with clanking glass panes. She tried to lie very still on her pillow so as to hear the child clearly. Any rustle of her blanket or her hair obscured the voice. It bounced and echoed as if the speaker was traveling through rooms or turning his back to her.

*I'm hungry,* he said. *My stomach's rumbling,* he said. *What's for supper?*

Angel stiffened, didn't breathe. She opened her eyes wide and waited for the blur to clear. She looked around her room, wondering if someone was there. The room was dark and humid, but there was no one in it but her. *What are you making for supper?* the boy said. *Can I have a cup of milk?*

Angel's stomach rumbled then and her tongue thickened with thirst. Angel became aware of a fortitude and boldness building in her own body, as though she were about to leap over a wide creek or jump from a tree branch to the ground. She felt like herself, but she felt like something else too. Something bigger, lighter, ghost-like. Then, in her dark, solitary room, she opened her mouth and whispered, "I can feel your hunger. I remember you." She could smell the rancid odor of her own breath. She wondered if she was dying, but she was not afraid.

*Did you hear that?* the boy said to someone else. *Are you talking to me, Mother?* he wondered.

"I'm here," Angel whispered again. Her teeth chattered. "I can hear you. Can you hear me?"

*Who is that talking in my head?*

"I'm very sick. I might die." Angel closed her eyes. She imagined the boy turning and looking and spinning.

*I hear someone,* the boy said. *No,* he said. *Someone else.*

Her gut seized and she retched up a drop of black, wiry spittle. She smiled, pleased in a way to have such power. "If I die, I'll haunt you," she whispered.

*Who's that?* the boy said. *What do you want?*

Then, just as suddenly as the magic had come over her, it was gone. The door creaked open and Angel's mother walked into her bedroom, carrying another tray.

The boy's voice was lost.

"Who are you talking to?" she asked.

"Just my prayers," said Angel. She felt hot and dizzy. Her eyes rolled back in her head, and then she fainted into black again. She came to and ate and went to sleep again and again and again.

Over the weeks, she remembered her mother preparing her a hot onion broth and bidding her to drink it all gone. She remembered the terrible stomachache that came when she ate it, but then the floating feelings, the dreams. She remembered her mother hovering over her, her father standing at her bedside, petting her head. She even remembered a priest coming and muttering prayers over her. Shortly after that, the soup's taste changed. It looked the same, but now tasted of salt and pepper without the metal and bile. Then, Angel knew, her illness was coming to an end, her punishment was over. She knew it was time to heal. Now when her parents came, Angel understood how to tilt her head and bat her eyes at her father. She knew how to look dotingly toward her mother, to thank her effusively. Without ever discussing it, her mother had communicated that all these days in bed, all these aches and illness, all the small poisons planted in Angel's body were a contract. Angel understood, somehow, that every sweet syrup, metallic powder, or bitter bite was a ploy, a plot, a hook between her mother and father. Angel accepted, very early, that her mother was poisoning her, and that her life for now was in her mother's hands. Angel aimed to be very, very good. She thought that if she was very, very good, then her mother might not kill her. And then someday she too might woo a man and feel a love that conquered sense.

But Angel had a secret she kept all to herself. She too profited from the sickness. In those hot, wet, drowsy days, Angel was turning into a sorceress or a prophet or a saint. She was making magic or miracles. She didn't know which, but she didn't care.

# 24

## The Story of the Swan

ONCE SHE LEFT HER PEOPLE, Big Waters found few causes for talk. All the talk of her previous life still echoed in her ears. She could hear the first sounds made by each of her children, the high, hungry cries in their first desperate breaths and first whiny days. Even in her old age, she was sure she would be able to single out her babies' cries in a place of a hundred crying children.

She could hear too, word for word, her mother's instructions before she was to become a wife. Those words were transferred in a long hymn from the mother's lips to Big Waters' ears one autumn evening as her mother oiled and twisted her hair, whispering in the home that, come morning, would no longer be hers. She would be a married woman with a home of her own. Knowledge of her mother and all her mother's mothers of the ages came to her that evening, and Big Waters had listened well and trapped all that knowledge so that even now, she hadn't forgotten.

This is how you dry the meat, the mother had said. This is how you waft the smoke to keep the flies from settling and laying eggs on the meat. This is how you store the corn so that the rodents and snakes will not get it. Off the ground and hung by a string. Even then, the little animals may find it and you will have to be vigilant or bring a cat to your home. A cat is best, but you will have to trade with the whites for them to bring you one, and you will have to pay many hides for it. Burn the leaves of nightshade to rid your home of a bad smell.

This is where you find the thin mud and the stinky leaf to protect the children's skin from mosquitoes. This is how to seal the seams of your home when the green grasshoppers come. But if the grasshoppers are brown and scream as one and fly as though in a cloud, these will eat through even the hides that cover the poles of your home. I have seen them eat the poles. If you see the screaming brown cloud, close all the flaps of your home and let the smoke fill it. Take your children and run to the water. It is the only safe place. Put cloth over your ears and faces. The smoke may keep them out of your home, and when they leave, you can return to it.

The moss on the north side of the rocks is the same as the sky before a big wind and ice. Call your children to you when the sky looks the way the moss looks. Always set up your home close to an overturned tree or large boulder. Then, if the fierce wind that looks like a dog's tail comes down from the sky, take your children and crawl into the hole where the tree once stood or burrow into the ground close to the boulder. You will be safe among the roots or near the rock.

This is the onion root to feed a child if he is constipated. This is how you make the paste if his insides pour out of him. If he touches a fire or steps on a hot ember, take him to the water. Others will tell you to put grease on the wound, but this will not ease his pain. Only the water will ease his pain. Do not believe the others, not even your husband's mother, if they tell you about the grease or fat or even plant oils. Those will not ease his pain either. Only the water. For the old ones with the brittle bones that pain them, prepare sun root with the blood of an animal and spoon it into their mouths each morning.

To catch a porcupine, throw a blanket over him and hit his nose with a big stick. Some quills will poke through the blanket and you can take them for sewing needles without harming yourself. Leave him a bit of corn cake as a gift.

This is the way a child's eyes go when he lies. Off to either horizon in a lie. This is the way a child's eyes go when he tells the truth. Up to the sky in truth. In a man it is changed because he becomes wise to his mother. But he is not yet wise to his wife. This is the way a man's eyes go when he lies. This is the way they go when he tells the truth. Watch closely, my daughter. This way in lie. This way in truth. Up to the sky in a lie. Off to either horizon in truth. It changes from child to man.

Sometimes in an old man it changes again, and he takes on the ways of a child once more. Remember these things so that you will not be fooled.

So many other words. So many that Big Waters didn't want to clutter the world with more talking. But with Clement, this child entrusted to her, now five summers old, Big Waters felt compelled to tell him the story of his beginning. If she didn't give him the story of his origin, who would? And so, once, when he was old enough to listen, she put him under the big window near the schoolroom and said, "Listen."

"Yes, Big Waters-Mama," he said.

"In my forty-eighth year, I was without a man or children and living here among the sick and orphaned. Every day I would cut curling toenails, clean waxy ears, soap bloody wounds, or wipe pus-filled eyes or otherwise do as the long-faced nun and the dog-faced priest told me to do. I worked and was happy working, but my spirit was not satisfied, and I was sad for the husband and children who had forgotten me. I prayed to God at every sunrise. When I was a small girl among my people, the missionaries in black clothing came, and though they looked poorly dressed and ill-prepared for cold weather, we listened when they told our people about Jesus and his father and his great spirit because it was our way to greet and make welcome people who may need help to find food and shelter. We smiled and nodded at the missionaries as they told of their big father above the clouds, and we understood and agreed among ourselves that the missionaries spoke of a god similar to our own. That night, a deer stag with magnificent antlers came to our village, and so we welcomed the missionaries and we began to talk some of the talk they used to their god above the clouds because it made them happy and more agreeable to live among.

"Each year, great white birds come from the north, and the sky is covered with them so that it looks like winter. They fly here in groups as big as a hill and descend upon the still waters to build their nests and hatch their young and feed them until the young can fly, and then they go to warmer places until the cold fades. On the first day of the great birds' arrival, an eagle shrieked in the sky and swung down upon the flock. The eagle split the flock in two, and by spinning and soaring separated one swan from its mate. Then the eagle rose above it and dove upon the great white swan. The eagle opened its talons along the back of a white swan, lost from its mate and its flock. The swan reeled back and dipped. The eagle lost its grip. The swan was hurt but fled from the eagle. She could not fly to the other swans or her mate. They had gone on without her, and she was injured. But she was a wise animal. If she flew back to her flock, she'd bring the eagle to them too, and she was kind, so she did not do that. Instead, she landed in that windowsill where my bed sits below. When I looked at her, I had a vision of eggs in her belly, and so I made a nest out of corncobs and reeds in the corner where the swan rested until it was time to birth her clutch. With much effort, because of her wounds and because these eggs were her first, she brought forth the eggs upon the nest that I had made. She sat on them and kept them warm until morning, when the eagle shrieked across the sky once more. The eagle had not forgotten its lost meal and would not go away until it had devoured the swan.

"The swan spoke to me then and asked me to care for her eggs, and I agreed. 'Look around,' I said. 'Do you not see wounded and orphaned of every kind already in my care? What's two more?' The swan craned her long neck to see the people I had tended and found my work suitable. She told me I was a good mother. The swan tapped her beak on each of the eggs in farewell and then hopped onto the windowsill and took pained flight, for she was still greatly injured. Before long, I heard the eagle shriek again. And I ran to the window. The eagle swooped upon the swan and gripped her in its talons. The swan did not suffer long because an eagle is a quick killer. For her sacrifice, the swan lives forever in the heavens and flies across the northern sky in the time of the turning leaves. From there, the eagle can never reach her and all on earth can look to her. She reminds us that though summer has ended, it will come again in the same way the swans come every year.

"Many weeks later, the eggs began to crack and open. One of the cygnets was hearty and cried out again and again. The other was quiet and small. For days, I fed them. The hearty one ate her own food and her brother's too, as though she could not be satisfied. The eagle appeared in the sky again, circling, hungry. I was watchful. But the eagle's eyes were keener than mine, they are the sharpest of all the animals', and they watched from very far away, so far that I could not see and forgot. The first cygnet was greedy and grew stronger and cried out louder and louder. The eagle waited for me to go and warm the milk, and then he dove to the window, and opened his talons, and lifted that cygnet into the sky. The other one was quiet and the eagle did not heed him and forgot about him for a while.

"I became more watchful then, to fulfill my promise to the swan I would be. I moved the little one into my bed, where I kept him warm and gave him milk. As he grew, I chewed up bits of fish and fed them to him. I kept him from all harm, and he became mine.

"This is why you have one eye of the earth and one eye of the sky, so that you remember your mother of the earth and your mother of the sky. Never forget the sacrifice the swan made for you nor the lesson the other cygnet teaches, with her greediness and complaining."

She pointed out the window, toward the house far away through the forest.

"There is where the greedy one was carried by the eagle. In the big house with the big people and all the money and food around them."

Clement looked and saw the huge house that belonged to the politician with the pretty little girl, the house that had only recently become visible because so many of the trees had been cut. He liked to see the house, but he hoped no more of the trees would come down.

"Be quiet and listen for the shriek of the eagle. Keep still in trouble and stay close to me."

Big Waters was spent. She closed her eyes and tucked her chin to her chest.

Clement went to the window and stared. He watched for the slightest movement. Though it was so far away, he felt he could see the girl's shape standing in the window and staring back at him. He raised his hand to wave. He was sure she raised a wing in return.

# 25

## The Beloved Child and
## His Whore-Mother

O N A PALLET IN THE CORNER of Miss Daisy's room at
the Red Swan Saloon, Davis Christmas lay looking up at
the ceiling and scraping his toe along the wall. Miss Daisy watched
him in the reflection of the mirror as she sat putting white powder
all over her face and chest.

She put down the puff. "Whatsa matter, dear?" she asked the
boy.

"Where's my mama now? Is she ever coming back?" asked
Davis.

Davis could be a real rascal. Only this morning, he had turned
over her expensive perfume bottle and used one of her best hair-
pieces to make a nest for the silly cat. And she had yet to bother
him about the gouge in her pressed rouge and the red smear across
the cat's back. She sometimes wondered if Davis misbehaved
because he was missing his mama or acted out and then missed his
mama coincidentally. Miss Daisy could never scold Davis when
he was missing his mama. She hated herself for thinking the boy
might use such a situation to manipulate her, but she'd never been
a natural mother and didn't know about these kinds of things.

"Davis, dear, you know your mama's in heaven," she said.
"Remember when Father Paul made the fancy ceremony over her,

and we all wore our best and then she was laid to rest in the pauper's cemetery?" She turned around on her stool and faced him. She put out her arms. "Come up here, hon. Miss Daisy wants to hold you."

Davis pouted his lips and shook his head. "I only want my mama," he said.

"Well now, you're breaking my poor, poor heart," said Miss Daisy. "I'm so sad I could cry." She pretended to heave a little and pressed a tear out of her eye. Miss Daisy too knew how to be manipulative.

Davis sat up and crawled over like a baby. He made baby noises and put up his arms to be held, as an infant would. "Hold me," he said in his best baby voice.

"That's a good baby," Miss Daisy said. "Come up here now, dear, and let's be happy today." She picked up the boy and cradled him and rocked him. She put her nose in his hair and inhaled deeply. He smelled of face powder and tobacco smoke, of her. And if a person who didn't have eyesight could see them, she thought, that person would believe that they were natural mother and child. If that blind person didn't have eyes to see her painted face or the indent above her eye where a man had punched her so hard, he crushed part of her eye socket, that person would have no sense that she wasn't a natural mother. She tended him like a natural mother. She's the one who had put whiskey on his gums when he was teething. She's the one who had splattered flour on his bottom when he had nappy rash. He was hers, and she loved him better than any other mother could love her own child.

Sometimes, while Miss Daisy rocked Davis, she wondered about her old beau. She wondered if he now had children with his wife. She wondered if he was brutish to his slaves, even to the children among them. She sometimes let her imagination conceive of him ripping a child from its mother's arms, and then she would get mad at him and think to herself that she was very lucky not to have married him after all. Even if she thought about his family's big house, with pillars and marble staircases and the rose garden and colorful carpets and velvet drapes and floral settees and silver platters and crystal stemware, she'd then imagine him taking a cane across the back of a black mother, and she'd be very, very happy she wasn't his wife, that she never had the opportunity to wear that lilac taffeta gown with the tiny pink flowers embroidered down the sleeves, which a seamstress had made especially for Miss Daisy's wedding day, or the heirloom ruby ring with the tiny crystals all around it that had belonged to his grandmother, which surely would have become hers that day. Miss Daisy'd think that she'd choose this life, here at the Red Swan, rather than be wife to such a beast, even if he had all the money in the whole world and she could wear the best dresses and fresh, lacy undergarments and have meals made and brought to her room when she was feeling ill or tired, even if she would be invited to all the best balls with the most handsome men and women in all the South. Miss Daisy'd think that she'd prefer life here, with Davis, even over the comfort of her own mother and father and sisters and brothers, all of whom avoided her like leprosy once she was jilted and the rumors began about her lost maidenhead. Davis didn't care that she was a whore. Davis didn't care that she sometimes got sad and stayed in bed in an opium stupor. He loved her no matter what. He hugged her and sometimes in his sleep called her Mama, and she would go to him and hold him, so his dreams would be the best and as real as possible.

"I've got a good idea," said Miss Daisy. "I think we should go down and practice your piano scales." She sat him upright. "Would you like that?"

He nodded. "Is the bartender going to yell at me for making a racket?"

"Not while I'm there," she said. "I'll hit him with a stick if he does." She tickled Davis's tummy.

He giggled and squirmed. Then he asked, "Will Mr. Hatterby come today?"

"I'm sure he will," said Miss Daisy. "We better straighten up this room a bit." She fixed her pillows and smoothed the duvet.

Davis opened the door and hung from the knob. He leaned back. "Will I have to stay downstairs while he's here?"

"For a while." Miss Daisy went to her vanity and checked her face in the mirror.

"Will he bring me a treat?"

"I'm sure, sweetie," she said. "He never forgets his favorite boy." She worked an earring into her lobe.

"Am I really his favorite boy?" Davis swung on the door, kicked the wall, and swung back.

"Yes, yes!" said Miss Daisy. "He takes good care of you and me."

"He likes us?"

"He sure does." Miss Daisy hugged him to her, then stood him in front of her and spoke to him gently. "Mr. Hatterby is a very important and good man. We must be as helpful to him as we can."

"Are you helping him when I must leave the room and he sits on your bed and you close the door behind me?"

"In a way," she said. "I guess so. Yes. I'm helping him so he can help others."

"You must be very important," said Davis.

Miss Daisy wanted to laugh, but didn't. The repetitive work of attending to the men who needed a bedding grew boring. And the women of the Red Swan weren't welcome in town among other women and honorable townspeople. So Miss Daisy grew lonely and eager for excitement. She felt giddy when she heard that another "guest" was coming, and she believed this work at the Red Swan was important. For the help that they rendered to the occasional escapees in the form of protection and lodging and transportation and silence, she and the other women at the Red

Swan received much in return, she thought. She felt useful. She felt needed. She felt righteous, even. And, with his money and protection, Barton Hatterby made their little operation possible. "I guess so," she said. "Let's go now. Downstairs with you." Davis was getting so big that she wondered about taking him to the school Father Paul had told about, where the nun taught the Indian children and the orphans. Surely she wouldn't mind a black child too, especially one as smart and light-skinned as Davis.

# 26

# Nanny and Angel

W HEN MR. HATTERBY AGREED to calm his wife's fretting nerves by bringing her along on a month-long trip to Chicago, Angel's brain hopped with glee and scheming. The Hatterbys would leave Angel in Nanny's care, and Angel was careful not to react with too much eagerness. She played the part. She cried. She pouted her lips and asked her mother not to go. She hung on to her mother's waist and wept. But beneath the pretense, she couldn't wait for Mother to go and Nanny to come.

When Nanny arrived, Angel stomped her foot, shouted, "You're not my mother!" and ran upstairs to her room. She slammed the door for good measure, knowing how pleased her mother would be. As a good mother would, Mrs. Hatterby raced up the stairs to comfort Angel one last time and bid her farewell.

"Mother will bring you a nice new gown and a pretty new dolly," she cooed.

Angel was silent. *Just go,* she thought. *Go away.* When she determined that she'd pouted the appropriate amount of time, she turned over and pecked her mother on the cheek. "I'll miss you very much," she said.

"Of course, my darling Angel," she said. "And I you."

Once they were gone, Angel scrambled downstairs and ran to

the kitchen, where Nanny was already pulling down tins of flour and sugar from the shelves.

"I didn't mean it!" Angel said.

Nanny turned and gave the girl a wry smile. "Well, yah," said Nanny. "I know tat already witout you telling me." She clomped a tin of alum onto the tabletop and then put on her apron. "You should be one of tem actresses on stage." Nanny took Angel's face in her hands and turned it this way and that. "So pale! Have you been sick again wit the stomach ailments? I just don't understand it." She dropped her hand. "Well, I better get to work making you healty again. You never get sick on my foodt."

"Do you think I'll find a husband if I'm so pale?" said Angel. "I want a good one. Like Father."

"Yah," said Nanny. She sighed and put her hand to her heart. "Tat's all I ever wantedt too. Until my childrent came. Then chiltrent are ta most important thing. They are a credit to all ta good work teir motters put into tem. Now let's make kringles."

Angel chewed the inside of her cheek.

Nanny's fish soups and beef stews and braided breads and tart pies steamed the windows of the house and infused a lively aroma through every room. For Angel, whatever Nanny did breathed life into the big house. Corners that once looked dark now showcased a watering can of spring wildflowers or grasses. Formerly quiet rooms now filled with Nanny's humming. Nanny took Angel on walks into town where she had seen other children, which was against the rules, but Angel had promised not to tell. One morning a few days after her parents had been gone, Nanny entered Angel's bedroom early and pulled back the heavy curtains, though it was only barely daylight.

Angel startled from a dream, rolled over, and moaned.

"Today we are going to visit all ta little childrent who don't have a motter to take care of tem," said Nanny. She pulled open drawers, grabbing fresh underthings for Angel.

"Mother says to keep the curtains closed while I'm dressing." Angel stretched her limbs. "Where are their mothers?"

"Most of tem diedt," said Nanny. She tossed a few silky things onto Angel's bed. "And now ta goodt sister and Big Waters take care of tem all. How's your tummy today? Your color is pink and rosy."

Angel sat up. "I feel wonderful." Her dark hair cascaded like a glossy mudslide. "That's nice of tem to take care of all tose children." She flopped back down in the blankets. "Are tay your friendts?"

Nanny came to the bed and smacked the tops of Angel's feet. "Ton't talk like me or your motter will not let me take care of you anymore. Say *them*, not *tem*. But yes. Tay are my friendts." She pulled Angel up by the arms. "You are getting too big to have me dress you, young lady."

"I like having you dress me," Angel said. "Am I wearing something beautiful today? I want to."

"All your gowns are beautiful," said Nanny. "You are a spoilt little girl, you know. Some girls only have one dress for ta week and one dress for Sunday." She pulled a brown silk dress out of the drawer and snapped the wrinkles out.

"I didn't know tat," said Angel. She looked out the window and wondered if anyone could see her.

Nanny smacked her feet again.

Angel giggled. "I like to talk like you do," Angel said. "I like the way it sounds. How do you know these women?"

Nanny pulled the nightgown over Angel's head. "When my husband and children diedt, I got very sad. My mind was not right. I heard ta voices of my childrent all night. I tought I saw tem aroundt ta house. Finally my neighbors took me to ta sister and she took goodt care of me. Andt now I repay her kindnesses and bring her food for all her orphans."

Nanny pulled Angel's arms to stand her up and slip on her dress. "You heard voices?" Angel asked.

Nanny thought for a minute. "I tought I was. But I was just mourning. Sometimes I tink I can still here my little Olga. She was ta baby. But. It's my mind playing tricks."

"They aren't real?"

"No, my childrent are deadt andt in heaven with their fotter."

"I don't hear dead voices either," Angel said. She lifted her arms.

"Well, I wouldt hope not," Nanny said. She slipped the dress over Angel's head.

Angel scooped her hair out of the dress's neckline. "Does the sister have any of her own children?" She put a strand of her hair in her mouth and sucked.

"No. Her heart is reservedt for ta orphans." Nanny worked at the buttons on the back of the gown.

Angel looked out the window, across the way, where she could see the top of the infirmary in the distance. "My mother says to stay away from those orphans because they are filthy and naughty and will get lice in my hair."

Nanny exhaled. "Goodt Lordt," she whispered. She pulled the strand of hair out of Angel's mouth. "Let's brush tis mop."

"Make it like yours," said Angel. "With the coiled braids on either side, like breakfast bread."

"Whatever you say, your highness." She brushed and then parted Angel's hair, lovingly, Angel thought. Nothing felt so good as Nanny's fingers in her hair.

"Do you miss your children, Nanny?" said Angel.

Nanny rested her hands on Angel's head for a bit. Angel could feel the weight of them, heavy and grave. "Yes," she said. "Very much."

"What happened to them?"

Nanny's fingers moved again. "Two summers ago." Nanny took three sections of hair and began twisting. "My husbandt andt I had just finishedt our woodt house. It was very nice. Very clean. Very straight andt bright. We movedt all of our tings andt our girls, Hannah andt Olga, from ta dugout to ta house. Tay were so happy!" She held on to the end of Angel's braid with one hand, pulled a tie from her apron pocket, and secured the braid end. "We were in ta house but a week when a big storm came in ta night. My husbandt said to take Olga andt he grabbedt Hannah. We opened ta front door. Hail. Rain. A terrible, noisy windt." She spun the braid around its base andt secured it with pins. "We ran for the oldt dugout. But we didn't make it. The windt was too strong. The roof of our house blew apart. It hit my Jan andt Hannah. I was hit in the back of the headt wit—I don't know what. Olga was torn from my arms andt up into ta sky. I foundt her the next day in ta prairie. She looked as if she were only sleeping." Nanny turned Angel and began braiding the other side. "But her neck was brokedt."

Angel's face felt hot. "I'm sorry, Nanny," she said.

"Oh Angel." She tied the end of her braid. "Tank you. All we all can do is go forwardt. Forever and ever, forwardt." She coiled up the braid and secured it tight. "Go forwardt or die. Remember tat, Angel, when hardt times trouble you."

# 27

## Angel and Clement

CLEMENT'S LIMBS TWITTERED. He couldn't sit still. He thought about taking a stroll in the woods. He liked to walk, to wander, to see new sights, meet new people, but only if someone came with him. Mother St. John was always too busy. Big Waters was willing, but too slow. Big Waters said he was like a tree, always wanting to climb higher and spread outward and sway on the wind, but only when secured safely to the earth. Clement liked that comparison and thought it a right one.

Clement sat in the window, wiggling a loose tooth. He stared up at the big house, hoping the girl would come to the window. Each time he saw a movement behind the glass, his heart would thump, and he'd strain his eyes to see if it was her, but he hadn't seen her in nearly a week.

"You need to find something to do," said Mother St. John. "It's not healthy for a boy to sit and gawk out the window all day." Then she came and put her hand on Clement's head. "Open up. Is your tooth loose?"

Clement clamped his mouth shut.

"Open up, I said," said Mother.

"Don't pull it out!" said Clement.

"Well, I won't, but you've got to keep your fingers out of your mouth. It's filthy."

"All right." Clement pointed out the window. "Mother, do you know the people who live in the big house?"

Mother St. Johns looked out. "Yes, dear. I do." But she offered no more details, and Clement didn't ask. She had the look of a woman with a lot on her mind and a lot of work to do. She often had lines of worry around her eyes and mouth and two wrinkles of concentration between her eyes. Often lack of sleep left dark circles beneath her eyes, particularly after nights of whispering, coffee making, shuffling across the floorboards, and moving in weary travelers, many of whom spoke emphatically of their gratitude in deep voices heavy with the accent of folks from the South, until Mother St. John shushed them and told them of the dreaming children in the orphanage.

Clement knew he should not be curious, that it was a sin to be nosy, but these nights thrilled him out of his bed and to the door of the room in which he slept. He'd watch through the crack to see Mother St. John leading Negro men first to the kitchen, where she'd feed them, and then out the front door into the night without a lantern. Then Clement would sneak to the window and try to see. He'd press his ear to the glass and try to listen. He'd see nothing and hear little but the rustling of branches and leaves and the scrape of a door being opened and then closed.

"Mother, who was that who came into the orphanage last night?" Clement said.

"Why are you restless today?" Mother St. John said. "Sit still and say your rosary if you can't think of anything better to do than bother me."

Clement longed for the day when he'd be privy to all the knowledge he wanted, the day when if he asked a question, he'd get an answer. Childhood seemed like one unanswered question after another, met by various ploys to distract him. He told himself that he'd ask Big Waters later. Her answers were intolerably long and slow and encrypted in stories of animals and weather, but after he thought on them some, they usually revealed morsels of truth. "Yes, Mother," said Clement. "Our Father—"

"That's a good boy," said Mother St. John. Then she walked away.

Clement mindlessly chanted his prayers, but he was thinking about the girl in the big house, and he was thinking about the voice. A soft, high, but serious voice, one that at first felt like a moth flutter in his ear and sounded as light as bat wings in the night. He didn't know for sure whether the voice came from a ghost or a trickster or a saint. He had no proof that the voice belonged to the girl in the window, but he felt that it might, and that hope made him less afraid of it. He was determined to be bold and ask the voice the next time he heard it. He would be courageous and demand an answer. He feared that the voice might ignore him or distract him, the way the adults did, and that again he'd have to wait to know.

Waiting too was another thing he longed to grow out of. *When I'm an adult,* he thought, *I won't have to wait.*

Mother St. John appeared with a pot of oatmeal. Clement articulated another Hail Mary.

"Say them like you mean them or they don't count," Mother St. John warned. Then she whispered, "I'm doing my best." Clement knew that she herself was talking to the Virgin.

Clement prayed louder. "Holy Mary, Mother of God . . ."

"The Virgin Mary's not deaf," said Mother St. John. She shifted the pot from one hip to the other. "Your words must come from within, from your inner spirit."

"But why do I have to say so many?" Clement whined.

"It's our tradition, child," said Mother St. John. "It's the way we've always done it and the way we'll always do it."

"It's boring," he said.

"If it's boring, you're not praying hard enough," she said, her voice rising.

"Can I do them outside at least?" Clement said. "Under the trees, where it's interesting?"

Mother St. John paused, sighing. "I suppose," she said. "I can't see the Virgin Mary having any objection to a boy saying his rosary outdoors under the protection of the world God created. Go ahead."

Clement ran toward the door.

"On your knees, please!" Mother St. John shouted after him.

Outside, Clement picked a tree and knelt. In this tree lived a particularly interesting pair of squirrels who were thieves. He'd seen them climb into other trees, enter other squirrels' knots, steal nuts, and scurry back to their own knot in this tree. He started his prayers while looking around, hoping to spot them doing something worth watching. Clement was nine prayers into a decade when he heard the voice trilling through the rustling of pine branches and over the warbling of spring birds, cardinals, sparrows, and chickadees. His heart quickened. He recognized the voice. He stopped chanting his prayers and listened.

"Do you think the other children will like me?" the voice said.

He wondered if the voice was real or in his head.

Another voice, a different and older one, said, "Yah. If you're nice andt not naughty or spoilt."

"Do you think they'll think I'm pretty?" The familiar voice again.

Clement's waiting was over. It was her. He sucked in his breath and tried to calm his heart, which was beating like thunder. He sat very still as the voices approached the Home for Orphans and Infirmed.

"Well yah, but that's not the most important ting in the worldt, you know."

"It is to Mother."

"Goodt Lordt," said the older voice. "You shouldt go to ta

school here andt learnt to readt," said the tall woman. "Readting is important."

"This place is a school too?" asked the girl. "And a place for orphans?"

"Yah, it is," said the tall woman. "You shouldt be here every day filling your mindt with sense."

"I don't think Mother would allow me around the dirty children."

And then he saw the pair through a break in the tree trunks. A tall blond woman holding the hand of a girl, his own age, his own height, gliding through the trees, their skirts waving and boots crunching. His skin rippled like the surface of a lake in a shower. *Speak*, he thought. *Speak again.*

"I feel strange," said the girl. She put her hand to her waist.

Clement felt strange too. The voice was hers, the ghost voice he sometimes heard. The glassy sound was gone, but the voice was certainly the one that haunted him.

The tall woman slowed down and then stopped.

"Oh no," she said. She took the girl's face in her hands. "Your tummy feeling sick again?"

Clement watched and listened, mesmerized. He thought he should call out to them, to let them know he was there, but he couldn't. He hoped they were real but searched the figures up and down to be sure. Were they walking or floating? Were they solid or see-through? Did they have eyes or dark holes? Was that hair or the cloak of a spirit? He didn't move but felt a strong urge to urinate. He held it back.

The girl shook her head. "No," she said. "Not like that. Something else." She grabbed her own arm. "I feel like something's pulling on me." Then she scratched the bun above her ear. "And this one feels too tight. Like my hair's being grabbed out of my head."

"Well, I can loosen tat," said the tall woman. She pulled the girl close to her. "Let me see."

The girl scratched some more. "No. Leave it. It's fine." She stepped back and looked around. "I think it's just the air."

"Oh," said the tall woman. She put her hand to her shoulders and looked at her feet. "I droppedt my shawl." They both turned and looked behind them. "There it is," said the tall woman, pointing back from where they came. "You go on up to the door andt knock. I'll catch up." The woman ran back and the girl stood alone. The girl started again down the path, toward the building, toward Clement.

The girl approached the clearing that led to the front of the infirmary. And then suddenly, she faced Clement where he knelt in prayer under the pine. She drifted nearer. In his mind, sun shone through the tree canopy, bathing the top of the girl's head in light. She glided closer. She was glorious. Her back was straight. Her hair knotted. Her limbs long. Her eyes ringed. She was pale and she was dark. She was small and she was huge. Old and young. And he knew her.

She saw him. Her dark eyes met his. She stopped. She on foot. He on knees. "Hello," she said.

Clement's heart opened and a flock of hopeful birds took flight. He stood and ran off into the woods.

# 28

# The Hatterbys

WITH HER MOTHER'S RETURN, Angel's stomach ailments and confinement to bed resumed. Through all of it, Angel could think only of all she had learned and seen while her mother was away. She thought of the school and of the nun and of the boy.

On her better days, Angel would lie in her big bed, with its velvet coverlet and plush pillows. She would set up her porcelain-faced dolls and imagine they were all at the school. And though she liked it when her father would come and check on her, letting her search in his pockets for the little treats he hid there, she wanted to go outside, she wanted to play, she wanted to have friends, and she wanted very, very much to go to school.

"Father, will you send me to school?" she whispered. "Please, Father."

Mr. Hatterby patted her head and hugged her close. "Girls don't need school, Angie. Girls need pretty dresses and dolls and shiny slippers to wear."

Angel climbed onto his lap and tugged on his ear. "Father, please. I want to go and see the children." She begged him desperately but knew her mother would protest, and she didn't want to upset her. It was hard to decide whether to protect her mother's feelings or voice her own desires. Angel had never felt such a strong feeling inside herself. She had never thought about one thing over and over again. She kept on with him, begging, "Father, I want to run and play and learn with all the other children."

Her father wiggled his mustache, which always made Angel laugh when she was a small child. She refused to laugh now. "Angie," he said, "you are a persistent little girl. I shall talk with your mother about this matter and do my best to be stern with her, but you know how she is. In the meantime, you be a good girl so as not to give her any reason to say no." He kissed her on the forehead and plopped her back on her bed. "How's your tummy these days? Are you well enough to go to school?"

"I am perfect, Father. I will be uncomplaining and very well if I can go to school and play with the children and learn to read too," said Angel.

"Learn to read!" He laughed. "Such big ambitions, Angie. I will speak to Mother. Play now, and rest."

The next day, she heard her father tell her mother that in September, Angel would go to school. She heard her mother protest and say that she was too sick, too frail. But her father pressed her mother with ideas about school, and every day her protests grew weaker. With that, Angel's determination to be strong, to be well, strengthened. Finally, her mother relented.

But within a week, though she tried to hold it back, for she knew what it meant, Angel retched uncontrollably over the side of her bed into the chamber pot. Her nightgown clung to her bony body, drenched with her own sweat. Her wet hair snaked around her pale face. Her stomach seemed to be trying to come out of her mouth. On the precipice of death, as delirium swirled, she again had visions of the boy emerging out of the trees. *Where are you?* he asked. *I can't see you. I want to see you. How are you talking to me?*

"I'll try and see you soon," Angel said.

"See," said Mrs. Hatterby to her husband, tending Angel like the best of mothers. "She's too sickly. And delirious." She put a rag in the water basin, wrung it out, and dabbed her daughter's forehead. "Mother will take good care of you, my darling Angel."

# 29

# Beaver Jean's Bad Luck
# Along the Bad River

MEN LIKE BEAVER JEAN bowed to the weather's whims, roamed with the river beaver, hitched themselves to phases of the moon, tethered themselves to wandering buffalo cows, and listened to the switching seasonal winds. In this way, men like Beaver Jean had forged the way west and written the maps. He intended, of course, to find the runaway pair, to locate his wife, and to rear his child up right. But he was patient as time passed and accepted it when new adventures or interesting tributaries moved him in different directions. He didn't panic when, a few days after arriving at the fort, his horse, Alice, lay down in the dirt, kicked her skinny legs a bit, shook her head, expelled great air from her hind end, moaned sadly, and died, leaving Beaver Jean and his wives stranded with a cart full of furnishings, worthless beaver pelts, a couple of copper pots, steel knives, some sugar and coffee, and a barrel of hard apple cider.

"Well, ye women," he'd said. "Looks like we're stranded in the fort for a term. Look around at yer new home."

In the Trees danced around like a girl, thrilled to be among so many she knew. "I can see your happiness, In the Trees, which makes me happy too," said Beaver Jean. "Ye are often unbearable in yer antics, but ye do have a round, comely face that does lighten my heart now and again."

The Girl with Friend Eyes unpacked the poles. In the Trees unrolled the skins and darted off occasionally to chat with people she knew. Beaver Jean dug a sorry hole outside the walls of the fort for his Alice. The ground was hard and gray and crumbly, not at all like the black, moist, fragrant earth near Stillwater, the type of earth one could imagine eating up the corpse of a horse and turning it into something useful. Beaver Jean wondered what would happen to his horse's body in this kind of earth. Someone loaned Beaver Jean a horse and cart and they wrangled Alice's carcass onto it. Beaver Jean led the procession through the fort and out the gate to the gravesite, a spot chosen for its clear view of flat endless land to the west. He cried unbridled, like a newborn, as he tied a rope around Alice's hooves, walked to the opposite side of the hole, and with the borrowed horse tugged her toward it.

"I feel mighty winded, ol' Alice, ye dead nag," said Beaver Jean. "Ye seems more portly in death than ye were in life." Beaver Jean heaved the horse again toward the hole. She slid off the cart a bit. Beaver Jean bent over and breathed deeply, trying to cough up and spit out a bit of phlegm that had been clogging his wind. Then he surged all his might into one final pull. The horse's back end fell into the hole, but in death she had stiffened and thus didn't fold over nicely into the grave the way Beaver Jean had hoped. Her top half poked straight up out of the grave. She looked to be rearing up, as in life, and Beaver Jean cried some more at the sight of her looking so lively.

Beaver Jean collapsed onto the ground to rest. "Oh Alice, ye always were a stubborn animal." Sweat gathered on his forehead, and he felt it dripping through his chest hairs. He stood up again and then knelt at the lip of the grave. He pushed on Alice's head and neck to get her in. He sat on his bottom and kicked at her until she tumbled down.

"It doesn't surprise me one bit that I had to reinjure my wrecksome toes in a last act of kindness toward ye," he said.

Beaver Jean then remembered his pappy and wondered what he might say about the way Beaver Jean buried his horse. "That looks mighty wrong indeed," Beaver Jean imagined his pappy saying, "the wrong way is the way ye deposed that poor animal. That wrong-way grave wouldn't be a proper resting place to bury a cross-eyed cat."

Beaver Jean looked around. The words were so clear that he wondered if the ghost of his pappy had come down to earth to help Beaver Jean through this niggling time. But as far as Beaver Jean looked and looked, he saw nothing but slow, low hills and those clouds coming in fast. He blinked a time or two. It seemed to him that his vision was becoming spotty. He felt hot and cold at the same time.

"I sure do wish ye were breathing yet, Alice. We rode out many a bad weather, the two of us together," he said into the wind. "I was countin' on ye having a good many miles left in yer legs to help me find my wife and boy. Now it gives me a powerful sorrow to think of teaching that boy to ride on a different horse." Bulbous clouds rolled in, casting a cool shadow over the grave scene. "Looks to be a spring storm coming this way." A soft lone snowflake landed on his nose. Beaver Jean's sight failed him. His knees buckled, and he fainted at the grave of his horse.

Between dumping his horse in the hole beneath the clouds and opening his eyes in a steamy tent with a flapping canvas, Beaver Jean remembered nothing. He opened his eyes and had a feeling familiar from the time he awoke on the nun's floor. He wiggled his toes, trying to determine how many he had on each foot.

"Don't move!" a voice shouted. The monsignor leaned over him.

Beaver Jean smacked his lips and moved his tongue around. "Do ye practice healing as well as priesting?" Beaver Jean whispered. He coughed and tried to remember the last thing he could remember. Alice.

"You have devil breath," said the priest. "My God. Open up. You must have a rotten tooth in there."

Beaver Jean blinked his eyes. "Am I still at the fort?"

"I suppose you didn't suffer any loss of wit since you appear to be as intelligent now as before you nearly froze to death in the spring snowstorm after burying a horse halfway," said the monsignor. He stood and pulled a small, dry tuber from a cord strung across the tent. He turned to Beaver Jean's wives, who appeared as smiley and compliant as he'd ever seen the pair, and said, "Boil this in water. Add pepper. Bring it to me when it's ready." They took the tuber and scrambled out of the tent and into a warm afternoon.

"Musta warmed up sudden," said Beaver Jean.

"Nah," said the priest. "You been dying, recovering, talking nonsense, and sleeping for three weeks or more. After that last late blizzard, spring's here for good now."

Beaver Jean tried to get up, but his head felt like a boulder.

"You lie back down, you big dummy," said the priest. "You're not going anywhere for a long while, I says."

"Who says?"

"I says, you dummy," yelled the priest. "You are hereby quarantined with the rest. None of us is going anywhere till we're dead or this godforsaken disease is long gone."

"I got work to tend to," said Beaver Jean. "I gotta locate my wife and boy, for one."

"You sired a child?" asked the priest. "Good Lord." Then the priest seemed to resign himself to it. "Well, it'll have to wait. We can't spread the pox beyond this fort. Do you want to wipe out the entire population of America?"

"I've made it a point not to abide the bristly laws of the religious."

"Don't you dare debate with me, traveler. Before I turned from my wicked ways and made my vows to the Church, I led a force of Choctaw warriors under the advisement of General Andrew Jackson. You know who he is, don't you?"

Beaver Jean thought hard. "I believe he was president for a time."

"You're damn-tootin' he was!" yelled the monsignor. "And he owes me a favor! And I'll tell you what. If you try going after those two you're after or try leaving this fort before I tell you you can, I will send a letter to Mr. Jackson, and you don't want to know what will be in it."

"Would you ask him to imprison me?"

"Maybe worse. Now lie down and stay there."

Beaver Jean rolled onto his side and attempted to sit up, but he fainted and fell back again.

Beaver Jean slept for the better part of a month and tried not to aggravate the blisters erupting on his arms and chest. The monsignor told him he was lucky, that the pox was often worse, and deadly. When Beaver Jean regained his strength, the monsignor put him to work finding food for the fort.

"You call yourself a trapper? Get out there and find us some food without getting yourself killed in the process!"

At first Beaver Jean went for short walks out onto the prairie. He took along one of his wives to lean against when the weakness came to his knees or he ran out of breath. Coming back to full health was an exercise in patience. He trapped little rabbits and ground squirrels.

"These can't feed one child," the monsignor shouted at him. "Get out there and find something substantial."

Beaver Jean couldn't help but notice some similarities between the monsignor and his pappy, but he found himself liking the monsignor nevertheless. He yelled a lot, but he worked hard and could tell a good story too.

Beaver Jean soon found he desired to please the little priest. Luckily, he was able to shoot a buffalo with a lame leg. With the help of his wives and some women from the tribe, they butchered and brought the meat back to the monsignor's camp. Upon receiving the meat, the monsignor reached his hand up and put in on Beaver Jean's shoulder. "Now that's a good boy. You've done a real good thing here."

Beaver Jean had a feeling in his chest that he hadn't had since he was a youth at his mother's skirt. He resolved to remember the act and the words and impress them upon his own son someday, after he found him. He tried to keep the exact inflection of the priest's voice intact: *Now that's a good boy.*

Later that day, a soldier came and offered Beaver Jean a nice sum of money for the buffalo pelt, which the soldier thought he'd take with him on his way to Texas, which had been annexed by the United States.

"What do ye mean, 'Texas, which had been annexed'?" asked Beaver Jean.

"The United States has annexed Texas, sir," said the soldier.

Beaver Jean turned the word over and over in his mind. *Annexed.* It sounded interesting and terrible at the same time. "What do ye mean, 'annexed'?" asked Beaver Jean.

The soldier looked nervous and blinked. "I don't know, sir," he said. "That's just what I heard before I received orders that my company was to get down there and help clear the wilds of some surly Indian tribes."

Beaver Jean smelled an opportunity. His missing Negress and child now had too much of a head start on him to be worth the trouble and cost of finding them. He needed a new venture. The word *annexed* sounded exciting and mysterious. He had to get down there and see what it meant. He perked up and felt more virile than he had in weeks. "Do ye think them Indian nations will be in need of supplies while the army removes them to their new homes?"

"Oh, I'm sure of it, sir," said the soldier. "From what I hear, they're a sorry sight to be seen."

"Would ye mind terribly if my wives and I accompanied you United States army men to Texas, which has been annexed by the United States?"

"You'll have to take your query to the company's captain and to the monsignor, sir," said the soldier. "No one goes anywhere without his say-so."

"I will do that, young gun," said Beaver Jean. Then he put his hand on the soldier's shoulder and told him he was doing a good job. "Now, can ye point me in a way where a man might make a trade for a good horse?"

He dreamt that night of Lydian. She was running wild, with her red hair flapping behind her like a flag in front of a small clay building. Cowboys and rancheros cheered her on, and she danced wilder and wilder until she fell to the dusty ground, laughing. In the dream, Beaver Jean turned to the man beside him and asked, "Where is this?"

"Texas!" the man responded. "Texas, which has been annexed by the United States!"

When he woke in the morning, Beaver Jean talked with the monsignor.

"I have amended the purpose of my journeys. Now I will like to go to Texas, which has been annexed by the United States."

"And what, pray tell, do you intend to do there?" asked the monsignor.

"I will make dealings with the Indian nations, which will be in want of supplies on the reservations the United States has set up for them. Often, the Indians can't make do with what's on their reservation to feed their entire people and are in need of a good trader to bring them provisions and other necessities for living in rough and barren lands."

"Beaver Jean, given the right education, you could have been an orator," the monsignor said. Beaver Jean was quiet. "This god-damn country," the monsignor continued. He seemed to be think-ing of some great and oppressive burden. Then he sighed. "You are allowed to go, Beaver Jean, but if I hear of you cheating one Indian or hunting down one black soul, I will send that letter to President Jackson, who will order you shot and quartered."

"There will be no need for such measures, Monsignor. I have been an honest trader and trapper in most dealings and intend to proceed the same. I thank ye for the good care ye took in nursing me whilst I was ill and whilst my two wives proved fairly useless. Though this trip has not produced the intended effects, I am glad to have come on this adventure and glad to meet ye and will count ye a friend."

Beaver Jean packed up his things and attempted to saddle his new horse, Charlemagne, which snorted at him in grave disdain and high-stepped his back legs in poor cooperation.

"Ye best not have an uppity posture with me, Charlemagne. Ye is a beast of burden and will behave as such."

Charlemagne stamped at the ground.

Beaver Jean intended to get a head start on the army, shoot a couple of deer or buffalo, and sell the army the meat once they caught up. Before he took leave of the fort, the blacksmith he'd encountered on that first day in the fort accosted him once more.

"I sees yull still got that nasty beard on yull face," he said. He pulled a red-hot horseshoe from the coals and dipped it in water. It sizzled and fizzed and steamed.

Beaver Jean walked to the blacksmith, put his hand on his shoulder, and said, "Ye are completing that job the right way. Good work."

"I know dat, yull dumb animul trapper," said the blacksmith. "Now yull better get that paw off mah shoulder or Ima stick this horseshul up yull asshul." He smiled as he said it.

"Blacksmith, ye have not shown me much friendliness all the while I was here nearly dying of a terrible disease and losing my best horse too, but now ye seem to be changing yer heart toward a more agreeable manner."

The blacksmith shook his head and shifted his weight from foot to foot. He pointed at Beaver Jean's horse. "I bet Charlemagne here wull bust yull face into the back of yull skull before yull get half mull out dis fort."

The horse shivered the muscles along its black back, as if in agreement.

Beaver Jean patted the blacksmith on the shoulder and then waved goodbye to Fort Pierre on the Bad River. He was a man invigorated, a man headed south for Texas, which had been annexed by the United States.

# 30

# Angel Learns to Negotiate

MR. HATTERBY STUFFED boxes of cigars, bottles of French champagne, stiff boots, fawn-skin gloves, and silk nightclothes into a traveling trunk. Every time he moved away from the trunk, Mrs. Hatterby's cats would hop on top of the things and paw, nip, and scratch at them. As Mr. Hatterby searched the house for his long duster coat, which he needed for a couple of weeks on the windy prairie, he yelled at the cats and pointed at Angel to take care of them. One of the cats grabbed his glove fringes in its claws and began to bite and tear.

"I'm not supposed to touch them," Angel told her father. "Mother says not to touch the cats." Angel had just turned nine and had received a kitten, which she didn't like. Not that it mattered. The cats were for her mother, she knew.

"For God's sake," Mr. Hatterby sighed. He waved his arms at the cats. "Get the hell off those gloves, you nappy feline!" he roared. "Those are expensive gifts!" The cat whipped its tail and lazily jumped off the gloves and onto the floor. It slinked around the trunk and, as soon as Mr. Hatterby turned his back, jumped back onto the gloves and began clawing and biting the fringes.

Mr. Hatterby's coachman waited outside with the horses and carriage. His wage was determined by a combination of both the miles he covered and the minutes he spent. Mr. Hatterby, nothing if not thrifty, which is why he was an important man with an important job, was eager to depart.

"Where is that coat?" Mr. Hatterby asked.

Angel didn't understand much of what her father did to earn such a fine living, but she could see how other men respected him, deferred to him, and asked for his opinion on matters great and small. She sat on the steps of the grand staircase, watching her father scurry here and there, adding papers to his satchel, sweeping the cats away, and crushing a pillow into his trunk. She was used to the last-minute bustle and also the fuss her mother created each time her father had to leave. Sometimes Mrs. Hatterby feigned illness herself and made herself vomit. Sometimes she pretended as though there were important dates, such as imaginary church holidays, that her father would miss while he was gone. Once she claimed to have had a premonition, a dream, in which he was killed by wolves on his trip and which she was certain would come true. Another time she threatened to invite a common logger man into the house while he was gone to fix all of the things her father hadn't had time to mend: a loose floorboard, a window that wouldn't shut tight. She threatened to kiss the logger on the mouth. Sometimes she pretended not to care at all that her husband was leaving and would stay in her room the whole morning, emerging only when he had gone. Today she was in her room, throwing things around and crying loudly.

"Milly!" Mr. Hatterby boomed. He stood at the bottom of the stairs and shouted up toward Mrs. Hatterby's room. "Milly, what have you done with my coat?"

The wailing upstairs grew louder. It sounded mournful and high pitched, with bouts of choking. Her fake cry.

"Milly, I'm not going to ask you again! Time is money!"

Mr. Hatterby and Angel heard the knob turn and the door creak open.

"Find it yourself!" Mrs. Hatterby shouted down. "You don't

care about me! You don't care about us! All you can think about is statehood, statehood, statehood, running to that whorehouse, and being governor."

"Being governor!" Mr. Hatterby scoffed. "If word ever got out of Stillwater about the lunatic I've married, I'd not only lose the governorship, I'd forfeit my whole reputation and this house! Now where is my coat, woman?"

"You don't even care that Angel's been deathly ill all week," Mrs. Hatterby sobbed. "What if she falls stricken while you're gone?" Then she heaved and panted. "Oh my. I feel faint. I can't breathe."

Mr. Hatterby looked at Angel. Angel shrugged her shoulders and shook her head no.

"Angel's fine," said Mr. Hatterby. With his eyes closed, he inhaled fully and breathed out slowly. When he opened his eyes, he smiled. "Should I call for the priest?"

Mrs. Hatterby filled her breast with air and shouted, "No, I don't want the damn priest! I can't find my headache powders. Where are they?" The sounds of drawers opening and slamming shut came down the stairs.

Then the door opened all the way, and Mrs. Hatterby emerged at the top of the stairs. Her eyes were red and watery, but Angel did not worry because she had often witnessed how her mother would poke her own eyes to make them look that way. Angel had even tried that trick on Nanny to get extra treats until Nanny figured it out and gave her a spanking.

"My darling," said Mr. Hatterby. "My beautiful wife. Please come down here."

Mrs. Hatterby crossed her arms and pouted.

"You don't love me," she said.

"You are my life," pleaded Mr. Hatterby, softly, coaxingly. "Come down here now so I can talk to you." He waved for her to descend. She picked up her taffeta skirts and descended. Mr. Hatterby shook some papers from his satchel and held them.

"My dear girls. Do you know what these are?" The papers had big block letters on the front.

"We're not concerned with those," said Mrs. Hatterby. "We want to know when you're coming back." Her voice had turned low and soft. She stuck out her bottom lip. When Angel saw her mother act this way, she sometimes felt ashamed, even if no one else was near enough to witness it. Other times, Angel felt simple curiosity at how little or how much her mother could affect her father's words or behavior. She'd study her closely, watching the little eyebrow lifts and welling eyes and quivering lips. And other times, like today, Angel grew frustrated as her mother's behavior thwarted her own chance to hear about the interesting thoughts and actions of her father. Angel sometimes wanted her mother to go away so she could listen to what her father had to say about the world outside the big house, outside Stillwater.

"What are they, Father?" asked Angel.

"These, dears, are notifications in all the country's major newspapers about the organization of Minnesota Territory." Then he pointed to some words. "And right here? This is where it mentions the four major cities. See, Angel?"

Angel looked hard. She recognized many letters, but she didn't know the words. Then one stood out to her. It was the same word that was on many of the buildings in town and even on the carriage outside her house.

"Stillwater, Father?" she asked quietly. Her mother looked at the paper and at Angel and then at Mr. Hatterby.

"Yes, my dear. You are correct and very smart." He kissed her forehead, and Angel felt very warm.

He pointed to the word. "This one says Stillwater, our town. This one says St. Paul. This one says St. Anthony. And this one says St. Peter, which is far south of us on the prairie and where I have to go for a few days," said Mr. Hatterby.

"But why?" moaned Mrs. Hatterby. "Why can't someone else go?" She fanned herself and collapsed into his big chest.

"This is my responsibility, Milly."

"Father, what will you do there?" asked Angel.

"Well, there are four major buildings we must construct in the territory before the United States government will consider us for statehood and before we'll have a proper vote. We need to have a capitol building for the legislators to meet in, a proper university to educate our citizens, a prison to hold our criminals, and . . ." He paused and looked at his wife. "And a state asylum."

"What's an asylum for, Father?" asked Angel.

He patted her head. "Don't you worry about that. That's the one I'm going to convince the people in St. Peter to take, far away from us folks up here."

"Well, what are we going to get?" asked Angel. "The capitol building?"

"No," said her father. "St. Paul will have that. I'll fight for the university, but I'll settle for the prison."

"What would we do with a university?"

"People go there to learn to be doctors, lawyers, and scientists," said Mr. Hatterby.

"Did you go to university?" asked Angel.

"Yes, of course."

"Can I go to university?"

Mrs. Hatterby interrupted. "You won't have to worry about that. We'll find you a nice prosperous husband with a fine house and good inheritance and lots of servants."

"You know what else is in this paper?" asked Mr. Hatterby. "A woman has earned her degree to become the first woman doctor in the country!"

"A doctor?" asked Angel. "My goodness. She must be very smart."

"I know all there is to know about doctoring and tending the sick, and I never spent one day in any school," said Mrs. Hatterby. "Not one day."

"In any case, I must be off," he said. "Now where's my coat?"

"What will you bring me?" asked Mrs. Hatterby.

"Milly, I'll be on the prairie. There are no shops there, only country folks and country wares."

She fluttered her eyelids. "Then I don't remember where I put your coat."

"OK. How about this? They've got quite a large Lakota population down there. How about I bring you some beads and feathers, and then you can give them to the seamstress to sew into a new hat once I get back?"

She puffed up her cheeks and sputtered. "Anything else? Do they have anything else that's ornamental?"

"Not really. They're not so colorful and showy as some of the other tribes."

"All right then. Feathers and beads will do. Your coat's under the veranda." With that she turned and ascended the stairs. She called down, "Angel, go to Nanny today. Mother has a dreadful headache."

"Yes, Mother," replied Angel. Then she turned back to her father. "Have a good trip, Father. Try your best to get the university. I'd like to go there. Having a prison nearby sounds dreadful."

"I'll do my best," said her father. "But a prison brings good jobs and cheap labor, which attract businesses too. Now help Father fetch his coat out from beneath the veranda, would you?"

"Father," Angel said, "then will we be a state?"

"Well," said her father. "Not right away. The Southern states. They don't want to be outnumbered." Angel's father looked at his daughter, and his eyes softened. "They're nervous about the Negro question."

"What question is that?"

He kissed the top of her head again. "This smell is the one that always hastens me home," he said to her. "You're a good child, Angie."

After he left, Angel went to the steamy kitchen and sat watching Nanny prepare a lunch of roast grouse and sweet potatoes. Angel rested her head on the table.

"Nanny, who taught you to read?" she asked.

Nanny didn't turn from the stove but continued to stir the pot. "I went to school in Norway," she said. "My fotter tought it very important his daughters readt ta Good Book and ta newspapers."

"Why, though?" asked Angel. "Why is it important?"

"What?" She turned around. "So's you can make up your own mindt about ta events and not be fooled by contracts and important papers, tat's why!" She pointed a spoon at Angel. "When my husband and I get ta land here, we bot read the contract and signed ta papers. We both work, we both own. When he and ta babies die in the tornato, I sell ta land and get all ta money. If not, it would go to somewhere else. With dat money I have purchased ship tickets for three cousins from Norway to come here."

"I want to learn to read, Nanny."

"Ya! I tell your motter tat, and she got upset and treatened to hire a new nanny for you," said Nanny. She slathered the grouse with a thick spread of bacon grease, then she wiped her hands on her apron and went to Angel. "Is your motter sick in bed today?"

"Yes," said Angel.

"How's your stomach today? Hurt?" asked Nanny.

"No, it doesn't," said Angel.

"Tat's right. It never hurts when Nanny takes care of you," she said. She seemed to be thinking about something. Her blue eyes seemed to melt on the inside but grow hard on the outside. Her faint blond eyebrows came down. "Today we go visit the school again," she whispered. "We bring some of your old dresses and

some treats for the childrens, and you can sit in the schoolroom
with the other childrens. Would you like dat?"

"Very much," Angel whispered in return.

"But it's a secret, yah?"

"Yes," said Angel. She hugged Nanny, and some bacon grease
smudged her pinafore.

"Yah," said Nanny. "Now I make a plate for your mother. You
take it up and tell her to eat and rest. When she naps, we go."

Angel carried the tray to her mother's room, set it on the floor. She
knocked gently on the thick oak door before pushing it open and
picking up the tray. Angel was careful with it. She liked the sound
of the teacup rattling against its saucer. All the drapes in the room
were closed. A burning lamp cast a dim glow near the bed. On
it, her mother rested on her back, with her hands folded over her
middle. A crumpled cloth lay next to her. From it emanated a light
but distinct odor. Whatever it was that helped Angel's mother rest,
Angel knew its scent well. When she was small, her mother put a
cloth with that scent over Angel's mouth and nose when she cried
too much. After she inhaled it, the room would turn fuzzy, voices
became indiscernible, and Angel would want to sleep. When she
woke, she felt calm but nauseated.

"Come in, Angel dear," her mother said softly.

"I brought your food," said Angel.

"Set it on the table," said her mother. "Smells like sod-hut food.
That woman needs sophistication. When I regain my strength, I'll
prepare you proper meals. But I'm very tired now." Her mother
had changed into a thin nightgown and rubbed her rounded belly.

Angel noticed the bulging womb and wondered why she hadn't
seen it before. "Yes, Mother."

"I was dreaming about a beautiful dress, black silk, with a belt
made of feathers. Can you imagine it, Angel? Wouldn't it be grand
for funerals?"

"Yes, Mother," said Angel. "I'll come get your tray later. I'll leave you to rest now, Mother."

"That's a good idea," said her mother.

Angel turned to leave the dark room.

"Angel?" said her mother.

Angel stopped but didn't turn around.

"You understand we pay Nanny very well to take care of you," whispered her mother. And then she added very lightly, "Behaving as though she loves you is her job."

"Yes, Mother," said Angel. She left the room and closed the door behind her.

# 31

## *Weather in Heaven*

CLEMENT BIT HIS FINGERNAILS as a hushed but powerful quarrel between Mother St. John and Big Waters disrupted the orphanage. The boys, nine of them between ages four and fourteen, stood bare-chested in a line. Mother St. John had run down the line with soap and shears and a pail of water. Each boy received a washing and a haircut. Among the boys were three Indian children, two full-breeds from a chief who wanted his sons to learn English and Christianity and a half-breed, the child of a railroad prospector and a squaw who'd died in childbirth. Big Waters, seeing the three Indian boys with their sheared locks, flew at Mother St. John and pounded her fists on the nun's back.

"Big Waters!" Mother St. John raised her arms to protect her head. She turned and grabbed the old woman's fists in her own capable hands. "Stop that. What's gotten into you?" She shook Big Waters' arms. "What's gotten into you, I said?"

Big Waters yanked her hands back. She looked at the boys, whose eyes were wet and downcast.

"What?" said Mother St. John. "See how handsome they look." She put her hands on her hips and panted.

Big Waters shook her head.

"It's for their own good," said Mother St. John. She spoke quickly now. "Father Paul wants all the boys to receive the Holy

Eucharist and wants them to have clean faces and short hair and smart clothes."

Big Waters groaned and licked her parched lips. "Shame," she said clearly. She extended her withered finger and gestured for Clement to follow her. He glanced at Mother St. John, who nodded. He followed the old woman.

"But school begins in a half-hour!" Mother St. John called after them. She exhaled. "I did it for their own good," she said again, to no one in particular.

Clement followed Big Waters to the schoolroom. Sunlight coming through the window played over her face, and Clement realized that Big Waters was very old. She pointed for him to sit. And then the words croaked from her ancient lips.

"In the beginning, the Sky Woman gave birth to two children. One was Earth, in which all the good things took root and grew. The other was Wind, which was always moving and changing, threatening to destroy everything Earth had grown. Wind had no use for Earth. But Earth needed Wind, for without it the seeds of all growing things would not come. Wind grew bold and teasing, whispering to Earth and tormenting it, dropping seeds, but then blowing them away. Sky Woman grew angry at her child Wind. Out of Earth, she made Rock and Fire and cast them upon Wind in the form of clouds. Now when Wind drops seeds, Rock and Fire grow black and clap and shoot and release rain onto the seeds so that they take root in Earth."

Big Waters stopped. She motioned out the window. "Here she comes," she said. Clement looked and saw the tall woman and the girl approaching, again.

"Who?" asked Clement.

"Trouble on the breeze," said Big Waters. Then she left the schoolroom. Clement wondered if all mothers told as many story lessons as his did. He sometimes wished they'd talk straight. He sat at his seat and waited. He watched the girl. He pressed his feet into his boots to steady his nerves. *This time,* he promised himself, *I will not run away. I will be brave.*

Though the other dozen children poured in noisily—boots sliding, chairs scraping, voices bickering, the door slamming, noses blowing, and slates dropping—Clement heard only a whooshing in his ears, an underwater sound. She was coming. Though he opened his mouth to breathe deeply, his lungs took in only shallow, quick breaths. He was about to stand and run out of the room when someone moved behind him and then sat beside him.

It was her.

The scent of mist off a roaring river filled him. A strange contradictory sensation fell upon his body, like being warm and cold at the same time, the type of feeling he got when he sat in a drafty but sunny window in winter. He was cold, but sweating. He pretended to be studying the woodgrain of the table in front of him.

Then she spoke.

"Hello," she whispered.

Her breath rushed over him, as scent metallic but fresh like the air after rain. He was frightened and excited. His ears burned. His fingers froze. He swallowed and used his tongue to push the back of a loose tooth.

"Do you know me?" she whispered.

Her voice, at once familiar and foreign, pierced him. Sharp and high, but pointed and serious and soothing too. He pressed his feet harder into his boots.

He cleared his throat. "Yes," he said, but he couldn't even hear himself. He cleared his throat again. "Yes," he said, louder this time. "I believe so."

"I saw you sitting under the tree that one day," said the girl. "But you ran away."

"Yes," he said. The pounding in his ears subsided. "You're the girl who talks to me sometimes."

Then he turned his eyes upon her face. He kept his chin close to his chest, but he raised his eyes to meet hers. Hers were wood brown. She blinked quickly. He blinked slowly, to reveal the full effect of the anomaly. Now it was his turn to unnerve her, to show that she wasn't the only child with strange ways.

"They don't match," he said.

She moved her gaze from one eye to the other. "No," she said.

He lowered his eyebrows. "How do you do it?" he asked. And then he spoke more quietly. "Are you a witch?"

Her forehead furrowed. "No," she said. "I don't think so." She lifted her shoulders and dropped them again. "I don't know. I can only do it sometimes." She raised a finger and pointed at his eyes but then lowered it again without asking what she had wanted to ask. She continued to stare, and he stared back in earnest. He thought she was the most beautiful creature he had ever seen.

"I wish you did it more," he said. "I like to hear you." Then he breathed freely, having told the truth. "I'm glad you've come."

On that first day, Clement heard nothing of what the teacher said. He warmed in the light of the girl's white-blue skin and cooled in the shadows of her black hair and dark eyes. He watched her violet mouth when she spoke, and he knew from the one mirror in the infirmary that his looked the same. He intuited a link, and he had already begun the speculations. The stories of Big Waters, which he had once endured in politeness, now blushed like moon glow and star splatter over where the pair sat together in the far back corner of the classroom, alone, away from the rest. She was the swan of the story. In her was Wind from the Sky Woman.

"I'm Angel," she whispered. "That's my name." She cleared her throat and then added, "Like in heaven."

He nodded. "Clement is mine." He thought and then added, "Like good weather."

Already the two names seemed bound together. Angel and Clement. The pairing sounded perfect. He couldn't have chosen more suitable names for the two of them. He wondered if he'd always be so delighted. He wanted to know everything about her, but he also wanted to keep her mysterious and discover pleasant details about her one day at a time. How long could he make it last? Forever? He wanted to take her and secure her to him.

Already he looked with suspicion upon his classmates and friends, the children who'd been raised as his siblings. What if they too noticed how special she was? What if they too wanted to talk to her? What if they wanted to touch her? What if she decided to speak to them the way she spoke to him? Fear and anger rose in his chest like thunder and lightning in a storm. He had been raised to help, to share, to give everything. But he would not share her. He could not. She was his own.

"Some of these children are mean and selfish," he said. "I'll protect you always."

She looked around, wide-eyed, curious.

"I'm going to tell you a very important story about swans, which no one can tell you but me," he began.

She leaned in close to him to hear. While he whispered, the tendrils of hair loose from her braided bun moved with his words. He had her.

# 32

## A School Visit

WHILE HER MOTHER continued her private confinement, Nanny scuttled Angel to school each day. By the end of the week, Angel scarcely left Clement's side. In his presence, the blood in her body seemed fortified. She felt heavier, more certain, rooted. Each day he cleaved her to him with tales and traditions and, when she hinted that she was bored, he told her to follow him. While the other children ate their lunches and played outside, Clement led Angel through the woods.

"Where are we going?" Angel asked. The sleeves of her dress caught on the branches. Loosened leaves fell in her hair. "I'm afraid my mother will get mad."

"We're almost there," Clement said. He was careful now to hold the branches as he walked, so they wouldn't snap back and hit Angel. Water gurgled. "Hear that?" he said.

"Water?" she said.

"A little farther," he said. Then he stamped down the branches of buckthorn and dogwood so she could pass through and see the small shallow pond. "Come on," he said. "Watch out for poop."

Hundreds of white swans with black-banded eyes weaved across the water. The pond was encircled by heavy green pines.

"There's so many birds!" Angel said. "How did they get here?"

"They flew," said Clement. "They come every year."

"They look like snow," she said. "Like the snow and ice."

A pair descended from the pine tips.

"Watch!" said Clement. He pointed to the two flying swans, who lilted to one side, then another. They clumsily bumped into each other and then hit the water with a splash. They shook their wings, stretched, and then cut across the surface in perfect grace.

"Oh my," said Angel. A rumbly laugh shook her chest. "They're more graceful in the water than they are in the air."

"Yes," he said. "They're silly in the air." He reached out his hand, and she took it. His heart quickened. All his life, he'd sought the kind of feeling he now had, as though he was really, truly bound to another human. Even among the other orphans, he felt alone. Most of them had a brother or a sister or both, a real relative, in the place, but he had no one. The brothers and sisters always shared, always protected each other, always had someone's hand to hold, but Clement stood alone. Yet he always perceived that somewhere outside the orphanage his family was alive and searching for him. He didn't have the sense that his real mother or his real family was dead. He always imagined that someday, someone who belonged to him would walk up to the front of the Home for Orphans and Infirmed and inquire, "Is a boy named Clement Piety here? I love him very much, and it was a terrible misunderstanding and mistake to leave him without anyone."

"I wish I could have one," said Angel, "to keep in my room."

Clement imagined the giant birds fluttering around a fine room, knocking things over and honking noisily. "I don't think a swan would like to live in a house," said Clement.

"A stuffed one, I meant," said Angel. "Mother's got a peacock. With long purple and blue and green feathers. I wish you could see it."

He thought that he'd like to see the peacock too, to see the inside of the big house where she lived without him. He wanted to see if all those comforts he imagined were real. Did she have her own plush bed with smooth blankets and thick pillows? Her own cup and plate? Room to be alone? Books to read?

"She made a hat with some of the feathers," Angel said. "But she never wears it." Angel let go of Clement's hand and flapped it in the air. "Sweaty," she explained.

"I've got another place to show you," he said. "Come on."

They walked back toward the orphanage in silence. Clement felt like he was flying, funny. He led her through the forest, and she followed like his shadow. He turned around again and again to look at her, to make sure she was real. He wished she'd always be there, near him. He thought of a thousand ways to keep her close. Maybe he could go to live with her. Or maybe she could stay with him. Surely everyone would understand that the two of them ought not to be separated. He wondered if people who saw them together could see the connection, the similarities. He wondered if Angel noticed it. He hoped to share all of his deepest thoughts and secrets with her. No hidden thing should remain between them. He led her behind the Home for Orphans and Infirmed. Tall, snarly bushes reached out mangles of branches and vines.

He stretched out his hand again.

She waved it away.

He pulled it back and lifted a low branch. "Under here," he said. He crouched and crawled behind a bush.

She watched him. She looked around, as though wondering if anyone was watching. She smoothed her skirt.

"Come on," he said.

"I can't," she said. She folded her arms over her chest. "I can't get dirty."

He lowered his eyebrows. "It'll wipe off," he said. He picked up a clump of leaves and dropped them. "It's just dirt and leaves."

"OK," she sighed. She looked around again. She knelt and

crawled after him. Behind the bushes, she stood up and clapped her hands together. "Yuck," she said.

Mosquitoes buzzed in their ears and attacked their exposed skin. Angel smacked one on her cheek.

"My mother's going to be mad," she said.

Clement wondered if Angel's mother would ever get mad enough to make Angel stay at the orphanage. "Stand back," said Clement.

She did.

He passed his hands over the wall until his fingertips felt the slightly raised slats of a door in the wall. He pried his fingers into it and pulled.

"Do you know about slavery?" Clement asked her. He hoped not. He wanted to tell her everything.

"Yes," said Angel. "I do. My father is opposed to it. Me too."

"Me too. We're the same." His hands found her arms. He pulled her close to him, so close, they were nearly nose to nose. "You can't tell anyone," he whispered.

"Ouch," she said. "You're hurting my arms."

He released her, and he tugged and pulled the door open. "Sometimes we hide them here," he said.

From outside, the room appeared to be nothing more than deep and dark emptiness. Clement disappeared into it as though walking into the mouth of a monster. He reached out his hand to Angel. "Come in here." She put her palm in his. Clement held on tight. His fingernails cut into her hand.

"Not so tight," she said. "I'm coming. I'm scared."

"Look," he said.

Her eyes adjusted. The room remained dark but for the faint light the door let in. On the dirt floor stood a small bed and a simple table with a washbasin. A rag rug completed the scene. "People have to hide in here?" she asked.

"Yes," he said. "It's better than being with their evil masters."

"But it's so dark," she whispered. "And dirty. Why don't you put them in the infirmary with you?"

"Because it's a secret," Clement said. "No one can see them. No one can know. You can't tell anyone."

Angel was silent. Her head spun. She found it difficult to breathe. She imagined hiding in here, alone in the dark.

"Let's go back outside," she whispered.

Clement sat on the bed. "I know you won't tell anyone. You can't," he said. "Mother St. John and Big Waters aren't supposed to be doing this. They could go to prison."

"Where are the Negroes now?" Angel whispered. She looked at the blackest of the black space between the bed and floor. Could someone be hiding there now?

"We haven't had any for a long time. Sometimes we get two in a month, but sometimes we don't get any for a year. Have you ever seen a Negro? We have one who cleans the school sometimes. A boy. He's very light, but he's still a Negro."

She thought about the dirt floor. Her mother often talked of people who had dirt floors, but Angel had never seen one until now. "Yes," she said. "I have. Our horse caretaker is black, but he's his own man, my father says." She wondered if moles or snakes ever popped up from the floor in here. She shuddered. "Let's go," she said.

"I like to sit in here and hide from everyone sometimes," said Clement. "It's peaceful." He stood and went to her. He grabbed her hand and led her to a corner. "You stand here," he said.

"What are you doing?" she asked. She smiled at him, but it was a small, tight smile.

He walked to the door and closed it. The room went black as midnight.

Angel gasped. "What—" she started to say, but then quieted.

He shuffled to the far corner, opposite hers. "Are you afraid?" he whispered. The words moved unfettered in the dark.

Tears came. "Yes," she said. "Please—"

He sat down with his back against the wall. "OK," he said. "Now do it."

She heaved a cry. "Do what?" she said. "Let me out of here."

"Talk to me without talking," he said. "In my head, like you do sometimes."

Silence. Then he heard a choked whimpering and boots slithering across the floor. Suddenly the door opened, and she stood silhouetted in the daylight. "I can't. Don't ask me ever again." She heard branches snap and leaves crunch. She was gone.

"Witch!" he yelled after her.

# 33

## Nanny's Fate

ANGEL HICCUPPED ON THE WAY home. Her eyes hurt and felt swollen. Nanny walked with her arm around Angel's shoulders. Sometimes she gave her a squeeze. Nanny didn't ask questions but seemed to know what happened. She told Angel that boys sometimes were gruff with girls they liked, that they sometimes teased and insulted because they didn't know how to compliment and coddle. "When they get older, they act better," she assured Angel.

Angel tried to imagine her own father as a boy. Had he been mean and scary to girls? She remembered how he sometimes lost his temper with her mother. "Are you sure?" Angel asked.

"Oh ya," said Nanny. "Before we were marriedt, my husband once called me a fat piggy and spankedt my bottom."

Angel laughed and cried at the same time.

"He followedt me aroundt the school yardt, oinking at me too," Nanny added. "One day I turned around and slappedt him in ta face. Ten he stoppedt."

Angel gasped. "I couldn't do that!" She grinned. "Could I?"

"Smack him," Nanny said. "Or kick him in the boy parts. Or ignore him. Boys hate to be ignoredt most of all."

• • •

The door to her mother's room remained closed, so Angel didn't have to explain her dirty hands, face, or dress. She didn't have to hide her puffy eyes or the mosquito bite on her cheek. At night she lay in bed, thinking about Clement. She closed her eyes and concentrated. She stiffened her stomach muscles and panted. She tried to talk to him, to see if she could do it whenever she wanted.

"I didn't like that," she said. "You were mean!"

She waited. Nothing happened.

She put her fingers into her mouth and jabbed at the back of her throat. She gagged. She tasted the familiar bile.

"You scared me," she said. She waited.

Still nothing.

She slept. Her dreams that night were filled with the white birds.

Angel went back to school and tried to pretend as though she didn't see Clement or hear him even as he scooted closer to her on the bench or said her name or tapped her hand. At lunchtime, Clement presented her with a small purse made from fawn skin and decorated with beads.

"I made this for you," he said.

At first, Angel feigned reluctance. In the way she'd learned from her mother, she looked at the gift, rolled her eyes, and crossed her arms.

Clement offered it again. "Take it." He pressed it to her arm. "Please."

Angel turned her head. He stuffed the purse into the space between her arm and chest.

"Take it," he whined.

She took it and ran her fingers over the pattern, a pair of swans with their necks entwined. "It's beautiful," she conceded.

"I made it just for you," said Clement. He moved his hair out of his eyes. "Well, I put it together, but Big Waters made the pattern."

"Thank you," she said. She turned it over and over.

"Do you like me again?" Clement's chest tightened.

She kept her eyes on the purse. "Yes," she said.

He exhaled. "Will you talk to me like you did before?"

Angel put the purse to her nose. She sniffed it and crinkled her nose. Then she rubbed the smooth side of the purse along her cheek. "I don't know. If I can, maybe. But probably not."

"Please," he said. "I won't be mean to you ever again."

"Maybe," she said.

Angel's mother still remained locked in her room. Angel began to imagine that her mother had died in there, behind the big, heavy door. She imagined that now Nanny would come every day or perhaps even move into the Hatterby house and take care of Angel always. Angel wondered what it would be like to always feel healthy, to never have stomachaches, to freely go to school and not have to sneak there only when Mother was ill or pouting, to play unconstrained, to make friends, more friends than one. She wanted lots of friends. Girl ones and boy ones. More friends than only Clement. Would other children like her? Clement did. Would other boys like her? Would she one day have a boyfriend?

The possibilities excited her. She hopped from her bed and to the door. She opened it softly and slowly and slipped into the hallway. She sought the quietest path. She tiptoed past her mother's room. She heard voices from within. She stopped. The priest. Father Paul was here again. She heard him chanting. Last rites? She listened and held her breath. The sound of her mother's real cry, one that was deep and low and rocked her small body, rolled under the door and seemed to pool at Angel's feet and move in vines up her legs, her belly, her chest, and then clasp her neck. Her mother was alive.

Angel swallowed and returned to her room.

In the morning, Nanny slipped Angel to school. Alive with

curiosity and owl-eyed at the world outside her home, Angel planned to enjoy this day to its fullest. She had a vague notion that it might be the last one. Like the other children, she leapt to her feet at recess time and skipped outside and ate unfussy food and inhaled pine air and plunged a dipper into the water barrel from which all the other children drank. Her cheeks flushed, and she got a slight sunburn on her nose. She scraped her knee, twisted an ankle, and ran so fast, she got a side ache.

"Everyone gets them," Clement told her. "Just lean over and breathe." He rubbed her back.

When she stood up straight, she saw an unfamiliar person coming down the walk. He was black, but lighter than any Negro she'd seen before, and he was holding his hands out in front of him, his fingers lifting and falling as though playing a phantom piano. His face was slightly plump. He wore a tan shirt with a black vest over it. His boots were shiny.

"Who's that?" Angel asked. She placed her hands over her belly.

"Where?" said Clement. He followed Angel's gaze. "Oh, him. That's the kid who cleans the school. Davis. His mother dresses him like a dandy."

"A what?" said Angel. She licked her hand and ran it over the top of her head.

"He's a Negro," Clement said. "But not the enslaved kind."

"That's good," said Angel. She turned her back to the new boy.

"I guess so," said Clement. "He's all right, but he talks a lot."

Angel pushed her shoulders back. "Is he coming over here?" she asked Clement.

"No," said Clement. "Why?"

When Clement and Angel returned to the classroom with the rest of the students, Davis set his mop and pail in the corner and stood behind Clement and Angel's table.

Clement turned around. "You can sit here," he said. Then he

explained to Angel, "We're not supposed to, but we let Davis learn some too."

Davis was older than Angel and Clement, and taller and stouter. He sat beside Clement but leaned around him to look at Angel.

"Hi there, pretty girl," he said to her.

Clement put his hand on Angel's arm. "He talks a bit forward because he's been raised in a whorehouse," he said. He elbowed Davis. "Weren't you?"

"Can't deny it, but I don't mind it," said Davis. "Always something interesting going on there. How ya been, Clement, and who's your lady friend?"

"Knock it off, Davis," said Clement. "She's new and not used to your jokes."

"I think I been swept off my feet," said Davis.

Angel's cheeks flooded with heat.

Clement sniffed, as though in laughter, but his forehead and the corners of his mouth lowered.

All day, Angel and Davis glanced at each other, leaning around Clement to catch looks and smiles.

At the end of the day, just as Angel determined she'd say something to Davis, ask him a question or compliment him on his shirt, she walked out of the school to the clearing and lifted her head. There Angel's mother stood. The forest canopy darkened. Bird noises seemed to stop.

"Angel!" her mother hissed.

"I—" Angel started.

"You're fired," her mother said, lips barely moving.

Angel looked over her shoulder to where Nanny stood. Nanny pulled a bonnet over her head and looked at the ground.

It struck Angel as odd to stand between her tall, sturdy blond nanny and her small, delicate dark mother, round in the belly with a child. In the sunlight, her mother seemed tiny beneath the giant trees but so serious and threatening. Her mother looked from Clement to Angel and frowned. She held out her hand, and Angel tucked her head and walked toward her mother.

Clement shouted, "You can't take her away!"

Davis asked, "Who's that?"

Nanny stayed back, and she never again returned to the Hatterbys' house.

That night, when her mother brought her the soup, Angel slapped it off the tray and sent it splattering onto the floor.

"I'm not drinking it," she told her mother, with words that dropped like stones. "I'm not drinking it ever again." The bowl broke; pieces of it tottered along the wood floor. The soup splashed the walls and the legs of her bed and the bottom of her mother's skirt. One of her mother's cats crept along the wall and ran out of the room.

Her mother bent to pick up the pieces of the bowl and tossed them onto the tray. Then she stood, put an arm on her lower back, and stretched, popping her belly out far for Angel to see. She extended her arm, clamped her hand into a fist, and pounded herself in the belly. She gasped and then spit, "You are a dirty little abandoned bitch. If it weren't for me, you'd be a snot in that orphanage." She hit herself again and again.

"Stop," Angel said softly. "Stop it."

Her mother hit herself again and again. "You stop it," she said. "You stop it," she kept saying. Finally she leaned over and staggered out of the room, slamming the door behind her.

All night, moaning and wailing came from her mother's chambers. In the morning, a pail full of bloody rags sat outside her mother's door. After a few days, her mother emerged and her belly was flat again. Angel wondered about the baby, but she never saw one.

# 34

## Davis Learns His Place

WHEN DAVIS CAME HOME from school, he found a stray cat sitting on his bed. It had a fresh-from-the-forest look to it, its fur matted here and there, an eye pasted shut, and an angry cocklebur in its tail. Its other eye, gray-green, looked at him as though it was disgusted by his presence.

"Ma!" Davis shouted. He was growing tall and had hair under his arms and often felt full of unexplainable rage and strength. "Ma!"

Down the hall of the Red Swan, a door flew open and footsteps plodded on the hallway carpet. Suddenly, Miss Daisy appeared in the doorway, looking harried and disheveled.

"What's the matter?" she wheezed. Her hair was coming out of its bun. Her cheeks were flushed. She looked back toward her room and then at Davis again. "Is everything all right?" She held his face in her hands. "Why are you yelling? Are you hurt?"

He could smell the sweat and a man's cologne on her. As a boy, those scents hadn't bothered him. As he grew and came to understand what they meant, a fury had built in his bones: at her, at the men, at all of it. "There's a strange cat on my bed." He pointed to the feline, spreading like butter in the sunshine streaming through the window.

"Oh," said Miss Daisy. "That's Homer. He kept coming to the door for scraps and mewling to come in. He won't hurt you." She walked over to the cat and picked him up. She put him to her nose and smiled at him. The cat struggled and leapt from Miss Daisy's chest back onto Davis's bed.

From her room down the hall came shouting. "What's going on!" and "I paid a lot of money for this!"

In her cheerful lilt Miss Daisy shouted back, "Be right there!"

Davis rolled his eyes. "We already have a dozen cats," he said. "They're everywhere. I don't want any more cats stinking up my room."

Miss Daisy clenched her jaw and quivered her lips, which meant she was about to cry.

Davis sighed. "Ah, God. I don't mean to upset you, but we've already got so many animals around here." He pointed to the cat hair on his pillow and the carpet. "How are we going to feed this one too?"

More shouting from down the hall: "Get back here, you piece of filth!"

Davis stepped into his doorway. "Hey!" he shouted. "Shut your damned trap!"

Miss Daisy heaved up a big sob, and Davis turned and put his arms around her. He was now half a foot taller than her and still growing. He held on to her and hugged her tight until he was grabbed around the neck and yanked off his feet.

"Stop it!" Miss Daisy screamed. "Get away from him. He's just a kid."

A small, bald man, wearing only trousers and suspenders, stood over Davis, hauled back his fist, and landed it on the side of Davis's temple.

"You think I'm gonna let a little nigger talk to me like that?" he said. He popped Davis again in the same spot.

Miss Daisy grabbed hold of the man and tried to pull him away.

He shook her off and pushed her back. She fell into Davis's dresser and onto the floor.

The man reached back and punched Davis three or four more times, knocking him down, before the bartender appeared in the doorway, kicked the man in the stomach, encircled his waist, and threw him to the floor.

"Dirty nigger in here!" the bald man said. "Filthy whores and dirty niggers." He got up, went back to Miss Daisy's room, and appeared again with his boots and shirt and coat. "You just lost yourself a customer," he said before descending the stairs.

Miss Daisy, her hair and clothes a mess, cried like a child.

Davis touched his fingers to his temple and his eye. He looked at his hands and saw blood. "I hate this place," he said. "I hate it here."

Miss Daisy crawled to him and used her hem to wipe the blood from his face. "Shhh," she said. Tears fell from her face onto his own.

"I hate it."

"You just have to learn to be quiet," she said, "and hold your tongue." She pulled his head up onto her lap. "Get me some water," she called to the bartender. When he did, she dabbed a handkerchief in it and then blotted his face.

"For how long?" Davis asked.

She seemed to be thinking. She moved the handkerchief all around his face, carefully and tenderly. Then she welled up again. "Maybe always," she said. "I hope not, but maybe."

He pressed his face deep into her skirts and cried. He could smell the man scent and jerked away, revolted. He stood. "I hate this place." He grabbed Miss Daisy by the arm and pushed her out the door. "Get out. Leave me alone." He slammed the door. Then he went to the window, opened it, and took in a good breath of clean air. The cat sat lazing on his bed as though nothing strange had happened. Davis picked it up and threw it out the window.

He lay back on his bed and thought about all he wanted to do and see. He talked to himself. "I want to see the mountains and get some of that gold in California that everyone's talking about. I want to have an adventuring kind of life on a horse, with a gun and money. I have to get a horse. I will become a Negro cowboy, or maybe just a cowboy; maybe no one will know me and will think I'm light." He closed his eyes and saw himself riding into a western sunset on a big, strong horse with its nostrils flaring, chasing down a mountain lion or a black bear. He saw himself raising a rifle and shooting the animal and gutting it and then wearing a coat made from the fur. He imagined himself panning in a river, plucking gold nuggets as big as his hand out of the water and buying a pocket watch and a new saddle. He pictured himself on the new saddle, with Angel riding with him. He'd put his arms around her and hold on to the reins as they rode over the land. Davis put his hand down his trousers and awakened himself. He stroked and stroked, thinking of her reddish blue lips and pale skin. He stroked and stroked as he imagined the noises she would make as the horse carried them away.

# 35

# Big Responsibility

A S THE BURGEONING NATION wrestled over the rights
of fugitive slaves, Iowa and Wisconsin became the twenty-
ninth and thirtieth states in the Union, which for years left the
land west of the St. Croix and north of Iowa, including Stillwater,
as part of the United States but no state in particular. The tribes of
the region had called the place Minnesota, Land of Sky-Colored
Waters, as it was sometimes bluish and sometimes cloudy. Already
rumblings were heard about giving that name to the territory.
Some men wanted to push for immediate statehood, but the battle
would be tense. The thought of another free state sent nervous
tremors up and down the necks of the leaders of the Southern
states. Too many states wagging their fingers at the slave states
was not something the South wanted. To some escaped slaves and
abolitionists, a place in limbo, Minnesota Territory, was a good
place for people in limbo, and so dozens of fugitive slaves, with the
help of riverboat workers, free Negroes, whores, barbers, railroad
porters, an earless priest, an overburdened nun, an arthritic squaw,
and the bastard son of a fur trapper and a red-haired imp stepped
onto the shores of Stillwater.

Stillwater found itself on a twig's tip of a branch on a tree with
roots deeply planted in the South. Mother St. John's Home for
Orphans and the Infirmed had converted a well-hidden room into

a safe haven and resting place for weary travelers from the South. And although the boy Clement couldn't understand the politics surrounding the events that unfolded there, he understood that his job was important and should remain a secret.

Mother St. John woke Clement by blowing in his ear. She held a dim lantern to her face. For nine years now he'd lived here among the sick and motherless. He was a good boy and a comfort to Big Waters, who had raised him, doted on him, and reared him to do good and hard and humble work in the world.

"Wake up now," Mother St. John said. "I need you to collect our guest." Clement sighed and sat up. He dressed quietly so as not to wake the others. Mother St. John threw a satchel filled with biscuits and dried beef over his shoulder. "He'll be hungry, I'm sure," she said. She opened the door just wide enough for Clement to get through and handed him a bottle of whiskey. "For the conductor."

Clement considered asking for the muzzleloader that Mother St. John kept hidden behind her own bedroom door but then thought better of it. Instead he said, "I thought I heard a mountain lion yesterday."

Mother St. John said she hadn't heard of any big cats in the area and told him to say his Hail Marys on the walk to the river. Clement started out, his mind on nothing but that gun until he considered the consequence of not saying his prayers as Mother St. John had directed. He knew that as soon as she had him alone, she'd ask him about his prayers. And it was impossible to lie to Mother. She had told him once that nuns knew everything, a special gift from Jesus. He believed her. So, on the first decade, Clement dedicated each prayer to begging for a rifle. Six Hail Marys into the Joyful Mysteries, Clement froze in his boots. From the sky, two yellow eyes fell like embers from a torch and grew larger and larger. Clement gasped. The eyes became bigger and bigger, moving closer and closer, toward his head. He fell to the ground

and asked the Virgin to protect him as an owl dove past. The draft
ruffled his hair. He dimly saw a rabbit dashing in and out of the
leaves and branches, and then heard the high unnatural scream
of the creature rip through the dark as the owl seized it with its
talons and lifted it into the sky. The heavy wings flapped strongly.
Very soon the woods were quiet again. Clement breathed. If he'd
had a gun, he'd have blasted that owl. And maybe the rabbit too.
Probably he'd have shot the rabbit first and then the owl. Both of
them.

Clement began walking again. He knew these trees well and
the things that lived among them. He knew the hollow tree where
the bobcat made its den and kept its kittens. He knew the rock
upon which the garter snakes coiled into large mating balls each
spring. He daydreamed about Angel, and he grew briefly jealous
of Davis and the way he stole her attention. But before he knew
it, the rustle of the leaves and the creaking of the branches were
muted by the rushing sound of the river, where he knew to wait.
He settled near a cluster of birch trees. Birches were his favorite.
The way they grew into each other, strengthened each other, one
tree's bark melting into another's amazed him. He leapt up and
grabbed a low branch. He swung back and forth, suspended like
an opossum. He counted to a hundred and then dropped down.
His palms stung. He spit into them and rubbed his hands together.

Clement's mind wandered to guns and hunting. He made pis-
tols of his hands and pretended to shoot and holster. After a while,
he sat and leaned against a tree, waiting. He pretended he was a
stealthy hunter. He raised his arms as though handling a rifle in
pretend-aim at a bear or wildcat. He pressed himself against the
tree, imagining he was at war against restless Indians or wandering
robbers. He turned his head to one side of the tree trunk and then
the other, so that only one eye surveyed the area before him. At the
thought of the enemy, Clement dropped to his knees and then lay
on his stomach, making himself as small as possible, at one with

the earth. If he were a real soldier or sheriff, he knew, no one would see him. He leaned on his elbows and popped off a shot.

"Pow," he whispered. "Got you."

Soon Clement tired of his game, sat up, and rested his head against the trunk. He fell into a catnap. Not too deep. Enough of a rest to think about all the ways a boy could make a name for himself in bravery or honor. All around Clement, the world was changing. Men were inventing machines that made trains and boats go faster and farther, tilling land that had never been turned before and pulling great harvests from it, inventing guns that could shoot a mile away, organizing cities and states out of wild territories, discovering medicines for illnesses that had been incurable, and filling the newspapers with stories of dangerous fights against the Spanish in the South, battles against the weather in the Rocky Mountains, and discovery of gold in the place called California. Every man in the world seemed to be making a famous name for himself while Clement sat trapped in the little orphanage, under the tutelage of Mother St. John and Big Waters, who asked him a thousand questions about his whereabouts, his bowel movements, and his prayers, and hardly gave a boy room to grow up.

Clement wondered what his great purpose was going to be and how long it would take him to discover it. He wanted to be important now. He was again thinking of owning a gun and shooting a great big bear when he startled himself out of his doze in time to hear the almost silent pulling of an oar through water. Clement squinted to see the place where the little rafts sometimes appeared, seemingly exhaled out of the night sky.

He decided that there'd be no harm in showing this place to Angel the next time she came to school. He hoped she'd come back soon. But her mother had looked very angry. Clement felt sorry for Angel. He wondered what it was like to have that angry woman as a mother. Clement wondered about his own mother, his real one. The one who had left him, left them, if they were indeed twins, two eggs from the same mother swan. He wondered why. He wanted to know why. He wondered if he'd ever get to know. He thought that somehow, when he was big, he would know. He wondered why Angel wouldn't talk to him now the way he liked, in his mind. He felt it would be easier to get through the days if he could only hear her voice in his mind. He wondered if she didn't like him anymore, and that made his heart hurt. He wondered why not. He wished he hadn't closed that door. He tried to imagine the episode from her perspective. He realized that she was unfamiliar with the room, and some people were afraid of the dark. He thought that the next time she talked to him or the next time he saw her, he would tell her again how sorry he was. If only she would talk to him. He hated waiting. For now, like so much of his life to this point, he would have to wait to know what he wanted.

Soon a raft materialized from black shadow into a plainly visible thing creeping close to the shore. A man whose name Clement did not know poked a pole deep into the river and threw a rope to him. The man was one of the few free black men who worked on the river steamers.

"Got it, boy?" he whispered.

Clement scampered after it. He tied the rope around a fat tree trunk and slid down the muddy riverbank. The conductor jumped waist-high into the river. "Phew," he said. "River's mighty cold yet, and strong."

Clement started to move away from the shore.

"Stay back, boy," said the conductor. "Current's strong too. Don't want a mite like you to get pulled under." He pulled the raft toward the shore. When close enough, Clement helped him lift one corner of it onto land. "All right," he said toward a canvas tent on the raft. A tall black man seemed to unfold his long limbs out of it and then stood. He was taller than any man Clement had ever seen. Clement wondered how he had fit inside the tent and for how long he must've crouched in that small space. Clement held out his hand to steady the man as he descended from the raft to the shore.

"My legs is shaky," said the tall man. "Been cramped in the riverboat a long time. Thanks, son."

Clement nodded. A sliver of sunlight appeared on the horizon. The conductor untied the rope and wished the man luck. Clement took the whiskey bottle from his pants pocket and handed it to the conductor. He took it and slid back down the bank and onto his raft.

Clement turned to the man. "We have to hurry," he said. "Before it gets too light. Lots of people get moving at morning."

"Thank ya," said the man. "Alone out here?"

"Yes, but I know the way real good."

"Still, though," said the man. "Big work for a small boy."

"I'm not small."

The conductor disappeared as seamlessly as he had appeared.

Clement shook himself out of the straps of the satchel and tossed it to the man. "It's only a short walk, but you're hungry, I bet."

"That's a kindness," said the man. He opened the satchel and removed a piece of beef. He bit down on the leathery strip and tore a bite. "How old are you?"

"Nine," said Clement.

"Ya don't look no nine," he said.

"It's getting light out," Clement said. "We better hurry." He knelt and pointed to a rock where the man should climb. "I'm big enough to have a rifle."

The man laughed and found his footing on the rock. "Ya got one?"

"No," said Clement. He reached down to help the man up. "Not yet."

The man extended his hand and looked into Clement's eyes. He pulled his hand back. But then just as suddenly, he thrust it toward the boy again and grabbed hold. Clement helped heave him up the bank. "That the light playing on your eyes?"

"No, sir. That's just the way God made them."

"One brown, one blue?" asked the man.

"Big Waters says it's because I have earth and water in me."

"Big Waters your mama?"

"No." Clement noted the man's eyes, light brown like coarse sugar. "Your eyes are odd too."

"Yep. My daddy wasn't a nigger." He hummed a couple of notes. "I gotta boy like you somewhere with his mama, I hope. I haven't seen her in many years."

Clement thought of getting back to a big tin plate filled with pancakes and oatmeal, along with coffee. Big Waters made good coffee even when coffee beans were scarce. She ground acorns or dried beets and sweetened the concoction with cream. "We got good coffee back home for you to warm up with," said Clement. "And I'm sorry about your wife."

"Got along with the Winstons. Maybe she's been through here?"

Clement had never heard that name. "I don't think so," he said. "We haven't seen any ladies in a long while."

"'Spect not. It's a hard road and that was a long time ago."

The pair trekked over tree roots and mud clots.

"Where's your son?"

"Not sure," said the man. He leapt over a downed tree limb. "I never knew nothing about him except that he was goin' to be born. I guess he could be a girl, but I don't know. His mama is clever and he is clever too, I 'spect."

"That's good," said Clement. Far off, hammers pounded metal. And the sun was coming up. The Stillwater workday had started. "We're almost there."

The man stood. "Got a mill near here?"

"Yes, but that's the noise of the new prison going up."

The man started walking again. "I hope you get your rifle some-day."

"Mmm-hmm," said Clement.

"Let's get my papers," said the man.

"They're ready," said Clement. "And the priest's got some money from the rich man for your trip."

"You among some mighty kind folks," said the man. "Not many like 'em."

"I wish they'd give me a gun," Clement said. "I'd be real brave."

When they arrived at the infirmary, Mother St. John welcomed them at the door and quickly shuffled the tall man toward the back. "I don't mean to be rude, sir," she said. "But you never know who's watching. There are some fur trappers in this area who've taken up bounty work."

"Tha's all right," he said. "You can call me Christmas. That's my name. Jim Christmas."

"We don't usually share names, sir," said Mother St. John. "It's better that way."

"Pardon me," he said.

"We're going to get you fed and outfitted for the rest of the journey, which will start tomorrow night if all goes well. The priest has business with the archdiocese in Chicago, and you'll be riding with him." She pulled a horse blanket from a shelf and handed it to him. "Seems strange, I know. But we've got no way to go direct to Canada from here unless you want to set out on foot. I shouldn't ask, but Christmas, did you say? Seems familiar, but I can't quite place it."

"How many days walking is it?" he asked.

"Too many," she said. As she made up the bed, she explained that she'd made him free papers and that he'd be safe with the priest. She explained how they'd travel to Chicago, and there he'd have to choose. "You can stay there," she said. "The city's big enough now, with a large enough free population in which to mingle." She looked at him to make sure he understood. He nodded. "Or," she continued, "you can take a boat north to Canada through the Lake Michigan." He nodded again. "Or," she went on, "you can venture a bit farther east to Cass County, Michigan, where there's a city of free Negroes starting up with the help of the Quakers."

"Many of us stay here?" he said.

She sat on the end of the bed. "No. You can take your chances here too, if you want," she said. "Do you pass? You're lighter than most."

"Nah," said the man. "Tried that for years. Works for a while, but when the folks find out . . . they mad as wildcats." He rubbed his jaw and laughed at an old memory, it seemed, then straightened up. "My walk and talk give me away as a Negro."

Mother St. John nodded. "We've got a small population of free Negroes, fifty or sixty people, maybe. But since you're new, you'll attract attention and a lot of questions."

The tall man raised his eyes as though he was thinking about the possibility.

"But," said Mother St. John, "if I may, you might threaten the business we do here and be injurious then to any others who come here looking for help. The benefactor who funds this process wouldn't be agreeable to it, I don't think."

The man shifted his weight. "Awfully kind of him, to do this sort of thing."

Mother St. John got off the bed and gestured for him to sit. "Well, yes, I suppose it is." She stiffened a bit at the thought of the benefactor. She'd heard he was a scoundrel, using the system to build his own reputation, betting the country would be crying for freedom in a few years. She'd heard he wanted to be on the right side of that argument. She'd also heard that should he get discovered, he had friends in high and powerful places to help him. She doubted he'd be so generous toward those, such as Big Waters, Father Paul, the whores, the boy, and herself, who did the most dangerous work. "Yes," she agreed again. "Of course it's very generous. Sit."

He did. "I'll be on my way." He lay back. He was so long, his feet hung off the end of the bed. "I been wandering and traveling a long time, and I don't expect I'll stop until I find my woman and that child she was having. It's been so many years, I wonder if I'll recognize them when I see them."

"I wish you luck," said Mother St. John.

"Do you know the state of affairs in Mexico and the islands south of the state that they call Floreeda? I surely do not like this cold weather you have here. I hear it snows half the year."

"A lot. Yes. But not quite half."

"My father was a cowboy and my mama said she lived ten years in Haiti before being brought to America. I think I would like to go to either of those places, should they be agreeable to freedom for all peoples."

"I do not know much about the world beyond this small place, I'm afraid. But you can ask the priest tomorrow or the Quakers in a day or two. Perhaps our benefactor could answer some of your questions. He makes quite a few trips to the South and might have better knowledge of the politics there than I do. Someone will surely answer your questions for you. Now I bid you good night, for I must turn out this lamp."

"Yes, I understand. Good night and thank you."

# 36

## Davis the Piano Player

IN JULY OF 1855, a thick, damp heat settled over Stillwater.
Davis opened all the windows of the Red Swan Saloon as wide
as they'd go, but there was no relieving the heat really, though
the open windows did help with the pervasive smell of human
sweat and perfume and cat. Davis used sticks to prop the windows
open. He put a pitcher of water and glasses on a table next to
the door, stood in the doorway, and surveyed the sights. He bent
down, selected a shiny stone, and put it under his tongue. Two cats
wound around his ankles. He kicked each of them.

To the south, the St. Croix River lazed along, like a giant gray
snake hissing in the heat. A hazy combination of mist and humidity and mosquitoes hung above it. Davis rested his head against
the doorjamb and tried to think about something other than the
heat. But everything he thought of made him hotter. He was
eighteen years old and had his sights set on two things, adventure
and Angel Hatterby.

As if to jolt him from his daydreams, up the dirt path waltzed
Mr. Hatterby, the one person, to Davis's thinking, who best exem-
plified the type of adventuring life he'd like to lead himself, with
fine clothes, important friends, high-philosophizing talk, and
coast-to-coast traveling and sightseeing. That he was the father of
Angel did also occur to Davis.

When Davis thought about Angel Hatterby, a blood rush surged to his groin. He spit out the stone and tried to take a deep breath. He wiped the sweat off his forehead.

"Morning, Davis," said Hatterby. "Hot enough for you?"

"Yes, sir," said Davis. "It sure is hot enough for me. Is it hot enough for you, sir? I mean, are you finding ways to stay cool, sir? I myself was thinking about taking a dip in the river, but I see it's still quite high and running fierce, and I never did take the time to learn to swim, which was a mistake on my part, sir." He wondered if Mr. Hatterby could read his mind. Davis worried that his face somehow gave away his thoughts. He put his hand over his mouth and pretended to yawn.

*Don't ask about Angel,* he told himself. *Don't ask about Angel,* he repeated in his head. "How's Angel been these days?" asked Davis.

Mr. Hatterby untied his neckerchief and sat on the stoop of the Red Swan. "Did you say something, Davis?" he asked. He unlaced his boots.

"No, sir," said Davis. "I did not."

"I'm going to have Miss Daisy give me a cold bath. Would you fetch the water for me, son?"

"Yes, sir," said Davis. "Of course, sir. I will get on it right away."

"There's a nice tip in it for you."

"Thank you, sir."

"Start tonking that piano real loud in about a half-hour. Would you, son?"

"Yes, sir. Of course."

The piano had been a gift to the Red Swan Saloon from Barton Hatterby. He was a raucous lover and insisted that the piano be playing when he did his business, to drown out the noise. He also donated one to the school where Davis played and sometimes taught music lessons to other children. Mr. Hatterby himself owned the only other piano in town, though neither his wife nor Angel played.

When he threw parties at his mansion, Mr. Hatterby invited Davis to play, with these cautions: "Don't speak to anyone. Don't eat or drink anything. Don't touch anything but the piano. Don't ask to be paid. I'll leave the money at the saloon. Respond with a pleasant smile if spoken to." Mr. Hatterby appreciated discretion above all else.

Davis loved playing piano at the Hatterbys' mansion. Davis loved the white fence around the Hatterbys' property. He loved the stone staircase that led to the huge wood door, which had a lion's-head knocker. He loved the yellow paint and the white trim of the house. He loved it that the Hatterbys' gardener had planted red flowers beneath the windows. Davis imagined himself as king of the Hatterbys' house. He pictured the maid opening the door to him as he approached, taking his coat from him, and asking him if he wanted a brandy or coffee. And although Davis had never been up the grand staircase, he imagined ascending it, passing the stained glass window, and going to his bedroom up there, where Angel would be waiting for him, where a fire would be burning in the fireplace, where he would lie down next to her.

While Mr. Hatterby greeted guests and entranced them with his own ideas on abolition, which allowed for maintaining a certain natural hierarchy, while he explained that a certain order could be maintained without enslaving the darker race, Davis stared at Angel. He knew he ought to be interested in Hatterby's musings. The man was a respected politician who could very well affect Davis's life, whether he could earn the same wages as a white man, walk on the same sidewalk, sit in the same pew at church, legally marry a white woman. But Davis, wrapped in the cocoon of youth, wherein the fulfillment of every desire feels possible and deserved, thought only of Angel. He was dazed by the light that seemed to radiate from her pale skin. Aside from the natural nerves and follies and hesitations that rack a young man, Davis never considered not loving Angel Hatterby. Perhaps it was his bold mother's genes or the unrestricted love he received from the women of the Red Swan, but Davis didn't behave deferentially. He supplicated adults, catered to employers, and bowed to women because he'd been taught to be respectful, not because he was black. He loved Angel Hatterby, and he didn't feel guilty for it.

The first time Davis played for a Hatterby soiree, Angel smiled brightly, recognizing him. But her mother had yanked her arm and pulled her into the kitchen, and when Angel emerged, her expression had changed. At first, Davis had been hurt, but then he caught Angel stealing looks at him and he knew she loved him too.

So he didn't worry when she avoided him or turned her back to him when she caught him gazing. He grew giddy as the months and then years passed, and she became coy. She stood ever closer to the piano. Sometimes she'd stand next to it and study his hands as he played. She nodded at him, and he wondered. Was it a welcome into her heart? What should he do next? Should he smile or not? Should he pick a song to send a secret message? Which? He tried to think of something romantic, but his fingers began playing "I'll Be No Submissive Wife" before he could begin something else. He watched and saw Angel mouthing the words to the tune.

# 37

## Angel the Coy Mistress

MRS. HATTERBY USUALLY stayed upstairs during her husband's parties. Too many people in one place made her perspire and feel nervous, and she often claimed to be with child, though the obvious signs rarely materialized. Mrs. Hatterby had birthed two premature babies over the past five years, but Angel hardly remembered or thought of them. She didn't know, for instance, whether they had been boys or girls, whether they'd lived a couple of weeks or only a few hours. Their births and passings had been so quick, and Angel's own health had been so dire, that she couldn't recall exactly. And Angel wasn't sure whether the deaths were natural or not. And now, at fifteen years old, her own body seemed more interesting to her than that of her mother. She spun in front of mirrors, noting bulges and curves that weren't there before.

Angel was relieved when her mother chose to stay in bed. Even though her mother no longer bothered her about drinking the soup or confining her to her room, Angel felt an odd commiseration with the woman, as though she herself had somehow been responsible for her mother's illnesses, her own sicknesses, or maybe even the deaths of the babies. Angel didn't know. The presence of her mother made *her* perspire and feel nervous, and right now she wanted to dress. She wanted to be beautiful. She loved to be beautiful.

Angel chose for this party a peach gown with tiny green leaves embroidered all around the bodice. The sleeves were brown velvet, as was the trim at the hem. Angel thought this dress looked like the natural world. As she dressed, the piano music made the floor beneath her feet vibrate. It excited her to think that Davis was in her house. It excited her to think that Davis would be looking at her. She looked in the mirror. She licked her finger and then smeared some stray hairs away from the neat part she had made. There. Perfect. She put on her white gloves. She selected a flowered fan from her collection.

As a dutiful daughter, she first went down the hall to her mother's room and knocked lightly.

"Come in, dear," said her mother. Angel opened the door and went in. Her mother was sitting up in bed with a blanket pulled up over her. She was paging through a picture book.

"Hello, Mother," said Angel. She curtsied. "What are you reading?"

"Sit down with me for a moment, dear." She rested the book face-down over her belly. It was the same one she always looked at, *The Married Woman's Companion*. She couldn't read, and Angel could recognize only a few words, but they both liked to browse through books and newspapers, especially those with pictures of dresses and ads for slippers, corsets, and stockings. Mrs. Hatterby patted the bed.

Angel approached and sat down. Her mother's sanctuary smelled of decayed flowers and sour feet.

"I love the sound of silks as they move," said her mother. "Are you happy about the party?" She straightened Angel's already-straight belt.

"Yes," said Angel.

"You like parties?" Her mother squinted at the belt, as though something about it perplexed her.

"Sometimes." Angel looked at it too and found it to be perfect.

"You're growing up, Angel. Soon it will be time to find you a husband."

Angel sat up straight. She took her mother's hand.

"Then you'll leave me too," said her mother. "Then no one will be here at all who loves me. There will be no one here to take care of me." She squeezed Angel's hand hard, her sharp nails like little reminders of all they'd endured together. Angel remembered a time when Clement had clutched her hand in a similar way.

"I'll always take care of you, Mother," Angel said. "I promise."

"I hope so, dear." She let go of Angel's hand. "I remember the day I took you away from that awful place. I shudder to think what could have become of you if I hadn't saved you. You'd be a dirty, motherless urchin. But never mind. And never speak of your origins to anyone," said her mother. "No properly bred or moneyed man would marry a girl out of the poorhouse, with unknown origins. Sometimes when I look at you, I wonder about the nasty woman who left you. I wonder if she was a savage or some other kind. You've got such dark hair and eyes. Be sure to always powder your skin. Keep it light."

"Yes," said Angel. She wanted to ask about her real mother, to know who she was. She wanted to ask about Clement too, to find out why they looked so much alike. She wanted to know every small detail of her own birth, but she was afraid to know too.

"I suppose you're eager to leave me and get to the party." Her mother's mouth formed a tight smile, but her eyes were piercing.

Angel said, "No, Mother. I'll stay with you as long as you like."

"No," her mother said. "Go on. Enjoy yourself. You look so beautiful. You must take advantage of this fleeting beauty before it's gone." She laughed. "Look at what's happened to me."

Angel did. Her mother was still quite beautiful. Fair skinned. Pink lipped. But her green eyes flickered with unsettling intimidation. "You're the most beautiful mother in the world. Sleep well," said Angel.

"How can anyone sleep with that saloon music in the house?" her mother said. "Kiss me before you go." She reached out her arms to Angel.

When Angel leaned over to peck her mother's cheek, the woman grabbed the back of Angel's head, pulled her hair, and pressed Angel's face to her chest. At first Angel resisted, but then went still, though she panted a little.

"Listen, Angel," said her mother. She pushed Angel's face hard to her bony chest. "That is the beating of a broken heart." Then she let her go, waved for Angel to depart, and picked up her book.

Angel rushed out of the room.

In the hall, she leaned against the wall and caught her breath. She straightened her hair and stifled a sob. She thought about running away, about how to escape this house.

She felt guilty for thinking such things. The woman was, after all, her mother. She had made many, many sacrifices for Angel. She thought about Davis. Angel knew she couldn't marry a Negro, but still felt tied to him somehow.

Angel descended the staircase to the compliments of her father's friends and to the consternation of their wives. Angel was too pretty for them to like her. She smiled at them, insincerely and shyly, in a way that showed off her small teeth and hurt her cheeks. Angel mingled among her father's guests, acting the hostess. She listened as the men argued over the details of a treaty with an Indian band called the Ho-Chunk and the ignorance or intelligence of chiefs named The Coming Thunder and One That Stands and Reaches the Skies, who had agreed to forfeit the lands and payments to any among their group who were ill-behaved, drunk, or unsuccessful as farmers. She eavesdropped as the men

NICOLE HELGET                    241

debated the righteousness of the actions of a violent abolition-
ist named John Brown, the legality of the freedom claims made
by a slave named Dred Scott, the impact of a book called *Uncle
Tom's Cabin*, which had supposedly made Queen Victoria cry, the
bloody implications of the Kansas and Nebraska Act, the prob-
ability that the civil war in Kansas would spread to all the states
and territories, the certainty of statehood for Minnesota, the rules
of a new kind of game called rounders, or baseball, and all kinds of
wild and wonderful things happening in the world. Angel wanted,
more than anything, to ask questions, to know more. She watched
her father carefully and admired the passion with which he spoke.
His words sometimes sounded like poems or sermons. Once in
a while, she saw the other men roll their eyes, though, and she
wondered why. Their apparent disloyalty made her angry. But it
also made her study her father more closely. She searched for signs
of disingenuousness in his words. He looked as honest as he did
when he kissed the top of her head and said that the smell of it was
what brought him back home again and again.

She found the men's attractive wives and asked about their children, about who made their hats and where they'd found their perfume. They answered politely but shortly and returned the same
small smile she gave them. Behind her back, she heard the women
whisper about her crazy mother, saw them raise their eyes toward
the stairs, where they correctly supposed the crazy woman was
kept.

She excused herself to give directions to the cooks, the maids.
She did all the things a proper hostess should do, all the while
withholding her gaze from Davis. She sensed his presence but
did not look directly at him. She turned her back to the piano and
tried to ignore him. She tried to start conversations with the wives
again. The sister of Thomas Lawrence, a wealthy lumber baron,
remarked to her about the song Davis played. Then Angel turned
to look upon him. He was already mooning at her.

Angel ran her fingers over the ribs of her fan and wondered if Davis knew what it meant—"I'm thinking of you." She decided he probably didn't. Later, she brought the fan to her forehead and used it to swipe away stray hairs and then fanned herself quickly—"My heart is yours." *I wouldn't do such things if he understood,* she told herself. *I wouldn't behave so forwardly.* But to express these feelings in some way felt good. She couldn't talk of it. The memory of how she had once spoken with Clement through her thoughts passed through her mind, but she blinked it away. She didn't want to think of those days anymore. Those were childish days and these were not.

Around eleven, she excused herself to retire to her room, as proper etiquette required of young ladies. The party went on for another couple of hours. When at last the music stopped and the voices quieted and only the sounds of the servants cleaning up could be heard, Angel sneaked down the stairs and out the kitchen door. She looked around in the dark. Finally, someone stepped from the shadows.

"I wait out here after every party, hoping you'll come out and talk to me," whispered Davis.

Her skin prickled. She reached out. "It's so dark, I can hardly see you. Where are you?"

Then she felt a hand take hold of hers. His skin was mealy, but she didn't mind. She rubbed her thumb over his hand. Calluses hardened his fingertips. His hold was strong but gentle too. It was warm and large. It felt safe and strong. It felt new and essential. It was perfect. They stood that way, not speaking, until the kitchen lamps were lit for the morning chores. They barely spoke except to note a falling star or the sound of night animals moving.

At first light, Angel let go and waved goodbye. She went inside and walked directly past the nosy housekeeper. Angel had a brief notion to barter with the woman for her silence but decided not to. More and more, especially since the release of her nanny, she'd noticed the servants seemed to collude with her. She hoped that sitting outside the whole night with a Negro wasn't pushing the boundaries. Maybe the housekeeper hadn't seen him. But for now, Angel didn't want to ruin the moment, the first wholly happy time she'd had since she'd gone to school, since she'd played with Clement. She decided that all the waiting was worth it. She'd choose one night with Davis over every day with Clement, every time. She wondered if that was cruel. She couldn't care. This was different. She wanted to keep the memory of Davis's hand in hers for the rest of her life. But she wondered if maybe she too lacked sincerity, like the men at the party or the women who'd smile at her and whisper once she turned away. She truly felt that she wanted Davis's hand in hers forever, but what if she actually wanted it only for now? How could people tell the difference? She'd once cared for Clement in such a way too. Angel supposed that all these complications meant she was a woman.

# 38

## Big Waters Begs

BIG WATERS RELEASED HERSELF from Clement's slumbering hold on her and set her feet on the cool floor. She covered him up and tiptoed out of the room, past the kitchen, and out the front door. Once outside, she stretched and moaned in pain. She was old, and her bones rubbed and her skin sagged with age. In the night, Clement had crawled in beside her as he used to as a small boy, held on to her, and sobbed into her chest. The heat of him had felt good, but she had tried to remain still all night so as not to disturb his sleep. Now she walked, her muscles relaxed, and her mind got working. She thought about the boy's hurting heart, and how her own heart seemed to be bleeding too. A mother is only as happy as her unhappiest child.

She knew why he cried. And she knew that her own love was not enough for him. This hurt her, but she forgave the boy for it because he could not help his heart's desires. Since the first day his sister had been taken from him, she knew the pain in this life would be great. It is not natural to separate those who have wombed together.

Big Waters waited at the back door of the Hatterbys', and she would not leave even when the caretakers and housekeepers and horsemen shooed her away. Finally, the woman of the house, Mrs. Hatterby, herself appeared in the doorway.

The woman sneered, stepped out the door, and then closed it behind her. "Just what do you think you're doing here?" Her eyes darted. "What do you want, old woman?"

In the monotone way of those who rarely speak, Big Waters strung together these words: "The children are of one womb and would do better to visit with each other." Then she stepped back and rested her arms across her chest. She was tired. Along the side of the house, in the shadows, she spied the girl watching and listening.

Mrs. Hatterby stepped down from the doorway to a step. "Who do you think you're talking to?" she said. "Get away from here, and you better keep that filthy brat away from my daughter."

"Your daughter emerged from another," said Big Waters. "And by her, a brother to whom she owes much. Bringing an unwanted child into your arms is right and good, but you were not right and good in leaving the other."

Mrs. Hatterby thought for a moment, then curled her lips into a wry smile.

"What is this?" she scoffed. "What could I or my daughter possibly owe to that boy? You're mad."

Big Waters remained at the door.

Mrs. Hatterby fished in her pockets and pulled out a couple of coins. "All right. Is this how we're doing it? Here's money for your dirty children and your niggers you feed at your dirty little shack. You think I don't know? You think I don't know what my husband's up to? What your nun is up to?" She pressed the coins to Big Waters' chest and let them fall. "Don't mess with me, old woman. I could bring the wrath of hell down upon all of you. Now get out of here and don't come back." Mrs. Hatterby went into the house and slammed the door behind her.

Angel came from the side of the big house and picked up the coins. She pressed them into Big Waters' palms. "You may as well take them. For Clement. We have plenty more."

Big Waters closed her palm over the coins. "You have given me a fine gift, and I have only this to give you in return. Listen. I was there on the day you were born in a small room to the red-haired child wife. You came first and were pink and noisy and full of black hair, which is strong and means a long life. The boy came second and was small and quiet like a naked bird. His life will not be long. In the womb, you devoured your mother's strong blood and will live long but will also be greedy. You left your brother very little and now his life will be hard. He hadn't even enough blood to darken one of his eyes. For this gift of long life he has given you, you owe it to him to make his days pleasant. It is your duty as a sister to do this."

Angel's lashes closed over her eyes. "Where is our mother? The red-haired woman?"

"I only know that the hairy trapper with the Indian wives once sought her."

"Does Clement know?"

"He knows you are his sister. But I have not told him the rest," Big Waters said. "He is not strong enough to know all the truths."

The wind rustled, and Angel began to fear that her mother might check to make sure the old woman left.

"I'm supposed to—what—be his friend or his sister? What am I supposed to do?"

"Keep him happy."

With that, Big Waters left.

# 39

# Fantasies and Realities

THE NEXT MORNING, Angel sat on the piano bench. She recalled the events of the night before. The excitement of the men's world delighted her mind. She envisioned clamorous gatherings of important men shouting radical ideas, explosions in mountains where railroad tracks would be laid, slaves in the South grabbing their masters' whips and tossing them to the ground in pure rebellion, and colorful, noisy, deadly clashes of soldiers and Indians on the prairies. She thought about her brother, Clement. He was her brother. The old woman had said so. And her real mother had red hair. Red hair! She wondered what had happened to her and who the hairy trapper was. To suddenly have so much information made her feel grown-up. After years of boredom, all at once her life was accelerating. But what could she do? What could she choose for herself? It seemed as though her father and mother were making all the important decisions for her. She wondered what Clement would do with his own life. Would he become a soldier or fur trader or timber man or railroad man or gold prospector or Indian fighter or cattle rancher or whaler or farmer or world traveler? The possibilities for men were so vast! Then she thought about Davis. What would he do? Would he leave here, and her, for somewhere more interesting and exciting?

She placed her hands upon the piano keys and swore she could feel Davis's residual heat. She closed her eyes and imagined him kissing her. She parted her lips. She tried to sense him the way she could sometimes sense Clement. She thought about him. What might he be doing this minute? Maybe he was thinking of her. She felt sad to realize how little she knew about him. She wondered if it was crazy to imagine touching him and kissing him when she didn't know his middle name, his favorite color, where he came from, or where he was going.

"What are you doing?"

Angel opened her eyes and closed her mouth.

"I said, what are you doing?" her mother repeated. She was descending the stairs in her nightdress, something she never did. "Get away from there." She ran to Angel's side and pulled her arm. "Don't even think it."

Angel nodded.

"It's a dirty, filthy thing you're imagining."

Angel nodded again. There was nothing else to do when her mother got angry like this. Her mother pulled her to her feet and walked her to the kitchen. She prepared a tea.

"Don't you ever think about how I sat with you and nursed you back to health all your life? Does that ever cross your mind?" asked her mother. "Or how I've kept you away from the riffraff who could ruin your life? Do you ever thank me for that?"

Angel nodded.

"I got so little sleep! I sat up with you night after night, rocking and humming and feeding. And you're ready to throw all we've done for you away on an orphan or a nigger. Shame on you, Angel." She stirred the tea and handed it to Angel. "Do you know what would happen if word got out that you were born in a dirty hut to a woman who abandoned you? Do you know how slim your prospects would be? Do you think you'd be wearing dresses of silk or living in a house like this? You better wise up. You better not ruin our chances at a good match. You better not embarrass me."

Angel watched her mother's hands shake, rattling the cup and saucer.

"Your father and I have arranged a marriage for you. A good one. And don't even think about declining the offer. Thomas Lawrence. Do you know how many women in Stillwater will die of envy?"

"I like him," Angel whispered. "Davis."

Her mother corrected her. "You like him for now. A girl's heart has the freedom to be fickle until she marries. Like him. Fine. But that's it." She huffed and put a hand to her breast. "You think I didn't have other suitors? Of course I did. But once I married, I became completely devoted to your father. That's what wives do. Husbands above all else."

Her mother handed her the tea. Angel smelled it. There was the old odor. Tears boiled her eyes. Her hands shook.

"But Father likes Davis," Angel said. "He does. And you said yourself he supports emancipation. I heard you."

"Because it's convenient, Angel, you stupid girl. Because he thinks that emancipation is a position that will secure him an elected or appointed position." She laughed. "What your beloved father really supports is colonization, like the British. The only reason he doesn't want slavery here is because it appears uncivilized." She waved her hand. "He supports it everywhere but here."

Angel's heart beat fast. She felt her face flush.

"You think I'm stupid, don't you?" her mother went on. "It's a game, girl. To play silly."

"I don't believe you," said Angel. "I don't believe it. It's not true. Father likes Davis." Then she couldn't talk. She was crying.

"Take a drink and calm yourself," her mother commanded. "I've already ordered a new gown, and your father has begun construction on a mansion as your wedding gift."

Angel sipped. Her mother's voice went on and on but seemed to be receding. She drank some more. She didn't care. The ones she loved were always taken away from her. She tipped back the cup until the last drop touched her tongue. "There, you crazy witch," she said to her mother. She grew dizzy and lightheaded.

Her mother smiled, unfazed by the insult. "You go on upstairs and climb back into bed."

Angel did as she was told. In her bed, she lay back on her pillow and felt the room spin. She drummed her fingers on her blanket and waited. Then she heard a faraway but familiar voice. He was saying prayers, a rosary.

Nausea swept over her. She gagged over the side of her bed. She heard him saying, *Holy Mary, Mother of God—*

"Aren't you a good boy," Angel mocked. She panted and drooled onto her pillow. Her stomach clenched up like a bear trap. "Oh God."

Silence.

"Don't be afraid," she said. "It's only me. It's your Angel."

*Angel? I knew you hadn't forgotten me. I love you, Angel. I love you very much. Say you love me too. I want to hear you say it.*

Then her mother came in.

"You're not going anywhere until your marriage," she said. "And you're not to see that orphan or that nigger ever again. If you do, I'll make sure they suffer for it. And you. You'll regret it, I swear."

When Angel was better, she couldn't remember if the memory of talking with Clement was real, nor could she recall exactly what her mother had said. But the words of her nanny did come back to her: go forward or die.

# 40

## The Voyeurs

AFTER THAT TIME when she'd interrupted his prayers, Angel had not returned to Clement. He'd been impatiently expectant for nights on end. He paced and wouldn't sleep for fear he'd miss her. Then from Mother St. John he'd heard that Angel was getting married, and he fell into a deep melancholia. On the day of his sister's wedding, Clement sat among the tree stumps near Stillwater, which had once hovered over the town in protective canopy. He sobbed like a child and gazed up into the sky, asking God why. The sun beat on him, and his skin reddened and burned. Because of this, he'd be peeling skin like a snake. For this pain he blamed Thomas Lawrence.

A reckless timber man, Thomas Lawrence owned nearly every acre around this town, and he had razed nearly every tree standing more than a man tall. The stump Clement sat upon was one of thousands still wet with the sap and moisture that had fed the towering forest. Clement mourned the trees. He mourned the displaced hawks and owls, eagles and woodpeckers. The river, once a living body of movement and laughter, now sat clogged with Lawrence's logs, waiting for their turn at the sawmills. The whole town stank of sawdust and rotting wood and charred timber. The only trees left were the birches around the Hatterby house and leading to the river behind them, the small grove around Lawrence's new mansion, and the dense woods across the river from his place, a haven of untouched trees for Lawrence to enjoy as he sipped his morning coffee on his balcony.

The wooded paths where Clement used to stroll were now strewn with cushions of shredded bark and squirrel backbones and bird wings, victims of the harried clearing. Clement sometimes came upon deer standing lonely among the stumps, looking at him as though confused. Once he stumbled over the skull of a horse, worked to death and left to decompose rather than properly burned or buried. And Clement had heard of men run over by the towering sleighs of logs and knew of a boy who'd broken his neck falling from a treetop he'd been sent to hack. The boy survived and now lay in a bed in his mother's house day and night. Clement knew this because he'd seen him with his own eyes. Mother St. John and Big Waters had heard of the woman's plight and sent Clement to her weekly, with foodstuffs and laundry for the woman to wash and press. She was a German and prideful. She would not take the food for free, would only exchange it for labor. Where her man was, no one knew. She was alone out there with a houseful of children, the oldest paralyzed, with no word of apology or offer of care from Thomas Lawrence.

Most men in Stillwater were beholden to Lawrence, in one way or another, for their livelihood. And Lawrence was literally burdened by the weight of his wealth. Clement had seen him drop a coin on the dirt street and not bother to pick it up. He could have any woman he wanted. Why Angel?

Thomas Lawrence used things up and then discarded them. Now he was marrying Clement's sister. Clement could hardly stomach it. All morning, he'd felt sick in his gut. When Big Waters tried to rouse him from his bed, he'd snapped at her to leave him alone. She'd brought him a plate of bread and ground cherry jelly, his favorite, and he'd slapped it off his bed and onto the floor. Uncomplaining, she cleaned it up. When he saw the old, withering woman on the floor, using a thin knife to scrape up the jelly, he'd risen.

"I'm sorry, Big Waters," he'd said. "That was foolish of me." He'd put his hand on her knotty back and bid her to sit on his bed. Then he'd taken the knife from her and scraped up the rest of the mess. He carefully gouged the jam out of the crevices between the boards, knowing what a stickler Big Waters was for clean floors.

"I can't figure out why she'd marry such a fool," Clement had said. He liked talking to Big Waters. She rarely said a word, but she seemed to be a good listener. When he had finished, he kissed her cheek and said he was going for a walk. Big Waters patted his thigh and then let him go. Clement considered leaning against her and having his cry there, but he was a grown man now and couldn't do such things anymore. He trusted Big Waters and knew she'd never scold or scoff at such a sign of tenderness, but even in her eyes Clement wanted to be considered a man.

Mother St. John had been nagging him for more than a year about finding his calling. He knew it was time to move on from the care of the women, but he didn't know what to do or where to go. He moped and blamed his long-lost mother. If she had stayed and raised him and Angel up the way she was supposed to, with a husband in a house, then Clement would have learned a trade from his father or grandfather, like other boys. Maybe he'd have inherited a business. Maybe some money. Maybe he would have found a nice girl to love, and maybe he'd be getting married too. But none of that was happening, and it was all her fault. Thinking about being abandoned by his mother and the expectations of Mother St. John and Big Waters drove Clement to tears. Thinking about Angel marrying Thomas Lawrence caused him to heave and cry hard.

After his wailing in the woods, Clement composed himself and thought to witness this union for himself. He wondered if Angel would perhaps come to her senses and not marry Lawrence. He wondered if he'd be able to see her face, to ascertain if she was marrying him for love or for money. Perhaps she was reluctantly following the will of her parents. This seemed likely to Clement, but he was impatient of her sense of daughterly duty. Angel was not a natural child and should not be bound to the rules that apply to natural ones. Her natural place was as his sister, as a partner to him, as a confidante. Why couldn't she see that? He began to grow angry. She was an abandoner, like their mother.

He imagined her escaping through the big wooden doors, racing down the steps, and diving into his own arms. But what would Clement say to her anyway—don't marry Lawrence? How might Clement reply when she asked, "Why not?" Mention that he's the richest man in town? Then Clement had to laugh at his own foolishness. He had no job. He had no station in life. He had no money. He had no inheritance. He had nothing, no prospects. Why should she listen to him?

And even if she did, Davis would probably swoop down in an instant to corrupt her before Clement could convince her of Davis's reprehensible and ridiculous intentions. Clement had seen how the two of them looked at each other. Growing up among whores who coddled him as though he was as beloved as the Savior had made Davis too confident and bold. He behaved as if he didn't realize that he was not only an orphan, but also a black one. He had fewer prospects than Clement did, but he appeared to ignore this fact. What would happen if Angel didn't marry Thomas Lawrence and Davis pursued her? She was too naive and simple to foresee the dire consequences.

Clement had to accept this marriage for now. He had to position himself in such a way that he could help Angel when she grew wise to Thomas Lawrence. He had to find a purpose, so that he could show Angel he was a man too and could take care of her.

Then they could run away together, find their mother, and learn the truth, so that they could be whole and begin again.

All morning, Davis's stomach had rumbled as though a wildcat and a dog were wrestling over a rabbit inside him. He'd been crying, to boot. The night before, he'd cried his eyes red on his bed. Miss Daisy fluttered around him, sick with worry, finally convincing him to drink some whiskey to calm his nerves and dull his broken heart. He'd drunk a quarter of the bottle, and now the liquid was wielding an awful effect on him. Though Miss Daisy had warned him not to, and even offered to make an excuse to Mr. Hatterby, Davis had agreed to play the piano at Angel's wedding, and now was the time to rally his senses and do it.

Davis had arrived early to tune, but found he had to race to the church's outhouse. He sat in there, looking at the knots on the boards and coming close to tears again when there came steps and then a pounding on the door.

"Go away!" he said. "I'm busy here."

Someone pounded again.

"Go somewhere else," he yelled. "This one's in use by an afflicted soul!"

"This would be the church's property," someone said, "and I've got to empty my bowels in a terrible way."

Davis knew the voice. "Father Paul?"

"Yes, child," said the priest. "Davis?"

"Yes, it's me hurting in here," said Davis.

"Hurry out of there now. What are you doing here anyway? What's wrong with the outhouse at the Red Swan?"

Davis stood and wiped his bottom with a corncob from the basket. He tied up his pants and unlatched the door.

"I'm coming out, but don't say I didn't warn you to stand back," said Davis. He opened it and faced the priest. "My guts are bothering me terrible." The priest waved him out of the way and rushed in. "I've been passing awful odors all morning," Davis said.

Once inside, the priest slammed the door and yelled at Davis, "The bells are ringing, and I've got to officiate at this ceremony. Come back later."

"I'm here to play the piano and witness this union."

"You're going to get yourself killed." A fierce and unpleasant series of noises expelled from inside. "Does Thomas Lawrence know how you feel about Angel?"

"Nah, nobody does. But Mama. But you. But a coupl'a friends and some folks at the Red Swan, but I'm playing it close to my chest," said Davis. He leaned against the outhouse wall.

"Could you give me some privacy, please?" said the priest. He sighed. He blew air. He groaned and whispered, "Oh Lord."

"Sure, Father," said Davis. "I'm sorry."

"We'll talk soon, just not now," said the priest. "I understand your heart is hurting. But don't make a commotion. Thomas Lawrence could ruin you."

Davis smacked his head against the outhouse.

"I'm sorry, Davis. If it helps, I know how you feel. I loved a girl once too, believe it or not."

"Thanks, Father."

"And Davis," said the priest.

"Yes, Father," answered Davis.

"I'm sorry about this. I wish I could say something to comfort you, but the world is not yet what we wish it to be and choices for many of us are limited."

"Thanks, Father."

Midway through the ceremony, an awful smell wafted from the area near the piano and the altar and the couple kneeling before it in prayer. And though none of the guests coughed or remarked about it, Father Paul, while consecrating the Host, twitched his nose and grinned.

# 41

# Angel's Wedding

ANGEL TRIED TO FOCUS on the matter at hand, getting married, but the ether had long-lasting effects. She'd only meant to calm her nerves but perhaps had overindulged. The church spun. Father Paul's words echoed. She tried to appreciate the years of planning her mother had put into this moment. She tried to remember the names of her father's friends from all over the country who'd come to watch her wed Thomas Lawrence, who himself had a long and impressive guest list. The ether had left a thin iron scent in her nose and taste in the back of her throat. Angel looked to her right, at the stocky man with graying hair at his temples, and giggled. She hardly knew him and tonight they'd share a bed. It seemed silly. She felt woozy. Thomas Lawrence reached over and put his hand on her back to steady her. She giggled again. She knew he thought her beautiful. He had told her that many times when he courted her in the parlor. On the eve of her eighteenth birthday, he'd knelt on her mother's carpet and asked for her hand. She had picked a cat hair off his shirt and said, "Yes, thank you," just as her mother had insisted.

Angel burped softly. "Pardon me," she whispered.

Thomas Lawrence rubbed her back harder.

Her mother cleared her throat from the first row.

Angel rolled her eyes and giggled again. She rocked back on her silk slippers, ordered all the way from Paris, France, along with the gown she wore, light pink with brown trim. Angel had wanted to wear white, but her mother had said that white was garish and made her look like a corpse.

Father Paul consecrated the Host. A rotten aroma filled the church.

"Smells bad in here," Angel whispered to Thomas Lawrence. He stifled a laugh too. They looked at each other. Angel thought that he was quite handsome. But then she thought about Davis. Was she fickle? Was her heart disloyal? It was impossible anyway. Davis had to know that. She felt a little guilty, but she was excited too about Thomas Lawrence. She was proud that such a man found her desirable. She lifted the handkerchief to her nose again and sniffed. "Ohhh," she sighed.

Her mother cleared her throat again.

Angel looked over her shoulder toward the woman. "Oh stop it," Angel said, a little too loudly. Thomas Lawrence again put his hand on her back. He rubbed his thumb against her spine. She liked it. "That feels nice," she said to him.

*What feels nice?*

Angel's throat thickened. Clement.

*What feels nice?*

Angel brought the handkerchief to her nose again and breathed lightly. The ether dulled the proceedings. The priest looked thin and effervescent. The whole church seemed to be perched on a cloud. Only the hand of the man she was marrying anchored her in the here and now.

"Not now," she whispered.

*Don't do it. Don't marry him.*

Angel looked at Thomas Lawrence and smiled. He nodded at her. Angel thought of Davis and was suddenly ashamed again. "Oh," she said.

*I'm miserable too. This is wrong.* Clement pleaded with her for the entire ceremony. She ignored him.

# 42

## Beaver Jean Returns

IN JUNE OF 1858, Beaver Jean had been sitting in a San Francisco saloon, clutching a three of diamonds and a five of spades to his chest. All morning he'd been flipping cards with a man who claimed to have been a general in Santa Anna's army, a German who hardly spoke English and held a cigar with the burnt ember pointed toward his palm, and a Chinaman named Fu, who had taken Beaver Jean's buffalo blanket, best stirrups, and pemmican pouch already and was poised to annex Charlemagne if the river didn't reveal a favorable card.

Charlemagne stood outside, steady and honorable as a knight in King Arthur's court. The horse had an uppity way, but it had led Beaver Jean and his wives across many miles and through many peevish circumstances in Texas, which had been annexed by the United States, though Mexico claimed to own it. The weather there had been pleasant, but by 1848, Beaver Jean couldn't tell who was American, Texan, Mexican, or mixed breed, nor which Negro persons were free and which were slaves, nor which Indians were hostile and which were friendly, nor where the boundaries lay or what laws applied where.

Figuring out right and wrong was a complicated matter. There was plenty of work in the tracking department, but the area was flooded with bounty hunters, rangers, and people claiming to be law who were organizing posses, arresting ne'er-do-wells, and hanging them up in trees. Beaver Jean, with only Charlemagne's help, had grown too old and couldn't compete with the energetic likes of the bounty hunters of the South. For a while he looked around for Lydian. He checked out the brothels and always asked for the red-haired foxes, of which there were many, but none were ever her. He wondered, by then, if he'd recognize her when he saw her. So Beaver Jean had packed up his wives and hopped onto Charlemagne and lit out for the city of gold, where he thought that at least he could make a fortune for his son, even if he hadn't been around to rear him up right.

They had passed through the Great Salt Lake settlement, where Beaver Jean stayed for a while among those who called themselves The Saints. They lived a life pleasing to Beaver Jean in all ways except for exaggerated praying and propheting. He didn't like that and kept moving west, over mountains and through deserts, and finally arrived in California, where there was gold to discover and railroads to build. In California, Beaver Jean had made a living doing what he knew how to do best, trapping beaver.

Though for the rest of the world, beaver fur was out of fashion, for the gold prospectors and rock blasters who worked all through the cold winters, beaver fur blankets, coats, hats, and gloves were practical, warm, and durable. As quickly as Beaver Jean trapped them, his wives turned the beaver furs into every necessity a body could imagine. With some of the money, the wives, who in their own advancing age quit bickering and began to connive together in moneymaking conspiracies the likes of which Beaver Jean had not known women could plot, bought a dozen hogs and started up a pork supply to the restaurants of San Francisco. They kept themselves busy and profitable in their business affairs and made enough so that Beaver Jean could finally put his feet up for a while and let the women do the work. Each week, for his entertainments, they allotted Beaver Jean some money, which he often took to the brothels and gambling parlors, since both places were full of the world's best excitement and greatest sinners. When he ran out of money at the poker table, he'd throw down whatever was in his satchel, attached to his horse, or sitting in his cart.

Now Charlemagne was on the pot, and Beaver Jean was sweating fiercely over the matter. He knew if he lost Charlemagne, his wives would beat him silly and keep his allowance from him. Then he'd have to get back to the rivers and back to work.

"Your horse be in Fu's wok by dinnertime," said Fu. The flop had shown an eight of clubs, a ten of spades, and a jack of spades.

Together, a three and a five made the age of Beaver Jean's third wife, the little Lydian, who would practically be an old woman now. Beaver Jean promised himself that if the cards turned up favorable, he'd take Charlemagne away from here before he was slaughtered for stir-fry and get his wives out of this backward, sinful land, where women bossed men, and get back to the pure air and morality of Stillwater. Maybe after her hiding and travels, Lydian had settled down there with his boy. He'd read in the paper how Stillwater had become part of the thirty-second state in the Union: Minnesota. Beaver Jean liked that name very much and remembered hearing it a long time ago. He was quick to correct all the European foreigners who couldn't pronounce it properly, especially the big German sitting across from him, grinning confidently and holding his cards in his fat sausage fingers.

"Not Minneee-sota," Beaver Jean would say, "Minnesota, is the right way." He'd point to his mouth as he pronounced the name. "No, not Minesoooota. Minnesota." And "Not Mine-sota, like a gold mine. Minnesota."

"Why you still talking about new state Minnesota?" asked Fu. "Play cards, you something bitch."

"Son of a bitch, is the right pronunciation," said Beaver Jean.

The turn had shown a six of spades.

The general from Santa Anna's army went out. The German too. Fu went all in.

"What about you, Beaver Jean? What you do? You fold like scared whore?" said Fu.

"I have my only horse in the pot and now I shall throw in a fine wife as well. She is fair and good-natured and thrifty. I intend to win this hand."

The general from Santa Anna's army said, "Well, we may as well see them." He opened his hands and bid Beaver Jean and Fu to show their cards. Fu flipped over his hand, the king of hearts and the ace of clubs.

"I put your wife on a boat to Shanghai before the day is done. She bring good price."

Beaver Jean's stomach pitched. He put down his cards, his three of diamonds and five of spades.

Then the general dealt the river. The queen of spades stared up the men. There was a pause. And each man sat thinking about implications.

"The dirty bitch queen of spades?" said Fu. "You joking me!"

"Flush beats a straight, Fu," said the general.

Beaver Jean, with his purse full of Fu's money, decided to head home.


After two and a half years of walking eastward, through California, Utah Territory, Kansas Territory, Nebraska Territory, the unorganized Dakota Territory, and finally into Minnesota, Beaver Jean and his wives arrived, once again, in Stillwater, now part of Minnesota. They looked around and around. Beaver Jean wondered what in the hell had happened to the town he'd left behind. Had he really been gone so long a time? Long enough to see all the trees come down? The buildings go up? Who were all these white people? Where did they come from? How was it that soaps and candles and kettles and pepper could be so abundantly available? Who had started up the newspaper? Who was it the newspaper was talking about? Where were the trappers such as himself? Where were the old army men? The old Indian chiefs? The stiff religious types? Beaver Jean stood in the middle of the thoroughfare and turned around and around, looking up at the buildings scratching the sky, out across the water cut up with riverboats, down the streets thick with mud and horse dung and ox manure.

"You better move away from there if you don't want to get trampled by a stagecoach," said a young man with a downcast countenance. Next to him walked a Negro man with a lively gait.

"Thank ye for yer counsel, young'un," Beaver Jean shouted after him. The young men turned around. They stood against the sunset and looked like shadows against the orange horizon. "Ye know anyone to be hiring an elder like myself?" Beaver Jean asked the men.

The Negro shouted back, "It's either get labored by St. Croix Valley Lumbering, seek employment at the prison, which has had some troublesome times, or join the army, which is what these sad fools is off to do." Then they turned around again and began walking away.

"Watch yer backsides, boys," said Beaver Jean. "I been down into the Kansas Territory, and I'd steer clear of that away if I were ye, especially ye darker-raced friend. There's some mighty rascally devils down there intent upon making a big war. I'd also steer ye clear of the southlands of this place they now are calling Minnesota and the lands directly west of here, which we trappers used to call the Dakotas, but I don't know what the name for that area is now. All in them lands, the Indians are mighty unsettled and dissatisfied with their treatment by this state and government, so's ye best watch yer backs and maybe reconsider yer intentions and get back home to yer mamas before ye get shot or scalped."

"Worry about yourself, old-timer," shouted the white man. "I'm off to get outfitted with a gun and find glory and purpose. I am off in the tradition of all great men to fight other men! Hurrah!" His voice was mocking.

"And I'm off to keep him from getting his head shot off," said the Negro.

"Suit yerselves," said Beaver Jean, "and thank ye for yer advisement again."

The young men had been swallowed up by the people and traffic of the street. Beaver Jean's spine itched beneath the skin, as though responding to dry lightning. He felt a faint desire to remember this moment and keep it. He thought to review it later. He looked around at the sights and sounds for later consideration. He noted his boots. He thought about the lost toes. He listened for the crunch of gravel beneath his feet. He felt a quick shadow pass over him. When he looked up, he watched an enormous swan glide overhead and dive toward the water. That was a thing easy to remember, he thought.

Then Beaver Jean walked to the prison and introduced himself as a trapper and a human tracker, occupations that interested the warden.

# 43

## Clement and Davis Enlist

Now AND THEN, when he could take the silence no more, Clement would go to the Thomas Lawrence mansion, Angel's mansion, and stand outside, under cover of the few tall, full trees that remained. He had to be near her. Her presence felt vital to him. Sometimes she saw him standing there and motioned for him to go to the back, where she'd be friendly and polite, but dismissive too, as though she wanted him to leave.

"We're getting too old for this, Clement," she'd said. "Someone's going to see us."

"Too old for what?" he'd asked. "Who cares who sees us?"

"I've got a family now," she said. She looked toward the house. She rubbed her belly. "I'm expecting."

"Expecting what?" Clement asked.

She laughed at him and raised her eyebrows. "A baby."

"What?" he said. He took her all in and tried to see if she looked different. Yes. She was fuller. And rounder. And not quite as pale. She was changing. She was leaving him behind. "Oh. That's wonderful." Clement's stomach dropped. His throat thickened. "Can I come in? It's cold, and I know Thomas is up north."

Her eyebrows came down and her cheek muscles pinched. "I don't think that's a good idea."

His heart quickened. "Why?" he said, his voice high and demanding. "Why not?" He went on about how they were finally adults, how she was finally out from under the thumb of that crazy woman, how she was free to make her own decisions about who she did and did not want to be with. "Unless you don't want me," he said.

"Clement," she said. "Life goes on. I'm married now."

"To him?" He scoffed. "He's hardly even here! He's off smashing down the continent."

"He's working for his family, and he's building a country."

"Give me a break. Would you say that to Davis, if he was here?"

"Shut your mouth, Clement."

"Or wait. Maybe he is here? Is he inside? Is that why I can't come in?" Clement feigned looking in all the windows of the big house. "I've heard rumors. Everyone talks about you in this town. I even heard you're a witch. I wonder how that got started."

"Stay away from me," she said. She left him standing there in the dark with his questions.

Clement convinced Davis to volunteer with him for the war, which was easy as soon as Clement told him that Angel was with child. They went to the courthouse in Stillwater to sign on with the Stillwater Guard of the First Minnesota. The men there had given Clement a gun and Davis a bugle and ladle. "No guns for Negroes," they said. "Direct orders from the president." From training at Fort Snelling through the trip to Washington, D.C., Clement and Davis stuck together. They met men from the logging camps of the northern woods, men from the Great Lakes area, men who farmed in the south, a couple of short-haired Indians from the reservation, and others who were schoolteachers, carpenters, railroad workers, newspaper writers, husbands, and fathers.

"You look mighty baby-faced to be going to war, son," said a mustachioed fellow on the train. "You sure your mama knows where you are?"

"I've got no mother," said Clement. "She abandoned my sister and me when we were just born. I was left in an orphanage with lots of other children, a lot of sick people, and a nun and an Indian woman. My sister got raised in a rich family but they didn't want me, so I . . ."

Davis giggled. "We all got stories, Clem," he said. He put out his hand to shake the hand of the mustachioed man. "My name's Davis, and this is Clement, and we're off to kill some rebels and find some excitement. What about you?"

"I'm an expert war veteran," said the man. "Sick of farming, mostly. Get sick of it every time I don't have a war to go to." He knelt. "Don't know many Negro men heading south. You got a death wish?"

"Can't have the girl I love," said Davis, "so I may as well go get myself killed." He smiled and elbowed Clement.

"What's your station?" the man asked.

Davis pulled the bugle from his bag. "I can't even play this thing." He turned it one way, then the other. He pretended to blow into the wrong end. He perched it on his head as a hat.

Clement laughed.

"Then why'd you take it on?" asked the mustachioed man. He pulled some bison jerky from his pack and handed Davis and Clement a strip.

"It's the only way they'd let me come along," Davis told him. "This, and act the cook. But I can't cook either."

"You must be crazy to want to come to war," the man said. "But I'm crazy too. I been on the Texas side against the Spanish, then on the Texas side against Mexico. One of these days Texas will want to fight the United States too. That's how them Texans are. I don't read the papers. Did Texas pick a side in this national argument yet? I'll bet my life it's on the rebellious side for sure. Those Texans are some combatsome individuals." He used his teeth to peel a strip of meat, and talked and chewed at the same time.

His mustache danced like a broom. "But I learned an iron gut on all those campaigns and can eat practically anything that's been grown or killed." They talked on and on, all the days it took to get from Minnesota to the East. Clement and Davis both liked the mustachioed man and hoped to stick with him.

War wasn't as glorious as Clement hoped it might be. Rather than fighting Confederates, Clement spent half his time drilling and the other half protecting Davis from the wrath of their own First Minnesota company boys who directed all their grumblings toward Davis. They were dissatisfied with both his work as the company cook and the company bugle-player. They accused him of softening boot leather and serving it. They accused him of cooking muskrat and opossum meat and passing it off as beef and pork. They accused him of making broth with tree bark and mud and making dumplings from bacon grease and sawdust. One soldier said he found a human tooth in his stew and charged at Davis with the butt of his gun before Clement stepped in and calmed him down, telling him, "It's only a kernel of dehydrated corn," though it really was a human tooth. Although some of deeds and deficiencies the soldiers complained about were true, Davis couldn't help it. The Union food stores were totally depleted, and deliveries over the muddy roads from the bowels of the bureaucratic beast that was Washington, D.C., were sparse and unreliable. Davis feared for his life every time he served up a meal. Along with those three fearsome moments, Davis also feared for his life every time he was ordered to sound the bugle for drills. The men would emerge from their tents with scowling mouths and would threaten to do violent things upon him, in some cases with the very bugle he blew. The regiment had many reasons to feel frustrated, and since it wasn't possible to vent those frustrations on the weather, the leaky tents, the ruts and gullies, the maggoty food, the long marches, the lonely nights, the weeks without mail, the army, the secessionists, the commanders, or the president, they took it out on Davis.

Here away from home, Clement had grown to depend upon Davis's friendship. He was a funny fellow with good stories about life in a whorehouse and gossip about people they both knew back in Stillwater. To be near Davis was the closest thing to home that Clement had, which made Clement protective of him.

Against the insults and threats, Davis tried to be brave and understanding and sometimes even make a joke of them. Clement had hardly ever heard the kinds of sentiments that were now directed at Davis from soldiers on their own side. He felt especially bad because he'd been the one to convince Davis to come along for the adventure and glory that war was sure to bring. Also, it'd keep both of them from having to make a living in the employment of Thomas Lawrence, a thing neither wanted to do but both might have to do if they stayed in Stillwater.

But Clement's plans for making money weren't coming to fruition just yet. The Union had a terrible time getting their boys paid on time. For all the effort the government had taken in encouraging boys to sign on, it didn't seem well prepared to have them. None had a proper uniform to wear. Some women back home got together and sewed proper coats and sturdy pants that had a standard look to them, but not every soldier received them. Clement got one of those coats, but he could hardly convince himself to put it on, for fear he might wear it out. Instead, he put it under his head at night and before the lamps went out would stare at the stitch work and try to imagine the woman who so carefully had pulled and drawn the thread through the cloth. He still wore the pants Big Waters had made him years ago, which now had a hole in one knee, rode a half inch above the tops of his boots, and were nearly worn through in the backside, but he was very fond of them. They made him wish that he had been better to Big Waters. His time away convinced him that family was indeed the most important thing in the world, and eventually he intended to go home and convince Angel of the same.

Finally, in June of 1861, a partial payment of thirty dollars came, which was more than Clement or Davis had ever earned in their lives, so they decided to take a walk and see what they could find among the commodities of the local farm wives.

"I saw a boy come back with a big hack of juicy pork tucked between soft bread," said Davis. "I'd like to find that woman and buy some of that off her."

"Yeah," said Clement. "That sounds good." They smelled the air, warm and fragrant with apples and peaches. They came upon a yellow farmhouse with a big white veranda. Pies sat on a table, cooling. A sign that read PIE, 50 CENTS hung above them. An old Negro man sat shelling peas in the corner of the veranda. He lifted his head and turned his ear toward their footsteps.

"I hears you comin'," he yelled. "Come on up and buy a pie from my mistress."

"We're coming," Davis shouted back to him. "But we were looking for a bit of pork."

"Dat all gone now," said the old man. "You too late. Got pie."

"He looks a hundred years old," Davis said to Clement.

"Yes, sonny," said the man. "I am a century and seven years old. You will like this'm pie." The man's eyes were glazed over and his sparse hair was metallic silver. Then a young white woman came to the door.

"Who you talking to, Mose?" she asked.

"Can't see 'em, but I 'spect some young Yanks," he said.

She wiped her hands on her apron and waved for Clement and Davis to come up the steps.

"You want a pie?" she asked Clement. She was yellow-haired, with tan skin and freckles on her nose. She spoke with what they called the Virginia croon.

"We'll each have one," Clement said. He tried to think of ways to get her to talk more. The long vowels and softness on the consonants pleased him. "If you're selling."

"I'll sell you one," she said, "but I can't sell one to him." She nodded at Davis but didn't look at him.

"I'll buy two then," said Clement. He talked quick, before Davis could question her motivations and ruin their chance at something sweet to eat. He pulled the money out of a small bag. "But you ought to be a little friendlier, especially if you're charging fifty cents for a pie."

"I'm friendly enough," she said. She took the money, looked at it to make sure it wasn't Confederate, Clement supposed, and put it in her apron pocket. "I'll sell you two. What you do with the second, I don't have to know, and you don't have to tell my husband. And you better mind your manners or the price will go up to three dollars a pie." She trained her eyes, greenish brown, brightly at him and raised her pale eyebrows.

"Don' mind her," said Mose. "She barks but don' bite hard."

"I can agree to those terms," said Clement. He looked at Davis, who nodded. "I'll take two peach, if you have them."

"I have them," she said. She turned away from him and toward the pies. She used her apron to pick them up. "What's the matter with your eyes, Yankee?"

"Peach pie was a favorite of General Washington," Mose interrupted. "My mama was a nigger in his house, which is the God's hones' truth of the matter."

"Shush now, Mose, with your stories," said the woman. "You'll exhaust yourself talking." She brought the two pies back to Clement and shrugged her shoulders. "He's been saying that since I was small. I don't know. It's possible, maybe. These're hot on the bottom."

"God's hones' truth of the matter," whispered Mose.

"Huh," said Clement. "I was born with eyes like this." He took one pie by the rim and handed it to Davis. He took the other for himself.

"They're pretty, your eyes," she said. "Unusual. You boys come return my pie tins when you're done. And come back tomorrow if you want more pie." She fixed a strand of hair behind her ear. Clement was mesmerized by this simple gesture. He thought about how long it had been since he'd really looked at a woman besides Angel. He wondered if he had ever noticed another woman besides Angel.

"Tomorrow," she said, "I'll have biscuits and chicken too, and maybe some fried fish, if Mose can catch something instead of talking and scaring them all away."

"Thank you, ma'am," said Clement. He felt brave. He stared at her some more. She looked warm, as if she'd been standing in the sun. She looked full of health. Her yellow hair spun around in curls, softly, wildly, free from the bun she must have twisted up this morning. Clement couldn't help but compare her to Angel, with her pale skin and dark hair. He'd not thought before that women could be beautiful in different ways, but beautiful still. "What's your name?"

"Mrs. Milton," she said. "June."

"That's a beautiful name," said Clement. "Where's your husband, if you don't mind my asking?"

"That is none of your business," she said sharply, but in fun too. She put her fists on her hips.

Mose mumbled.

"Quiet, Mose," she scolded. "You boys don't belong here. Get yourselves home as quick as you can. Bad days are ahead, I'll assure you that. This ain't going to be no quick war like they say." Then she told Clement and Davis to get off her porch so she could get back to her cooking.

Clement and Davis stepped down the creaky stairs.

"Bye, now," Mose cried after them. "'Specially you, young nigger. God bless your work in this world. I hope it turn out all for the bes'."

"Thank you, Mose," said Davis. Davis walked with Clement,

but he turned around again and again to look at the man on the veranda.

The men walked about a half mile and settled against a fence post to eat their pies. They were afraid that if they brought them back to camp, they'd have to share.

"You believe that old man?" asked Davis. "Over a hundred years old?"

"I don't know," said Clement. "Doesn't seem possible."

"Hmm," said Davis. "Was he a slave or just working for that woman?"

"Don't know," said Clement. "She was a handsome woman, wasn't she? Hard to believe she'd side with the rebels, but she sounded mighty rebellious to me."

Davis scratched his ear. "Though they don't say it, I expect lots of these locals side with the rebels," said Davis. "General Lee is from just across the river, and he took up with the rebels readily enough."

"That's true," said Clement. "I wish he'd have stayed on our side."

"Me too," said Davis. He swatted a moth fluttering near his head. "One thing I like about Maryland over Minnesota is that there aren't so many mosquitoes here."

"I've been thinking about that too," said Clement. "Why do you think we have so many in Minnesota?"

"Don't know. Probably has to do with all the lakes, the standing water."

"You're probably right," said Clement. "Still waters are good breeding places for all kinds of things. Even mosquitoes."

"They're pesky," said Davis.

"But the frogs like to eat them," said Clement. "And the fish like to eat the frogs. And I like to eat the fish. So, I'll stand 'em."

"You sure got a way with words," said Davis. "You thinking about talking that woman out of her skirts?"

"No, but I'm sure it's crossed your wicked mind," said Clement.

"Nope," he said. "I didn't like her disposition. You gonna eat all that pie?"

"No," said Clement. "My stomach's a little queasy. You can have the rest."

"You're a good friend to have in this war, Clement Piety. Don't let anyone tell you different."

That night, Clement and Davis both came down with a terrible stomach ailment, which rendered them so weak and dehydrated over the next few days that both were sent to a Union hospital to recover. At first, they wondered whether the blond woman had poisoned them, and then they wondered why. Had she been trying to help the rebels, or had she been trying to keep them safe from the big battles? But soon other members of their regiment came down with the same symptoms. There they stayed for weeks, as the healthy members of their regiment prepared and suffered through their first real battle, at Bull Run. Missing out on the first serious action of the war pained them and the others from their company who were sick. Most of them blamed Davis's cooking, though more than likely the ailment had been picked up from civilians and then spread through the regiment's tight quarters, where boys from the isolated farmlands of southern and western Minnesota, who'd hardly been exposed to a cold in their lives and so had never had opportunity to grow impervious to the various diseases, now slept mere feet from their sick neighbors.

"I'm gonna cut your balls off, nigger," said a soldier, a Swede from southern Minnesota who'd been throwing up and shitting for days, to Davis. Between puking and sitting on the pail, Clement could hardly keep from laughing at the man's lilting accent.

Davis tooted out a couple of notes on his bugle and grinned at Clement.

"You settle down, you big oaf," Clement said to the complainer. "He can't help it the Union sends him that tack to prepare. Save your money and buy yourself some of that fiskbullar you're always blathering about."

"I got no money!" shouted the soldier. He made heaving noises, but nothing more came up. "I'm gonna make you eat that horn the next time you think to blow on it."

"You're healing now," said Clement. "And Davis's poisonous food probably saved you from certain death at Bull Run. You'd ruther be one of those boys with a leg or head blown off?" Davis's horn playing was an assault to anyone with ears, but it was amusing, at least.

All the boys in the hospital ruminated over the slaughter at Bull Run and the terrible casualties among the First Minnesota Regiment. It was hard to believe that after months of random, almost playful fire with the Confederates, that real war had finally befallen them. The guilt of missing the battle while so many others paid with their limbs and lives affected Clement's sleep, and surely the sleep of the others, and their mood grew sour and caused them to question all things of big purpose: why were they here, why had they been spared, who was to blame, when would the next battle come?

# 44

## Gut-Shot

CLEMENT AND DAVIS LAY among the sick and the
wounded. And they'd seen friends die. When the wounded
first came in, those who could jumped from their beds and aided
the overwhelmed doctor. Among the first was the mustachioed
man they both remembered from the train ride east.

He'd taken a minié ball to the gut in the battle where the First
Minnesota, led by a confused commander, was ordered to sit and
wait to fire while a Virginia company took up position against
them and fired upon them. Though the Minnesotans were brave
and held for a time, the day's battle went to the South, as the Minnesotans, along with the other Union regiments, retreated. When
the scene calmed down, the mustachioed man was gathered up
and carried by horse to the hospital. He had ripped his shirt and
pants away from his body already. His whole right side was bloody.

"Oh hellfire, man," the surgeon said. "Didn't anyone tell you not
to get gut-shot! Goddammit. There's not a thing I can do for your
life."

"It's not my gut," said the mustachioed man, his voice high and
unnatural. "It's my hip, isn't it?"

"Let me look closer," said the doctor. He leaned in as the man
tried to lie still, pushing his head back into the mattress and grip-

ping the sides of it. "I see your point, but to me this wound looks closer to the gut than the hip. But, yes, there's a good amount of damage to the hip too. But by my judgment, you are definitely ruined, sir."

Clement and Davis went to him and watched. The wound was the size of a hand and shaped that way too, as though there were a palm and then fingers spreading out on the flank of the man. The ball had clipped the hipbone, which stuck out of the wound, and other pieces of the man that ought to be inside the torso were spilling out.

"Damn!" said the doctor. He arranged his spectacles closer to his eyes. He pointed with a metal instrument at the slimy innards. "This is part of your intestines, son. And this looks to be your pancreas or liver, maybe. You can't live without either of those! Oh damn you. You're a goner."

"Can't you put it back in?" said the man in high desperation. "Can't you try?"

"Oh son. My heart hurts every night over ones like you. Kinds like you have impaired my Christian beliefs and doomed me to hell, I'm afraid."

The doctor pulled a blanket up over the mustachioed man's torso. Then he pulled a brown bottle and cloth from his pocket. He dabbed the cloth with the liquid in the bottle and put the cloth over the man's mouth and nose. The man stopped pressing into the mattress and calmed.

The doctor turned to Clement and Davis.

"You friends of him?" he asked. He looked at them over his spectacles. His eyebrows were like wild weeds.

"Yes, sir," they said. "We rode over with him on the train."

"Talk to him. Keep him comfortable. He's got an hour or so."

The mustachioed man moaned a deep but soft noise. "I wish I'da stayed on the farm," he whispered. "Write my ma I'm sorry."

Davis went to a corner and puked in a pail.

Clement held the man's hand and talked to him. "I'll tell her," said Clement.

The man squeezed Clement's hand.

"I always like Minnesota the best of all the states there is," Clement went on. He remembered how Mother St. John talked soothingly to sick children or the impaired or the injured or the old. He spoke that way now to the man as his breath slowed. "It's got the prettiest sky and blackest soil where all good things can grow. The trees are the straightest and sturdiest and make the best wood for strong houses and rocking chairs."

"Keep talking, friend," the man whispered.

"On Saturdays, all the mothers wash the children's nappies and hang them on strings swung between trees to dry in the breeze, which smells like lilacs in spring and fried walleye in summer."

"Yes, walleye," said the man. He laughed a bit, but fierce coughing overtook him. When the man calmed, Clement said, "In fall, the giant trees turn the colors of all the metals you can imagine and drop onto the surface of the shimmering lakes."

The man licked his lips. Clement signaled for Davis to get a ladle of water. Davis did, and they both helped the man have a drink.

"Talk some of the ladies," the man said after he'd been quenched.

Clement thought for a few seconds. First, Angel came to mind, of course. Followed by Mother St. John, and then, strangely, he thought of Big Waters.

Davis pointed to the man's wound, where the water he had drunk now came out in a dark pink gush. Clement pulled a handkerchief from his pocket and sopped it up.

"They got the freshest breath because the Minnesota air is the healthiest there is in the world. The winter freeze kills everything bad which could ever hurt a body. In the spring, the ladies emerge from their winter cocoons with bright and clear eyes, wearing dresses like flower petals." Clement thought some more. "All of them tend their little babies in the way the loveliest mother, the Virgin Mary who sits now in heaven waiting to draw all children to her bosom, taught them to do with her example. The Minnesota ladies got the virtue of saints and voices like angels when they sing."

The man's eyes were closed, and he was very still. Clement wondered if he was dead already. But then the mustachioed man said, "That's right. I think I can go now. I can hear them already." He paused. "I hear singing." Then his muscles relaxed; the strain was over.

"God bless you," Clement said. He extended his hand and made the sign of the cross over the man's chest. "Mother Mary, lead him to your Son." Then Clement crossed himself and sat quietly with the dead man for a few minutes. He felt Davis's hand on his shoulder.

"Where'd you learn to talk like that?" Davis said softly. "You spoke real nice to that man and sent him to his death happy."

Davis and Clement spent several more weeks tending the sick and the dying and the recovering. Often, Davis would remark that he felt like a coward now, seeing what the men had endured while he'd been on a hospital bed with a stomachache.

"Some of these men are fighting on my behalf," he told Clement.

Clement dabbed the forehead of a soldier who'd lost his hand to amputation and would have to endure another, to at least his elbow, the way the gangrene looked to be spreading. "What do you mean, 'on your behalf'?"

"For my people," said Davis. "The Negro race."

"Your people?" asked Clement. "Since when? I never heard you talk about being a Negro before." Clement dipped a washcloth into a bucket of water and twisted it. The water ran pink. He didn't feel angry toward Davis. Clement was only curious at his friend's new perspective. In the past, Davis's indifferent attitude toward his own race had bothered Clement some, though he wasn't proud of that fact and now knew that he had often held Davis's race as a wedge between Angel and him. But since they'd first boarded that train, Davis had become dearer to him than practically anyone else on earth. Though Clement had written dozens of letters to Angel, he hadn't received a single one in return. Though she'd sent small trinkets to Big Waters to include in packages to Clement, she had not penned one kind or encouraging word to him. Now he turned to the people he could depend upon. Here, that person was Davis, his true friend. Clement would have laid down his own life for Davis, as a brother might do.

"Can you find some clean water?" Clement asked him.

"All the water looks that rosy color. Even the drinking barrels," said Davis. "We all been drinking the blood of our regiment brothers." Davis sighed. He reached down and closed the eyes of a dead man. "I'm changed. Something's changed in me." He pulled a blanket up over the man's face; his feet remained exposed. "Can't they even provide us with blankets long enough? All these men fighting and dying. Really dying, and for what? They must have reasons. Why have I never before had a purpose that I would risk my life for? How have I gone nearly twenty-five years without one?"

Clement had been asking himself the same questions. If he was going to be here, fighting, what was he going to be fighting for? "Probably some of these men are fighting for personal splendor," he said. "Maybe some of them to preserve the Union. But not too many are fighting for Negroes, I don't think. Not the Minnesotans anyway. We don't have so many raising those issues in our state."

Davis came to the bed and sat between Clement and the patient he was tending.

"You talk like you know something about it," said Davis. His eyes narrowed to slits, the way they used to when he asked about Angel. A nervous look, but serious too.

"If our statesmen have abolition on their minds, the wise ones work at it quietly and under the cover of dark," said Clement. "Just what I read."

"Yeah," said Davis. "Me too. Just what I read."

The two men looked at each other. Clement stared in a way that urged Davis to be quiet. His eyes, those strangely colored orbs, looked hard at his friend. Even here, among Yankee comrades, they both had heard disloyal sentiments voiced. Some boys from an Illinois regiment had said that if President Lincoln freed the slaves or armed a free Negro, they'd defect and join the Confederacy. An Irish man from New York had told Davis that if the opportunity presented itself, he'd sell Davis to a Southern plantation owner without a second look. It was not safe to assume that all Northerners were abolitionists. Even the president seemed unsure as to whether he supported emancipation of the slaves. He had said that if he could free all the slaves and preserve the Union, he would do it, and if he could not free one slave and preserve the Union, he would do that too. Most of the soldiers supported the Union. They did not know, personally or publicly, how to feel about the slave question.

"Well," said Davis. "I guess some things just remain mysterious."

"You got that right," said Clement.

"I'm glad I came here with you, Clement. I have learned something about the world and about myself, and I intend to live my life better, for as long as it lasts."

"The best thing you can do is live and avoid the fighting," said Clement. "You've got the music talent, which is a gift from God, and you ought to take care of it by not getting your hands shot off."

"I don't think I will," said Davis. "My eyes have been opened. I feel a larger purpose now. These men dying for honor or Union or emancipation or whatever they're dying for have moved me. I feel different."

Clement felt different too. Though he still missed her and wished she'd write, Clement hadn't thought of Angel nearly so much while he'd been among the sick, injured, and dying. His hands and mind were doing the good work of healing bodies and preparing souls. Despite all the gore and pain around him, he swelled with a sense of goodness. But he wanted more glory, recognition. He wanted to go home a man and restore faith in family and home.

"I keep thinking about how you talk to those dying men," said Davis. "Not everybody has those words of comfort in their head. You got the mouthpiece of a priest. That could be your purpose, if you could stand the lifelong chastity."

"Maybe," said Clement.

"There's honor in small everyday goodnesses too," said Davis. "You don't have to get killed to be a hero."

The company marched toward the Potomac River to protect a landing near Edward's Ferry along an important supply line. There they found a pleasant pastoral respite, albeit a lot more waiting. Since they now knew how difficult and deadly the battles would be, they couldn't understand why their army just didn't get after the rebels. Waiting for the next battle was the hardest part. Though the weather was warm, the winds were sweet, and the victuals were more regular and better tasting, each man was encumbered by what lay ahead. Here at Edward's Ferry, they could see and even shout to the Confederates across the river, but aside from a small skirmish or two, no one caused any trouble. Once in a while, a Confederate might shoot across the river, but the bullets dropped into the water halfway across.

Davis and Clement sat under a tree, sharing a cup of good, strong coffee as Clement wrote a letter to the editor of the newspaper back home. Clement's gun lay across his lap, as he was also on guard duty, watching the harmless rebels on the other side of the river.

"See 'em?" Clement asked. He nodded across the river.

"Yeah, I see 'em," said Davis. "They look small."

"I read their soldiers are an average of ten pounds lighter and one inch smaller than us Yankees."

"I believe it. On average. You're about that small, though."

"That's just because I was sick in the hospital for so long."

"You didn't lose any inches of height in that illness. You're as short as you ever were."

"Well, you're as dumb as you ever were," said Clement.

"Just let me hold it," Davis pleaded. He scootched closer to Clement and tugged on the butt of his gun. He kicked his bugle. "I'll let you toot my horn."

"No," said Clement. "Quit asking." He bent over his paper and wrote intently.

"Read it to me," said Davis. "Read me what you got so far. I wish I could read better, but I didn't pay very good attention at school."

"You were too busy with piano playing and looking at Angel," said Clement. "All right. Here's what I got so far." Clement cleared his throat. "Ladies of the North, heed my request!"

"Yeah," said Davis. "I like that. Talking to the ladies. They's the only ones that think about us from back home."

"Your boys wounded while fighting in the South are in desperate need of blankets, pillows, and tin cups. Search your cheery houses high and low for any home comfort that can be spared! Wonder whether your children couldn't drink from one cup and contribute the others for the parched lips of a First Minnesota boy, another mother's son, who has lived without a roof over his head for nearly a year, has used his own cupped hands to drink from rivers running red with blood, has endured the knife, bullet, and bayonet of the enemy, and now lies in wait for recovery or death and only desires a cup to drink from!"

"Things have been sorry around here, but I haven't seen no rivers running red," said Davis, "but you surely have a storytelling way about your writing."

"Unpack your needles and thread and sew together scraps of coffee sacks, aprons, petticoats, and the baby's dresses for blankets or little cushions for the weary heads and pained limbs of the injured!"

"Yes, I surely would like a pillow," said Davis. "Keep reading."

"And do not let one lemon or lime wedge or bit of salt flavor your food until you have considered the festering wounds and hacked stumps of soldiers in desperate need of their sanitizing qualities, which will drive the rebel infection into retreat. Every bit of lemon, lime, and salt you can spare is needed to save lives now!"

"For what?" asked Davis. "What do we want that stuff for?"

"Cleaning wounds, I think," said Clement. "So they don't get infected. I don't know. I heard some doctor talking about it."

"Tell them to send a lemon cake instead," said Davis. Clement folded the letter. "Who you gonna send that to?" asked Davis.

"Probably Mother St. John," said Clement. "She'll take it to the newspaper." He stood. "I'm going to get it mailed."

Davis put his hand on the butt of Clement's gun. "I'll hang on to that rifle while you're gone."

"No."

"I'll give you first pick of food."

"That tack is beyond mastication. Disgusting. No."

"You don't even use it."

"I'm gonna blast a hole in you if you don't quit asking me."

Clement jabbed him with the barrel and smiled. Davis feigned taking a shot in the gut and lolled his tongue and fell over.

· · ·

A couple of days later, the captain ordered the men into the river for baths. He said they stunk like hell and that their mothers would die of humiliation if they caught one whiff of the stench. He stood on top of the hill and watched as the First Minnesota and Davis stripped to their underwear, if they had any, and waded in. The water felt good yet wasn't cold. On the other side, Confederates shouted over at them, "We'd shoot your fishing tackle off but we can't see it!" and "That ass is as nice a bull's-eye as any!" They shot a couple of harmless bullets that dropped into the water no harder than a thrown pebble. Clement, a good swimmer, stroked around and dove beneath the surface. He pulled Davis's feet out from under him. Davis went under, and they emerged at the same time.

Davis sputtered. He gasped. "Don't do that!" he yelled. He splashed at Clement.

Clement laughed and splashed him back.

Davis rushed forward and pushed Clement. "I'm serious," he said. He looked around as if to see whether anyone else was listening. "I can't swim."

"What're you talking about?" Clement wiped his eyes and tilted his head to get the water out of his ear. "Everyone can swim."

Davis began making toward the shore, but the captain yelled for him to get back out there, that he could smell the stink on him from up there, that any Confederate from here to Mississippi would know he was coming by the smell of his dangle. All the men laughed. The water boiled with their feverish cleansing and horseplay. Then the big Swede lunged toward Davis and dunked him. Clement was about to tell the galoot to lay off, that it was enough, when the giant lifted Davis out the water and tossed him out to where the current ran faster, where the river was deeper. Davis splashed in, and never rose.

Clement swam out to search. He kept expecting to see Davis's head appear here and then there, this second and then the next. Clement dove deep. He was a good swimmer, but the river was full of downed trees and pieces of sunken pontoon bridge. He mean-dered among them, but he saw not one sign of his friend. He came up for air. The rest of the company stood where they had been, watching. Clement wondered if they and Davis were playing a trick on him. But he saw no smirks or twinkly eyes. Their faces looked solemn, as though they were holding their breath.

"Help me!" Clement finally said to them. "He can't swim!"

The men looked around, and a few of them dove under the water too. But there was no sign of Davis. Even when the captain ordered the company out of the water, even after they all ran up and down the shore looking for Davis, thinking he might have landed somewhere down the shore, even after the Confederates who had lazily shot at them helped by searching their side of the river for the cook and everyone came up empty, even then Clement couldn't believe it. He couldn't grasp how a person could be there one second and gone the next.

But he was. As though he'd been sucked into a hole, Davis was gone.

That night, Clement had a dream. In it, Angel was talking to him, crying. She moaned that she couldn't endure it, wondered when it would end, and prayed for the Lord to take her life.

"Angel, are you dying?" he'd said.

A scream. A pant. *No.* A breath. *I'm living.*

Then he heard the squall of an infant and the happy sigh of relief of a new mother.

"Are you there?" he'd said. But there was no answer.

# 45

## Letters from Home

CLEMENT AND THE REST of his regiment wintered at Camp Stone through the remainder of 1861. He wrote many letters home, to Big Waters and Mother St. John, to the newspaper, to Angel. He told her of Davis's death. Still, he received nothing from her. In the spring, the regiment moved to Camp Winfield Scott, near Yorktown, and Clement received a package containing a blanket, a warm shirt, socks, a rosary, and applesauce from Big Waters and Mother St. John. Clement felt, sometimes, that packages and letters from the women were the only thing keeping him alive. He wrote them his thanks, telling them of the impending fights the First Minnesota was promised to see.

In the letters that followed, his words grew morose and pointedly hopeless, a response to both the deteriorating circumstances of the war and the loss of his friend. "I miss him each day," he wrote, "and often think I would eat opossum meat every day if it was Davis that made it." His next letter told of the indecently buried bodies on Malvern Hill, how some of the men's legs, arms, and even heads were left uncovered. Some hadn't even been buried at all, left with their bellies wide open as their ribs "grinned like mad teeth." He told of the four bald eagles he'd seen near the Chickahominy River, a scene that reminded him of home until he got closer and saw that they were scavenging the corpse of a white-haired Negro man in Union dress, who reminded Clement of a man they'd helped many years before, though he couldn't recall the name of that man.

In their letters, the women wrote of the Stillwater mayor's adulterous affair with the wife of Stillwater Prison's warden, the fish the children had pulled out of the waters, the rainless summer, the poor harvest, the persistent clashes between hungry Indians and new settlers in the southern parts of the state. They wrote of the fear that all the citizens had for the safety of their soldiers and for themselves. The women always reminded him to say his prayers.

Clement wondered if some of the regiment ought to have stayed home to manage affairs in Minnesota. Finally, in August, the First Minnesota was ordered back toward Bull Run, where Major General Pope was in need of reinforcements. Some of the men were eager to have another shot at Bull Run, to reverse the outcome of the first battle. But by the time the soldiers arrived, Pope was in full, humiliating retreat. The president dismissed him and sent him west, to Minnesota, to manage the conflict between Indians and settlers, which had already killed five hundred. Upon hearing such news, Clement typically would have felt concern for the safety of the orphanage and also Angel, but this time he could only think, "I can go home. If a general is going, I can go too." He couldn't explain why, but until now Clement had thought that an impermeable barrier existed between Virginia and Minnesota, between soldier life and civilian life, as though a sky-high brick wall or hell-deep ditch separated them. But with the general's departure, those ideas fell away. He realized it was physically possible to get from here to there. Clement realized that he too could simply walk away from the war and go home.

He could just begin heading west. He could do it. He counted up how many miles he had marched since he'd been away. Surely as many as it would take to go home. To return to what was left of the trees he loved, the rivers and lakes he fished, the home he craved, the mothers who tended him best, the warm room, the soft bed, back to Angel, his own sister. He promised himself to fight one more battle. He would volunteer for perilous duties and fight bravely, and if he lived through it, he would earn his right to go home, if only in his own mind.

One month later, in a cornfield near Antietam, Clement Piety earned his walk.

Part IV

# MYTHS

# 46

## *The Escapee*

IN THE LATE FEBRUARY afternoon, the inmate Clement
Piety stood on the surface of the frozen St. Croix River, staring
at a hole in the ice. When the ice first began to break up and the
guard fell through, Clement had eased away from the fissure and
away from the unfortunate man battling the current to stay afloat
in the winter water. The waves coiled around the prison guard like
snakes come up from the center of the earth in some apocalyptic
event. Clement searched the heavens for horsemen or thundering
trumpets or another sign of rapture. Seeing and hearing nothing
but the regular ways of winter on the river, he looked again to the
guard, holding himself to the unbroken ice with one bare hand, his
glove lost to the water. The guard's wool coat, which only minutes
ago the prisoner had coveted in this weather, was now soaked.
Its weight tethered the man to the depths of the St. Croix. The
guard's eyes beseeched Clement for help.

"Oh Jesus," Clement said. The guard heaved one whole arm
atop the ice shelf. Clement heard the slap of soaked cloth. "The
ice is breaking up," he said to the guard. "I knew we shouldn't have
been out here. I told you so."

The guard made no indication that he'd heard. Clement
stretched out his arms. In his hands, he still held the chipping

tools he'd been using to cut blocks of ice. He tried to spread his legs, his weight over the precarious ice.

"I can't help you," he said. In a tentative approach toward the riverbank, he slid his boots along the rime. The drowning guard watched him.

"No," Clement said to unasked questions. "I can't."

The guard hung there, heaving and slipping and readjusting his grip.

Clement shook his head. "I'm sorry," he offered as explanation.

From early afternoon until this gray twilight, the hazy sky had showered Stillwater with soft rain and sleet, had alternately thawed and frozen the surface of every tree, animal, and man who chanced to be out of doors. All creation lay still, entombed in ice, swathed in that time near the end of winter when spring fights to break through, with its melting rains, only to be blown back again with the northern gales. Clement told himself there was no way to help the guard. That man was a goner. He turned his back to the guard slowly and eased his boot toward shore again.

Clement slid over a gray mass bulging from the ice, a squirrel trapped and dead, as if the Lord had planted this creature as a symbol for him to interpret. Like the women who raised him, this prisoner was forever finding cryptic signs in nature meant to test his intelligence and morality. Though spring was near, small mammals—bats, moles, squirrels, skunks—were most likely to freeze or starve at this time of year, fooled by fleeting moments of sunny warmth into waking from their deep sleep and leaving their dens.

He didn't want to look over his shoulder, but he felt he had to. He hoped there'd be no man there, only a hole in the ice. He turned. The guard was watching him. Clement sighed. "I warned you to stay on the shore," he said. "I did. I told you the ice was thin."

The man in the water said nothing. He closed his eyes in deference to deep thought or exhaustion. The guard had led him to the river on the warden's errand, to chop and collect a sled full of ice blocks for the warden's personal icebox, in which the rich warden was supposedly keeping a tall white cake with currant jam, a gift for his wife's birthday the next week. Whereas most prisoners would have welcomed this occasion to stretch legs accustomed to a cramped space measuring five feet by seven, to breathe clean air into lungs accustomed to inhaling dust mites and the smell of shit and dirty feet, to open their sorry eyes to a bit of blue sky rather than bars, stone, and guards, it was an errand unloved by Clement Piety, a thin man sensitive to cold and prone to shivering, to chills in his bones and sickness in his lungs and weeks of headaches after such an outing. Even now, the wet air seemed to penetrate his cotton coat, his striped prison issue, his itchy flannel, to settle upon his skin like a premonition of impending demise.

But now there was the matter of the guard in the water. Instinct had moved the prisoner away from the open hole, away from the drowning man. His own desire to live cautioned him against helping. Clement clenched his jaw. He looked away from the hole and toward the safe shore, a few more feet away. There was no time, no rope, nothing long enough to reach the guard while keeping himself out of harm, except the pick in his hand. It would do.

If he and the guard weren't back to the prison in half an hour, the warden would have the dogs out, and he'd be answerable for this event. And what could he say? How was it that he, the prisoner, the one charged with being on the ice, had not gone under? How was it that the watcher had? A month in the prison basement, at least. There wasn't a speck of God's light down there. There wasn't a unit of the devil's celebrated heat. That basement was a no place, worse than hell, worse than any war camp or battlefield.

Fractures, webbing from the hole in the ice each time the fallen man adjusted his grip, crept toward the prisoner. He perked his ears, chary of the high-pitched crack he'd heard before the guard dropped from sight, that brief note of warning the ice gave before crumbling beneath the guard's feet, delivering the poor man to his probable doom. Yet as Clement Piety, Stillwater Prison inmate 1024, convicted of murdering a man with an ax on the banks of this very river, regarded the scene before him, he observed the guard holding strictly to the ice and not succumbing to the rushing water. Clement's heart beat like a ringing bell in his chest. His breath rose like cannon smoke. He lowered himself to lay the pick and hammer on the ice and rid himself of the extra weight. As he crouched, he looked to the guard again, who was looking at him. Both were silent but for their haggard breathing. Fifteen feet separated them. And fifteen feet lay between Clement and the shore.

He rose slowly and backed away again. "I can't," he said again. The guard closed his eyes. Here was his chance to run. Or his second chance to save a drowning man.

That the handle of the pick was long enough to reach the guard was a truth plain to Clement. He could try. The guard was a decent man, one who talked with the prisoners in the dark, solitary rooms of the prison basement, one who would shake dice or flip cards with the inmates through the bars, one who asked about the prisoners' families and offered to write letters for the inmates who couldn't write. This was the guard who, upon first seeing the wild-eyed vulnerability of Clement Piety when he arrived at the prison seven years ago, spread news of his mammoth wrath and unpredictability among the rest of the inmates, in hopes of securing a measure of fear and respect for the scrawny man with the strange mismatched eyes. Eyes, the guard had told the others, that were a devil's mark, a demon's gift. The guard told Clement what the stronger, bigger men did with the smaller ones. The guard said he didn't like men turning worse than animals, away from their religion. The guard said he had hoped to spare him, and Piety had been spared. This was the guard who had written the letter of appeal to the state's attorney general, Barton Hatterby, on Clement's behalf. And the guard who checked the mail each week for the pardon that never came.

Clement Piety remembered those kindnesses now. He bent again to grab the pick. "I'll probably end up same as you," he told the guard. "A dead man, frozen like that ill-fated squirrel there." He twirled the wooden handle toward the guard and kept the pick end in his hand. He crouched and spread his feet as far apart as possible, as he'd seen the old bullfrogs do on lily pads. He waited until the guard opened his eyes again and looked him square in the face. "Once you're out, I'm off." Clement raised his eyebrows. "And I don't expect you to follow me, understand?" He extended the pick to the man in the hole.

The guard was silent but for his choppy breath. But his fingers inched toward Clement and the pick.

# 47

## Clement Goes Underwater

CLEMENT TOOK A BREATH of the cool, moist air and heaved again. He wasn't pulling as hard as he could. He was tentative, afraid to burden the ice shelf with too much weight all at once. In truth, he didn't believe this act of saving the guard had a chance in hell of working.

"I can't see us both coming off this still breathing," said Clement. The ice seemed to be sizzling with cracks and bobbing beneath him.

"Here we go," said Clement. "Hang on." He gripped the pick and heaved with every sinew in him. The ice, the entire sheaf from the middle of the river to the bank, gave way into dozens of pieces shaped like maple tree leaves. Clement teetered back and forth on a slab, and though he tried to steady it, the venture was hopeless. He went under, swallowed by the river.

Clement dropped the pick and kicked to the surface. He got one big breath before the guard grabbed him by the collar and pulled him back under. Clement blew out all of his air and swallowed a mouthful of the water. The guard tucked Clement under his arm like a parcel and used his other arm to navigate the water, sometimes bobbing up between ice chunks for air and then going under the long, jagged sheets again. Thirty or forty seconds later, the water slowed and warmed in a depth where Clement could set his feet down on the firm bottom. The two men stood and walked to the shallows. Clement threw the guard's arm off him.

Clement breathed heavily. "I thought you were trying to kill me."

The guard's lips and eyelids were purple. The whites of his eyes had turned gray, and the irises rolled back into his skull. The guard's knees folded under him, and he collapsed back into the water. Clement grabbed the back of his hair and pulled his back against his own knees. Clement grabbed him under the armpits and dragged him toward the shore. He was as heavy as a dead horse. Clement dropped the man onto the bank and rolled him out of the water. Clement fell beside him, coughed, and caught his breath.

"Get your coat off," Clement said. His teeth chattered like a beaver at a stick. "You look nearly gone already, but you might make it if you get these wet clothes off." He unbuttoned his coat and raised him a little, to get his arms out.

The guard coughed up a big black spew of water and let it run down his chin. He sat up, grabbed Clement by the coat collar, and pointed to his eyes. Clement needed no translation.

"I know it," he said. "Hard to disappear with eyes like these. But I'm off." Clement patted the guard on the shoulder. The guard nodded, then vomited again. Clement used the guard's shoulder to heave himself up the slope. He gripped the trunk of a small willow and was off into the forest, a rare wonder and thick with pines, an easy place for a small man like Clement to disappear. He looked like a creature meant for those trees.

# 48

## The Good Sister

ANGEL HATTERBY LAWRENCE stood at her window, wringing the baby's diapers in soapy water, rinsing them, and laying them over a cord she'd strung from the mantelpiece to the curtain rod above the window. The housekeeper would be horrified by the makeshift drying line in the middle of the parlor, by the water dripping all over the handsome carpet. But she didn't care. She'd dismissed all the servants and the nanny for the day. Most of the time, she appreciated them and liked their company, even if they didn't speak to her and talked about her personal matters all over Stillwater. Angel Lawrence was a lonely woman, and the simple presence of the help and simple noises of their work made her feel safe, made the days pass a little faster.

Today she'd wanted to manage things in the big house herself. She'd been having trouble getting her daughter to tinkle in the little chamber pot, and she didn't like the nanny's advice about tying the girl down until she went, so she dismissed her along with the rest, including the housekeeper, who was best friends with the mayor's housekeeper and whispered everything she heard about Angel to the mayor's wife. That was how so much tattle about Angel had spread around the town. Sometimes Angel felt like screaming from the rooftops that the mayor's wife sold herself like a regular prostitute to him, that she'd only bed down with him for trinkets and sweets, and see how that old witch liked the same treatment.

Angel stared out at the bare, twisted trees around her house and gazed into the pine forest beyond. Beyond that, the St. Croix River was strung like a silvery necklace over the valley, and Stillwater Prison sat on the hill, somehow menacing and comforting at the same time. It both pained and soothed her to know her brother was there. She lifted her fingertips from the water and placed them on the window, where they bit into the frost and left small dots of clear heat. She scraped away frost to get a larger look at the Minnesota landscape. She hated winter here. She hardly left the house, beyond going to the stables and carriage house, from the time the first snow fell until the last flake melted and floated away down the St. Croix. She felt imprisoned by the weather and thought she might visit her mother.

Although Angel's husband considered his mother-in-law a madcap embarrassment and hoped against hope that her fits would not fall upon his wife, he had benefited well from his father-in-law's political position and the negotiations Hatterby had made on behalf of his business. The timber industry was growing in importance, and he appreciated the influence of Barton Hatterby. Still, he wondered whether he had been tricked—he first met his mother-in-law at his wedding to Angel, perhaps by design or just by oversight. Prior to the engagement, Hatterby had touted his wife's lineage, descended as she was from the French aristocracy in French Haiti. When Thomas made inquiries about this, he discovered that it was true. Shortly thereafter Thomas Lawrence had produced a ring for the girl's hand.

Every second Saturday afternoon, Angel took great care to have the nanny bathe and powder and dress the girls warmly and smartly in their lace pantalettes and fancy dresses: a blue silk style with a matching jacket for Roseanne, a velvet black dress with a high collar for Dorothea, and a burgundy silk with a white apron

of embroidered flowers on the hem for little Goldenrod. Angel
herself chose between a visiting dress of blue watered silk with the
full hoops and her tiered dress of black lace over emerald silk. She
lately opted for the tiered piece, as she felt that the hooped style
was going out of fashion, though she liked the material and color
of that gown more than the other. The driver would take the four
of them to St. Paul to attend prayer with her mother, in the chapel
her mother had commissioned on her own property, and then dine
with her in the old territorial governor's mansion, which the Hatterbys had acquired through favors that Angel's father had done
for some friends.

Angel was careful not to allow her mother to be alone with
any of the girls. She had come to attribute her mother's peculiar
behavior to a tumultuous early life, without a mother of her own
to guide her. But Angel's knowledge of her mother's sins and her
mother's knowledge of Angel's origins bound the two in a powerful complicity. Each kept silent about the other's secret, but Mrs.
Hatterby had the upper hand. She kept Angel chained to her.

Yet Angel understood that in her old age, her mother needed
the company of her daughter and grandchildren. In a way it
pleased Angel to show off her own plump, vivacious daughters to
her mother, as if to say, "See. I know how to do this. I know how to
keep them alive and healthy. I have succeeded where you failed."

The world outside Angel's window stood absolutely still, as if
all that had once swayed on the wind or opened and closed with
the rising and falling sun or moved with the mood of the moon
had been switched for glass replicas. Everything looked exactly
as it had the day before, and the day before that. The same icicles
hung from the eaves of her enormous home, warning any friend
or neighbor away. The same brick fence licked around the yard.
The same trees stood bare. The same pale sky like dead skin over

the earth. The minute the river froze, the entire town filled with the walking dead.

Her daughters had been holed up like nocturnal animals for far too long. Their skin looked blue for lack of sunlight. Purple half-moons cradled their eyes. Where they once had muscles in their arms from swinging in the trees, they now had pallid sheets laid over bones. Unable to go outside or attend lessons or play games with the nanny, the girls were bored and constantly looked at Angel in expectation. "Go play," she'd told them a thousand times today already. "You're underfoot," she'd said as she shooed them away from her skirts.

Angel's heart fluttered and her breath came short. Perspiration gathered on her upper lip though her fingertips were frozen. She had an odd feeling. She placed her hand on her chest and pressed.

She felt a breeze on her ear. She held her hand to the window and ran it all along the sill, checking for a draft.

*Breathe deeply. Keep going.*

Angel's heart thumped. She swallowed. "Girls?" she said. "Did you say something to Mama?" She turned and spotted the children playing.

"Nothing, Mama," said one of her daughters, her head tipped quizzically.

Then she heard the faint but unmistakable voice again. *Jesus. Blow into your hands. Rub your arms. Keep moving.*

*What was happening?* she wondered. She exhaled and tried to remember the last time she'd heard this voice. She tried to remember the last time she'd heard this voice in this way. Clement.

Angel spun around. She looked up at the ceiling and down to the floor. But she knew where the voice was coming from, and it was not from inside her house. "Calm down," she said. She pressed her fingers to her temples.

*Don't tell me to calm down, goddammit.*

"Don't cuss at me," she said softly. Clement had grown some teeth, it seemed. She tried to remember if he had ever before sworn at her. Angel could hear teeth chattering, though the sound was distant and tinny. "Oh my Lord," whispered Angel. "Clement, are you dying? This only worked for me if I was nearly dead."

She listened, but she heard nothing for a long while. Then, just as her shoulders drooped, she heard him again.

*Is this how you did it? Did you have to nearly die every time?*

"Yes," she said. She was calm now. "Yes. Where are you?"

*Am I dying?*

The cold sweat spread to her neck and her chest. She panted and spread her hand over her chest. She willed warmth and safety to extend from her hand to him. "I can't," she said. "My girls."

*I'm so cold. I'm freezing to death out here. You owe me something, Angel.*

As she got ready, pulling on long stockings and tying boots, she thought of her worldly comforts. These clothes, this house, a fire in the fireplace. She had always possessed every material content-ment imaginable, and yet her life had not been easy either. She had never had peace or the protection of a mother. Clement had grown up poor, but the old women had loved him and shown him every kindness. What could she owe him? And yet, she felt she must go to him now. As much as she tried to occupy her mind with man-aging the house and arranging the gardens and rearing the girls, her brother and his trials always lay on her chest, a heavy, tangible weight of guilt and obligation and resentment and anger.

Angel's daughters scurried about her feet. Roseanne and Doro-thea stomped after a mouse in the corner, trying to trap it in a tea-cup. "Roseanne," Angel said. She took a breath and exhaled slowly. Her voice became calm, even lazy. She would not alarm the child. "Watch your sisters." She pulled her shawl from the nail by the door and then changed her mind and took the stunning swan boa out of the armoire instead. She wrapped it around her shoulders.

He'd recognize it, she thought. She selected a red fox cloak for Clement, as well as clean warm socks, pants, and boots.

Angel smiled at her daughters. "Leave that mouse alone. How would you like to be trapped in a cup?" She patted Roseanne on the head. "I'll be back soon. Stay in the house."

Angel walked out the door and toward the stable. She was worried and angry and urgently fed up and concerned all at once. More than anything, she wondered if she'd ever be rid of him, this constant tether to the old, to what wasn't and couldn't be, to dead parents and imagined connections. Go forward or die.

On a winter day like this one, they had entered this world together, one after the other, through the skinny legs of a nymph-girl mother who abandoned them both. Angel had once loved him more than any other in the world. But she grew up. She married. She had her girls to think of. There was no love that trumped her girls. There was no person.

She could let him die. She didn't have to go. She wouldn't have to worry about him exposing her as a mutt, threatening her marriage, undermining her daughters' future.

But he was her brother, her own blood and sinew and bone. And if he could speak to her now, what would keep him from haunting her when he was dead?

Angel rode out and decided that this day would be the last. She'd save his life and then let him go back to prison. If he said things there, if he told of her birth, what did it matter? Who would believe him? He was an orphan. He was a criminal. No one would listen to him. No one would believe a single word he said.

# 49

## The Virgin and the Convict

ATHIN AND SICKLY MAN, malnourished after seven years of prison potatoes and moldy bread, Clement Piety stood, dripping wet and heaving for breath, in what was left of the great northern wilderness. From scalp to ankles, goose pimples covered his skin. He flipped his long hair away from his eyes.

Behind him the St. Croix River rushed on, breaking away ice in great masses and carrying them down the current. On the other bank, a half mile or so away, loomed Stillwater Prison, home to Clement Piety no longer. And though he was finally free of it, Clement felt a strange obligation, a familiar tug to return. "I'm not going back," he said to no one. The roar of the river soaked up his words. He bit his lip to control his quaking jaw. He drew blood. The taste of blood iron verved him a little. He felt warmer and turned toward the woods.

Though a small man and prone to contracting every kind of disease, at that moment Clement felt like a tall tale, strong and giant. He felt cocksure and hallowed, surely saved for some very important purpose.

He dodged into the giant firs and hustled for a long while. The forest floor was frozen yet, but much of the snow had melted. Clement easily picked his path through the trees. They were familiar to him. He'd played here as a boy, remembered when this tree was yet a sapling and that one hosted a owl family, when this one's trunk leaked sap, and that one held a dead deer over a low-hanging branch, dragged up by a cougar. He felt light-footed and swift. He'd leave no tracks and wasn't worried. Running felt warm and freeing for a while, but after a mile or so his chest grew taut, and Clement thought he'd better rest. He stopped alongside a big pine and bent over. His thoughts wandered, darted from his life as a poor orphaned boy raised by Big Waters, to his reunion with his sister, to his trials in the war, to his row with Angel, to the death of the old man, to his imprisonment, to the fact that Angel never once visited him or brought him any worldly comforts while he suffered on her behalf. He wondered what she would say when she found him, which he knew she would do. Surely she'd come now, when his situation was so dire. She'd not abandon him.

"Jesus," Clement said to himself. His heavy, soaked clothes clung to his body. He wondered whether Angel actually would come. Whatever power had infused him before seemed to dissipate, and a serious weight and fatigue settled upon his shoulders, as if someone had put a timber across his back and told him to climb a mountain.

He thought of the Lord and his cross. "Jesus Christ almighty," he said to himself. Talking to himself was something he'd picked up in prison. It didn't feel strange to him now. "I've got to get ahold of my wits. I'm goddamn alive and free." Tears came to his eyes. They were sensitive to the daylight and raw from the water. He rubbed them and squinted past the trees.

"Holy Christ." The raging river worked up some anger in him over his lost years, his lost sister, his lost mother, his lost life. He talked at the prison. He swore at it. He'd learned some fierce language in prison and liked using it, but now wondered if taking the Lord's name in vain would keep him from entering heaven. Clement put his hands on his hips and toiled for air. He breathed so deep it made him dizzy. He swayed. He rested along one tree, then another. He pulled himself along by this branch, then that one. He grew cold again. The winter winds, though carrying warmer air across the state, hit him frigidly. He became aware that he could be freezing. He clenched his fists and curled his toes the best he could. He coughed and shivered and thought of poor Jesus' trek to Golgotha. He thought that at least the Good Lord had a warm climate to suffer in and a mother to encourage Him along. Clement's body fought him hard then. He tried to control his thinking, for it seemed the more he thought about being cold, the more he shivered. Soon violent tremors overwhelmed him. His legs would not walk one step more. Clement knelt in the dirty snow beside an animal path and a mound of deer droppings.

"Angel, you better find me quick," he said. "I better get dry." He dropped his britches. "This ought to come off too." He plucked at the buttons of his coat and shook it off his arms. He worked at the buttons of his shirt. He swore at his fingers, which, once clenched, didn't want to open. He looked around at the trees, one of the last forests untouched by the loggers. A whip of mist floated just above his head, blurring the treetops. Wherever he looked, tree trunks stood like sentinels. He heard mice or gophers or squirrels scurrying beneath dead branches and needles, fooled into thinking spring was here. *Stupid rodents. Better get back to sleep or you'll be at the mercy of winter yet.* He heard birds scratching in the tree above him. He suddenly warmed over, as though his blood had been peppered and now raced to his ears and fingertips. His hands and feet suddenly burned. A fire warmed the top of his head. And his eyes were heavy. He was exhausted, so he sat down in a cushion of needles. *I'll take just a short rest and catch my breath,* he thought. He huffed and exhaled. He wasn't feeling cold at all. He dug his hand into the earth beneath him and wondered if he could burrow down some and get comfortable, like a dog on a rug in front of a fireplace. He wondered where the deer that had left those droppings had gone to. Was it a buck or a doe? If it was a doe, did it have a fawn? Maybe he could cuddle alongside them if he could find them. But he was too tired to move. Perhaps they'd come back. Perhaps he could take a short nap and wake when the mother and fawn returned. He closed his eyes and the scent of roses mingled with the pine aroma. *Haven't smelled roses in a long while,* thought he.

The forest went silent at that moment, and he wondered if something had gone wrong in his ears or his head. He opened his eyes and couldn't see but a bit in front of him. He waved his hand in front of his face to clear away the haze. He shouted, "Hey!" but made no sound that he could hear. "Where'd you animal noises go?" he thought he shouted, but he heard nothing. Clement used the tree trunk to pull himself up and stand. His britches were still pooled around his ankles, and he stepped his feet out of them. He had one boot on and one off, lost in the river probably, but he couldn't be sure and couldn't remember. He wondered why he didn't remember running without a boot on. His shirt hung from his shoulders, a strange weight, like dead deer limbs. *Why's this shirt feel so heavy? Water must be heavier than I thought it to be. I feel like I'm shouldering the whole world, like Atlas. I best sit back down and rest a bit more.*

It was at that moment, Clement Piety later insisted, while he was slowly freezing and being enticed to succumb to his death, that an apparition of the Virgin Mary, the mother of mothers, saved him. Clement said that out of the silence, the cooing of what he thought was a winter bird enticed him into a clearing, where it was as warm as a summer kitchen. The cooing became a lullaby a mother would sing to a baby. The fog was transfigured into a woman, and Clement said she told him, "Behold. I am the Mother of God."

For the remainder of his days, Clement would offer as evidence a long red fox cloak, which he said the Virgin removed from her own body and put upon his, and which he toted along with him out of the forest that day and for the rest of his life, a cloak upon which believers cried their tears, touched their arthritic hands, or rubbed their unhearing ears, a cloak upon which the barren prayed for fruitfulness, the decrepit pleaded for healing, and the poor begged for food. When the people would inevitably ask why Clement did not pray upon the miraculous cloak for the return of his own sight, Clement Piety would smile, roll his milky eyes, and remark that the lovely face of the Virgin was the last earthly vision he had desired and so she blinded him. Believers went away thinking that Piety'd been marked by the Virgin herself, in the way that Moses came away from the Lord with a head of white hair and a tablet of commandments.

Angel discovered Clement beneath a canopy of fir trees, bare and shivering, babbling loudly, practically deaf, and nearly unconscious. He was wet but had known well enough to get his clothes off in order to live. Though she knew no one saw her, nor did she want anyone to see her, she arranged the long white feather boa over her shoulders, in a way becoming a baron's wife. To wear it that day seemed especially appropriate. White feathers, so hard to come by, nearly impossible. White for her name. White for the snow. Feathers for the way she'd fly from him, finally.

She stroked the boa and said to him, "You're not coming with me. It's not even a consideration."

She hopped down from her horse and unlaced the satchel she had tied to the saddle. She threw it down next to him. He reached for it. He looked up into her beautiful face, her ebony hair, her perfect skin.

"And don't start up about being abandoned and all that business," she went on. "You had the same chances as I did to have the life you wanted. You think life's been easy for me?" She looked around to be certain that no one was watching or listening. She leaned over him. "Well, it wasn't." She straightened up. "Isn't," she corrected herself.

Clement's ears felt full, as though water were swishing from one side to the other. He didn't hear much of what his sister said. He smiled at her though, despite her ornery look. She reached beneath the boa and untied her cloak and swirled it off her shoulders, thin little things like those Clement supposed their mother had. He wondered if she was thanking him for taking the blame for the old man's murder, for sitting in the cold prison all those seven years.

"Here," she said. "Take it."

He reached out and wrapped the heavy coat around him. The fur smelled of her, roses and something like a woodstove.

"No one will believe an escaped criminal over me," she said. "No one." She helped him up and put her hands on both of his shoulders and stood face to face with him. He liked it that she was his exact same height and that he could look directly into her brown eyes. He often wondered why it was he who got the inept eye, but then he was happy his sister didn't have to bear that burden. He'd told her that he was happy to bear the burden of disfigurement for them both. Now he tried to collapse into her and let her hold him up. She pushed him upright.

His ears weren't working right. He watched her mouth form words. She pointed to the satchel. Something about the Red Swan and Big Waters following him and then something that looked like "Don't follow me." She was crossing her hands, making a big imaginary X in front of herself. He pointed to his ears. He yelled, "I can't hear you. My ears are funny acting." She was shaking her head at him. Dread came over him. She was going to leave him.

She helped him dress with the clothes she'd brought. A wool shirt. Pants. She was rough. His mouth wasn't working either. He tried hard to think. He squinted so he could think his concentrated best. *I love you best,* he tried to tell her with his mind. He was sure she could hear him. *I love you best,* he thought again. *Don't you love me best too?* And then he thought, *Remember that we're twins.* No two people in the whole world were closer than twins. The most important thing was that they be together forever and ever and that no one ever could come between them again.

She stroked her boa again as if it were a charmed thing. She saw in his face a recognition then. She saw him wonder about white feathers. Then she turned from Clement and mounted her horse. She kicked the animal and galloped away.

Clement thought hard: *Where are you going? Come back here.* But she kept going, the strands of the boa fluttering behind her like wings. He felt the earth pulsating subtly beneath his feet, the horse hooves pounding and taking Angel away from him. Clement stood there for another minute. His ears were coming back to life. He sat down and pulled the boots and socks from the satchel. He thought about what a smart sister he had, one who remembered socks as well as boots. He smiled that she still knew him best, knew what he was thinking, knew to come and find him. They had a special connection. One of miraculous proportions. A gift from God.

He wondered why she had left him this time and when he would see her again. He pulled the cloak around him and looked about.

Clement Piety walked through the last woods. No movement had yet commenced from the prison. But in time, the warden would look for him, and with his anomalous eye, he would not be difficult to find.

Clement Piety walked in the twilight and dark. The cloak was warm, but his feet were numb. His hearing came back to him, as well as the familiar routes through these woods. He walked into the infirmary, right into the waiting arms of Big Waters.

# 50

# Big Waters Cleaves Clement to Her

B IG WATERS HID CLEMENT in the dark room. She prepared a strong-smelling concoction and coaxed him to lay his head upon her lap. He was as pliable as soft leather. She petted him in his sadness.

"The water will call you, so long as you have its eye."

She pried his eyelids apart with her fingertips and dripped lye onto his pupils, one after the other. He cried out a little, but she put her hand over his lips and he stopped. The lye would burn away the top layer of his eyeballs and create a white coating over the irises. In a few days, he would be gauzy-eyed and sightless. He didn't resist in the slightest and trusted her cruelty completely.

The process gave Big Waters a measure of satisfaction. To hurt him a little felt good, for he had been a neglectful and ungrateful child who had grown into a neglectful and ungrateful man. But he was hers, in any case. And it felt good to her old hands to be the one to fix his problems again, to care for him a bit longer, to be needed as a mother.

Still, he called out for Angel.

Big Waters was too old to go and get the selfish one. Clement would finally have to be satisfied with Big Waters and remain with her. He would finally have to show gratitude to her for caring for him, to accept that she was the one who loved him most.

• • •

It was while he lay recovering in Big Waters' care that the memory
of the Virgin came to Clement strongly. He talked incessantly
about her, working out the details of the story. In the woods that
day, Clement said, the Virgin Mary converted his heart from lone-
liness, sin, and sorrow to joy, devotion, and purpose. So forever
after, he would forget many of the fortuitous events that led to
his escape that day in February and ascribe it to the Virgin Mary,
Queen of Heaven and Earth, the one woman who never threw
him out in the cold to the ravenous wolves.

He'd go on about this for hours, talking day and night as a fool
might.

Big Waters listened. Clement sat prattling on and on. She
wanted to tell him, I never abandoned you. I raised you when you
were abandoned. I adopted you when you were left by a simple-
ton girl and when no other mother wanted you. I kept you warm
with my own body. Here I am. I have spread poultice on your eyes
and protected you from capture. And you are nothing but trouble
to me and remain ungrateful. You do not see how I suffer, how
my body fails me, how now my hand will not close or how my
leg drags on the ground. You do not know about the sparks that
bother my mind. How each one is brighter and renders me more
useless.

She finally brought Mother St. John to see him.

Mother St. John had scolded Big Waters over Clement's eyes,
wondering, "Have your wits gone astray? You've made a useless
mole of him." But she as she listened to the wild tale pouring from
Clement's mouth, her heart danced. Perhaps finally, after all her
hard work in the woods, God was rewarding her with a visit from
the Virgin, a great miracle in the forest, a blessing unparalleled.
With permission from Father Paul, who tore the wanted posters for Clement off the walls of every building in Stillwater, she
thought to widely disseminate the tale, to draw more people to the
true Church, to the true mother. Father Paul balked at drawing

attention to an escaped convict, but he then imagined the droves of believers swarming his church, bringing offerings. He arranged a meeting with the mayor and the warden, a difficult thing to do, considering their heated relationship. He begged on Clement's behalf, begged pardon for his own and Mother St. John's participation in hiding him, explained that imprisoning a man who had experienced such a miracle would only hurt the interests of everyone in the town. The two men, eyeing each other suspiciously, hardly heard a word the priest said. They nodded and agreed, though. They waited patiently through the priest's supplication, and as soon as he left, they tore into each other, breaking a vase, a cigar box, a jaw, and a hand while scrabbling over the virtue of each other's wives.

When Father Paul returned to Mother St. John, he only said, "Yes."

Mother St. John wrote down the story Clement spun:

*The Virgin Mary appeared to me alongside a fir tree in the forest alongside the St. Croix River. Moments before, I had escaped death by falling through the ice into the freezing waters and swimming to shore. I made for the trees and stripped out of my clothes. Standing there, I began to sob and fear death. The beautiful Virgin Mary, Mother of Jesus, appeared to me then and wrapped a red fox cloak around me. I was a sinner at that time, with many mortal sins on my heart, which would have surely bound my soul to hell if not for Her divine intercession at that moment.*

The narrative contained effusive gratitude to the Virgin, as well as long, descriptive paragraphs about her beauty and grace.

*Her hair rolls in gentle waves down her breast, at which one can imagine the infant Jesus suckling his first nourishment. In her gaze, I could imagine the smiles she produced upon the infant Jesus as He looked up at her, transfixed in the moments just after His*

*birth in that humble stable on a cold Bethlehem night shiny with
stars but unwelcoming to a bare babe. How fortunate He was to
have such a Mother to cover Him and press Him to Her heart! Her
voice, a lullaby of soft whispers, singing love songs in His infant
ear! Her face, a beacon of love and steadfastness, a face bespeakt
of devotion and allegiance. A Mother's Love for the Ages for Jesus
and for all the sons of the world!*

In this way, *Our Lady of the North* came to be printed, bound,
and distributed, and by his death in 1878, Clement had recounted
again and again, all over the new country, his miraculous encoun-
ter with Our Lady of the North. Pilgrims traveled great distances
to fold their hands and listen to the blinded man tell his tale. They
were enraptured by his tale of the Virgin Mother, sitting on a low
tree branch in some accounts and floating on a cloud in others,
wearing a white gown or a blue gown, a crown of roses on her
head or a ring of roses around her waist, depending upon Clement's whim. They were transfixed as Clement described how she
covered him, saved him, and told him a prophecy that he was to
reveal only at his death.

On the morning of his death in 1878, at the age of thirty-eight,
Clement Piety drank chicory coffee and ate a piece of bread with
Big Waters. He stood and said, "We can't wait for miracles to
occur. The greatest wonderments manifest themselves as we walk
the blade's edge between life and death." He picked up his guiding
cane and walked out the door and toward the river.

Big Waters, her mouth suddenly lax and her eyes blinded by
flashes of light, let him go.

# 51

## Lydian

THOUGH SHE TRIED AND though she wanted to, Mother St. John couldn't bring Big Waters out of her listless and silent bereavement in the days after Clement's disappearance into the waters of the St. Croix, from which he had so miraculously emerged twice before. Her mouth, and her eye and the extremities of her left side, hung low. She drooled and wet herself. With so many children now, coming by trainloads from the East in some months, and so many sick to tend, and so many new nurses and teachers to supervise, Mother St. John felt helpless in regard to Big Waters, her old friend, and she admitted to Father Paul that the old woman needed more help than she could give.

Father Paul arranged for a bed at the nearby Convent of St. Joseph of Carandelet, where a new passel of nuns had for more than a decade been assisting the deaf and the mute and the old and the unwanted in a way not so dissimilar from Mother St. John's work with the orphans in Stillwater. Big Waters would be a fine fit there.

Big Waters made no objection or fuss as she was moved. Mother St. John patted her hand and kissed her on the forehead and that was it between two women who had raised more children together than anyone could ever count.

· · ·

The Sisters of St. Joseph of Carandelet began their ministries in France at the onset of the French Revolution and grew so that they spread to St. Louis in the late 1840s and grew again so that they were able to send a contingent up the Mississippi to St. Paul in 1860, where they established St. Joseph's Help for the Deaf and Dumb. Here is where Big Waters arrived, carried into a large kitchen in the arms of Father Paul.

Standing at a table lined from one end to the other with nut cakes and fruit pies and sugar pastries was a nun dressed in the regular black-and-white habit but dusted with flour and sugar. She smiled at the old woman and said, "One thing to know about the French is that they know how to make a sweet." She hacked a slice off a round cake and put it on a plate. "You eat this now, old one, and I'm going to sample this one I've just got coming out of the oven. You arrived just at the right time."

Nearly thirty years before, a pair of old German bachelors named Schmidt went out to check their traps and happened upon a girl crumpled in a snowdrift. Crimson blossomed from her. The men lived in a simple one-room cabin with two doors and two windows, finished their supper at three o'clock, cleaned their fingernails with toothpicks while their food settled, then washed the dishes and dried them, and put on their coats to walk to the place where the warm spring fed the river to check their muskrat traps. This evening, they each closed the curtain on their respective window. They walked out their respective door. They locked its lock with the key they each kept in their coat pocket. This evening as they approached the bank where everyone knew the Schmidt brothers laid their barrel traps in the water, the one brother said to the other, "Looks liken someone's thieven our skins." In truth, all he could see through the trees and with what little daylight was left, was the shape of a body spread out along the river's edge a few feet from where he knew his trap sat, more than likely full of one or two or maybe even three animals. The skins brought a good price, and the brothers stewed the meat with parsnips and onions and pepper if they had any.

"Better notten be if he knowsen what's good for him," said the other. The brothers picked up their pace as best they could along the icy path, well compacted and slick with the mist that came off the river. They squinted to make better sense of what the one thought he was seeing: a man curled up on the ground near the place where their muskrats congregated. Both men had eyeballs full of cataracts. For the thin brother, even on the clearest day in the brightest light, the world was cloudy at best, as if cold milk had been poured over his pupils and he was expected to see through it. For the fat brother, the world as seen through his eyes was full of black holes surrounded by halos. He sometimes described this phenomenon to his brother as "Polka-dotted. Like Ma's Sunday bonnet." But with their German sensibilities and inborn distrust of anyone but the other of them, they assumed a thief was raiding their animals. The Schmidt brothers were forever on the lookout for people trying to rob them, and they had lived a long life rarely being victim to such crimes. They attributed this fact to their intense vigilance.

"You besten putten those muskrats back where you founden them!" yelled the fat one. "What do you seen?" he said to his brother. "Tellen me what he looks liken."

The skinny brother tightened his grip on his walking stick. He thought he may have to wield it against the thief. He approached the bank.

"Hey, you!" yelled the fat brother.

Both brothers sat down on their bottoms and slid down the bank on slides made by beavers. The one brother pointed his walking stick like a gun at the thief.

"Hey, I saiden," said the fat brother. "We're talken to you. Are you deaf? Gotten wax in your ears?"

The thin brother used his stick to steady himself as he stood.

The fat brother was out of breath. The thin brother helped him to his feet.

"Oooh. I'm stiff as a board," said the fat one. He placed one hand on his hip and raised the other into the air. "Thaten smarts." He twisted one way and then the other until his back cracked. "Well, let's go seen," he said. They walked a bit and got a good view of the body.

"It's bad for him," said the fat to the thin. "He's been out heren a while, sure. Also he looken to be a girl."

The thin brother leaned in to get a better look. They knelt beside her and touched her cheek. She was cold, but clouds of mist arose from her mouth. She was breathing.

"Is she deaden?" said the fat one.

The thin one shrugged his shoulders.

The fat one touched her shoulders. "Shesen breathing," he said. "And shivering." He pointed to her skirt and to the snow around her. "And she's bloody in them neverparts." He eased closer to the girl. He put his face nose to nose with her and breathed warm air over her nose. "My. My. My. What happenden to you, little girl?" Then he slapped her gently on one cheek and the other. He sat back. "We're gonnen picken you up and carryen you home, so don'ten be scared," he said. "Can you hearen me?" he said.

The girl fluttered her eyes a little. And the men came to life at that. The fat brother moved behind her and perched her up in his lap. The girl seemed to be trying to say something.

"What's that?" asked the fat. "Can you talken louder? I don'ten hear too well."

"I fell down," she said.

"You fellen down?"

"May as well check the traps so long as we came all the way," said the fat.

"Makes sense to me," said the thin. "Nothing for you to do but wait until I get back anyway."

The two old bachelors brought a great bounty of muskrats to their humble home that day. And Lydian took the fat one's bed, and he took to the floor. She stayed with them, getting strong, learning to sing German songs about bells and towers and castles, listening to fairy tales about dwarves and forests and trolls until the fat one died the next year and cataracts in the thin one's eyes blinded him completely. He sold the cabin to the lumber company and moved to St. Joseph's Help for the Dumb and Deaf, which is where he thought would be the most practical place to go. The girl accompanied him and began the life of a sister in the Convent of St. Joseph of Carandelet, whose work on earth was to tend to the deaf, the dumb, and now the blind. She'd always thought it would be nice to be a sister anyway.

Big Waters moved her gums but said nothing. Father Paul helped her onto a stool and pushed the plate in front of her. Big Waters pinched a corner off the cake and lifted it to her lips.

"You look quite familiar to me," said the nun. "But I just can't place you."

Big Waters chewed on the side of her mouth that worked. Tears welled. What was the use of being so old? she wondered. What had been the use of any of these years? What had it mattered? Who had she helped? She sniffled.

"Come, come now," said the nun. "I'm going to take good care of you. And the Lord shines upon all who enter here. I was a mournful woman too. My heart was near broken until I happened upon this place and turned my heart to God and to the service of the needy. I have been serving in his ministry for so many years now that I can't even count them. I'm a natural born mother, even to old ones like yourself." She put her arm around Big Waters' sloping shoulders and squeezed. "I'm going to love you just like a mother would." The sister talked about how she would wrap her up and feed her treats and tell her stories and rub her feet. The sister said, "Even when we're old, we need to be mothered."

Big Waters thought that was true. Big Waters looked hard into the nun's face and was certain she recognized something familiar, though she could not place it. The eyes of the nun were fringed with red lashes and the irises were a warm earth color. *Clement,* she thought.

# Epilogue

THOUGH THE MORNING had been dark, the remaining snow now glowed in the dusk. Near Stillwater, on an unnamed pond fed by the St. Croix and under the shelter of a rare tamarack stand, a swan patrols the nest where her gray cygnets sleep, heads resting, beaks tucked. Their backs rise and fall in mute slumber, and they bandy dreams of clear skies and gentle winds and plentiful pondweed and tadpoles. The mother swan has chased away the spring animals, the skunks, geese, frogs, and even the curious weasels and beavers that threaten her baby birds. She's ferocious and attentive, a good mother. Again and again she glides over the place where a human body lies beneath water, caught in the weeds and tree trunks. He rests face up, motionless but for the pond's mild whims of buoyancy. Through a memory imprinted somewhere in her fowl brain, she remembers him.

# Acknowledgments

 Thanks to the Minnesota State Arts Board for the generous grant toward the completion of this book and to the citizens of Minnesota who passed the Minnesota Clean Water, Land and Legacy Amendment, which guarantees persistent stewardship of our state's natural resources and artistic culture.

And thanks to the following people:

To Pam Becker, my office mate who serendipitously has in her head a wealth of information on the lives of fur trappers.

To all my colleagues and students at South Central College in North Mankato, Minnesota.

To Minnesota State University, Mankato, particularly the creative writing department and the Good Thunder Reading Series, for continued support.

To the people at the Washington County Historical Society and the Warden's House Museum in Stillwater, Minnesota.

To Jeremy and Erin Drews at the Ann Bean Mansion in Stillwater, Minnesota.

To Ted Genoways, author of *Hard Time: Voices from a State Prison*.

To Richard Moe, author of *Last Full Measure: The Life and Death of the First Minnesota Volunteers*.

To William Lass, author of *Minnesota: A History*.

To the photographer who took "Log Jam at Taylor's Falls, 1884," the photo that inspired the whole project.

To Trampled By Turtles for the music that put me in the mode to imagine Beaver Jean.

To The Pines for more foresty mood music.

To Frederick Manfred and *Lord Grizzly*. Victor Hugo and *Les Misérables*. O. E. Rolvaag and *Giants in the Earth*. Ken Burns and *The West* and *The Civil War*. Willa Cather and *O Pioneers!* Walt Whitman for everything. The personal narratives of missionaries and settlers and the recollections of Joseph Farr. I liked poking around in your lives.

To Faye Bender, my agent and advocate.

To Jenna Johnson and all the folks at Houghton Mifflin Harcourt.

To my writing group, Nick Healy, Tom Maltman, Aaron Frisch, Nate LeBoutillier, great writers and my first and best editors.

To my mom and Janet Lohre, my grandma, and Pat LeBoutillier.

To Nate, always, for the encouragement and edits, for inclement and clement weather both.

To Isabella, Mitchell, Phillip, Violette, Archibald, and Gordon, my little Minnesotans, lovers of the dirt and bark and critters and insects and winter skies and summer humidity, who've provided me with endless mothering experiences that have inspired details in this book and who force me again and again to go outside.